D0043290

A DEAL WITH THE DEVIL

"Suppose we strike a bargain," Youngblood said with a smile.

Morgan gave him a suspicious glance. "I told you once before, you can't buy me out."

"I wasn't thinking of buying you out. There are other things we might bargain. You have three months before you're due to leave the Red Rock Ranch, right?"

"Three months and four days," she corrected.

Youngblood grinned. She was counting the days. Was it because of him? Did she, too, lay awake every night, her body aching for his touch? "It's simple," he said. "If I persuade you to make love with me during that time, you give up your share of the ranch and never return." Youngblood heard his heart pound with dread as the words came. No matter how he tried to deny it, he wanted her here. And the worst of it was he was beginning to think he might want her here forever.

To her surprise, Morgan found herself silently considering his outrageous offer. If she agreed to his plan, he'd do everything in his power to get her into his bed. Morgan's pulse raced as she imagined how he'd go about melting her resistance. If she was smart, in three months and four days she could be sole owner of this ranch. But the question was, was she strong enough to do battle against such a seductive opponent?

ROMANCE REIGNS
WITH ZEBRA BOOKS!

SILVER ROSE (2275, $3.95)
by Penelope Neri

Fleeing her lecherous boss, Silver Dupres disguised herself as a boy and joined an expedition to chart the wild Colorado River. But with one glance at Jesse Wilder, the explorers' rugged, towering scout, Silver knew she'd have to abandon her protective masquerade or else be consumed by her raging unfulfilled desire!

STARLIT ECSTASY (2134, $3.95)
by Phoebe Conn

Cold-hearted heiress Alicia Caldwell swore that Rafael Ramirez, San Francisco's most successful attorney, would never win her money . . . or her love. But before she could refuse him, she was shamelessly clasped against Rafael's muscular chest and hungrily matching his relentless ardor!

LOVING LIES (2034, $3.95)
by Penelope Neri

When she agreed to wed Joel McCaleb, Seraphina wanted nothing more than to gain her best friend's inheritance. But then she saw the virile stranger . . . and the green-eyed beauty knew she'd never be able to escape the rapture of his kiss and the sweet agony of his caress.

EMERALD FIRE (3193, $4.50)
by Phoebe Conn

When his brother died for loving gorgeous Bianca Antonelli, Evan Sinclair swore to find the killer by seducing the tempress who lured him to his death. But once the blond witch willingly surrendered all he sought, Evan's lust for revenge gave way to the desire for unrestrained rapture.

SEA JEWEL (3013, $4.50)
by Penelope Neri

Hot-tempered Alaric had long planned the humiliation of Freya, the daughter of the most hated foe. He'd make the wench from across the ocean his lowly bedchamber slave—but he never suspected she would become the mistress of his heart, his treasured SEA JEWEL.

Available wherever paperbacks are sold, or order direct from the Publisher. Send cover price plus 50¢ per copy for mailing and handling to Zebra Books, Dept. 3067, 475 Park Avenue South, New York, N.Y. 10016. Residents of New York, New Jersey and Pennsylvania must include sales tax. DO NOT SEND CASH.

THIS WILD HEART

PATRICIA PELLICANE

ZEBRA BOOKS
KENSINGTON PUBLISHING CORP.

To my grandchildren,
Timmy, Jackie, Andrew and Anthony.
I love you all.

ZEBRA BOOKS

are published by

Kensington Publishing Corp.
475 Park Avenue South
New York, NY 10016

First printing: July, 1990

Printed in the United States of America

Chapter One

New York City, 1886

The lush sounds of a dreamy waltz permeated the air with seduction. It added, as if the evening weren't heady enough with scent and warmth, to the romance of the night as the music carried over from the huge ballroom, through opened French doors to the darkened stone terrace.

In a shadowy private corner, half-hidden behind a large potted fern, a young couple stood entwined in a heated embrace. Hungry lips, desperate for further tastings, barely parted from her sweetness before they once again lost themselves in the magic that was her mouth. God, but she was sweet. His body strained forward, hard and vibrating with need. Without her noticing, he had backed her more securely into the corner. Her body was lush, full, and dizzyingly soft. He couldn't hold on much longer. He had to make this woman his.

What matter was it if they should come together before the vows were spoken? No one would know. In any case, she would soon be his wife. Damn it, why couldn't he break down her resistance? How could she remain so cool, so in control, even while his passion blazed? God, he doubted his sanity if he was forced to wait much longer.

"Morgan, God," he gasped as he tore his mouth free of her sweetly pliant lips. His breath was hot; it hit her face in desperate pants as he strove for control. His mouth nibbled with erotic tastings at her cheek, her temple, her ear, as Bradley deliberately used all his well-practiced skill to see his ends met. "I can't stand this. Come to my rooms tonight. I want you so bad, I hurt."

Morgan smiled the secret smile known only to women so obviously loved. The moment was exquisite and would forever remain in her heart. He loved her beyond bearing. Had anyone ever known this delight? This joy? How did one manage to absorb such emotion without flying free of the earth's gravity to forever float above their fellow man?

"Please," Bradley coaxed, his confidence in her acquiescence growing, in leaps and bounds, when no protesting murmurs came forth. "I love you," he rasped desperately as his arms tightened and once again his mouth took hers in a kiss that threatened to relieve her of the last of her resistance. Had they been anywhere that offered a bit of privacy, it might have.

Bradley almost smiled in triumph as he heard the soft moan come from her throat and felt her relax further against his body. It never failed. The words, as always, were the magic formula in this game men and women played. No woman could resist after hearing them.

His arm holding her securely at her waist, he bent her back so his mouth might take full advantage of the swells of lush breasts, showing just above the gown's low neckline. Silently he blessed the gods of fashion that allowed him this delightful liberty.

With practiced ease he enticed. With teeth, tongue, and lips he coaxed, and had they been anywhere else, Morgan knew she would have lost her feeble, silent struggle against his desperate need. Mentally she cursed their present position, for she wanted above all to give in to what this man craved.

6

It was with more than a touch of regret that Morgan finally managed the words. "Oh darling. I wish I could, but . . ."

Bradley sighed as he leaned his forehead against hers, his arms falling to his sides as he strove to control the pain that twisted his belly into knots.

"You're going to marry me, you know."

Morgan smiled, her eyes sparkling with happiness as she nodded.

"It will have to be soon." He trailed trembling fingers over the exposed portion of her breasts. "I need to see these. I need to see all of you."

"I love you," she returned. "My father will be home tomorrow morning. Come and speak to him then, and we can be about our plans."

But if Morgan thought the next morning's visit would hold the answer to all her needs, she was destined to suffer a measure of disappointment.

Pacing the floor of her room, Morgan waited for an extraordinarily long time after Bradley left, and still no summons came from the library. A slight frown marred the smoothness of her forehead as she wondered about the delay. Perhaps her father was busy. Morgan gave a brilliant smile. That was it, of course. He had another appointment and hadn't had the chance as yet to tell her the wonderful news. Nervously she waited another half hour and finally, with her patience at an end, she took it upon herself to end this agony.

Morgan ran down the stairs, a smile lingering upon her lips. "Harrison," she whispered, spying the manservant just closing the door as he exited the library, "how much longer will father be with his appointment?" Lord, but she was anxious to hear the glorious news. She couldn't wait to tell the world her happiness. She smiled as her eyes lowered to the silver tray held in his capable hands, silently telling as it boasted a coffeepot and two empty china cups. But Morgan was mistaken when she supposed the two most important men in her life had shared the coffee in companionable leisure. Indeed, the meeting had not gone at all as she imagined, and both were already soothing their respective anger and disappointment in drink.

For the first time in his life, the early hour didn't matter. Andrew Wainright knew he would soon face his daughter's fury. And although many would quiver at one of his dark threatening looks, he knew his daughter held not the slightest fear of him. Indeed, the opposite might be closer to the truth.

"Mr. Wainright is alone, miss," Harrison explained, his expression as always carefully blank, even as he wondered why the young woman would assume her father occupied this early in the morning, when all knew his hours of business wouldn't begin for yet another hour.

Morgan blinked her surprise. Alone? Her father was alone? Why hadn't he called for her then? Didn't he realize how anxiously she awaited the news?

Andrew Wainright was a man of great wealth and power. There was nothing within that power he would not give to his one and only child. With one exception.

Andrew was not ignorant of the fact that he had overcompensated for the loss of her mother. Many believed Morgan to have a strong stubborn and at times reckless streak, much like her father. Andrew supposed that was true, but he knew in his heart it was more than that. He had foolishly spoiled his daughter. Spoiled her rotten, in fact. Idly he wondered if he wouldn't have done the same had Nancy lived. For, since birth, Morgan had been a beautiful creature. Her beauty, combined with her pleasant, if strong, personality made an overwhelming picture. Indeed, she had never given him a moment's trouble. Well, not many, in any case. It had been so easy to give in to her gentle requests. Too easy, Andrew sighed as he took another long swallow of whiskey, for he knew

8

his daughter's usual sweet temper would soon be a thing of the past. Instinctively he knew her fury would have no equal. He wasn't far from wrong.

"You can't be serious!" Morgan gasped her shock. In all her life her father had never refused her anything. Why in the world did he choose to do so now? "Don't you realize how important this is to me?"

"I'm afraid I am serious, Morgan, and yes, I can imagine how important you believe this to be."

"I don't imagine my feelings, Father."

"I know you don't," he returned almost miserably.

"Then why? Why have you refused?"

"The man is a blackguard, damn it! A wastrel! Not fit to wipe your boots. He will not suit."

Morgan shrugged aside the words, not for a moment believing them true. "Will any man suit, Father? This is not the first time you've found fault with my beaus."

Andrew nodded his agreement. "I realize I haven't been as liberal as I might have been in that regard. Still, any one of them would have been preferable to the man you've finally chosen."

"I doubt it. I think you would have done the same with any."

"Morgan, that's not so." He shook his head, hating to do this.

"Exactly what is it about Bradley that so offends?"

Andrew breathed a long weary sigh. "Morgan, he is a womanizer and a braggart to boot. All know of the masterful ways he convinces those unsophisticated lambs to his bed."

"I don't believe it."

"I never thought you would."

"He loves me. He never even looks at another."

"If he told you that, he's a goddamned liar. No one loved more than I did your mother and I looked. Everyone looks."

9

"What I meant was—"

"If you think he's waiting to take you to his bed," Andrew interrupted, "you're mistaken. I can give you names, if you like."

Morgan's eyes misted, her chest twisted with pain. "I never thought you cruel, Father. How can you purposely hurt me like this?"

"It's better, I think, to hurt now than suffer the agony of his infidelities later. I love you. I don't want to see you unhappy."

Morgan gave a wry humorless laugh, her pain giving way to anger. "All done in the name of love? I wonder how many lives were ruined on that pretext."

Morgan knew this man seated across the desk better than most. Once he made up his mind, it would take an act of God, or perhaps the devil, to change it. What she didn't realize was that she could have used the very same words to describe herself. Her lips thinned with growing anger. "I will do as I wish, in any case. I wanted your permission, your blessing, but I don't need it. I'm past the age of consent."

Andrew had wondered when her shock and disappointment would turn to anger. He almost smiled at her show of spunk. "No, you don't need my permission. You can do as you wish," he readily agreed. "But if you go against me, know this. I'll not give you a penny."

Morgan gave a bitter laugh. So it came to this, did it? A battle of wills? Well, we'd see who'd come out the winner here. "I have no need of your money. We both know I have my own. And Bradley"—she smiled victoriously—"why, he's almost as well off as you."

"I'm afraid you're wrong on both counts." Andrew shook his head. "The truth of it is, the monies you call your own wouldn't, for six months, keep you in the silks and satins you're accustomed to, and Bradley is nearly broke."

"Ridiculous!" She laughed without a glimmer of humor. "His family's business—"

10

"Is in ruins, thanks to his gambling."

"Gambling? What gambling? Are you trying to tell me that an occasional hand played in cards makes him a gambler? Father, is there no limit you'd go to ensure your ends?"

"I'm afraid not. But in this case, I hardly had to try."

"Meaning?" And when no answer was immediately forthcoming, Morgan felt a twinge of real fear pierce her heart. "What have you done?"

Suddenly she was out of the chair, facing him with as much fury as he himself ever possessed. She leaned across the desk, her once sweet lips curved into a snarl. "Tell me!"

Andrew knew, not for the first time, this woman would be a powerful adversary, or ally. "Sit down."

"I said tell me, damn it!"

Both father and daughter would have been amazed at her casual use of profanity, for ladies of New York's polite society simply did not indulge. They would have been amazed, that is, had either heard it. But two sets of identical blue eyes clashed, and neither heard anything over their own determined thoughts as each sought to win this, the most important battle of her life.

"Sit down and I will tell you."

Morgan forced herself to relax by degrees, knowing she'd get no information until he was ready to tell her. Finally she almost slumped back into the chair.

Andrew cleared his throat and forced aside the chill he felt at the silent menace in her glare. "After some discussion, Redgrave and I have come to a meeting of the minds."

Morgan made a snorting sound that clearly bespoke her disgust. "Which mind? As if I don't already know."

Andrew ignored her sarcasm and continued, "We've decided to give your relationship time."

"How much time?"

"Six months."

"Six months!" Morgan gasped, unable to believe what

11

she'd heard. "You can't be serious! What am I supposed to do for six months?"

Andrew's eyes narrowed with thought. He didn't trust that bastard Redgrave. Although he doubted the man had the balls to go against him, there was always the outside chance Redgrave might take the money and Morgan. If he disappeared with her for a time, Andrew would have no option but to allow the union, or witness his daughter's disgrace. The best thing to do would be to put Morgan out of the man's reach. Suddenly an idea dawned. "I was thinking you might enjoy a visit to the ranch you've inherited from your mother's friend." And at Morgan's look of incredulity, he added, "Aren't you the least bit curious to see the country? After all, it's where your mother and I came from."

Morgan's beautiful nose wrinkled ever so slightly with distaste. "Hardly."

Andrew grinned at his uppity, willful daughter. For as long as he could remember, he'd catered to her. Lord, but this little lady was in dire need of a man's strong hand. And Redgrave was about as strong as piss in the wind. No, he wasn't the man for her. A moment later, Andrew made his decision. "Well, I think it's time you did."

Andrew felt oddly surprised at the anger that suddenly filled him. He would have thought, after all this time, his resentment toward Jonathan Banks a thing of the past. But amazingly that wasn't the case. His wife was ten years dead and still he felt raging jealousy simply because the man existed.

At times such as these, it didn't matter that Nancy had chosen Andrew over Jonathan. That she had been involved, that she had nearly married the man, that she had once gone to bed with him, was enough for Andrew to feel a renewal of almost insane hatred.

Morgan laughed. "And just what do you think I'd do on a ranch? Rope wild steers? I'm sorry, Father, but I won't wait."

"I'm afraid you have no choice. Even now"—Andrew

consulted the gold timepiece slipped from the pocket of his vest—"he's no doubt packing . . ."

"Packing?" Morgan gasped, her heart suddenly racing in her chest. "For where? Where is he going?"

"I thought it best if he saw a bit of the Continent, before—"

"You thought?" she interrupted with a sneer. "Damn you to hell for your interference."

Andrew forced aside the smile that threatened at her choice of words. Indeed she was growing more out of his control daily. He gave a slight shake of his head. Imagine a lady using such unbefitting language. Still, as long as he held the purse strings, the girl had little choice but to obey.

Morgan came suddenly to her feet, her silk skirt making a swishing sound as it moved against her stiff horsehair petticoat. She was almost at the door before he thought to ask, "Where are you going?"

"I'm going to Bradley. If he's leaving, so am I."

"Elope, you mean? He won't do it, you know."

Her hand was on the doorknob when she turned to face him. "You don't think so?" She smiled in victory, for she alone knew how terribly in love they were, how desperately they wanted each other.

A flicker of doubt flashed in Andrew's eyes. For a moment he wondered if he hadn't misjudged. Did the man truly love his daughter all that much? Did he love her enough to put aside his life-style? Andrew shook his head, knowing the truth of the matter. It had taken little effort on his part to convince the man to wait. If he were truly in love, no amount of money would have made a difference. He never would have accepted the sum Andrew had offered, nor agreed to a half-year's wait.

"Go to him, then. See if you can convince him to go against me."

"You think you have all the answers, don't you? You think you know everything, have the right to control people and the way they live." Morgan's voice lowered to a growl, her stance belligerent. "I'll convince him, all right. We don't need your money. I'm an adult, Father. You'll have to learn to allow me to make my own decisions."

"Darling, you shouldn't have come." At her look of surprise, he quickly added, "But I'm so glad you did. I didn't want to leave without seeing you one more time." Bradley smoothly turned her so her back was to the divan, upon which lay the ruffled drawers of the lady who now occupied his bed. Silently he cursed that Morgan should have chosen to visit his rooms now. How many times had he tried to convince her to come? Only to find her banging on his door in tears at a most inopportune moment.

"You're not leaving. Surely you told him that," she asked hopefully.

"I'm afraid I must." Bradley sighed as he watched her eyes mist prettily.

"I can't be apart from you for six months. I can't bear the thought."

"If we want his blessing, we must accede to his wishes."

"We don't need his blessing. I'm of age. I can marry whomever I choose."

Bradley held her close and cradled her head against his chest, praying that in her distress she wouldn't notice the whore's heavy scent that no doubt clung to him. "I know, darling, but he swore to cut you off without a cent if we didn't—"

"We don't need his money," she interrupted. "I have my own."

Bradley knew the paltry sum of which she spoke. Did she think him a fool? How were they to live on that?

"Money aside, darling." He almost laughed aloud at his words, for there was nothing that he could imagine more important. "Imagine the scandal it would cause. He

14

wouldn't come, you know. Who would walk you down the aisle?"

"We could elope."

"Morgan, you're not serious!" he gasped, clearly astonished that she should harbor such thoughts. God almighty, he'd never be able to live it down, should he so foolishly accede to her wishes. "We'd never again be able to show our faces. Our friends would snub us. Doors would forever be closed to us."

"Is all that so important to you?"

"Not to me darling," he murmured the lie. "To us. I'd never forgive myself if I saw you suffer because of a whim. We can wait. You'll see. Six months are nothing compared to a lifetime of sharing.

"God, when I hold you like this," he groaned, unable to finish his thoughts as her temptingly lush form pressed closer to him. With a sigh that bespoke his torment, he loosened his hold and took a half-step back. "Perhaps it is just as well that I'm going abroad. I couldn't bear to see you and not have you."

"Why? Why are you leaving the country?"

"Family business, my dear," he lied shamelessly, knowing it to be nothing of the sort. He was being paid handsomely to keep his distance. The idea irked. Shit, he hated for the bastard to win. Still, if it weren't for Wainright, he wouldn't be looking forward right now to the fleshpots of Europe. Bradley grinned as he blew at the feather in her hat that insisted on poking him in the eye. He would have it all. Six months of the most licentious living. God, he grinned into the silk flowers of her hat, imagining two maybe three at a time sharing his bed, and then marriage to one of New York's most eligible young ladies. That she was no doubt also one of the richest only endeared her more to his heart. Yes, if he went along with her father's plan, he'd have it all.

"I'll be back, sweetheart. And when I return, nothing and no one will keep me from making you mine."

"Nothing need stop you now," she whispered, her

cheeks flaming at her daring.

Bradley groaned. Christ almighty! Why now? He'd tried for months to bring her to his bed and now, of all times, she suggested they wait no longer. For a wild moment he thought about the woman inside. Surely she'd have no objection to the three of them together. Bradley gave a long sigh, knowing Morgan would be horrified at the thought. Damn, he groaned again. And it could have been such fun.

He had to think. It wasn't nearly as easy as it should have been since the idea of Morgan and the whore together caused all rational thought to flee. He felt himself growing hard at the thought. "We can't. Think, Morgan," he finally managed. "God forbid you become with child. I'll be in Europe. I couldn't stand the thought of your disgrace."

Morgan knew the truth of his words. For one wild moment she almost wished she was with child. Her father couldn't have separated them then. For a spiteful moment she relished the pain she would cause him. It could still be done, she silently reasoned, but almost instantly she thought better of it. No, Bradley was right, that would be a most irresponsible act.

Morgan sighed, knowing she had no choice. She'd wait out the time. She'd visit that stupid ranch and no doubt curse her father for every mile that separated her from her home, her friends, everything she loved. Morgan gave another long sigh. She'd do what had to be done, but in the end, she'd be done with domineering men. Never again would a man force her into anything. She was going to live her own life and marry whomever she chose.

Morgan couldn't have been more mistaken.

Chapter Two

Nevada, 1886

Morgan groaned against the discomfort. Actually, *discomfort* was too mild a word. She'd never before suffered as now. With no real hope of protection, she nevertheless tugged at her wide-brimmed hat in a fruitless attempt to shield herself from the worst of the slashing onslaught. The action did little more than stretch the already drooping brim to her shoulders. Morgan trembled as rain water sluiced over her and ran in shivering cold rivulets beneath the jacket of her traveling dress and down her back. God, would it never stop?

Morgan had thought the ghastly train ride to be a jarring, unbearable task. Followed immediately by the horror of four days traveling by a speeding, rattling, dangerously swaying stagecoach from Elko, where they had departed the train, south the two hundred or so miles to Sweetwater. She had suffered choking dust, unbearable heat, and endless monotony and yet all her previous discomfort was as nothing compared to this.

Despite the padding of frilly drawers, two petticoats, and a thick velvet traveling suit, her bottom felt personally acquainted with every sharp rock and rut the wagon bounced over, while slashing rain had soaked through the many layers of clothing, chilling her, within minutes, clear to the skin. She was a sudden mess. Already covered with layers of dust from traveling, she imagined the dust now turned to mud upon her face and clothes. She was wrong. The heavy downpour had already washed away the grime.

Lord, what she wouldn't give to be clean and dry. Morgan grimaced with remorse. Here she was complaining silently, but complaining nonetheless, while her companion suffered the worst of it. Morgan shot a guilty look toward the woman who huddled beneath the only available slicker in the back of the wagon, knowing the woman's discomfort was her fault. Guilt lay heavily upon her conscience, for it wasn't Morgan whose stiff joints became agonizing centers of pain owing to rheumatism enflamed, no doubt, to an alarming degree by these cursed elements. No, it was Martha. Poor dear Martha, her nurse since childhood, her companion once Morgan had become an adult.

Granted, Morgan had been anxious to see this journey brought to a close, but God, why hadn't she listened to Mr. Mackey's advice? Why was she so stubborn? Why hadn't she spent the night in Sweetwater? There were rooms to rent above Daisey's saloon that could have been taken for a day or so. Both she and Martha had been exhausted from the journey so far suffered. Surely they could have used the rest. But had she allowed it? No, she had stupidly insisted that she reach the Red Rock Ranch today. She'd hired a wagon at the livery and Mr. Mackey to drive, while ignoring his warnings of a storm. Damn. When was she going to think before she so foolishly acted?

"How much farther?" she again dared to ask.

"A ways yet," was all she could get this dolt of a man to answer.

They had been traveling almost three hours and Morgan doubted the man had said more than two sentences in all that time. "You don't speak much, do you?"

"Nope."

"Is there a particular reason why?"

"I figure, when I got something important to say, no one's goin' to listen if I rattle off at the mouth."

Morgan groaned in silent despair. Was this a sampling of the mentality of these people? Were those at the ranch as peculiar in their way of thinking? Morgan shuddered, imagining herself forced to contend with these people for six months' time. She, who loved the gay parties of New York and the many friends she had acquired over the years, was destined to grow mad if quartered with people like this. But she wouldn't be quartered with them, she silently corrected with unbound relief. She'd have her own place to stay, while the men slept in the bunkhouse. She knew at least that much from the penny novels she'd read.

Lord, she prayed there were neighbors living nearby. How was she to stand little more than her own company for six months?

The wagon gave a sharp lurch as it slid into a deep rut and Morgan cried out as her stiff fingers clung fiercely to the seat. There was no road, at least none that she could detect. Nothing but mud and ruts and still more mud. How did he know they were going in the right direction? Morgan dared to raise her eyes to the downpour. She could see nothing but an almost solid curtain of gray water and flat, desolate, empty land.

Perhaps a quarter of an hour later, Morgan felt her heart flutter with excitement as they mounted a small rise. Despite the dusk of evening and almost blinding rain, she could detect ahead the distinct outline of three large weathered buildings. Red Rock. They were here at last. Morgan offered a silent prayer of thanks. Never could she remember feeling this measure of relief just knowing her journey at an end. Morgan closed her eyes, a whisper of a smile curving her lips as she imagined herself dry and comfortable sitting at last before a roaring fire.

To be sure, the buildings didn't look like much, but that was no doubt due to the distance involved and inclement weather conditions. The problem was that the closer they came, the worse the buildings appeared, until Morgan watched with a sinking heart as the wagon stopped before what one could only call a shack.

The main house was made of stone, red stone, if she wasn't mistaken. It was small, very small, but that wasn't what horrified her. It was the roof. A roof made of sod, and what was left of it slumped sickeningly at its center as if it had finally given up its struggle to the elements. The door was closed, if indeed the sparse slabs of rough wood constituted a door, for in its present state it could hardly offer a measure of protection from the wind and rain. It took no effort for her to see light through its wide cracks. Windows were broken and covered with tar paper or irregular chunks of wood. Morgan breathed a sigh of despair. She had no reason to believe the house wouldn't be as equally unacceptable inside as out.

Along the front of the building ran a narrow covered porch. At one end the roof of the wooden structure sloped as well as the floor leaning down toward the muddy ground, until it resembled a ramp. Morgan wondered how the whole of it had managed to remain standing, for it appeared unable to withstand even the gentlest of breezes. Fearfully she wondered if it would accommodate even her slight weight. She was loath to put it to the test.

"Ain't much." Mr. Mackey gave a slow shrug as he watched her push back the brim of her hat. Her eyes were wide with horror.

Morgan had left New York with the mistaken impression that, although she wouldn't be living near Virginia City, a thriving and notorious metropolis, surely Nevada offered many smaller cities that could compare. One glance told her the fallacy of that assumption, for Sweetwater boasted of no stately mansions, no fine restaurants, no luxurious hotels. Lillian Russell and

Sarah Bernhardt had never come within a hundred miles of this godforsaken place. And yet nothing in her wildest imaginings had prepared her for this.

Morgan glanced at the man at her side, wondering if he realized the degree of his understatement. It took her a full minute to gain control of her emotions, for she wanted nothing more than to sit there and cry. How could her father have sentenced her to this? Surely he hadn't realized the disreputable conditions she'd be forced to suffer.

Father's insistence or no, Morgan knew she and the Red Rock Ranch would be parting company. Her first impulse was to order the man to drive them back to Sweetwater with all haste, but a quick glance at Martha's shivering form and tightly pinched face and she reconsidered. Tomorrow would surely be soon enough. Somehow they would make it through this horrible night. And after they spent a few days recuperating in town, they would again begin their journey. Only this time they were going home and she didn't care if her father ranted from here to kingdom come. She was going back to New York where she belonged.

Her voice was low and husky, filled with no real hope, when she finally managed, "Perhaps you might direct us to more acceptable accommodation, Mr. Mackey."

He shrugged his skeletal frame and offered, "There's the bunkhouse."

"I think not," Morgan answered quickly, for she'd gladly brave these elements and more before she'd consider sleeping with the dozen or more men she knew managed this place.

Mr. Mackey shrugged again and Morgan wondered if the man ever spoke without first making that movement. "The barn is dry. Can't say how warm, though."

Morgan shook her head, knowing that her delaying the inevitable only caused Martha further pain. "No doubt it's warmer inside than it appears."

Mr. Mackey jumped to the muddy ground and was

tying the reins to a wobbly hitching rail when the door to the shack opened and a man stepped out to the shaky porch. Morgan couldn't see his features, for besides the fact that the rain had yet to abate, the man stood silhouetted in the light from within. His bulk nearly filled the doorway. Idly Morgan wondered how his spindly legs could support such weight.

"Who's there?" he called out, his voice slightly slurred, Morgan imagined from sleep.

"I've brought you some company, Seth," Mr. Mackey returned as he came around to aid Morgan in her descent.

Morgan hurried to the rear of the wagon and helped Martha to her feet. The two women then moved toward the sorry shelter.

The man staggered forward, lost his balance, and fell. Morgan cried out her alarm as he crumbled as if dead to the floor.

It had taken all three men summoned from the bunkhouse to bring Seth inside, a task easier by far than carting him back to his bed. With much groaning and grunting, they heaved a thankful final sigh that his bulk was finally settled upon the bed. Morgan had followed the straining men as far as the bedroom door, leaving Martha to huddle before the fire. She stood in the narrow hall, off of which were three doors in all, each she imagined leading to bedrooms. But even the hall wasn't far enough away. She had no need to ask what ailed the man, for none among them could deny the unmistakable stench of whiskey that permeated the air.

"We didn't figure you'd be comin' till next week, miss," one man, the oldest of the three, offered in sheepish apology, leaving Morgan to assume he believed it was all right to drink oneself into a drunken stupor if you weren't expecting company. A moment later the man wiped his hand on the leg of his pants and offered it to her in welcome. Morgan didn't think but to take his hand. A moment later she'd have cause to reconsider that impulsive action. He cleared his throat. "Name's Johnny," he said as he pumped her hand with all the delicacy of a cowboy pushing a steer into its holding pen. "This here is Luke and Matt."

Morgan's wet flopping hat fell forward, almost blocking her view of the two shyer men. Her eyes widened at the gregarious greeting her slight form was taking. Lord, she wondered, did he expect her to spout water if he pumped hard enough? Apparently Johnny realized his strength for he suddenly let go of her hand. He turned beet red and cleared his throat again. "There'd be extra rooms." He nodded down the hallway behind her.

Morgan nodded and smiled politely. "Thank you, Mr. Johnny."

"Just Johnny, miss. No need to stand on ceremony this far out."

Out of what? Morgan silently wondered as she sighed in despair. What on earth had she gotten herself into? Why had she ever agreed to come to this godforsaken place?

All eyes turned as Seth moaned from the bed. Morgan, standing just outside the room, longed to ask if this was his usual habit, but decided it was none of her concern how the men on this place chose to live. In any case she was leaving in the morning. Her spine stiffened with determination. Just let anyone try and stop her.

Morgan had harbored the hope that a fire would take the chill from her bones, and it surely should have, especially since she had created a nearly roaring inferno in the fireplace. But in the end the flames lent little warmth to the room, since most of the heat fled through the giant open patches in the roof.

Finally, with teeth chattering, Morgan made her way to the bedroom she and Martha had hastily cleared. She was exhausted. It had been weeks since she last found herself in a comfortable bed. A moment later she slid beneath the covers.

Thank God, the roof didn't leak in this room. Morgan couldn't say the same for the kitchen and parlor. She shook her head with disgust, for pans of every size and shape dotted the floors of those two rooms.

Morgan snuggled against Martha's warm back, greedily absorbing what she could of the older woman's body heat. Lord, had she ever felt so cold?

Sometime later, perhaps only minutes later, Morgan came awake to the sounds of Seth's thunderous snores. Good Lord! How could the man sleep with all that noise? It was amazing he didn't wake himself up.

She felt chilled and reached for the warm body that was supposed to be lying beside her. But Martha's side of the bed was empty. Vaguely she remembered Martha telling her she was going to the outhouse. It was totally dark. Morgan couldn't see a thing. She shivered beneath the thin wool blanket, less from the cold than the darkness, for Martha had taken the lantern with her when she left. Morgan's lip lifted in a self-mocking sneer. It had been a long time since she was afraid of the dark, but this eerie, decrepit house easily transported her back to a childhood where ghosts and goblins occupied every corner of her bedroom. In truth her fears were less of the supernatural and more of what might lurk outside her bedroom in human form. "Hurry, Martha," she murmured to no one as she lay curled tightly upon the feather mattress, her body tense, her eyes fearfully searching out the dark corners of the room.

Morgan heard the soft sound of a slippered foot. She breathed a sigh of relief and felt herself relax. She rolled from her side and snuggled her head deeper into the pillow. Her eyes were closed as she remarked, "What took you so long?" An instant later she gasped and emitted a sound that much resembled a choking squeak as out of the dark a heavy weight landed full upon her.

24

Youngblood grunted a startled curse as he felt something, or more to the point someone in the bed. His hand brushed against a full breast. His hips nestled as though purposely aimed between the sweet delight of soft thighs. His cheek against thick smooth hair. Instantly his mind registered softness. Womanly softness. A frown creased his brow. What the hell was a woman doing lying in this bed?

Youngblood came immediately to his feet, and if his hands fumbled in the dark, touching her where he had no business touching, he couldn't really be blamed. Could he?

The whole thing happened so fast, Morgan began to wonder if she hadn't imagined it; one second he was there, the next he wasn't. Perhaps she had been dreaming.

She heard the sound of a lantern's chimney being lifted. Suddenly a match flared to life and the small room took on a soft golden glow. Instantly she knew, of course, this was no dream.

Youngblood's eyes widened with amazement. So the face matched the body in beauty. While he had fumbled in the dark, the thought had crossed his mind to wonder at the possibility. "I would have come sooner had I known you were waiting for me."

At the sound of the obviously male voice, Morgan shot up as if catapulted from the bed. She had hoped it her imagination or perhaps a dream. If not, it had to be Martha who had stumbled over her. For one wild, near hysterical moment she had prayed it to be so.

Unconcerned as to her mode of dress, or to be more precise, her lack of dress, she faced the now grinning man who had fallen upon her in the dark.

Morgan's eyes rounded with fright. Her heart pounded so hard she couldn't quite get her breath. An Indian! A half-naked savage was standing not two feet from her. Where had he come from? What was he doing here? Dear Lord, she cried a silent prayer, help me! There wasn't a portion of her entire body that didn't tingle with terror. The shadows of the small room began to swim around her. She was going to faint. No she wasn't! Morgan gasped for air. She couldn't allow herself the luxury. There was no telling what he would do if she fell at his feet.

Joseph Youngblood looked down with amazement at the tiny woman as she shook a mass of heavy blond curls from her eyes. He forced himself to ignore the fact that they fell in silky golden waves to her waist. What the hell was she doing here, so soon? They'd been notified only this week that she was on her way. He hadn't expected her for at least another week.

His eyes were dark; in the dim light of the lantern they appeared black. But the light wasn't dim enough for Morgan not to notice where they had come to rest. For the moment Morgan cared not at all about her lack of modesty. She was too scared, in any case, to do anything about it.

She glanced toward the bedroom door and knew instantly she had no chance of escaping, for the huge Indian blocked the opening. Idly she wondered if she could make it to the window and out to the bunkhouse before he grabbed her. She took a step back, only to find the Indian had moved as well.

"Who are you?" he asked. His gaze clung to the sheerness of her nightdress. Beneath the lacy fabric was the clear form of womanly fullness and the hint of dark rosy nipples. Unconsciously he wet his lips at the delicious sight.

"Mor . . . Mor . . ." She shuddered with fright and finally managed, in a voice half-strangled with fright, "Get out!" She took yet another step, only to find him maintaining the distance between them.

Youngblood grinned; startling white teeth flashed against a bronzed face. He knew full well the terror she suffered and silently applauded her control. "What are you doing here, Mor, Mor, get out?"

26

Morgan blinked in confusion, never thinking to answer his question. Was he teasing her? Certainly not. Indians didn't tease, did they? Indians killed. At least she'd heard they did. Why hadn't she thought to find out? God, how had she allowed herself to wallow so deeply in her private misery of a lost love—temporarily lost love, she silently corrected—not to have looked into the conditions here? First the uninhabitable housing and now this!

Were the Indians in these parts friendly? Did they still go on the warpath? Lord, she should be ashamed at her ignorance, and perhaps she might have been, had she not been half out of her mind with terror.

"Who are you?" Morgan asked, and thanked God that her voice hardly trembled at all. Silently she prayed he wouldn't notice, for she somehow knew herself at a distinct disadvantage if this Indian recognized her fear.

She was a good two minutes too late.

"Youngblood. Who are you?" he asked, knowing full well who she was.

Morgan ignored his question. "What do you want?" she asked as she took another step, inching her way toward the window and praying Johnny slept within easy reach of a gun.

Youngblood grinned, wondering what her reaction would be if he told her exactly what he wanted. Purposely he forced the smile from his lips, knowing full well her intent, for her eyes darted toward the window again and again. He shrugged, and in an attempt to calm her fears, he purposely stepped back and set the lantern on a small table that should have held a pitcher and bowl for washing. In a movement meant to imply his lack of menace, he crossed his arms over his chest and leaned his shoulder against the door jamb.

Had Morgan not been filled with almost debilitating fear, she might have noticed his stance held no aggression, but was one of pure male confidence as he shifted one leg over the other. "What have you got?" His

27

dark gaze moved to her heaving chest as she struggled for every breath.

Youngblood cursed the lack of light. When he'd lit the lantern, he hadn't thought to turn it up all the way; now it did little more than hint at what lay beyond that soft frothy lace. Suddenly his gaze returned to hers. Jesus, she had the most beautiful eyes. They were huge and as blue as a clear sky. Idly he wondered what they'd look like half-closed and filled with passion. And that mouth. He felt a distinct stirring in his groin. Was it as soft as it appeared? For a second the wild thought came to sample those pale pink lips and know firsthand his silent wonderings. Purposely he shook himself from the tempting thoughts, knowing she'd no doubt awaken the entire ranch with her screams if he were to make such an obvious move toward her. He forced a deliberately nonchalant shrug. "Indians have been known to trade most anything."

Morgan looked wildly around the room. Trade! That was it. He had come to trade. Only she couldn't imagine what would interest him. Suddenly she dashed toward the table beside her bed and grabbed the extinguished candle and holder. In a moment she was back, almost tripping over the hem of her gown "Here, take this."

Youngblood grinned and shook his head as he placed it upon the table. "I already have one."

A flicker of renewed fear mingled with desperation darkened her eyes to midnight blue. Suddenly they flashed with hope anew as she realized he'd want something more substantial. "A saddle! That's it! In the barn. Take one." She amended that. "Take two."

Youngblood's eyes widened with mirth. It was amazing how generous this woman could be, especially since everything she'd so far offered already belonged to him. "I've one of those as well."

Morgan, desperate to see the last of him, spied her one and only blanket. She ran to it, grabbed it up, and forced it into his hands. "Here," she exclaimed as she pressed it upon him. "I insist. Take it."

"That's very nice of you, but won't you be cold?"

"I'll be fine. Just take it and go."

"You want me to leave?" he asked as if the idea had never occurred to him.

Good Lord, but that was an understatement. She not only wanted him to go, but wanted never to see the likes of him again. She could live a long time without this particular brand of terror.

Wrapped up in her thoughts, Morgan never realized just how close she was standing to this man. Suddenly, without thinking, he reached out and his fingers slid through the heavy mass of curls and waves that had fallen over her shoulder. Silently he watched as one curl wrapped with enticing silkiness around his roughly calloused finger.

Morgan shuddered as she recognized his interest. In her terror, she'd never noticed the sexual hunger that had entered his eyes. Why had she taken her hair down? It had been wet, came a reasonable voice from the back of her mind. That's no excuse, she countered. If she'd left it up, he might not have noticed it at all. It was so light, so different from his own, it was bound to bring a certain amount of interest. He might have left her, satisfied with the one and only blanket she and Martha had between them, if she'd had the sense to at least braid it into a more sedate style.

Morgan trembled as one thought refused to abate. Did Indians still take scalps? Oh God, she thought wildly, if only she'd thought to keep her hat on! In bed? she silently questioned. Ridiculous. No one went to bed with their hat. Morgan groaned at her nonsensical thoughts. Here she was facing certain disaster and all she seemed capable of was allowing her mind to ramble on about a hat.

Her hat! Why hadn't she thought of it before? Indians were known to like pretty things. And her hat was pretty, what with all the flowers and that beautiful blue bird perched upon it. At least it had once been pretty before the torrential rains had turned it into a sodden mess.

An instant later she nearly flew to the opposite wall and wrenched the wide-brimmed hat from a nail, almost tearing it in the process. She pushed it at him. "Take it," she insisted with such force as to nearly ram it into his stomach.

Youngblood dropped the blanket at his feet and fingered the absurdly adorned apparel. His lips twisted into a grin. "Interesting," he remarked, his laughter at the monstrosity barely restrained. "Have you anything else you might want to give me?" His eyes sparkled with humor. "That little concoction you're wearing, for instance?" He was tempted to tell her just how thin the material was, almost useless in fact, but knew she'd immediately seek cover if she realized the truth of the matter. He might not be able to see all he wished, but what he could see was better than nothing.

"What?" she asked in astonishment. Morgan again blinked, while color rushed to her cheeks at his unmistakable inference. He definitely was teasing her and no doubt had been all along. Why had she allowed herself to become so frightened that she did not notice before? Lord, but she'd made a complete fool of herself, running around the room like a mindless idiot, while he stood there watching, never offering a word to relieve her fears.

Morgan breathed a long steadying sigh, realizing at last she had nothing to fear from this man. "That was most unkind, wouldn't you agree?" she asked as her hands came to her hips and she glared at his grinning face.

"Perhaps, but your performance was entertaining to say the least. I was beginning to wonder what else you'd be willing to give up. Especially since nothing here is yours."

Morgan nodded as she digested his words. He knew too much to be a casual visitor. "You work here, I take it?"

Youngblood shrugged. "You could say that."

Blood pounded in her brain. "Is this what you people call Western hospitality? Scaring someone half to death?"

Youngblood chuckled. "What did I do? All I wanted was to go to bed. Seth fell asleep in mine. I thought I could crawl into the only spare bed here. It was you who insisted I take half the contents of this place."

Morgan was filled with a fury she'd never quite believed possible. Damn this man and his obnoxious grin! Obviously he didn't know who she was or he wouldn't have dared this charade. Her lips grew hard with a victorious sneer, suddenly anxious to see just how prone he'd be toward laughter when he found out he was fired. Tomorrow she'd talk to whomever had been left in charge. She couldn't wait to see the last of this one. For some reason his good looks only added to her wish to see him gone from here.

She'd liked to have given him a piece of her mind, but dared not. Although for the moment he appeared without menace, she didn't trust a strange man—and indeed he'd have to be strange to run around at night dressed like a savage—to the sharpness of her tongue. No, tomorrow would be soon enough. Tomorrow she'd let the foreman handle this brute.

Now that her fright had passed, Morgan allowed her gaze to move over this stranger. She never considered herself particularly small, but he was so big as to make her feel tiny in comparison. Nearly naked, but for a breechcloth and moccasins—no doubt the reason she had not heard his approach—he was bronze all over. And she did mean all over, for owing to his near-naked state, there was little left to her imagination. His hair was black and glistened with faint blue highlights even in the inadequate light of the lantern. It wasn't short, but still not nearly as long as she imagined Indians usually wore it. It was held from falling in his eyes by a plain band of rawhide around his forehead.

His chest was wide, unbelievably so. His belly flat, the

31

entire upper half of his body was ridged with muscle she imagined hard to the touch. A whorl of dark hair surrounded his navel and dusted what looked like smooth skin of his chest and arms. *Hair?* Weren't Indian's supposed to be without? Her lips tightened further with clear disapproval. So he wasn't an Indian, after all. But for the slight slant of his eyes and the darkness of his skin, and of course, his ridiculous costume, she wouldn't have been fooled at all.

Morgan silently cursed her stupidity. She should have known simply by his manner of speech. This man was no savage, at least not in the true sense of the word. He was obviously educated. Now that she thought on it, she knew that accent, even if he deliberately tried to hide it. Soon she'd remember where she'd heard it.

"You're not an Indian. Why do you dress like that?"

"What makes you think I'm not?"

Morgan refused to go into detail. Her cheeks grew hot at the very thought. No matter her usual daring and almost madcap antics, it was quite beyond the realm of possibility to speak openly about parts of the human body. She stated simply, "I know you're not."

"Sorry to disappoint you, honey, but I am."

"But I thought . . ." she began, only to interrupt herself by pursing her lips in a tight straight line.

"What? What did you think?"

"Nothing," she returned, growing decidedly more uncomfortable the longer they stood there. Didn't the man realize his half-naked state? Didn't he know she could see nearly everything? How could she be expected to carry on a casual conversation while he . . . while the both of them, for that matter, stood there more than half undressed? Morgan gasped as she realized at last her own state of dress. Quickly she snatched the blanket from her feet and held it against herself. Good God, she'd been so terrorized she'd unknowingly given him quite a show. Her lips thinned in anger as she watched his mouth soften in a teasing, all too wicked smile, a smile that had no doubt softened many a heart. Damn him, she silently railed. Not once had he commented on her state of undress, and from the look in his eyes, she knew he had obviously enjoyed the display.

He had to have known he had frightened her nearly out of her wits. Frightened her, in fact, into forgetting everything but his most unsettling presence. Somehow she doubted he'd still be smiling tomorrow. She, on the other hand, was going to laugh herself silly as she watched him thrown off this place.

No sooner had Morgan spread the blanket over the bed again, than she heard a bloodcurdling scream cut eerily short. In a flash she was running toward the sound, only to be stopped dead in her tracks by the sight of Martha's limp form cradled against Youngblood's chest.

"Does she belong to you?" he asked as he nodded toward the woman lying unconscious in his arms.

"What have you done to her?"

"Me?" Youngblood grinned. "Not a thing," he protested in all innocence. "I think something scared her."

"I can't imagine what," she returned snidely as the quite obviously amused man moved into her room.

"Nor I." Youngblood grinned again as he laid the woman upon the now smooth blanket.

"Do you get a particular thrill out of scaring defenseless women, Mr. Youngblood?"

"Can't rightly say, honey," he shrugged. "Never done it before."

Morgan's eyes widened at the sudden change in both tone and accent. Gone was the educated eastern flavor, replaced by a decidedly western twang. Absently, she wondered why, then dismissed the thought as insignificant.

"Till tonight, you mean," she said.

He shrugged again and, in lieu of an explanation,

offered, "Don't usually find the place crawling with womenfolk. A man can pretty much dress and do as he pleases around here."

"So it's my fault that you run around naked, scaring everyone in sight?"

"Naked?" he asked with a grin as he allowed his gaze to wander down the length of his body. "I wouldn't consider myself naked, honey."

"Well, you're as close to it as I care to see."

"How do you know?"

"How do I know what?"

"How do you know you wouldn't care to see more."

"Because I just told you so."

He opened his mouth, but she hastily cut him off, "I think this sorry conversation has reached its conclusion, Mr. Youngblood. You may leave now," she remarked, her tone as frosty as a winter day.

Youngblood chuckled, a low and silky sound, as he nodded in her direction. "Yes, ma'am." His gaze fell upon the blanket. Suddenly he leaned down, fingering the material. "Is this all you have?"

Morgan nodded.

"What the hell is the matter with Seth? Why didn't he give you more?"

"It appears Seth is temporarily indisposed. I didn't know my own bedding was wet until I opened the trunks. By that time the men had left. No doubt they were already asleep."

"There are blankets in the trunk." Youngblood nodded over her shoulder. "It was a damn fool thing for you to come out here in the first place. You should have known a ranch was no fit place for the likes of you."

"And what likes is that, Mr. Youngblood?"

"City folks." His voice and expression told clearly his aversion. "Especially ladies with citified ways," he continued, his voice heavily laced with disgust.

Youngblood didn't know it at the time, but that one statement sealed his future. Morgan fumed at the

34

condescension in his tone. How dare he put her on the defensive simply because she had been born in the city. How did that fact make her inferior to this savage? If anything, she reasoned silently, her place of birth only put her above this beast. Morgan glared her resentment. Her head snapped up, her small chin jutted forth, her whole continence ready to do battle. "Oh? And by 'citified ways' I assume you mean by expecting people to wear clothes."

Youngblood grinned at her rising anger, her obvious sarcasm. He ignored her question and remarked, "No problem. Someone will take you back to town in the morning."

"Will they?" she asked snidely. "Whatever for?"

"So you can take the next stagecoach back to where you came from." He shrugged. "The train depot in Elko, I expect."

Morgan's smile was totally lacking in humor. "And why would I want to do that?"

"You ain't tellin' me you're stayin'?" he asked in obvious ridicule.

"No, Mr. Youngblood, I'm not telling you I'm staying." She smiled as she watched him breathe an obvious sigh of relief. "I'm not telling you that because it's none of your business."

Youngblood's eyes narrowed threateningly. "You stayin' or not?" Unbelievably he felt a surge of terror, but immediately squashed the feeling. What did he have to be afraid of? Certainly not this snippy, smart-mouthed, city woman.

Morgan bristled at his audacity. Her chin rose a notch, her eyes glared her contempt. "How dare you presume to question me? Do you know who I am?"

"As a matter of fact, I do. Your father's people sent word you were on your way."

"And you thought to welcome your employer with the most outrageous display of rudeness she'd ever seen?"

"You ain't my employer, honey."

"You got that right, and I'll make a special effort to thank the Lord tonight for his abundant mercy." Her eyes were as hard as blue chips of ice. "I want you off this place first thing in the morning."

Youngblood grinned. So she wanted him out of here, did she? Well, not any more than he wanted her gone. Jesus, this was just what he needed. What the hell was he going to do with this woman?

One thought came to mind, but he quickly discarded the delicious idea. Not a chance. He wasn't going to get involved with this one. He knew her kind all right. They were poison. He might be attracted, but that didn't mean a damn thing. He was attracted to plenty of women. Had been since he was little more than a kid. Had more than his share since then, too.

Damn! He didn't need the aggravation this little snip was sure to cause. He didn't need to feel this stirring when he looked at her. She was trouble, this one, but the most beautiful trouble he was likely to every lay his eyes on. The thing was he wanted more than to lay his eyes on her. Hell! He had to get rid of her and right away, before . . . before . . . Youngblood couldn't finish the thought, for he had no idea why it was suddenly so important. He just knew it was.

There was no possible way someone like her could fit into a place like this. All she could do was cause trouble.

In an effort to deny how deeply she affected him, his eyes hardened and his fists came to rest on his naked hips in a threatening stance that had frightened off more than one man. But none of his belligerence registered on Morgan as her eyes widened, for his hips had tilted forward in the most disgraceful and flagrant display of masculinity she'd ever seen. "And who's going to make me?"

Morgan glared at his stance and shivered as her gaze was helplessly drawn to his long bronzed length. God, what was the matter with her? She wasn't afraid of this beast. Not now. Not since she realized he had been

36

playing with her fears. Why then did the sight of him send shivers down her spine? Morgan forced aside the sudden fluttering in her chest, swearing the cause of her suddenly sweaty palms and rapidly beating heart was not standing before her. She shot him a confident grin. "I'm sure once I have a word with the sheriff—"

"Why would you want to do that?"

"Because I'm the owner of this place and—"

Youngblood flashed her a cocky grin and interrupted again. "The sole owner?"

Morgan's mouth opened and closed, twice. She knew she must look ridiculous, but for the life of her, she couldn't seem to utter a sound. Her mind worked at full speed trying to absorb his meaning. It couldn't be, of course. No doubt he was trying to upset her further. Please, no, she silently cried. It couldn't be that she and this terrible man owned equal shares of this place! He couldn't be her partner!

But he was. Somehow, deep inside, she knew he was. Why hadn't she been informed of this before? She knew, of course, she had inherited only half-interest in this ranch. But she had supposed her partner to be an absentee owner. He was a miner, wasn't he? Hadn't her father's lawyer said as much? What was he doing here then? Why had it taken an abominable trip to a godforsaken corner of this earth before the truth was known? God, she gave a soft groan, what had she ever done to deserve this? She'd been a good child, an obedient child. She gave a quick grimace and the slightest of shrugs. Well, perhaps she hadn't been all that good or obedient, she silently admitted, but Lord, she'd never been this bad! Why had her father seen fit to throw her into this nightmarish hell?

It was bad enough she was forced to go without the simple amenities she'd known. This house, a house that was closer in fact to a hut, had no gas lights, no running water, no servants. No telephone, not that she knew anyone within a thousand miles she could call. Morgan's sigh was filled with self-pity at her misfortune. Lord, she had to use an outhouse! Could anything be more uncivilized? All of this was surely bad enough, but what was worse—far worse, she was beginning to realize—was she'd have to contend with this most obnoxious character for as long as she stayed.

Both of them looked down as Martha began to moan, each registering some surprise to realize they had completely forgotten the woman's presence.

"Guess I'd best be gettin' out of here. Wouldn't want to scare the lady again." He glanced across Martha's prone body and grinned at Morgan's still astonished expression. "Night, honey."

Morgan's lips grew tight with displeasure. "A word of warning, Mr. Youngblood. If you call me 'honey' in that disgusting tone again, I won't be held accountable for my actions."

Youngblood laughed aloud at her threat. "Now that does sound interestin', honey. Just what actions might those be?"

His amused gaze held hers for a long breathless moment as he silently dared her to do her worst.

Morgan gnashed her teeth with the effort it took not to rail at him. She wouldn't give this no-account the satisfaction of knowing how greatly he had upset her. No, he didn't deserve even that much consideration. Her head pounded with impotent, almost blinding fury as she fought to control her expression. She sighed with relief as he finally turned and sauntered, calm as you please, out of the room. She cursed the soft echoing laughter that floated in his wake. The sound mingled with Seth's snores long after he was gone.

Chapter Three

"I don't mind telling you, it scared a good ten years off my life."

Morgan smiled, listening to Martha's ramblings as the woman finished fastening the last of the tiny cloth-covered buttons of Morgan's shirtwaist. It wasn't yet light. Still, from the bedroom, the two women peered with some interest through a window thickly coated with dirt. In the cool, quiet predawn, they could hear the grumbling sounds of sleepy men as they stumbled from the bunkhouse. Again and again the door to the outhouse slammed shut. The pump handle squeaked, water splashed. Someone cursed and another barked out a laugh.

It was quiet inside the house. Seth had at long last given up the ghastly grunts, snorts, and snores and had drifted into a more peaceful sleep. Too late, Morgan thought. The jarring broken sounds had caused her to lie in the dark for hours before she fell back to sleep, only to awaken before light at the sudden and complete silence.

Morgan smoothed her blouse into the high waistband of her skirt as she walked into the parlor, while shooting a glaring, resentful look at the bedroom door behind which Seth now peacefully slept.

The nearly see-through door and glassless windows did little to prevent the delicious smells of breakfast from

39

drifting into the shack and the sudden impolite rumblings in Morgan's stomach reminded her that she and Martha had not eaten since noon yesterday.

With no little dismay, Morgan glanced around the large rough rooms that served as both kitchen and parlor. The house was indeed larger than it had appeared last night, but no matter its size, Morgan couldn't in all honesty call this sorry structure a house. "I can imagine," Morgan remarked, remembering her first reaction to the man in question.

"You'll never know what I felt when I saw him walking out of the room swinging your hat. I thought . . . I thought," Martha shuddered, unable to put into words the terror she'd known.

Morgan reached around the older woman's shoulders and closed her in a tender embrace. "It's over now, Martha. You have no need to worry. Mr. Youngblood, although thoroughly obnoxious, is harmless enough."

"I don't know if I'd go that far," Youngblood remarked, appearing suddenly in the short hallway. "No man likes to think he's harmless."

Morgan's blue eyes fought a silent duel with his black ones until a soft flush covered her clear skin. She had been almost asleep before she remembered his remark about finding her in the only spare bed. At the time she'd been angry enough not to have cared. She was still angry enough. No, she wouldn't feel guilty putting this man out of his bed. In truth it had been Seth who had done that. No doubt he had made himself comfortable enough on the floor somewhere. Actually, she didn't care if he had or not.

Her gaze lowered to his chest and Morgan gave a silent groan at the sight of him. He was wearing tight Levi's, popular among miners since the days of the California gold rush, leather chaps, boots, and an open leather vest. A bandanna was tied at his throat. In his hands he held a hat. Damn the man! Had he an aversion to proper clothes? Why wasn't he wearing a shirt?

Morgan felt shivering sparks of excitement race up her spine as her gaze took in his exposed chest. Suddenly her lips tightened and she knew it wasn't Seth's noisy sleep that had kept her awake most of the night. She had lain awake for hours cursing this man and his abominable arrogance. And when she had finally slept, her dreams . . . well, she didn't want to think about her dreams right now.

Morgan turned her back to the man, suddenly unable to face him lest her eyes betray the disgraceful thoughts that had come unsuspectingly upon her in sleep. Her cheeks grew a guilty pink, while tiny pinpricks of undefined sensation spread down her spine. He was staring at her, no doubt wondering why she was suddenly reluctant to meet his eyes. She could feel his gaze as surely as if it had been his hands running the length of her back. Morgan was pretending to adjust the already smoothed waistband of her skirt when she heard him introduce himself to Martha. A moment later he apologized for the scare he had given her.

Morgan turned, her eyes wide with amazement, for she hadn't missed the soft gush of sound as Martha nearly cooed her reply. "Oh, that's all right. I realize now it was silly of me, but at the time I thought—"

"It wasn't the least bit silly of you, ma'am," Youngblood interrupted, his voice as smooth as silk. "And I can well imagine what you thought." He grinned at the obviously besotted woman. "If I'd have known you were here, I would have made sure to dress more appropriately. The last thing I wanted to do was to scare two ladies."

My ass, Morgan mentally ranted, taking great pleasure in the crass, if silent, expression so often used by her father. This beast had found delight in scaring her. He'd even been obnoxious enough to admit her terror most entertaining.

"If you're hungry, breakfast is ready. I'm afraid we take most of our meals outside, weather permitting. I

41

hope you don't mind."

Martha smiled. "Of course not." Morgan's eyes widened as Martha actually giggled like a young girl when he offered her his arm.

"Please, help yourselves to whatever you like," he remarked as his eyes met Morgan's gaze over Martha's head. His lurid grin left her with no doubt as to the double entendre in his words.

Wisely Morgan chose to ignore the taunt, but at Martha's sickening simper quickly forgot her intent. "How kind of you, Mr. Youngblood." Her small chin jutted forth in a show of belligerence, her lips tightened with disdain. "How very kind, indeed, to offer what is already mine."

Youngblood grinned. "And mine," he added, no doubt just to aggravate her.

Martha's round gray eyes moved from one to the other, silently wondering why the tension between them. Could it be they didn't like one another? How was that possible on so short an acquaintance? Martha sighed. It would have been so much easier if they could have gotten along, especially since it seemed they were destined to share the same living quarters. A peacemaker at heart, Martha disliked arguments of any kind and would go out of her way to avoid hostilities. Her eyes narrowed as she studied Morgan. What was the matter with her? Why was she so obviously angry? Mr. Youngblood seemed a nice enough sort and he sure was easy to look at. Martha couldn't remember a man who was easier.

Her stomach rumbled. Well, she was hungry. Whatever was the matter with these two would have to wait till later. "Are you coming, dear?"

Morgan tore her stormy gaze from Youngblood's. "No. You go ahead. I want to speak to Mr. Youngblood."

Martha shrugged and left the two of them alone.

"I take it you want something." Youngblood faced her, his legs spread, his thumbs tucked in the waistband of his trousers. Gone was his tender expression, his softly

42

spoken words.

Morgan's top lip lifted in a mere semblance of a smile, for what she truly wanted was never to see this man's face again. "I need someone to take me into town. Would you ask one of the men?"

Youngblood was instantly filled with mingling emotions. She was leaving. Thank God. He felt almost weak with relief. Why then the burning ache in his chest? It was that damn stew he'd eaten last night. For the hundredth time he cursed the fact that Bailey had married and started a small business in town. The ranch had been for three months without a decent cook. In desperation, Seth, who took care of the barn and the odd jobs around the place, had taken over Bailey's chores. The only problem was Seth didn't know the first thing about cooking.

Youngblood nodded after a long silent moment. "When are you leaving?"

"Whenever someone can take me."

"What's the stagecoach schedule?"

"Why? What has that got to do with anything?"

"The stagecoach only stops in these parts twice a week. You wouldn't want to miss it."

Morgan heaved a long sigh, straining for a patience she was far from feeling. "I imagine I wouldn't, if I were taking it, Mr. Youngblood."

Youngblood's lips tightened with annoyance. This conversation was getting them exactly nowhere. Apparently his supposition that she was leaving was incorrect. Finally, since she offered no information, he asked, "Why do you want to go into town?"

"I'll be needing building supplies and a team of men to fix this house."

"You figure on stayin'?"

Morgan grinned at his look of astonishment, more than happy to see he didn't take kindly to the notion. Suddenly nothing was more important than annoying this man. Of course, she could have told him last night

43

that no daughter of a Wainright backed down from a dare and he had as good as issued her one with his scathing remarks about her not fitting in here. The truth was, if he hadn't said it, she would probably be readying herself right now for the trip home. "I'm staying, Mr. Youngblood. No doubt that doesn't sit well with you, what with my coming from the city and all, but the fact of the matter is, no half-dressed savage is going to scare me off my own land."

Youngblood's astonishment evaporated in an instant. His eyes hardened as he forced aside the sensation that vaguely resembled happiness. He wasn't glad. It didn't matter how his heart hammered in his chest, he wasn't ever going to admit to being pleased to hear she was staying. He didn't need, didn't want this thorn in his side. He wanted her gone, but if this spoiled, haughty city-bred woman was determined to stay, he wasn't going to make it easy for her. He was going to put every obstacle in her path until she gave up this ridiculous plan and cleared off his land. He wouldn't be able to breathe easy till he saw the last of her.

"How about a deal?"

"What kind of deal?" she asked, her eyes narrowing with distrust.

"How much would you take for your share?"

Morgan laughed, her eyes hardening with spiteful pleasure just knowing he didn't want her here. "There isn't enough money in the world. I love it here."

"Damn you!" he breathed, almost on a sigh. "I'll get it. Just name your price."

Chips of ice burned bright in her eyes. Her hand balled into a fist as she raised it threateningly. "If you ever curse at me again, I'll put my fist down your goddamned throat." In her anger Morgan never took into account the impossibility of her threat nor did she realize her own less than ladylike words.

Youngblood's lips twitched at the sight of this tiny bundle of fury. If the situation weren't so desperate, he might have laughed. "What the hell do you want to bother with this house for? You won't be stayin' that long. After you've had your little fling, you'll head back to New York."

Morgan was about to ask him what business it was of his how long she stayed, but forced aside the nasty taunt. Instead, she gave a great telling sigh as she strove for calmness. "You might thank me, Mr. Youngblood. After I'm gone, you'll have the use of decent living quarters."

"What do you mean, after?"

"What do you mean, what do I mean?" Morgan sighed again as she strove to bring her ever-rising anger under control. "You will have the use of the house once I'm gone," she finally managed, her tone clearly that of one speaking to another of lesser understanding.

"Thanks." His mouth twisted in sarcasm. "But I reckon I don't mind sharing it while you're here."

Morgan's eyes widened, for she hadn't imagined even this savage capable of such gall. "Quite impossible," came her stiff remark, with a dismissive shake of her head. "I'm afraid you and I cannot share this house. It would be unseemly."

"Unseemly!" Youngblood gave a hoot of ridiculing laughter. "I'm afraid I don't give a damn." Youngblood returned. "If you'll pardon the expression." His shrug made it all too clear he didn't care in the least if she pardoned him or not.

Morgan's eyes grew bright with fire. "You will not live here until I leave."

"Won't I? Where do you expect me to sleep?"

Morgan longed to tell him exactly where she'd love to see him sleep, but instead suggested, "Use the bunk-house."

Youngblood laughed without a shred of humor. "I'll say one thing for you, honey. You got guts and then some coming here and ordering me from my own house."

"I can't share it with you!"

"Afraid it might damage your reputation? Don't

45

worry, honey. I wouldn't touch you if you were the last female in these parts."

"That's very comforting, Mr. Youngblood, but I'm afraid it will not do."

"If you don't like the living arrangements, leave."

"How is it I wasn't informed of your presence? I was led to believe a miner shared ownership in this ranch." Her eyes narrowed with suspicion as she waited, obviously hoping to catch him in a lie.

Youngblood shrugged, just as obviously unconcerned. "Can't rightly say."

"Why would Mr. Banks have deeded you half?"

Youngblood shrugged. "He was my uncle. Figure that gives me some rights. Don't you?" His dark eyes dared her to call him a liar.

"You are a beast!" And at the widening of his suddenly lazy grin, she continued, "Use it then, but take my advice, Mr. Youngblood, and stay out of my way."

"Or what?"

Morgan had no real answer for she knew her threat to be an empty one. "Or you'll be sorry."

Youngblood laughed out loud. "Honey, you got me shakin' in my boots somethin' fierce. But you're right about one thing. I'm already sorry. Sorry I ever laid eyes on you."

Morgan gritted her teeth. Lord, at this rate she'd have no more than stubs in six months' time. "That makes two of us, Mr. Youngblood."

Martha's hand slapped sharply at Morgan's back. Tears ran freely down the younger woman's cheeks as she struggled to dislodge the thick, heavy hot cake that had cut off her breathing. How could food smell so appetizing and yet be so obviously inedible? Morgan refused to credit her suddenly closed throat to the man who danced his horse not fifty yards away. Still it was impossible not to acknowledge his audacity. There it was, in plain sight.

46

Her hat was hanging from his saddle as if a prize taken in battle.

Morgan's eyes narrowed with fury. God, but she despised that man. How dare he laugh, how dare he finger the brim almost lovingly as he joked with the men about the lady who had given, no, forced him to take it so he might remember their night spent together. His suggestive remark nearly brought her to the brink of madness. Why, it was all she could do simply to sit there when what she wanted more than anything in this world was to throw her plate to the ground and attack him with her fists.

But no, she wouldn't give in to a need so strong it nearly caused her physical pain. She wouldn't give him the satisfaction. He'd never know how easily he could upset her. Besides, if she lost control and did something foolish, the men would know about whom he spoke. And regardless of her denials, they were bound to believe the less than discreet innuendos already imparted.

Morgan gave a silent groan as she lowered her eyes from his mirth-filled and oh-so-superior glance. One hundred and seventy-nine days to go. Surely she could do it. Of course she could, she silently insisted, but right now, she couldn't swear which one of them would survive the ordeal.

Morgan lamented her willful ways as she again consulted the timepiece pinned to her bodice. An hour and a half. Yesterday it had taken three hours and more to reach the ranch. Curse her insistence. Why hadn't she listened to Mr. Mackey and stayed in town last night? There were ample accommodations above the saloon. Surely, although it might have been a noisy affair, she and Martha would have been safe enough. At the very least they would have been dry and at best she never would have suffered that encounter with Youngblood.

She and Martha could have started their trip this

47

morning rather than brave the worst rain she'd ever known. God, when was she going to learn to listen to the advice of others?

The town of Sweetwater, Nevada, was aptly named as it nestled on the shore of a gently flowing river that was surrounded on both sides by cottonwood and swaying willow shade trees, permitting its shores to remain grassy and cool. A most inviting place to while away an afternoon.

Other than its beautiful location, the town was indistinguishable among hundreds that dotted the West. It boasted two rows of mostly wooden, unpainted, weathered buildings, some two stories high, which faced each other across a wide dusty dirt street. The street itself was littered with spring carriages and buckboard wagons, plus an occasional cowhand who had come to town for one reason or another. Running children played in the slow-moving traffic, darting out before trotting horses while riders cursed to their screams of pleasure. Ladies, weary from endless labor, their arms filled with packages, went about their business of gathering needed supplies to last until their next visit to town, while a handful of men sat idly by or stood leaning against the buildings' walls and watched the town's traffic as they conversed in small groups of three and four. Horses were tied with slipknots to the hitching rails that stood before every establishment.

A boardwalk of uneven wood ran a foot off the dusty ground and stretched along both sides of the entire length of the town.

Morgan left Seth with a jaunty wave before the Emporium to pick up the supplies Youngblood had ordered. Before she began her shopping spree—the first one of many, she imagined, considering the abominable condition of the home that would be hers for the next six months—Morgan decided it only polite to introduce herself to the sheriff, since she was new to the community. No doubt, he would direct her to those most

48

capable of seeing her needs met.

A bell tinkled as Morgan pushed open the door, above which hung a sign saying SHERIFF'S OFFICE. Inside the small room a man—a very handsome man, Morgan could not help but notice—sat with pen in hand, leaning over a desk almost overflowing with papers. Engrossed in his work, he never looked up as he remarked, "Grady, get your drunken carcass over to Libby's for a bath. I ain't going to suffer through another day with you stinkin' out this place. The garbage you drink every night is bad enough . . ." His words dwindled to an awkward stop as he suddenly raised his head and fastened amazed dark eyes on the loveliest woman he'd ever seen in his life.

Morgan grinned. "Do Mr. Grady and I so closely resemble each other in scent, Sheriff?"

Marshall, for the first time in years, turned bright red as he stumbled awkwardly to his feet. He swallowed twice before he could get out the words. "Oh Lord," he groaned, trying desperately to remember exactly what he had said. Had he insulted her? Obviously not, if that beautiful smile was anything to go by. "Can I help you, Miss . . . ?"

"Wainright. Morgan Wainright." She laughed as she moved farther into the tiny room and extended her hand in greeting. "And I expect you can, Sheriff . . . ?" She ended the sentence on an expectant note waiting for him to fill in his name.

"Marshall."

Her eyes widened with surprise as they glanced toward the star on his chest. "Oh, I thought you were the sheriff."

"I am. It's Sheriff Marshall," he returned, cursing again how ridiculous that sounded.

Morgan grinned. "And if one day you should become the marshal?"

"Please," he groaned, a smile teasing his pencil-thin-mustached lip. "It's taken this town four years to come to terms with my name and title. I don't think they could

49

stand further confusion.''

Morgan laughed again and Marshall's stomach twisted at the sweet low sound. Gently he guided her to a seat before he leaned his hip on the corner of his desk, his dark eyes never for a moment leaving her face. "How can I help you?''

Morgan explained who she was and what she intended to do. When she was finished, she asked if he might know if there were any builders in the area.

Marshall shrugged. "Well, you'll have to remember this ain't the city, Miss Wainright. Folks around here don't have much call for a builder. What they need, they usually take care of themselves." At her crestfallen look, he quickly injected, "But there are a few who can swing a hammer and more than a few who could use extra money. I don't think you'll have a problem." He smiled at her obvious relief. "Tom Barry is probably your best bet. He's the town cabinetmaker. He would know about ordering supplies and could gather a crew for the job.''

"I don't know how to thank you, Sheriff,'' Morgan remarked with a beaming smile as she came to her feet.

"You could thank me by allowing me to take you to dinner.''

"Oh, I'm afraid I couldn't.''

"I'm sorry," Marshall remarked quickly, wondering if he had somehow insulted her. She didn't come from around these parts. Maybe she considered it improper for a lady to dine alone with a gentleman. "You probably have better things to do.''

Morgan smiled and shook her head in the negative. "Not better, Sheriff. It's just that I have so much to do before I return to the ranch.''

"I could help you.''

"Oh, I couldn't take you away from your work.''

"Helping you is part of my work," Marshall replied, and grinned engagingly, praying this woman was half as susceptible to his charm as was every other woman in town.

In his twenty-nine years, Marshall had had plenty of experience with the ladies. With his dark good looks and trim hard body, he had no problem finding his way into many a bed. So he was more than a little surprised to feel his body react almost violently at her touch. A tingling sensation shot straight up his offered arm as she placed her hand at the crook of his elbow. It sped through his chest and stomach to settle with unnerving precision in his groin. He looked at her with eyes gone wide with amazement. Jesus, he swore, as he forced aside his body's trembling reaction to her touch, he was staking his claim on this one, right now. She didn't know it yet, but he was going to become a permanent part of her life.

Morgan couldn't remember laughing so much. Over a light dinner and hours of shopping, Marshall had kept up a constant and amusing narrative as he described the people and events in his town.

"Stop, you'll make me drop everything," she gasped breathlessly as she leaned against the wall of one of the town's many wooden buildings. She bent slightly forward as she pressed her elbow to her side and held tightly to the packages in her arms. "It can't be true. You're making it up."

"Never," he said, grinning. "I assure you I haven't so great an imagination. As I said, the ants were crawling up her legs and she thought, what with her mama and papa out back, the house was empty. Technically speaking, it was."

Morgan giggled as she imagined the poor man's startled reaction to seeing a lady running stark naked, even if the room she entered happened to be her bedroom. "What did he do?"

"You mean when he saw her?"

Morgan grinned, not at all sure she believed him, for it would take more than a few ants to cause her to rip her clothing from her body the moment she entered

51

her house.

"Well, like I said, he was painting the windows, standing on a ledge just outside her room. When he saw her, he jumped with surprise. The pail went flying. The problem was when it came down it hit his head and he was covered instantly to his toes with white paint. The blow to his head caused him to lose his hold. Off balance, his arms swinging in the air, he screamed. I imagine he looked like a big clumsy ghost."

Morgan giggled at the imagined sight, her blue eyes twinkling with delight.

Marshall smiled, priding himself that she should find such obvious enjoyment in his company, and continued with his story. "Apparently she heard his screams and forgot she wasn't exactly presentable. Without thinking, she made a mad dash to save him. Reaching out of the window, she grabbed at his shirt, but he was already falling and much too heavy to pull back. Instead, his weight yanked her right out of that window. Stark naked, she fell with him into the rosebushes."

Marshall shook his head and grinned at Morgan's laughter. "The story goes, it was months before they got all the thorns."

She giggled again.

"And that's how the schoolmarm got herself married. Even on their wedding day, which I might add came only days after this, their first meeting, the bride and groom were taking white chips of paint from their hair and thorns from their . . ." He left the sentence unfinished.

"You're terrible. That poor lady would just about die if she knew you told me that."

Marshall laughed. "It's common knowledge around these parts."

Morgan dumped her parcels upon the already over-flowing wagon. Marshall added those he had offered to carry. Together they quickly arranged the packages so none would be lost on the jarring ride back to the ranch.

It was almost dark. Seth sat impatiently upon the

52

wagon's seat, waiting to start back.

"I want to thank you, Sheriff. You've made a day filled with chores completely enjoyable."

I could make more than that enjoyable, given half the chance, he silently returned. "Can I see you again?" he asked, and then held his breath awaiting her answer, amazed at the need he suddenly knew. Marshall cursed at the almost pleading note he heard in his voice. Where had his usual self-assurance gone? Damn, he didn't want to appear unsure of himself. Women were attracted to a man who possessed a measure of confidence.

But Marshall had unwittingly struck just the right note with Morgan. After Youngblood's arrogance, his attitude was just the tonic she needed for her badly shaken emotions.

Morgan smiled at the young man before her, while silently comparing him to Youngblood. He wasn't as big or as handsome and he possessed none of Youngblood's nearly overpowering presence, but his sense of humor and good looks were most appealing. Morgan's eyes widened, aghast at her thoughts. What was she doing? Why was she comparing him to Youngblood? Why wasn't it Bradley who first came to mind? After all, it was Bradley she loved. Curse the savage! There was nothing about him that was superior to another. In truth, she couldn't even stand him. Obviously that was it. He was simply so obnoxious that it was impossible not to compare all men to him. "I'm sure I'll be coming to town regularly," she ventured, knowing by his disappointed look that her response wasn't exactly what he had in mind. For some reason his reaction made her happier than she'd been in weeks.

"Maybe I could drop by the ranch." And at her expectant look, he added, "When I'm making my rounds, that is."

Morgan smiled, finding his apparent lack of confidence refreshing. For just a second she wondered what Youngblood would say if the sheriff came to call.

Instantly, she disallowed the thought. It wasn't his business. It wasn't anyone's business but her own. "That would be nice. Seth tells me our closest neighbors are the Harringtons and their place is at least twenty-odd miles north of the Red Rock spread."

Marshall wasn't particularly overjoyed to hear she held him in the same regard as any neighbor. He wanted much more than friendship from this woman. He wanted passion. Intense, sizzling, gut-wrenching passion. He'd wanted it from the first moment he'd seen her walk into his office. He'd thought of nearly nothing else all day.

If she'd given him half a chance, he would have already had her in his bed. Silently he swore the day wasn't far off. Not if he had anything to say about it, and judging by the ease he usually had convincing women to see to his wants, he very definitely would.

It was long past dark by the time the buckboard rattled beneath the triple R sign that marked the beginning of the Red Rock Ranch. Slowly it made its lumbering way up the slight incline a half mile to stop at last before the darkened barn. The moon had come up and cast eerie silver light over the entire ranch. The buildings looked forbidding, especially the main house with its partially empty pockets in the roof. Tonight no lights burned within.

In this light, she could not discern the red stones, taken from the Valley of Blood, which had been used to build the house. And had given the ranch its name.

The only sign of life came from the bunkhouse, where laughter could be heard and dim yellow light shone from the windows.

Morgan glanced toward the house and shivered at the darkness that awaited her. Even though it was fully dark, she knew it was too early for Martha to be in bed. "I wonder where Martha is. Everything is so dark."

"It took you long enough," came a low voice from out

54

of the shadows. "Seth, go tell the men to get out here and unload this stuff." He nodded over his shoulder. "They can put it in the barn for now."

Morgan gasped as strong hands lifted her without warning from the wagon's seat and settled her effortlessly before him. She knew without looking who held her. Who else would dare keep his hands positioned at her waist, pressing her close enough that their bodies nearly touched.

Almost immediately Seth disappeared into the shadows. "What took you so long? I was ready to ride into town and see if there was trouble."

Morgan disengaged herself from his hold. "No trouble," she remarked noncommittally as she ignored the wild beating of her heart and forced her breathing under control. Morgan could feel her anger bubble instantly to the surface. Valiantly she fought to rein in the words that threatened. She wouldn't give him the satisfaction of knowing his actions were even noticed. But they most certainly were. How dare he touch her like that? Who did he think he was? "Where's Martha?" Morgan asked again, glancing toward the darkened house, while forcing aside her need to rail at his cavalier treatment.

"She's in the bunkhouse, playing cards."

Morgan, despite her annoyance at his high-handed ways, felt her lips twitch with humor. "Cards? You mean those men play hearts?" Morgan asked with no little surprise. For some reason she assumed the rough men she saw this morning swaggering to their horses wouldn't hold much interest in the game.

"Not hearts. Poker. The last I saw she was betting to an inside straight."

Morgan giggled at the absurd notion. Why, the woman didn't know the first thing about poker. She could only assume Youngblood was teasing her. "Be serious."

Youngblood sighed. Martha wasn't exactly the subject he'd pick to discuss right now, but the woman wouldn't

55

be satisfied till she'd heard it all. "I'm afraid I am. It seems, after she scoured what she could of the house, she had some time on her hands this afternoon. The men put up a bit of a stink, what with her invading their territory and all, but she ignored their grumblings, arriving with broom, mop, and pail to clean that 'pig sty,' as she called it. Before I knew what was happening, she was dealing stud."

"Stud?"

Youngblood grinned for a moment, tempted to show her firsthand the meaning of the word, only what he was thinking had nothing at all to do with cards. "One of the variations of the game."

"But she doesn't know how to play."

"She does now," he returned as if the notion was not at all ridiculous.

Morgan looked around, feeling suddenly ill at ease, for she realized, for the first time, that they were alone in the dark. "Why is the house dark?"

"Probably because no one lit a fire."

"Why not?" she snapped. "You own half this place. How is it you take no pride in the fact? How could you have allowed the house to go to such disrepair?"

Youngblood's shrug belied his menacing tone. "What the hell do you know about anything? Did you ever think I might be working myself to death just to keep the ranch in the black? Did you ever think there is no extra money?" he lied outright for there was plenty of money in his accounts at both the bank in town and the one in Elko. More than enough, in fact, to build twenty new houses. But Youngblood was more interested in the size and condition of his herd of Mustangs than the house in which he lived. He shot her a look of pure scorn. "Maybe I don't need some piece of fluff telling me how I'm supposed to live. Maybe I like it fine just as it is. Maybe I'll insist you leave the place as is."

"Maybe you can go to hell. If I want to fix it, I'll fix it."

A long moment of angry silence followed her wild

outburst. Finally Morgan sighed. Curse this man. How did he cause her to lose all reason and blurt out such unladylike things?

"So what took you so long?" he repeated.

Morgan's lips tightened with annoyance. Who did he think he was to question her comings and goings? It was none of his business. How dare he press her for an answer? He was her partner in this ranch, nothing more. They couldn't even consider themselves friends. She owed him no explanations. Still, Morgan found herself answering, albeit reluctantly. "Not that it's any of your business, Mr. Youngblood, but I had a great deal of shopping to do."

"It didn't take you eight hours. What else did you do?"

Her anger at his audacity was quickly growing out of all proportion. Lord! How did this man bring about such extreme emotions? Granted, there had been one or two people in her life she hadn't taken to, but this fury he brought at his every word, nay at his very presence, was startling to say the least. "If you must know, Sheriff Marshall took me to dinner. Satisfied?" Morgan glared her resentment that she should be forced to explain her actions.

"I think the question is, was he?"

"What is that supposed to mean?"

"It means that the good sheriff never was one to let a hot little thing like you escape his bed."

Morgan gasped. Without thought, her hand swung upward, but was stopped none too gently in flight before making contact with his cheek. Her lips thinned and she spoke through clenched teeth. "He was a perfect gentleman. Too bad I can't say the same for you."

"Can't you?" Youngblood taunted her. "What would you say then?"

"I'd say you're an uncivilized beast."

Youngblood chuckled and then nodded. "So I've been told."

"Let go of my hand." Morgan strained as her free hand tried to pry his fingers from her wrist.

"And let you hit me?" he chuckled again.

"I won't hit you," Morgan replied, already ashamed of her unthinking reaction to his nasty remark. No matter that the man had the filthiest mind alive, no one deserved violence.

"Damn right you won't," he grunted as his hands took both of hers and twisted them painlessly behind her back.

Morgan's only excuse for not fighting what followed was sheer surprise. With a startled gasp she found herself pulled up hard against an unyielding chest. Her eyes opened wide with incredulity. She never realized she suddenly felt warm all over. That the warm clean scent of his breath was making her knees wobble. She never knew her body softened against his. She didn't think till later that she should have tried to wrestle free of his hold. After all, she would eventually reason, she couldn't have fought the touch of his mouth if she had no warning she'd find it suddenly attached to her own.

Huge blue eyes blinked with amazement as she silently watched his mouth crash into hers, hard, almost brutal, denying both of them the slightest tenderness. From somewhere in the back of her mind, she knew the sudden pressure against her teeth had split her lip, but she felt no pain. She felt nothing but shock.

But shock and surprise had little to do with what happened next. Morgan's face would burn red for days when she'd remembered her disgraceful reaction. If she'd only known, she might have been able to fight, but she was so caught up in her surprise, she hadn't realized his intent.

His lips parted from hers moments after the bruising kiss. He almost groaned out an apology as he realized what he'd done, for he tasted the blood, but the words never came as he noticed the softness in her eyes.

She'd deny it, of course, and would till her dying day, but she had no excuse then, for he had released her

58

hands. She could have walked away, for he held her not at all. Their bodies touched, but nothing but her own sudden yearning held her in place.

Her eyes clung to his and she watched in silent breathless fascination as he fought some inner battle and finally muttered a low curse as he gave in to his need and his head lowered again. Slowly, almost tentatively firm lips sipped at the moistness his mouth had left behind. He asked for nothing and demanded less as his lips whispered sweet, soothing, unheard words upon her mouth.

And at her soft sigh of wonder and delight, a sigh she had no knowledge of giving, his lips fastened to hers and the gentlest of touchings grew to a kiss that would rock the very foundations of both their worlds.

He opened his lips over hers and sucked gently, filling his senses with her scent, texture, and taste. His head shifted slightly so he might better take advantage of lips so lusciously soft and pliable he felt himself tremble with the need to devour. His tongue gently soothed and Youngblood groaned again at the delicious heat he found just inside. Gently he probed, seeking further admittance, hungering for the delightful warmth that lay just beyond his reach. He sipped, he soothed, running his tongue over the inside of her lips. Back and forth, again and again, until he was almost drunk on the taste of her. But it wasn't enough. He had to know all of her mouth. He had to taste and feel everything. His tongue moved beyond the smooth barrier of her teeth and he heard his own growl of satisfaction mingle with her soft sigh as it slid thick, hot, and hungry into sweet silky heaven.

Morgan moaned as he filled her mouth with his dizzying taste, his warmth, his scent. God, but he tasted wonderful. She moaned again as she savored the wonder. How was it a man could taste this good?

Later she would convince herself she had only reached for his shoulders to steady a world gone slightly off balance. She had felt no need to touch him. And if her fingers had suddenly found themselves threaded in the

59

black silkiness of his hair and then entwined together around his neck, she swore it wasn't her doing. He had probably made her do it. No doubt when she wasn't paying attention he had moved them there himself.

But unless Youngblood had suddenly grown another set, that notion was highly unlikely, for his big hands had found her waist and then the slenderness of her back, never stopping their deliciously thrilling wanderings until they settled with a groan of approval on her rounded backside. Gently he kneaded the succulent, firm flesh he found there.

Now Morgan had been kissed many times, for she was no longer a girl but a lady of twenty-four years who was engaged to be married. If the truth were told, Morgan was more experienced than most ladies of her station, for she was extraordinarily beautiful and had had since the age of sixteen many a suitor who hungered for a taste of that oh so intriguing mouth. She knew what it was to have her mouth meet another's, but never in her life had she known anything to compare to this erotic sampling. Her head swam dizzily. She tried, but she couldn't bring her senses back to normal. She was lost to a need she never knew she possessed and found herself a desperately eager partner in this wild beating of hearts, this straining of strong healthy bodies.

Morgan groaned as Youngblood's tongue penetrated fully into her mouth. He was devouring her. She could feel herself being drawn into him and she wanted it, wanted it desperately. She never realized the near-violence in their movements as each sought out the other, as each hungered for more of this sudden fury. She scratched at him, her hands against his bare chest, her senses reeling at the touch of hard, naked flesh. She tried to pull him closer; she was dying to know all she could of this heat.

He was a trickster, of course, this wily, oh so handsome Indian. No doubt he knew what would happen if he kissed her. He knew she'd never notice till hours later how his hands had parted her thighs. Reaching low and around from behind he had lifted her, tilting her hips toward him as he rubbed against her. And because she didn't notice, she couldn't very well have stopped him as his fingers moved over the sensitive insides of her legs. Sliding back and forth they sent shivers of anxious, glorious sensation into the pit of her belly, until they met at last, pressing up and brushing over her most sensitive parts, tearing a sound from her throat that resembled a thankful groan.

Well, of course it wasn't a thankful groan. How ridiculous. As a matter of fact, she doubted she'd groaned at all. It was probably him making all that noise. And if by some miracle it was her, she only made that sound because . . . because. Well, she'd think of an explanation in a minute. Well, maybe it was better not to think about it, she finally reasoned. It was better to make believe it had never happened in the first place. Much, much better.

They were gasping for breath when he released her at last. His hands reached out to steady her when he saw she had little control in her legs. She took a wobbling step backward and then was suddenly against him again.

Youngblood breathed a heavy mournful sigh as he tried to regain his breath. "That shouldn't have happened." His arms pressed her closely against him as he breathed in the clean scent of her hair and allowed his hands to memorize the delightfully slender shape of her back, the delicious fullness of her bottom. "It'll be all the harder now."

It took a long moment before she realized what he had done. What she had allowed him to do. Morgan opened her mouth, refusing to share any of the blame, ready to rail at his unconscionable actions, but the words died on her lips, for the men he had sent for were finally, if grumpily, coming from the bunkhouse. No doubt they were a mite upset at having their game interrupted.

As far as Morgan was concerned, they didn't know the meaning of the word.

Chapter Four

One hundred and seventy-eight days. Morgan shuddered. How was she to bear it? Morgan's eyes narrowed, spouting venom as she watched from the door of the house, while her tongue unconsciously soothed the injury he had caused her lip. In truth, it wasn't just the cut inside her mouth that so bothered her, but the fact that her lips were still swollen from his kisses, even hours after she'd received them, and anyone, with only the slightest imagination, could well realize the cause.

Morgan gave a disgusted silent curse as the wild Mustang almost threw Youngblood off his bucking back. Drat! The men cheered as he hung fast, while she would have done easily as much if he'd broken his neck.

Lord, she couldn't imagine disliking a man more. What right did he have to so abuse her? How dare he take it upon himself to kiss her? Who did he think he was? Curse the man!

Morgan was filled with almost debilitating impotent rage. A rage she had no means of easing as long as she allowed her mind to return to last night. And for as long as she lived, she doubted her ability to forget that all too mortifying moment, spent in the dark shadows of the barn.

At the men's arrival, she had stalked off into the darkness, unable simply to stand there so close to the villainous beast and calmly watch the unloading of her purchases and the supplies for the ranch. How could he act as though nothing had happened? How could he laugh and joke with the men, laugh and joke as if Morgan's world had not been tilted on its axis?

Later he had found her at the corral fence, petting the nose of the huge gray stallion he now rode. She had stood there for some time, waiting, hoping that this peaceful night's tranquillity might lend a soothing balm to the ragings of her soul. Morgan couldn't find the courage to enter the ramshackle house. Somehow she knew he had yet to retire. And fearful of encountering him again, only this time in the close confines of the dark, silent house, she couldn't force her feet to move.

Her gaze returned yet again to the spot where they had stood, kissing each other, touching each other with a desperate urgency that could be compared only to insanity. Lord, what had come over her that she should act so out of character?

The men had long ago gone back to the bunkhouse and Martha was no doubt busy preparing herself for bed; perhaps she was already asleep. Still Morgan lingered outside, unable to shake herself of the wild upheaval of emotions that assailed.

Morgan listened as the heavy silence of early evening slowly grew into a chorus of nocturnal sounds. An animal howled somewhere in the distance, while crickets appeared to chirp their musical reply. An assortment of insects provided background to the bullfrog who down by the yet unexplored riverbank croaked out his impatience for his mate's appearance. She hadn't heard his approach and yet some sixth sense told her he was standing behind her. Her shoulders grew tense and a prickling sensation ran down her spine.

She wasn't at all surprised when the low sound of his voice whispered behind and above her. "Perfect gentleman or not, Marshall is a womanizer. All he wants from you, from any woman, is to get under her skirt."

63

Morgan spun around to face him, hardly able to credit his unbelievable arrogance. Had she heard him correctly? Did he dare accuse another when his own actions proved him false? Morgan ignored the sudden thumping of her heart as she realized just how close he was standing. She disavowed the shiver that raced up her spine as his dark eyes gleamed with remembered hunger. She refused to admit his scent, so raw, so male, so deliciously different from her own, affected her in any way. She glared her contempt that he should dare defame another after his damnable actions. "While you, on the other hand, never allow the repugnant thought to enter your mind."

Youngblood chuckled at her sarcasm. "Well, I wouldn't go that far." He grinned as he took a step closer, backing her up so that the fence was now pressed to her back. "I've never been one to turn down an available opportunity."

"Get this straight, Youngblood," she said, her index finger suddenly poking hard at an equally hard chest. "I'm not available and most certainly not to the likes of you." She took a deep calming breath.

Youngblood's whole body tensed and his eyes clouded with disappointment as he prepared for the insult he knew was coming. Hadn't he spent half his life swinging his fists in blinding rage over the names she was ready to spout? His father was a Hopi Indian, his mother white. Combine this with the fact that they had never married and it left a multitude of insults many were delighted to impart. As far back as he could remember, he'd been called half-breed and just about every other name a body could think of. Yet for some reason he hadn't expected this woman to join the rest.

Unable to leave the words unsaid, he prompted, "What do you mean, the likes of me?" His voice was low and filled with menace when it became clear she had no intention of finishing.

Morgan shot him a look of disgust, so overcome with

64

her own terrifying emotions she never noticed the threat in his eyes or the whispery anger in his voice.

Morgan breathed a long sigh of disgust. "You know, Youngblood, you really have nerve to act so innocent after what you did."

"What did I do?"

"You kissed me, that's what!" she exclaimed in self-righteous anger.

Youngblood grinned, almost sighing with relief. So she was talking about a kiss. Had it affected her as much as it had him? Is that what had got her so riled? "And you've never kissed a man before?"

"Not one such as you."

"Meaning?"

"Meaning a gentleman would ask a lady's permission, not attack her in the dark!"

"Did Marshall ask?"

"It's none of your business."

"Did he?" he asked again, while moving closer still. Morgan found herself swallowing a pithy remark. He loomed above her almost threateningly. She didn't trust him in this particular mood and she wasn't about to give him reason for losing what little control he seemed to be holding on to.

"No," she almost shouted. "No, darn you! Sheriff Marshall would never be so rude as to steal a kiss. He very politely asked if he might come calling." Morgan ignored the fact that she somewhat exaggerated the truth here. Although she suspected the man of hinting at such a thing, he had not come right out and asked. Still she wasn't about to let this beast get one up on her and for the moment this was the only way she could think to get the better of him.

Youngblood forced aside the annoyance he felt at her words. Mentally he promised to take care of Marshall later. Right now he wanted more than talk from this woman. And he, for one, had no intention of acting the gentleman. This time they wouldn't be interrupted.

"Why are you so upset? Could it be it wasn't so much that I kissed you, but that you kissed me back?"

"Of course not!" And at his silence she continued, "Why, the idea is ludicrous." And at his growing grin, she insisted, "I did not kiss you back!"

"Didn't you? It sure felt like you did."

"Well, it felt wrong then. I did no such thing. Why, I'd never kiss a strange man. I'm engaged to be married."

"Are you?" he asked, hearing for the first time of her plans to marry. "Where is your fiancé then?"

"In Paris, on family business."

Youngblood laughed. "He's in Paris? Alone?" He laughed again. "Are you always this trusting of your fiancés?"

Morgan watched him for a long moment, never realizing her thoughts showed clearly in her eyes. She wondered why she felt none of the torment that most any young bride-to-be would suffer at being parted from her love? She should be jealous, shouldn't she? Why didn't she fear that Bradley, in her absence, might turn to another? Why? Was it because she trusted him so much, or was it because she simply didn't care enough? Of course she cared. It was this beast she didn't care about.

Morgan suddenly found her thoughts forgotten as her gaze wandered at will upon the man standing before her. She felt herself drawn closer. Suddenly, unbelievably, she couldn't get enough of the sight of him. God, he was something, no matter that his eyes had hardened and his lips had thinned in ridicule. His skin was darkly tanned, his eyes appeared to gleam a black fire in the silvery night, while shadows brought his cheekbones into sharp prominence. Why couldn't he have been ugly? Why did he have to be so big? So beautiful?

Morgan fought a hard-won battle against the memory of him holding her in his arms. She wouldn't acknowledge the shivers that ran down her spine. It wasn't his presence that caused them, in any case, she silently swore. The night was growing chilly. She had best get inside before she caught her death. Only Morgan didn't feel cold, regardless of her insistence on the matter. She felt hot, almost feverish, as he took yet another threatening step closer. She found herself forcing the breathless words through a tight throat. "I refuse to continue this ridiculous conversation. It's none of your concern, in any case. I'm going to bed."

Youngblood watched her walk away with equal measures of relief and disappointment. Almost reflexively his hand reached out, knowing he'd find little resistance if he pulled her to him, but wisely, his hand fell back to his side. Somewhere in the back of his mind came a desperate, almost terrifying need for survival. A survival he somehow knew could not be had, in the comparative privacy of the night, alone with this woman.

Youngblood almost laughed aloud in denial of the nonsensical route his thoughts had taken. That would be the day, when a flighty piece of fluff could cause him a moment's pause. No way in hell could a woman like her affect him. Youngblood's lips twisted into a sneer. Despite her words to the contrary, he remembered her response to his kisses. Jesus, he'd be a fool not to take advantage of what she so clearly offered. And Youngblood was anything but a fool.

He'd been in a rage for days after hearing of her impending arrival. The truth of the matter was he hated her and all of her kind, but that didn't stop his wanting her.

Youngblood shrugged. He wasn't a starry-eyed kid any longer, but a grown man. He didn't have to like her to want her in his bed. And he'd known he'd wanted her there from the first moment he saw her. He'd kissed her, held her delicious softness in his arms, felt the heat of her response, and his brain as well as his body had nearly exploded with lust.

Youngblood's lips twisted into a menacing, evil grin. This was one woman he was determined to have and enjoy to the fullest. He would take her with relish and then when she thought him under her spell, he'd throw his hatred in her face. The thought of the pain he'd inflict was almost as delicious as her body. Pain for pain, he silently mused. And Jesus, he prayed she'd suffer a measure of what he'd so far endured.

This morning she had awakened at dawn. She had stood at the window to the parlor and listened to the men's low muttered curses as they went about the beginnings of a new day. She wondered if Mr. Barry would come today. There was much to be done if she was going to live here in comparative comfort.

Morgan had smiled as she imagined this shack, not only put to rights, but made over into a real home. She gave an indifferent shrug. It mattered not that she was spending huge sums of money for something she'd use for so short a time. It mattered only that she'd be comfortable and happy while she was here. Well, to expect real happiness was perhaps pushing things a bit far. Morgan doubted she'd be happy again. At least not while she shared her living quarters with this most unwelcome and unsettling man. No, she couldn't count on happiness until she returned to New York.

Morgan had covered her mouth as she yawned and then jumped as a low voice sounded almost in her ear. "Morning, honey. I imagine these early mornings must be a mite trying on you city folks."

Morgan's lips had twisted into a sneer as she spun about and faced her tormentor. She watched him for a long moment. Suddenly she knew, or thought she knew, the reason behind his actions. He was trying to get rid of her. Morgan almost grinned at finding him out. Well, he could try all he pleased, but she wasn't leaving until she was good and ready. "You might as well give it up, Youngblood, I'm not leaving here. No matter your badgering."

"Me? Badgering?" he asked in all innocence. "Why I wouldn't think of it, honey."

Morgan turned her back to his laughter and gritted her teeth. No matter, she reasoned. She'd be gone from here soon enough. She could stand whatever he dished out. For her own self-protection, Morgan's mind raced toward a solution. She had to find something that would bring him equal aggravation. Morgan grinned with relish, knowing that once she set her mind to something, it was a foregone conclusion. The day wasn't far off when she'd bring this beast to his knees.

"I hate to break it to you, lady, but I ain't breakin' my butt workin' this ranch while you lounge around like the idle rich."

Morgan squeaked a startled sound and gasped as she spun on her heels, one hand clutched to her throat in obvious fright. This was the second time in one day he'd scared her half to death. She'd thought she was alone in the house, while Martha even now stood over a huge pot of boiling clothes out back. She never heard Youngblood's silent approach nor, in her fright, realized the frustrated anger in his tone. Her brows raised in puzzlement at his fierce expression, then his words sank in.

"You're so crude!" she cried, suddenly blushing blood red. She did not want to think about his butt, so temptingly outlined by his tight dark pants, or any other part of him.

"Yeah, maybe. But at least I'm honest about what I want."

"And I'm not?"

Youngblood waved aside her question. "I ain't got time to bullshit the morning away. I've got work to do."

"And what do you think I'm doing with this broom, riding it?"

Youngblood laughed at her snotty remark. "The thought did cross my mind."

Darn! When was she going to learn to think before she spoke? She'd given him the perfect opening and had no one to blame for his quick come-back but her own wayward tongue. Determined to ignore his very presence, Morgan shooed him aside with the broom as she continued on with her chore. "If you don't mind, I'm busy. Shall we fight later?"

"So"—he moved aside and went on as if there had been no interruption in his original thought—"if you want half the profits, I'd advise you to do your share of the work."

Morgan took a deep breath and then sighed, refusing to let him anger her further. Was the man a complete fool? He could see she was working. What more did he want? Did he expect her to ride the range? Brand cattle? Collect his Mustangs? "I am working, Mr. Youngblood. In case you haven't noticed, at this very minute, I'm sweeping out the house."

Youngblood dismissed her remark with a shake of his head. "Martha can do that."

Morgan heaved a long weary sigh. "I take it you have something special in mind, besides aggravating me?"

Youngblood grinned his delight. He'd known his very presence was annoying to this woman, but to hear her tell of it was like a balm to his soul. At least he wasn't the only one suffering here. "I want you to cart that load of hay out to the east range. Drop a bale every hundred yards or so." Patiently he waited for the explosion that was sure to come.

Morgan glanced outside the opened door, her eyes widening with astonishment as she spied the huge pile of hay sitting near an empty already harnessed wagon. It was so high it towered over the barn. She stepped out to the sloping porch. She knew he meant for her to load it as well as unload it. "All of it? By myself?" she asked in amazement.

Youngblood shrugged. "Seth can help. I can't spare any of the rest. We're branding the herd of Mustangs we gathered last week."

Morgan laughed at what she considered a most ridiculous request. This was obviously just something else meant to annoy her. He knew what he asked was impossible. Not only did she not have the strength for this kind of labor, but she had no idea where the east range was. Even if she did, she wasn't about to jump to do this man's bidding and he knew it. What was this? Some sort of test? If so, the man was bound to be disappointed. She didn't have to listen to him. He wasn't her employer. Thank God! "Keep your profits, Youngblood. I don't need the money." And then she added snidely, "Use my share to buy yourself some clothes."

Youngblood laughed a most annoyingly low, silky, totally male sound. "What's the matter with the ones I've got?"

She shrugged. "For one thing, your pants are too tight." She made a small sound of disgust at her unthinking comment, wishing instantly to take back the words, but it was too late. Darn! Why had she said that? It not only sounded infantile, but was obviously none of her business.

"And?" Youngblood asked, realizing correctly she wasn't about to go on without some prodding, especially since she was biting that delicious-looking lip raw, no doubt trying to keep her mouth shut.

Morgan shot him a killing glare, not at all pleased to see he was finding enjoyment in her unthinking remark. Finally she sighed. What difference did it make? The beast would take her words and use them as he pleased, no matter her meaning. She might as well tell him the whole of it. "And you never wear a shirt. I can only assume you don't own one."

Youngblood grinned, his eyes narrowing as he wondered to what degree his style of dress affected this prim and proper lady. "What's the matter? Haven't you seen a man's chest before?"

"As a matter of fact, I haven't, till I was unfortunate enough to come here. Where I come from men are cultured and civilized. They not only wear clothes, they wear the correct clothes."

"Why the hell didn't you stay there then?"

71

They were shouting now, both forgetting for the moment their plan to calmly aggravate the other. Neither realized the avidly interested crowd of cowhands strolling, with no apparent intent, to within hearing range.

"Because I couldn't bear the thought of not meeting the great Youngblood," she snarled.

Youngblood's mouth thinned to a tight white line at her sarcasm. She knew he was barely holding himself in control, but she didn't care. "Now that you have, why don't you clear out?"

The broom dropped unheeded to the porch floor. Actually it was flung aside. She faced him, her hands on her hips, the sneer in her voice daring him to do his worst. "I'll clear out when I'm good and ready."

Youngblood fumed. "As long as you stay here, you'll do as I say."

"Not likely!"

Youngblood cursed himself for pushing her. Her open defiance would never do. His men stood within hearing and watched as he allowed control to slip through his fingers. If he kept this up, their respect would be a thing of the past. His voice lowered to a menacing drawl that sent shivers up Morgan's spine. "Back off, lady, or I'll give these men a show they'll not soon forget."

Morgan glared in return. "Don't threaten me, Youngblood. I'm not afraid of you."

Youngblood gave her his most insufferable, arrogant grin. "They'd appreciate it, I think, if I showed you just who's boss around here. I wonder if you'd like it as much?"

"Meaning?"

"Suppose I kissed you like I did last night?"

"Suppose you drop dead!" she hissed. Despite the fury that raged in her chest, Morgan realized she'd best keep her words for his ears alone.

Youngblood laughed, his thumbs hooked in the waistband of pants that already rode indecently low on his hips. His words were easily heard by the gathering crowd. "Make sure it's done by the time I get back."

"Go to hell!" she whispered between clenched teeth. Not trusting the glitter in his eyes, she took a step back. There was no telling what this beast would do, especially if he thought he was losing face with his men.

Youngblood's grin widened until sparkling teeth flashed. He gave a low mocking bow and whispered in return, "After you, honey."

The man was a monster. An egotistical, obnoxious boor. Actually, now that she had time to think on it, she couldn't find one redeeming factor in his entire personality. Not that she knew him that well, of course. Morgan's lips tightened with determination. And as far as she was concerned, she was never going to know him any better.

Morgan shivered and silently cursed him again. The men had listened to his commands. And they had laughed at her anger! Bastards all. Morgan's face reddened again as she peeled still another potato. As had been the case all morning, she found herself helplessly repeating the mortifying confrontation again and again in her mind. Damn him! And damn the rest with him. Damn all men to hell!

His parting shot had been meant to do the trick, of course. And it had almost worked. Had he not issued the dare before his men, she might right now be riding the east range. "If you can't do it, why not just say so?" he had said, oh so smugly. And then he gave her a long studious look. Finally, he'd nodded his head as if satisfied at some private thought. "You are a bit puny. Maybe—"

"I can do anything I put my mind to, Youngblood," she interrupted, while glaring a seething resentment that encompassed the now quieted crowd. Morgan took no little satisfaction at turning their grins into sheepish looks of embarrassment.

Youngblood, on the other hand, showed no sign of remorse at his vile treatment of her. His disparaging grin silently told her exactly what he thought of her boast.

Morgan's eyes glittered her hatred as she watched him mount his horse. It didn't help her humor any to see her hat still tied to the saddle. He gave a wave and was gone.

Morgan shivered despite the heat. Oh, he was dangerous, this man, and not as dumb as she'd like to think. He knew just the right strings to pull. She'd have to be careful, very careful indeed.

With a puff of breath Morgan tried to dislodge the stubborn curl from her sticky forehead. When that failed, she wiped at her brow with her forearm, leaving an incriminating trail of white powdery flour behind. She was kneading a batch of dough for bread. The kitchen was hot, almost unbearably so, but smelled wonderful. Morgan surveyed her handiwork. To her credit, and after hours of working, she had one huge applesauce cake, already cooled and sugared for tonight's dessert plus four blueberry pies, their still warm, pungently sweet fragrance delightful enough to rival the finest Parisian perfumes. Meanwhile a huge pot of stew simmered on the stove.

She smiled as she relished this newfound freedom. How often had she argued with her father over this very thing? And when she had dared to go against his wishes, what had he done? Lord, you would have thought she'd committed murder rather than baked some sweet confection.

Why couldn't he understand Morgan felt this no chore? She loved creating mouth-watering delights.

But no. No daughter of Andrew Wainright was going to soil her delicate hands. The kitchen was no place for a lady of New York's polite society. Not as long as he had anything to say about it.

Thank God, he didn't. Morgan smiled. She couldn't remember an afternoon when she had enjoyed herself more. And that was only part of it. She couldn't wait until the men tasted her efforts.

The table was lined with cooling oatmeal cookies. Morgan put the bread dough into pans and set them aside to rise for the last time before she took a cookie and popped it into her mouth. She leaned against the sink and savored the sweet flavor with relish as she closed her eyes and gave the slightest moan.

Youngblood had been watching her for some time from the porch. Silently he cursed the look of euphoria on her face as the sweetness of the cookie exploded upon her taste buds. Helplessly his body hardened at the sight. It was almost blatantly sexual, that look. He cursed again. Every damn thing the woman did reminded him of sex. He couldn't watch her move without imagining her beneath him. He couldn't listen to her speak without thinking the sweet sound low and husky, filled with yearning. He couldn't watch her smile without cursing the fact that she never smiled for him. And worst of all, he couldn't watch her eat, not with that look of ecstasy, without remembering what she had tasted like.

His mouth twisted into a sneer. Damn, he didn't like seeing her in that kitchen, with her hair curling at her damp neck and her cheeks all rosy from the heat. Her eyes sparkled. Her lips curved into a soft smile. She looked like she belonged. He didn't want her to belong. He didn't want her to even look as if she might.

"There ain't no need for you to cook. We've already got someone to do that."

Morgan let out a shriek and jumped as the kitchen's silence was broken by his snarling comment. "Good God! Will you please stop sneaking up on me like that?" She took a deep gasping breath and her hand came to her chest as if she'd soothe away the wild raging of her heart. "They'll be sending my body home in a box if you keep this up. Why don't you make some noise? Why don't I ever hear you?"

"Some say if you hear an Indian, it's already too late." He grinned as he moved into the room.

She gave him a long look and nodded in agreement. "I can safely testify to that."

Youngblood chuckled at her snarl as he moved to the sink and pumped a pan full of water. A moment later he was splashing soapy water all over the flour-dusted floor as he scrubbed his face, arms, and hands.

"You could have done that outside, you know. Now you've muddied the floor."

He glanced down at the pasty mess. "If you didn't spread flour all over the place, there'd be no problem. I told you, you don't need to cook."

"First of all, I intend to do as I please. And it pleases me to cook. Second, cooking is not the issue here. You've made a mess of this floor. Clean it up!"

Youngblood stopped rubbing at his face. Slowly the towel he had taken from a hook over the sink lowered as he shot her a dark look of amazement. "Are you talking to me?"

"Do you see anyone else here?"

"Cleaning is woman's work," he said flatly as if that solved the problem and then flung the damp towel on the rising dough.

Morgan snatched it away and hung it up again. "Then why did you tell me to bring the hay out to the range? Wouldn't that be a man's job?"

Youngblood shrugged. "Did you do it?"

"You can see for yourself I didn't."

"Well then, what's your problem?"

"Marvelous answer, Youngblood," she commented snidely. "Are you always this scintillating a conversationalist?"

"Don't get to talk much to the ladies. Can't remember any complaining about my lack of conversation though." Youngblood shot her the cockiest grin she'd ever seen. "Guess the ladies are interested in things other than talking."

Morgan gritted her teeth. "No doubt."

"Back to the floor."

"Were we on the floor?" he inquired, and then laughed at her growing anger.

"I didn't hire on as your slave, Youngblood."

He gave her a shrug. "So don't clean it."

"And just leave it?" she asked in amazement.

He shrugged again.

Morgan's lips compressed into a tight line. Her hands came to rest on her hips. "We're going to have to set some rules around here about sharing chores. Firstly and most important, if you mess it, clean it."

"We don't share the chores, lady. If we did, that hay would have been scattered over the east range today."

Morgan ignored his remark. "I'll take care of the house, the meals, the laundry. I'll even straighten your room. Just clean up after yourself."

"Stay the hell out of my room!" His voice had suddenly grown to a roar. "You commandeered this house as if it were yours alone. I'll thank you to allow me at least my own room."

Morgan realized she probably shouldn't have entered his room, but she'd be damned if she'd apologize for cleaning it. "Your room was a disgrace." She shook her head. "Imagine a grown man living in such filth."

Youngblood loomed over her in righteous anger. "I happen to like it that way."

"There were so many dirty clothes strewn everywhere, we could hardly find the floor. It took Martha and me most of the afternoon just to sort through the mess."

"From now on, mind your own damn business."

Morgan shrugged. "Fine. If you want to live in a pig sty, go right ahead." She shot him a look of disgust. "Put your clothes outside your door and I'll—"

"No need, Cindy does my laundry," he interrupted.

"Cindy?" Morgan asked, surprised by the odd sensation she felt that another woman had been doing that chore for him. Firmly she acknowledged the feeling as nonsensical and returned, "Well she's not doing much of a job then. Nearly everything you own was dirty."

"I wait until I get a good-size bundle before I bring it to her," he raged. "Besides, Cindy knows just the right thing to do with my clothes."

"Really? And what is that?" She should have known.

If she had stopped and listened to the suddenly low, silky, almost purring sound of his voice, she would have at least suspected.

"She takes them off," he replied with a wicked grin.

"Bastard!"

"Morgan!" Martha gasped as she entered the kitchen just at that moment, astounded that her young lady even knew such a word, never mind dared to use it. Her eyes darted between the two young people. As far as she could tell, she'd come just in time, because both of them, their bodies strained toward each other, looked as close to violence as she cared to imagine. "Good gracious! What's all this shouting about?"

Morgan shot Youngblood a killing look as she suddenly portrayed the innocent. "Nothing," she said, her voice as sulky as a child's.

"I'm afraid I made a mess of your floor, ma'am, which caused Miss Morgan to grow a bit upset." Martha's gaze followed the pointed direction of his gaze. "If I knew where to find the mop, I would have cleaned it right up."

Morgan gasped at the outrageous lie.

"Oh no, Mr. Youngblood. It's perfectly all right. You work so hard all day. It won't take me but a minute. You go sit down and rest. Dinner will be ready in a few minutes."

Morgan actually growled as Youngblood shot her a triumphant look. His eyes sparkled with laughter as he remarked, "I might just do that." Suddenly he added, no doubt to further taunt, "And thank you, Miss Martha, for cleaning my room."

Martha beamed at his praise.

He shot the silently fuming woman a look of complete innocence. "You won't forget to call me, now, will you, Miss Morgan?"

Morgan's lips curled over her teeth in a silent snarl. She almost choked on the words as she forced them out. "I won't forget."

Chapter Five

Morgan pulled the horse to a stop as a glimpse of movement disappeared behind a boulder. Each day she rode out from the ranch in order to practice shooting her newly bought gun. But after a week, target practice had begun to take a weak second place to her real reason for coming out here.

She had believed, at first, this place to be no more than barren wasteland. A place where nothing lived under the harsh brutality of a relentless desert sun. A place that could boast of no beauty. She'd been wrong. Each day she came to know more clearly the exquisite pleasure of green dotted desert, of wild flowers, of the pungent scent of sagebrush, of the juniper and pinion pine that dotted the hills, of a sky so clear and blue and endlessly magnificent it nearly took one's breath away.

And each day she eagerly rode farther over this wild, beautiful land she now called home, exploring with eyes wide with awe everything from its smallest cactus to the majesty of the stark, red-gray mountains that surrounded this small valley.

Morgan made every effort to watch carefully for the direction Youngblood and the men had taken, for above all she wanted no encounter with the one thing that continually marred her peaceful existence. She considered herself blessed that they saw as little of one another as possible. They shared a house and two meals a day, but nothing more. Rarely did they speak, lest a word or two grow into an argument. She didn't want to see him any more than was absolutely necessary. And he certainly had no right to know, nor would he care, about the markmanship she was slowly gaining.

For a moment Morgan thought she might have come across him despite the pains taken, but no. She sighed with relief as she realized the movement she'd seen was too small to have been Youngblood or any of the men. Perhaps it was a small animal, she thought and moved her horse closer.

Morgan felt a moment's trepidation and pulled the horse to a stop again. What was she doing? Why investigate? Suppose it was something dangerous, like a snake. Morgan shivered at the thought. Weren't these untamed lands known to be filled with deadly threats? Wasn't that why she'd taken to wearing a gun when away from the house?

But it was one thing to shoot at the numerous small rocks she'd placed upon boulders. It was quite another indeed to face off an attacking animal.

She watched as the top of a dark head came into view over the edge of the boulder. "Come out of there," she called, relieved she had decided not to shoot. Still, she pulled her gun from its holster, unsure of whom she faced. "Who are you?"

Huge dark eyes, wide with caution, peered over the top of the rock. To her amazement, Morgan watched as a young boy moved from behind. "Don't shoot, lady. I'll go back. I promise."

Morgan grinned, her eyes widening with amazement as she holstered her weapon. "Who are you?"

"Pedro," came the soft, slightly shaken reply.

Spying no means of transportation, Morgan asked, "How did you get out here, Pedro?"

The boy shrugged. "Walked."

"What are you doing here?"

"Looking for lizards."

Morgan shivered her disgust at the mere mention of the ugly reptile. "Did you find one?"

"Not yet."

She breathed a sigh of relief. "You want a ride?"

The boy shrugged again. "I reckon."

Morgan pulled the boy up behind her. "You'll have to tell me where to go. I'm new in these parts and don't know my way around yet."

Pedro gave her the directions. Almost an hour later she stopped her horse before an adobe mission. Surprised, she turned in the saddle. "You live here?"

Pedro nodded.

Morgan looked about her in surprise. The place looked like a church, not a building to house a family. On both sides of the largest structure, a high fence extended to the right and left and then turned back to form a courtyard in which stood a number of smaller buildings. How could he live here? Maybe his family were the caretakers, she finally reasoned. "I think someone should talk to your father. You shouldn't be wandering so far away. Why, anything could happen to you out in the desert alone."

"No, lady. Don't tell. I promise, I won't do it again." A moment later the boy was off the horse and running through the large, ornately carved wooden doors that lay ajar.

Morgan watched the boy disappear inside. She was about to continue on her way, thinking it was really none of her concern, when a priest clothed in heavy brown robes came suddenly through the doorway. "Good afternoon," he said with a hand outstretched in welcome. "I wanted to thank you for bringing him back. Would you like something cool to drink before you leave?"

Morgan smiled, leaned down, and shook the elderly priest's hand. "Thank you, that would be nice."

Morgan knew she deserved none of Father Mendez's

81

praise. What she'd done had been for purely selfish reasons. Her visit was over. She'd been at the door shaking hands with the kindly old priest, when Pedro had come racing around a corner and nearly toppled her, for she stood in his path. His hands twisted nervously behind his back. His eyes told clearly his misery. To be caught running was bad enough. To almost knock the lady down might very well result in no dinner tonight.

Morgan looked down at the boy and smiled at his terrified expression, ready to tell him it was all right. But something happened at that moment. Something fluttered softly in her chest when his huge, dark brown eyes lifted to hers and Morgan knew she wouldn't be leaving the orphanage alone.

He was eight, or at least Father Mendez had imagined him to be, for the sheriff had found the boy alone, half dead of starvation and thirst, four years earlier. No one had ever found a trace of his mother or father. It was imagined they had taken ill and died somewhere in the hills, perhaps among the hundreds that had left Mexico in search of a better way of life. Sadly, they hadn't found it. Somehow the boy had miraculously survived the cold nights and wild animals as he wandered alone into the desert.

"How long am I going to stay here?"

Morgan smiled at the amazement she read in eyes gone wide as he took in the ranch buildings along with the many-fenced corrals. The place might be a shambles in her eyes, but it was closer to paradise to this young boy. "I don't know exactly. Maybe six months."

"And then I'll have to go back?"

Morgan's heart twisted painfully in her chest at the suddenly defeated expression in huge brown eyes. Children shouldn't ever look so sad, she thought. "No, Pedro. We're staying here six months, but you're staying with me forever."

God, this one was going to break hearts, she thought as she watched a smile light up his face. His eyes grew even larger as they rounded with hope and dawning trust.

"And then where are you going?"

"*We* are going home."

They were making up a pallet for him to use for the night. Their voices were soft but filled with laughter and excitement as he questioned and Morgan told of the many things he'd see once it was time to leave the ranch, when a low voice interrupted. "Company?"

Morgan grinned as she realized they were no longer alone, for Youngblood stood just outside her opened door. "Pedro, this is Mr. Youngblood. He owns this ranch."

Youngblood's black eyes first widened with surprise and then narrowed with suspicion as they met hers. What the hell was she up to? Why hadn't she included herself as the owner?

"Thank you for letting me stay, Mr. Youngblood."

Again, black eyes lifted to blue and held until Morgan suggested, "The men are back, Pedro. Supper will be ready soon. Why don't you find Martha. She'll get you something to eat."

"A friend of yours?" Youngblood asked, nodding over his shoulder at the departing boy.

Morgan shrugged. "Not exactly."

"What exactly?"

Morgan felt again her annoyance rise. "Is it any of your business?" Darn, she silently ranted, could she never be alone with this man and keep her temper under control?

"Everything that happens on this ranch is my business."

"Everything except this. The boy belongs to me."

"What do you mean?"

"I mean the orphanage is unbelievably overcrowded. So I took him with me."

"Just like that?"

"Look, Youngblood, I don't need this interrogation. I wanted him. It's as simple as that."

"And what are you going to do with him when you don't want him anymore?" His smile was hard, his firm lips almost sneered. "When it's inconvenient to have him around. When you return to New York, to your fiancé and friends and the gala parties? Will you send him back?"

Morgan's eyes widened with surprise that he should so heartlessly defame her actions. Her feelings for this child had no part in this war they waged. How dare he accuse her of so dastardly an intent?

Morgan's surprise grew quickly to anger. Finally she gave a contemptuous smile as she shook her head. Her back straightened with resolve. "He won't be going back, Youngblood. He's mine. And I'll thank you to butt out of my business."

Youngblood lowered his gaze. If Morgan didn't know better, she could almost believe the man was sorry for that last comment. But she did know better. He hated her. Of that she had no doubt. Hated her, in fact, on first sight, or perhaps even before they'd met. What she wondered was, why?

A slight flush covered Youngblood's features. He felt a moment's shame and then only burning anger that she had caused him to feel embarrassed. Damn her to hell! Who was she to cause him to lose all control? Silently he cursed his thoughtless words. Christ, what had come over him to say such a thing? In self-defense he directed his anger toward his oh so worthy opponent. His mouth curled with contempt. "If you wanted a child, all you had to do was ask. I would have been happy to accommodate."

Morgan gasped at his outrageous and uncalled-for attack. Her hands balled into fists. Her body trembled with rage. For a fleeting moment she wondered if she mightn't explode into a thousand pieces as she tried to contain her anger. "You monster," she railed, wondering if she'd survive fury of this magnitude. "I'd kill myself before I'd let you touch—"

Morgan had no chance to finish. Her door was viciously kicked shut and huge hands, one step from violence, reached for her shoulders and pulled her hard against him. Her breath was knocked from her at the sudden impact. His lips were a hairsbreadth from hers when the imprint of her against his body actually registered and lust, the likes of which he'd never known, exploded in his brain. He never realized the vicious words were softened in a tone heavy with want. "I'd kill you myself before I'd let another—"

He kissed her then, interrupting his own words, and this time Morgan would find no excuses as her anger transformed suddenly into a passion gone wildly out of control.

His mouth was clean, hard, demanding, almost punishing as he hungrily sought to absorb the scent and taste of this small, spirited woman into the depths of his body. And Morgan in response nearly melted at the feverish heat that burst into flames just below her belly and spread its thick aching waves of almost violent hunger into every fiber of her being.

She was leaning into him, her hands moving frantically as she mindlessly sought the delicious texture of warm, hard, male flesh.

Beyond thought, she only groaned a greedy sound as her lips parted and his tongue filled her mouth. Her knees buckled as he took her warm sweetness and left behind his intoxicating taste and scent. She was tearing at his vest, her hands hungry for more of the heat that seared her palms.

Her hands slid to his shoulders, his neck, and buried themselves, as she moaned a sound of pleasure, in gleaming black hair. God, it had been so long since she'd touched him last. And now that she had, she couldn't stop her hands from moving.

She never noticed the sound as he tore at her shirtwaist. The fabric came apart at her back as if it suffered no obstacle. Buttons rolled unheard upon the floor. He pushed the material from her arms. Eagerly, mindlessly, she assisted, until it lay useless at her waist.

The delicate straps of her chemise disappeared beneath rough hands and Morgan groaned her delight as calloused

85

fingers reached for a heavy, milky white breast. She pressed tightly against him. There was no need to hold her in place, for she held on to him as if he were her lifeline in an exploding world of mindless sensation.

His hand slid to her bottom and cupped the soft fullness found there. Lower his fingers moved until they found the deliciousness of her heat. Effortlessly, held in the palm of his hand, he raised her, sliding her up and down, relishing the mindless ecstasy of her softness against his aching body.

With a tortured sound, he tore his lips from hers, raised her higher, and fastened his mouth upon the deliciousness of one sweet breast.

Heat! Morgan gasped her shock as searing flame licked at her flesh. She shivered. She gasped. She groaned. She arched her back as tiny sounds came from deep within her throat, wordlessly imploring more.

He bit her then, but the action brought no pain, rather it intensified the bright sparkling lights of pleasure that flashed throughout her body. The pleasure centered in the pit of her stomach with agonizing accuracy. Her head fell back on a neck too weak to hold. Her legs hung uselessly against him.

He felt her slump and knew a hunger unlike any he'd ever suffered. His hands reached beneath her legs, swinging her easily to his chest, his hungry mouth never parting from her softness.

Morgan groaned her pleasure as he pressed her beneath him on the bed. She clutched his shoulders, her nails biting deep into hard flesh, and gave a soft cry as he attempted to pull back. For she had yet to hear the sound, and the weight of him against her was an overwhelming aphrodisiac. She couldn't bear the thought that he would leave her now.

Youngblood sat at her side and cursed as the sound came again, but his eyes remained on the intoxicating sight of her. Her hair had escaped its pins and now framed her delicate face in a wild mass of golden curls. Her skin was smooth, milky white, and so damn beautiful he wondered if he had the strength to leave her. Her breasts were lovely and full, larger than he had imagined, for they were kept modestly bound within a tightly fitted bodice. But Youngblood had known her shape from their first meeting. He had wanted her then and the ache and pain of that wanting had not decreased in the long days that followed. Silently he swore that, before she left, he'd have this woman. Only then would he be free of this agonizing need.

Youngblood almost smiled at her still dazed expression, knowing once she came to her senses she'd hate him all the more for his loss of control. No doubt she'd blame him solely for what had just happened. He cared not at all, for he knew the passion that lurked just beneath her cool surface.

Unable to help himself, his hand reached to caress the tempting softness of her breast. He smiled and his voice was low, filled with husky sexual promise. "They're calling us to supper. Shall I help you dress?"

It took her a full minute to realize his words. Her face flamed as she noticed at last their position. Morgan blinked her amazement and looked down at the dark hand that almost casually held her breast. His fingers were possessively and gently squeezing and shaping her nipple into a hard bud.

It was beyond his power to resist. His head suddenly dipped and sucked at the rosy tip. But Morgan had once again her senses about her and the once delicious action brought nothing but horror to mind.

She pushed against his shoulders, causing a loud sucking sound as his mouth was taken from its prize. She was gasping for breath, astonished at the emotion that had flared to life and raged between them. Morgan relished the anger that rushed suddenly through her. It was her only means of self-defense. Forgetting her state of undress, her lips tightened to fury as she stated coldly, "Get away from me, Youngblood."

Youngblood grinned at the anger he'd known would come to replace her passion. But he couldn't help the taunting words as he reminded her of her lapse of sanity. "Have you changed your mind then? You seemed eager enough a moment ago."

"Far as I can tell, anything in a skirt would seem eager to you."

Youngblood chuckled, but his lips hardened to an angry slash, belying the lighthearted sound. "I suppose you're blaming me?"

"I most certainly am. You kissed me, did you not?"

"Honey, just because I kissed you, you didn't have to go all soft and hot in my arms," he callously reminded. "Why, I'd have to be less than human to resist, what with the way you were tearing at me."

Morgan's eyes rounded with astonishment. "Tear . . . tear . . . ? Get away from me!" she snapped as she pushed him aside and came to her feet. How dare he take a moment of insanity and throw it in her face? It was his fault. None of this would have happened if he hadn't touched her.

Unconsciously giving him a most delicious view, Morgan's chest heaved with righteous anger as she stood facing him. She knew she should cover herself, but at this moment she couldn't have cared less if she'd been completely naked. "Get out," she muttered, closer to violence than at any time in her life.

"Are you going to eat like that?" he asked, his voice breaking ever so slightly at her casual nakedness.

Morgan suddenly knew her effect on him. It was obvious he couldn't take his eyes from her. Slowly her anger came under control and her eyes hardened with spite. She gave a deliberate shrug of a slender shoulder, knowing the effect as her breasts swung before his hungry gaze. Youngblood swallowed uncomfortably. Morgan's smile was wicked with pleasure at his suffering. "Can't see how it's any of your business," she drawled, imitating his Western twang.

Sonofabitch! He'd thought to tease her into admitting her needs. How had she turned the tables on him? How had he become the culprit here when only moments ago this woman had wanted him and anything he could give just as much as he? He could feel his sex throbbing hard with excitement. His dark eyes filled with the luscious sight of her. Jesus, had a man ever wanted like this before? His hands itched to reach for her, and from the satisfied look in her eyes, she knew it.

The rebellious moment lasted mere seconds before Morgan pulled the cover from the bed and held it to her nakedness, her cheeks red at her own short moment of insanity. Still she dared to face him, glaring her disgust, her hatred alone carrying her through this uncomfortable moment. Her hands cupped her breasts, pressing the blanket to her, forcing the soft white flesh to strain above the covering as she unconsciously taunted him to near madness. And he couldn't do a damn thing about his wants, what with that goddamned Seth calling him again.

He gave a shrug, his eyes hard, his mouth twisted into a bitter smile. "At least the men will get a treat. I'm going to Cindy's. She's a woman who knows what she wants in a man and is honest enough to admit it."

Pedro watched in silent awe as the men moved in a haphazard line toward the huge boiling pots of chili. His mouth watered, but he wasn't ready yet to make himself completely at home. Martha brought him a bent metal plate filled with the hot saucy mixture and three pieces of bread.

"If you want more, just ask," Morgan said as she handed him a chipped cup that held cool lemonade.

After dinner one of the men brought a small red puppy to the two women and boy. Obviously shy and perhaps a bit embarrassed, he placed the dog in Pedro's lap. "Figured you might like one of Red's pups. Every boy should have a dog."

Pedro's delight was a sight to behold. His eyes glowed like dark brown jewels, his cheeks flushed with joy. "Can I have it?" he asked softly, almost fearfully.

"Of course you can have it," Morgan returned,

smiling her thanks at the man and then almost laughing as he turned nearly as red as the dog. "This is your home, remember? Maybe one day you can even have a horse."

"Do you mean it?"

Morgan smiled at the sweet hopeful expression. "Of course I mean it. Can you ride?"

Pedro's shoulders slumped as he shook his head.

"Would you like me to teach you?"

He nodded, unsure of what to make of this. He'd never in his life had anything that belonged only to him. Now he had a home, a dog, and maybe someday a horse. He didn't understand how all this had happened, but he was sure glad it had.

Morgan sat upon the sloping porch and gave a soft laugh as all four of the men hunched down before her tried to outdo one another with hilarious stories about ranching. From the corner of her eyes she watched as Youngblood raced his horse into the yard. Supper had been finished hours ago. She hoped he didn't think she'd left anything for him. Purposely, spitefully, and to Martha's astonishment, Morgan had dumped what was left of the huge pot of chili into the compost pile she had suddenly thought to make for her garden. She hoped he was dying of starvation. She hoped pains were ripping his stomach apart. No, she didn't. She couldn't have cared less what he did or didn't suffer. The man was a nonentity as far as she was concerned.

The long ride had appeased much of Youngblood's anger, but as he listened to the soft tinkling sound of her laughter, he felt his annoyance begin to build again. What the hell was so damn funny? He had taken care of his horse and was walking toward the house when he heard her laugh again. Youngblood's mouth grew tight with annoyance. "There's a break somewhere on the south range fence," he said to the four men, ignoring Morgan's presence. "I found two of our cattle, dead. They must have been at the springs." He rubbed the back of his neck and gave a tired sigh. "We'll have to find it first thing in the morning."

A moment later she found herself alone on the porch. Youngblood's words and hostile glare having successfully ended what could have been a most delightful evening. Morgan scowled, hating him all the more. Cursed beast! As it was, she almost never spoke to anyone except Martha. Did he have to take away even this small enjoyment? The thought of entering the house was out of the question. He was in there. She could hear him prowling around the kitchen, muttering curses as he moved.

Most of the men had gone into the bunkhouse with an eager Martha to play cards again. Pedro was sleeping on a mat of blankets at the foot of her bed. She knew she should go to bed, but knew as well she'd get no sleep this night.

Haunting pictures came again to mind. She could see them together, imagine well what they did. Her cheeks darkened with anger that she should care. It didn't matter what the man did. She certainly had no hold over him, nor did she want one. All she wanted was to be left in peace as she waited out this most unfortunate enforced visit.

Did he kiss Cindy the way he'd kissed her? she wondered. Again she denounced the thought. But she couldn't forget her hungry, desperate response to his kiss, his touch. She might put the blame at his feet, but she knew in her heart the truth of it. He was temptation. A temptation that caused a wildness before unknown to her heart.

Yes, she had often kissed Bradley. And in his kisses she had found sweet pleasure, but never the raging almost insane emotion she'd known in Youngblood's arms. An inferno of heat. A heat that threatened to swallow her in its flame. Is this what Bradley had suffered? Is that why he had so often begged her to come to his rooms?

Morgan breathed a heavy sigh. How could she go back to Bradley now, having glimpsed the passion that could rage between a man and a woman? How could she ever be satisfied? She shook her head. It didn't matter. Bradley was good and kind. She could forgive him if he didn't bring thunder to her heart, for he was the man she loved. Whatever it was she felt for Youngblood, it wasn't love. It was sinful and wicked. It made her act totally out of character and brought only shame to her heart.

She shivered at the remembrance. Morgan's lips tightened as she silently swore it would never happen again.

"Where the hell is the food?" Youngblood almost roared as something was sent crashing to the floor.

Morgan dashed inside. "Stop that noise! Pedro is sleeping."

"Didn't you eat tonight?"

"Of course I ate." Morgan almost grinned, while feigning wide-eyed surprise. "Didn't you?"

His eyes were hard when he forced a cold telling smile to his lips. "Cindy doesn't cook much. She excels in other arts."

The man was disgusting. She didn't care a wit about his carnal escapades. What bothered her was he saw fit to flaunt his animal urges. Morgan forced her pinched lips into a semblance of a smile. "What a shame. No doubt you should find someone who can cater to all your basic needs. After all, I wouldn't want to see you go hungry."

Youngblood ignored her sarcasm, knowing she'd be perfectly happy to see him starve. "So where's the leftovers?"

"Leftovers?" she repeated with exaggerated innocence. "I'm sorry. I didn't think you'd be wanting anything to eat. I poured what was left of dinner on my compost pile."

"What compost pile?"

She smiled all too sweetly. "The one I'm making for my garden."

"And you decided to start it tonight. Right?"

Morgan smiled again, her eyes wide as she blinked in feigned innocence. "How did you know that?"

Youngblood released a low heavy sigh that bordered on defeat. Unhappily, his visit to Cindy had not proven beneficial, as first hoped. Once in the woman's company, Youngblood seemed to have lost the urge that had brought him there in the first place. And instead of spending a not too memorable time in bed, as they had often in the past, they had spent the evening talking, a not unusual phenomenon since they were friends of long standing.

Now he cursed his lost opportunity to rid himself of the lust that threatened to overcome his very sanity. It might not have been a terribly satisfying experience, but at the very least it would have taken the edge off the emotion that even now raged painfully within his gut. Youngblood couldn't understand why he had refused Cindy's offer.

Now he knew himself for a fool. Why the hell hadn't he taken care of necessary business? Damn it! Had he followed his first intentions, he might right now be less inclined to cart this little bitch off to his bed. Instead, he could hardly think beyond the temptation of touching her, smelling her, tasting her, fitting his body into the tight confines of hers. Compound these urges with the overwhelming need to strangle her and it was no wonder he was in less than a jovial mood.

Mentally he cursed the distance between Cindy's small house and his ranch. For a second he considered a return and more satisfying trip, but instantly disallowed the notion. It was too far. He had work to do in the morning. Work that would never be accomplished if he spent the night riding to and fro.

Silently he promised his next visit to be more fruitful. He was going to take the willing Cindy again and again, until this ache in the pit of his belly was naught but a memory and his body so satisfied that he wouldn't remember this one tiny, smart-mouthed, irritating woman.

Youngblood vehemently denied the small voice that professed the uselessness of his intent. It would work. He wanted only physical relief. It didn't matter that the relief would come at Cindy's practiced hand. Anyone would do. He didn't crave this nasty, tiny woman who could face him with a temper that easily matched his own.

Only not tonight. Tonight she was as falsely sweet as he'd ever seen. And goddamnit! Even that appealed.

Morgan hid her smile as she watched him force his anger under control. Finally she said, "Look Youngblood. This isn't going to work. Suppose we call a truce. It's hard enough to live under the same roof with a stranger. We'll never make it with this kind of antagonism between us."

"So?"

"So"—she nearly choked on the words as she forced them out—"I apologize for how I acted this afternoon."

"Don't worry about it. You got me all fired up, but Cindy was happy enough to take care of the problem." He hadn't lied. Cindy would have been happy enough, but he wasn't.

Morgan's lips tightened, her anger coming full force again. That's what she got for trying to make peace with a savage. They didn't bother her, though, his crass remarks. Not really. She didn't care if he bedded down the entire female population of the world. As long as he left her in peace. So why then was a pain tearing at her chest? Why was it suddenly so hard to breathe? Morgan would have died before she'd allow him the knowledge that his actions were even noticed. She forced a bored, heavy tone to her voice. "How very nice for you. Still, I'd appreciate it if you kept your rutting practices to yourself. I've no interest in your personal business."

"I didn't tell you my personal business. I told you Cindy took care of me. I didn't say how."

Morgan closed her eyes and willed away the picture of him in another's arms. He was purposely taunting her and she knew it. What she didn't know was why he should bother, or why she should care. What was there that raged between them that turned him so mean? Her look was clearly puzzled when she asked, "Why do you hate me?"

Youngblood grunted in true Indian style. "You can't help who you are. Let's leave it at that."

Morgan's eyes flashed her anger at the unspoken but obvious insult. "And just what am I?"

Youngblood looked at her for a long moment, unable to hide the hunger the sight of her brought to the surface, while growing steadily angry at the need he couldn't deny. "You, lady? You're a black widow spider. You'd destroy your mate the moment you're done with mating."

Morgan gasped, her blue eyes wide with shock. "What a horrible thing to say!"

Youngblood shrugged. "The truth isn't always pleasant."

"Mr. Youngblood, I seriously doubt you'd know the truth if it hit you in the face."

"Wouldn't I?" he asked as he closed the distance between them in two long strides. Before she knew what was happening, his arms were around her slight form holding her firmly against him. "Suppose you tell me the truth, then. Or better yet, show me."

Morgan pushed against his shoulders, denying the surge of desire that tightened her stomach at his mere touch. "Take your hands off me!" Her breathing was irregular as she broke free of his hold. "I see no need to stand here trading insults. I apologized in the hopes of setting aside our antagonism. I should have known I'd be asking too much for us to be friends."

Youngblood almost laughed out loud at the ridiculous suggestion. Didn't she know it was too late for that? Was she so innocent as to believe the passion that raged between them could be easily put aside and friendship could take its place? Youngblood shot her a probing glance, trying to see beneath her beauty to the real woman behind those wide blue eyes. Finally he gave a soft grunt. She was good. She was real good, but he'd never believe her all that innocent. She'd come from the city. New York City. He knew the kind of women who lived there. Hadn't he lost his innocence in the hands of one such woman? Perhaps not innocence of the flesh, but an innocence of the spirit.

He had still been a young man when he'd finally gathered the money needed to finish his education. He'd gone east to New York. A young man who had limited experience with girls and none at all with eager, lusty sophisticated ladies. God, she had almost ruined him for life, pretending as she had. Again he cursed his gullibility, for he had believed she loved him. Believed it, that is, until he'd found out she had a husband. Believed it until she offered him to pleasure her friend.

Not again. He'd never be taken in again by a beautiful face and the seductive sway of a skirt. This one was engaged to be married. No one could tell him a woman with her background didn't know the touch of a man. But if she wanted to play at the game, she'd find no obstacle here, for he now knew the rules. Youngblood's imagination knew no limit as he pictured the many erotically delicious ways they could unify into a most satisfying friendship.

A burst of laughter came from inside the bunkhouse. Both Morgan and Youngblood looked toward the sound. He grinned. "Martha at it again?"

Morgan nodded, while answering his grin despite herself.

"I should probably stop the game before she ends up owning this ranch."

Morgan smiled, her gaze softening as she watched his grin. Something fluttered in her throat and chest as his black eyes gentled and came to rest on her smiling lips. Unable to face the warmth she found there, Morgan lowered her gaze again and whispered, "Good night."

Youngblood breathed a long sigh as a moment later he heard the door to her room shut softly.

Chapter Six

Youngblood's lips tightened with displeasure as he came thundering into the yard, creating a mound of choking dust. He squinted against the brown cloud, but never for a moment lost sight of the woman who stood laughing at something Tom Barry said. Their heads were still close together, while the drawn plans for renovating the house, placed on a table before them, fluttered momentarily forgotten in the breeze. Another wagonload of supplies had arrived since Youngblood had left this morning. Idly he wondered how much more would be needed before she was finished.

A team of men worked inside, while another was on the roof. They had ripped apart what was left of the rotting structure, while heavy beams were hoisted up the side of the building and then hammered in place to form the support for a second floor.

Youngblood reasoned that the house would be ready a sight sooner than he had expected. The once-sloping porch now stood even as another man dug what looked like holes for foundations nearby. His gaze drifted up again. The roof was no more than a skeletal structure awaiting the layers of wood and shingle that would protect the house against the elements. Youngblood's lips curled with contempt. The way she was spending money, one would think she intended to make this her permanent home. Jesus! Just the thought was enough to send chills of terror down his spine. The idea didn't bear thinking on. He didn't want a woman constantly underfoot. He didn't want a woman, period, except to occasionally see to his needs. He had to get rid of her, and he would, but before he did, he was going to make her his lover. There was no way he could live like this without sharing her bed. Not if he hoped to keep his sanity.

Youngblood never realized the scowl of annoyance that curved his lips as he dismounted. This woman was a mite too friendly with everyone but him. And he didn't like it, didn't like it one bit.

Morgan noticed his expression and asked as he moved to join her and Tom Barry in conversation, "What's the matter?"

"Why?"

"You look about to murder someone."

Youngblood shrugged and forced a lightness he was far from feeling into his voice. "My usual expression." He shook hands with Tom Barry.

"You're going to have some house here, once it's finished," Tom remarked proudly. "Look at the plans for renovation and the additions we've come up with."

Youngblood gazed at the papers held flat on the table. "What was the matter with the way it was?" Damn it, she was making the place so big, he'd be lucky to find her in that maze. And he had every intention of finding her and regularly.

"Nothing, if you don't count the walls, ceiling, and floors," Morgan returned, then smiled as she leaned closer, her gaze fixed on the drawn lines before her. "Isn't it wonderful?"

Youngblood caught a whiff of gardenia and fresh, clean woman and almost groaned. He had to force his hand to remain at his side, for he had almost forgotten they weren't alone.

"Isn't it?" she coaxed, trying to get a response from him.

Youngblood nodded. "Looks mighty big."

"It will be," Tom Barry returned. "After the upstairs is finished, you'll have two more rooms."

"What you fixin' to do with all that room?"

"Why, live in it. What do you think?"

Youngblood glanced down at the woman at his side. His eyes lingered on the fullness of her breasts and the taunting piece of flesh her two open buttons left exposed. *I think we could make love in every damn room in that house and I still wouldn't be satisfied.* He said nothing.

"Have you noticed they fixed the porch today?" And without waiting for an answer, Morgan continued, "When they're finished, it will be wider and run around the entire house. I've ordered rocking chairs and a swing from the catalog," Morgan said as she pointed to the plans before her.

"The outside will be painted white, with blue shutters. You don't mind, do you?" Again, not waiting for his answer, she said, "I'm going to have them rail the porch. Over there I'm going to try to grow some flowers."

"Not in this sun."

"I know. I've ordered two trees for the front yard. They should give off enough shade, once they're grown, that is."

Christalmighty! Did she plan on staying long enough to see a tree grow to full height?

Her eyes sparkled as she rambled on about the furnishings. In her excitement she touched his arm and Youngblood had a time of it keeping his hands at his sides. "Does owning things always make you this happy?"

Morgan stopped her chattering and thought for a moment. She smiled. "Not usually. But this is special."

"Why?"

"Because it's my home."

"For a time," he reminded her, and then cursed at the sudden awareness that filled her eyes.

"Yes," she agreed, losing a bit of her effervescence,

"for a time."

"The one you got in New York must be bigger than this."

"Oh it is, but that's not really mine."

Youngblood gave her a puzzled look.

"I mean, it's mine, but not something I had a hand in putting together. It's been in the family for generations."

Youngblood nodded and as soon as possible excused himself to see to the care of his horse. Wisely, he had come to the conclusion that had he any hope at all in retaining his sanity, he could do so only by maintaining some distance. Every day it grew harder, quite literally, he silently conceded with a wry smile, to see her and keep his hands from reaching for the delicious softness he knew to lurk just beneath those prim blouses she wore. His body ached to feel her against him. His fingers itched to touch her. His eyes devoured her trim curves. His mind thought of little else. Right now, at least for the time being since the two of them shared one small house but separate sleeping quarters, the hunger that constantly twisted at his guts and filled his mind whether asleep or awake had to be held in check.

It was more than time to visit Cindy again. And this time he wasn't going there to talk.

It was as if the old house had magically disappeared and had somehow spawned a new beautiful home in its place. It was accomplished with amazing speed. Youngblood hadn't a doubt the reason behind the unusual efficiency lay in the fact that its new owner was breathtakingly beautiful and every damn man almost killed himself trying to please her. In only a few weeks it was all but finished. Morgan was anxiously awaiting the delivery of the furniture she'd ordered. Curtains had been bought in town and hung, while rag rugs covered the shining new floors.

Youngblood watched as Morgan carefully applied a

coat of blue paint to the trim around the windows. A white smock covered her dress and her hair was protected from splatters by a bright red neckerchief. He smiled as he watched her shake her head with disgust as she wiped a spot of paint from the glass.

"You'd have less trouble if you used a smaller brush."

Morgan blew a puff of air at a strand of hair that insisted on escaping its binding and falling into her eyes and glared at the man who had made himself so scarce this last week. Why, she'd hardly seen him at all, since he worked away from the house all day. After dinner, a dinner he made it his business never to miss since that night she had thrown out all the leftovers, he left for parts unknown, not to return till the wee hours of the morning, and now he had the nerve to tell her how to paint. Her smile was fleeting and obviously insincere as she returned to her work. "Some people might have offered to help out, rather than criticize."

Youngblood chuckled. "I imagine some would. Especially if the owner of this house was a pretty lady." He grinned as a look of undisguised annoyance was shot his way.

"And I take it you make it a point not to please ladies. Pretty or otherwise."

Youngblood leaned his shoulder against the wall, far too close to where she stood, and gave her a wickedly suggestive smile. "I don't know. I've been accused of pleasing one or two in my time."

Morgan refused to acknowledge the fact that it took only his grin to set her heart pounding in her chest. Still, she couldn't deny his words caused her a moment's annoyance. Just how many women had he pleased? Morgan shook her head, trying to dispel the thought. It was none of her business if he pleased every woman in the state of Nevada. And if she was annoyed, it was only because she was trying to finish this before dark. A slight flush of embarrassment tinted her cheeks at his daring remark as she muttered, "No doubt."

Youngblood grinned, wondering if he read correctly her response to his remark. Did it bother her to know he'd been with other women? Did she imagine that was where he'd spent every evening for this last week? Did she bother to think about his disappearance each night? Did it make her wild with jealousy? It sure as hell bothered him to know she wasn't what she appeared to be. No matter her actions and mode of dress, no one could tell him she was pure. He knew her kind. Youngblood's black eyes narrowed as they took in the sweet slender curves of her back. Why did the idea of another man touching her bring about this ache in his belly? And a murderous rage in his heart? Hell! It wasn't as if he cared or anything. He was letting her get to him. He'd have to watch himself. Before he knew it, he'd be acting as ridiculous as those lovesick fools that had been drooling over her this last week. Just the thought of them sent his anger up. "If you don't want to dirty your delicate hands, why didn't you bat your eyelashes at one of those poor fools that have been doing your bidding all week? Surely one of them would have come to your aid."

Morgan turned and faced her tormentor, her features tight with anger. With a quick glance she took in his opened vest moving gently away from his body in the soft summer breeze. Legs apart, his thumbs were hooked inside his belt, in a supposed casual stance, but Morgan knew better. He was angry. What she didn't know, or care to know for that matter, was why. Her lips barely moved as she hissed, "Those fools, as you call them, have been paid well for their work. I've no need to bat my lashes at anyone to achieve my ends."

"No? Then why are you doing it now?"

Morgan shot him a look of disbelief. "That, Mr. Youngblood, is called blinking. I dare say, even you have been known to do it occasionally."

"My ass, lady. I know a come-on when I see it."

Morgan shook her head and sighed with disgust. "Mr. Youngblood, it is entirely possible you are in desperate need of spectacles. If not, you are obviously suffering some form of brain damage. Perhaps you met with an accident to your head today? Surely it is the only logical answer, for I cannot believe you expect every woman you meet to fall at your feet in adoration."

Morgan could hear his teeth grinding in anger and almost smiled knowing she was able to rile this man out of his usual cool biting anger. Suddenly she glanced over his shoulder. A moment later she seemed to have entirely forgotten his presence as she whipped her coverings from her hair and dress and shoved them into his arms. A wide smile curved her lips, her eyes twinkled their delight, as she watched Marshall come trotting into view.

But if Youngblood had known anger at their short exchange, it was nothing compared to the rage that filled his being when he witnessed her happiness upon receiving her first guest.

Marshall dismounted and tied his horse to the hitching post as Morgan moved quickly, anxiously down the steps to greet him. Youngblood couldn't hear their first words, but watched in silent growing anger as she offered both her hands to him in welcome. His stomach lurched as Marshall clasped her hands in his. Still holding one of her hands, he escorted Morgan up the stairs.

The two men glared at one another without offering even a nod of recognition. Youngblood's gaze moved to Morgan and he silently sneered at her obvious delight.

"It's more comfortable in the house," Morgan remarked as she led her guest inside. "Would you like something cool to drink?" she asked, ignoring Youngblood's snarling presence.

The door closing in his face didn't improve Youngblood's temper any. He threw the smock to the ground and fingered her kerchief. For some insane reason he raised it to his nose and breathed the clean scent of her hair that lingered. A moment later he slipped it into his

103

back pocket. Youngblood almost knocked the door from its hinges as he followed Morgan and the sheriff inside.

Since its renovation, the kitchen no longer shared its space with the parlor. Now the front and only door opened to a hall that ran the depth of the house. Directly to the right stood a huge kitchen and dining room, on the left the parlor. At night, for the temperature often dipped drastically after the sun went down, a fire could be set in either room for both boasted stone fireplaces. If the doors were left ajar, the fires could heat the entire house. Farther down the hall were two bedrooms. Overhead were two more.

The floors shone with a rich luster from constant buffing around the edges of brightly colored rag rugs. An Indian blanket hung on one wall in the parlor, while heavy brown leather couches and chairs with accompanying tables dotted the homey room.

Youngblood's eyes narrowed with menace as he stood in the hall and watched Morgan move happily around the kitchen. "You will stay for dinner, won't you?"

Marshall grinned. "I was countin' on you askin'. Word has already spread around town that you're the best cook in these parts."

Morgan blushed with pleasure at his compliment.

"It's surprising to find a woman from the city so happy in the kitchen, wouldn't you agree, Marshall?" Youngblood asked as, uninvited, he joined the couple.

Marshall shot Youngblood a look of distaste as he watched the big man settle himself at the oversized table that could easily accommodate all twelve of the ranch hands plus the two women.

"I don't know. I thought all women were proud of their accomplishments. Does it matter so much where they come from?"

"The ladies"—Youngblood's voice was tinged with undeniable disgust—"I've come across from the city wouldn't know a kitchen from an outhouse."

Morgan shot Youngblood a killing look. What was he doing here? Who invited him? He'd managed to keep his distance this last week—why did he now choose to join her as she prepared dinner?

Morgan ignored his presence and centered her attention on Marshall. "Are you making your rounds, Sheriff?"

"I am. Please call me John."

Two pairs of eyes moved to Youngblood as he snorted a sound that hovered somewhere between a laugh and a growl. His dark eyes were filled with disgust.

"Is something wrong?" Marshall asked, reading correctly the animosity in the dark eyes and answering with his own more veiled hatred.

"Not a thing," Youngblood returned, his voice low and smooth, his smile so false it fooled no one.

Supper should have been a delight. The fried chicken was crisp, tender, and delicious. The buttered potatoes sweet, the green beans fresh and slightly crisp. And yet it was a ghastly affair.

Pedro, who had been permitted to accompany the men as they rode one of the ranges that afternoon, was beside himself with excitement and anxious to relate his experiences. In his childish exuberance, he swung his arm and toppled an entire pitcher of milk into Marshall's lap. The room was suddenly pitched into shocked silence, broken only by Youngblood's low snicker of satisfaction. Morgan considered it nothing less than a miracle that the two hadn't taken that moment to charge at one another's throat. She could only thank John's more civilized nature, for she mentally watched her table being turned over and food scattered every which way.

Conversation did not flow smoothly. Youngblood sulked and only growled a response whenever any questions were sent his way. The men, noting their boss's decidedly unhappy mood, left the moment they swallowed their last bite, each and every one claiming themselves too full to indulge in dessert.

Youngblood seemed to ignore the entire fiasco along with the food on his plate and instead nursed a bottle of whiskey. Never offering their guest a glass, he couldn't have cared less that his actions were the rudest example of hospitality Morgan had ever witnessed.

She was fuming and felt only the greatest relief at leaving the oppression of her kitchen when Marshall invited her to step outside. "It's lovely out here," she remarked as they moved through the moonlit night toward the corrals. "Any day now the chairs and swing I've ordered for the porch will arrive. The house will look so pretty and the long evenings not half as uncomfortable when we're able to spend at least a part of them outside."

"Do you think it wise to share the house with Youngblood? People will talk, you know."

Morgan shrugged. "He's half the owner of the ranch. I couldn't very well put him from his home." Morgan didn't bother to mention she had certainly tried to do just that. "After all, it was his before I came and will remain his after I leave." Morgan smiled up at Marshall's unhappy expression. "Besides, I've Martha to chaperon. If you knew her as well as I, you'd have no cause for worry."

"Do you always eat with the hands?" Marshall asked as he maneuvered them into the shadow of the barn.

"It saves me a good amount of work to sit everyone at one table. I hear it's not the usual thing, but I enjoy their company. I'm afraid I'm not used to the loneliness of ranch life. It's not only informative but entertaining to listen to them talk about their work."

"Still, you've taken on an enormous job. You shouldn't be doing it alone. There are some young Mexican girls in town that could use the work. Would you like me to—"

Morgan interrupted with a shake of her head. "I've had my share of servants in New York, thank you." Morgan felt a moment's frustration as she remembered her useless existence, only a few weeks ago. She never did anything more strenuous than picking up her own discarded underthings, and even that small chore was sometimes done for her the moment they were taken off. She'd been pampered and petted. She knew nothing of real life till now. Suddenly she realized she'd never been happier since coming here and didn't at all look forward to returning to her smothering life in New York. "Believe me, I wouldn't be doing it if I didn't enjoy cooking. Besides, I don't do all the work myself; Martha helps."

It was late by the time Marshall left, but Morgan felt restless tonight. She knew she'd never be able to sleep, not when her mind wondered over the animosity she'd witnessed this night. She had waved as Marshall trotted his horse away from the ranch, but instead of returning to the parlor and extinguishing the light and then going on to her bedroom, she moved down the porch steps and walked toward the river that wound its way over her land some distance beyond the corrals.

She needed to think, and if her wonderings brought no answers to the upsetting and almost tangible hatred between the two men in her kitchen tonight, at least the short walk would allow her the peace and tranquility the evening had lacked. They had barely spoken a word to each other. Morgan was filled with curiosity. Why did they hate one another so? What was there between them that could bring about this almost violent emotion? And Morgan had no doubt both would have gladly given in to their baser instincts any number of times, if she and Martha hadn't been present. Was it a woman? Could it be both had cared for someone? She shook her head. Neither was seriously involved, at least not as far as she could tell.

Perhaps it was something related to their childhood. If so, what in the world could have happened to cause the hatred to last this long?

Morgan sat upon a flat-surfaced rock and gazed out over the large body of water. It was beautiful here at night. Silvery rays of moonlight shone upon a glasslike surface. Morgan decided to ask Tom to make a bench near the edge, so she could sit more comfortably on nights such as these. The water beckoned. It looked so cool and lovely.

Morgan glanced around. She was definitely alone.
Surely there was no harm. Morgan unbuttoned her high-
heeled shoes. She raised the hem of her skirt and petticoat as she rolled her stockings down her legs. On
bare feet she walked to the water's edge. With skirts
raised to just above her ankles she tested the water with
her toe. It was cool and inviting. She wished she had the
nerve to disregard modesty and disrobe in order to enjoy
the water to the fullest, but Morgan knew she'd never
dare.

Her mind was lost in thought on tonight's happenings.
Lord, supper had been a disaster. The only time she had
relaxed was when she'd joined John outside for an
evening stroll.

Silently she cursed Youngblood and his constant
sneering attendance. Why did she allow the man to upset
her so? And why, if it was his personality to be cruel and
nasty, did she think it had anything to do with her?
Because she'd seen him otherwise, she silently reasoned.
There were times when she'd seen him laugh with his
men. He was gentle with Pedro and with Martha
charming and sweet.

What was it about her that he hated so, had hated, in
fact, almost from their first meeting? And what was it
about him that brought out the worst in her character?
Traits she had no knowledge of till now.

Morgan in her innocence hadn't yet recognized the
passion that raged between them, nor the ramifications
of denying it. She felt only confusion that this man could
bring about such startling anger. That he could feel such
hatred.

For all her innocent experience with the opposite sex,
Morgan had never encountered anyone like him. She
wondered how he could provoke her as he did. How did
he know her so well?

The sound of splashing water brought her gaze from
her feet. Suddenly before her eyes, the object of her
thoughts rose from the depths of the water.

108

Morgan gasped as moonlight glistened off bronzed skin. He never hesitated, but made straight for her, his movements silently cutting through the water, his body straight, comfortable in the dark, his whole countenance reminding her of a nocturnal animal at home in its habitat.

The silvery light from above offered her a clear view. His chest was bare. Water trickled down his huge shoulders and arms. His hair was without its usual rawhide and hung gleaming black to his shoulders. His skin glistened wet, brown, and smooth, except for the light sprinkling of hair that covered his chest.

Morgan dropped her skirts, careless of the fact that they drank thirstily of the water. She took a small step back, then another and another, but for every one of hers, he advanced three.

The water was at his waist now. His hips. She took a gasping breath, dreading the moment when the water would offer no protection. Her mouth grew dry. She knew he wore nothing, knew it as surely as she knew her own name, and yet she couldn't take her gaze from the silvery magnificence that rose like a gleaming shadow out of the blackness.

Her heart thudded painfully in her chest, a pulse pounded in her throat as she watched him close the distance between them. The water was at his knees. She watched as rivulets ran from his arms to drop from his fingers. Morgan groaned a low sound of pain, for she hadn't been wrong. He was naked. Naked and so beautiful, proud and so very much a man.

Morgan had never seen a naked man before. Idly she wondered if all were as pleasing to the eye. For some reason she forgot her intent to retreat. He was standing before her now, almost close enough to touch, unashamed and at ease in his undressed state. Morgan could hardly breathe. Why didn't he say something? Why didn't she? What did one say to a naked man? she asked wildly and then called herself every kind of fool. Why hadn't she fled? Why didn't she still? Why had she stayed to watch? Why was she watching him even yet? Why didn't she simply turn away? And most of all why did she feel this overpowering need to reach out and touch him?

Youngblood smiled. For the first time since she'd met him, Morgan noted tenderness in his gaze. "You look like you expect a great monster to come along and eat you up."

Morgan said nothing. It was beyond her power to utter a sound. Her eyes were wide with fear, but she knew the fear wasn't of him but, for some unknown reason, of herself.

Youngblood misread the look in her eyes. "I won't hurt you."

"You shouldn't have come out while I was here."

"When you saw me coming, why didn't you leave?"

"I didn't know . . ." Her words faltered as her gaze drifted unerringly down his body, drawn to the mysteries that made him a man.

"You thought I bathed with my clothes on?"

Morgan shook her head and turned away, mortified that she had stayed. "I'm sorry. I shouldn't have—"

"I'm not. I wanted you to see me. I want to see you."

Morgan swayed at his words, at the low, husky tone of his voice. "Oh God."

He moved closer. His voice deepened, growing husky and uneven. "But that's not all. I want to see you. I want to touch you. I want to taste and kiss you everywhere. And I think you want that as well."

She couldn't move. It was as if her feet were glued to the ground. Her mind screamed, *Run! Run as fast and as far as you can!* But her limbs wouldn't obey the silent commands.

His hand reached out. One finger turned her chin so she was facing him again. He leaned forward and his wet lips brushed against the softness of her cheek. Morgan shivered at the contact. His skin was cool from his bath, but she wasn't. She was smoldering heat that awaited only his touch to burst into flames.

His finger touched lightly to her cheek, giving her every chance to walk away, but she couldn't. He might as well have been holding her, for she couldn't move. His lips teased hers. Back and forth, again and again, they came to brush upon her flesh until she groaned with the wanting only he seemed able to instill.

Her hands came to his chest. Timidly she touched the damp cool flesh. Her hands grew bolder at the sound of his groan and smoothed up over his powerful chest to his neck, to his wet hair.

His arms gathered her close to his nakedness and he ground his hips suggestively against her. "You taste so sweet. I can't get enough."

"Youngblood, oh God, I don't know." She heaved a long whispery breath as he released her mouth and nuzzled her ear and neck with sizzling kisses that sent chills down her spine.

"I do," he muttered against her silken flesh. "I know I want you like I've never wanted another woman. I know I can't get you out of my mind. I know I think about you in bed, just down the hall from my room. I know I lie there every damn night trying to sleep, trying to keep myself from coming to you."

Morgan sighed, her eyes glowing with joy as the wonder of his confession crashed its glory upon her. He loved her. He hadn't exactly said the words, but now that he'd come this far, he would. And Morgan knew, she finally knew the reason why this man was forever in her thoughts. She loved him too! They'd barely known each other a few weeks and yet she knew that despite the anger and confusion he caused, she loved this man.

"I think I love you too," she said shyly as she lowered her head and nuzzled the flesh of his neck.

A long moment of silence went by while Youngblood became absolutely still. Finally he managed to breathe. He felt as if he'd taken a blow to his gut. Jesus Christ! Was that what this little game was about? Did she need to hear him say the words before she put out? Well, she had a long wait coming. Not since Letty, in New York, had he said it and he wasn't about to say them now. If she needed sweet talking to coax her into bed, she could find another sucker. "Is that what you want, baby? You want me to say it?"

Morgan blinked her confusion at the sudden harshness of his tone. "What? Say what?"

His eyes were no more than slivers of black ice as he stared down at her. His lips were twisted in ridicule. "You want a man to tell you he loves you? Would the words make you feel better about what you're doing? Did Marshall say them?"

"John? Why would he . . ." Her eyes widened with confusion. If he didn't know better, he would have thought her an innocent, but he knew her kind well enough. He'd never believe that look was anything but an act.

Morgan took a stumbling step back. Her heart was pounding; her fingers came automatically to her lips to soothe their swollen state.

Youngblood cursed, his hands on his hips. He glared his resentment. So it was over, simply because he refused to join in her game. He wanted her, all right, but he wanted her without the usual trappings of meaningless words, without lies. "If you want to get laid, just say so. If you don't, get the hell out of here so I can dress."

Morgan cringed at the crude words and her heart shriveled with pain at the cruelty in his tone. She shivered with revulsion. Had she been out of her mind? How had she let this happen? How had she been so foolish as to allow those damning, mortifying words? Words that would repeat forever in her mind. She'd told him she loved him! Oh God, she shivered again. How was she ever to face him again?

Morgan would never again know a greater temptation to pack up her few personal belongings and leave this place forever. But stubborn to a fault, she also knew that was exactly what Youngblood wanted. No doubt it was the major reason she stayed.

112

Chapter Seven

Marshall wasn't Catholic. He wasn't a churchgoer of any sort. And yet every Sunday morning he made it his business to crawl out of bed, sometimes just barely having closed his eyes, and meet the lovely Morgan at the mission.

He sat beside her now, barely hiding his scowl as the kindly old priest preached the homily. Love your brother, my ass, he silently returned. Jesus didn't have a brother like Youngblood, or he wouldn't have spouted such nonsense.

He shifted uncomfortably on the hard wooden bench. Damn, he'd have to work fast. He had every intention of marrying this woman, and once he did, he was never going to set foot inside a church again.

Marshall breathed a long sigh of relief. It was over. The priest was giving the final blessing to the congregation. Marshall couldn't wait to get out of there.

"You will be coming for dinner, won't you?" Morgan asked, while holding on to his offered arm as Marshall walked her toward the buckboard.

Marshall smiled down at the lady at his side. He was going to kiss her tonight. Later, after dinner, he was going to ask her to step outside for a breath of air and then he was going to kiss her and maybe, if the mood was right, sweet-talk her into marrying him.

113

"I'll be right behind you," he said as he bestowed upon her his most devastating smile and lifted her up to the back of the buckboard.

Martha and Johnny were already seated up front waiting for her. Pedro tumbled in beside Morgan. Marshall mounted his horse and followed the slow progress of the wagon back to the ranch.

"What are you all dressed up for?"

"It's Sunday, Mr. Youngblood."

"So?"

"So I've been to church."

"What the hell time is it?"

Morgan eyed the shirtless man with the red eyes and as yet uncombed hair as he stumbled into her kitchen and fumbled in his pockets, obviously searching for his watch. Morgan consulted her own timepiece pinned to her bodice. "It's eleven."

Youngblood merely grunted in response. "Where's the coffee?"

"We finished it at breakfast. I'll make you a fresh pot, if you like."

"Good," he mumbled as he stuck his entire head under the water he was pumping into the sink. Youngblood's head was pounding. He'd never been so drunk as last night. If it wasn't for his horse knowing the way, he knew he'd never have made it back to the ranch. What the hell was he doing? He never drank in this much excess. What was he trying to prove?

Youngblood groaned at the pounding behind his eyes. Maybe next time he'd stay in town. Better yet, maybe next time he wouldn't go at all. Youngblood sighed with disgust as he rubbed a towel over his face. He was wasting his time anyway. All he ever had to show for a night spent at Daisy's was a god-awful headache in the morning. He was useless lately, couldn't service one woman never mind two. What had gotten into him last night? Why had he listened to the girls and their pretty pleas? He knew the moment he'd agreed he wasn't going to be able to do it. And now, damn it, now they knew as well.

Youngblood shrugged. He could pass it off as being too drunk to complete the act. Complete the act? he silently ridiculed. You couldn't even start it.

"What's that for?" Youngblood asked as Morgan moved about the kitchen preparing a tray of glasses and a pitcher of cool lemonade.

"It's for company."

"Who's coming?" he asked. "As if I didn't know."

"John is already here," Morgan returned. "I'd appreciate it if you could be polite. I'm getting a bit tired of your grunts and growls at my table."

"It's my table too and I'll grunt and growl at whomever I please." Youngblood scowled; Morgan turned her back to him as she squeezed another lemon. Jesus, this was just what he needed. Why, the man was here more often than in town. Obviously he had the hots for Morgan. Well, good luck to him. He hoped he got her and soon. He couldn't think of a better way to get her the hell out of here. Maybe then he'd find a moment's peace.

"Your coffee will be ready in a minute. Watch it so it doesn't boil over."

Youngblood grunted as he sat in one of the dining room chairs. He was getting the hell out of here. There was no way he was going to sit here all afternoon and watch Marshall make cow eyes at the woman. Jesus, he couldn't imagine a more useless way to spend the day.

"I hope you have enough for two more," Youngblood said as he ushered his guest into the large dining room, already filled with hungry men passing steaming platters of appetizing food around the table.

Morgan looked up at the sound of his voice, her eyes rounded with surprise as she came to her feet. This was the first time Youngblood had entertained a guest, since

115

Morgan had arrived. The lady at his side, holding tightly to his arm, looked uncomfortable and nervous. Morgan swore it wasn't jealousy that tightened and fluttered like a whisper of pain in her chest. Of course it wasn't. She'd probably indulged in one cup of coffee too many. Why should she care if Youngblood brought a lady to dinner? He probably only did it to aggravate her anyway. He was probably trying to show her he could have company as well as she. Well let him. Who cared what he did anyway?

Morgan instantly took pity on the woman, who looked decidedly uncomfortable, and Morgan gave her guest her most radiant smile. "Of course," she said gently. "There's always enough."

Morgan wasn't overly thrilled to find Cynthia Saunders sitting at her table, but she'd die before she let Youngblood know he had scored a point. After all, if she had a guest, Youngblood, as half owner in this ranch, had every right to bring whomever he wished to his table.

The meal wasn't half over before Morgan realized with more than a little surprise that she really liked this woman. From almost the beginning, she sensed Cindy cared about people, both men and women equally. She laughed at herself and joked with the men, and if she was a bit lusty in appearance, it wasn't so obvious as to keep her from being quickly accepted by all. When the meal was finished, she accepted Cindy's help in the kitchen without a thought, while the men moved outside for a smoke.

Deep in conversation, she never noticed Youngblood's scowl. This wasn't turning out as he had expected. Damn, nothing turned out as he expected when it involved this woman. He'd thought Morgan would be upset that he'd invited Cindy at the last minute, especially since he'd just about told her straight out that Cindy and he were lovers. Or maybe he hoped she'd be upset. He'd never imagined the two would form a fast friendship. Reluctantly he left them alone, while praying Cindy would have no cause to remark about his lack of attentions of late.

"I wish I would have met you sooner," Cindy said as she dried the dishes Morgan had washed. "It gets pretty lonely out here."

"You should have had Youngblood bring you over." Morgan grinned. "I'm just about starving for company."

They talked for a few minutes on the hard life women were forced to live out here and the loneliness all endured, when Cindy suddenly remarked, "I think Youngblood's taken with you."

Morgan didn't ask what she meant. Both women realized Youngblood's moodiness at the table. Moodiness that grew into snarling hatred every time Marshall had Morgan's attention. Only Morgan knew things weren't always the way they appeared. Her smile held a touch of sadness. "I'm afraid you're mistaken there. He dislikes me immensely."

Cindy laughed a low easy sound that had enticed more than one man to her bed. "Really? Then why does he practically eat you up with his eyes?"

Morgan stared at her with obvious surprise and then slowly shook her head. "I'm sure he doesn't. He's probably wishing me back to New York." Morgan shrugged a slender shoulder. "He can't wait for me to go. Sometimes I can't either. Whenever we're in each other's company, we fight."

"And that doesn't tell you something?"

"Sure it does. It tells me we can hardly stand one another."

Cindy laughed again. "Seems to me the two of you should sit down for a long talk."

"I'm afraid that wouldn't accomplish much. We snarl more than talk whenever we're together."

"How about when you're alone?"

Morgan didn't answer. She didn't have to, for her cheeks grew bright with the memory of those times.

Cindy grinned. "I thought so." She heaved a long sigh as she realized the truth of the matter. "Been wonderin' why the man made himself so scarce lately."

117

A moment later Marshall came inside claiming he was bored with men for company. The women soon joined the men outside.

Martha had disappeared again. No doubt she was once more involved in a game of cards with a few of the men. One by one the rest drifted off. Some intended to sleep the afternoon away, while others took their horses into town for some livelier action. Pedro was throwing a ball to an excited Rusty and laughing in delight as the dog brought the ball back. Finally tiring of the game, he called on the remaining four adults to join him in a game of catch.

Morgan and Marshall played while Youngblood and Cindy sat on the porch swing and watched. He couldn't take his eyes off Morgan. Every movement so fluid, so graceful, brought him closer to the point of madness. Her shrieks of excitement, her laughter filled him to overflowing with need. The sun beat down on golden hair as it fell from its pins, making his stomach twist with pain. Youngblood could only sigh his relief as they finished their game at last.

Youngblood continued to brood throughout the afternoon. Morgan shot him more than one look of annoyance while the three conversed around him.

"You feelin' poorly, honey?" Cindy asked, unable to ignore his silence any longer.

Youngblood broke into his first grin of the day. "Why? You fixin' on given me a taste of your home remedy?"

Morgan almost gasped at the sly suggestive tone and the wink that followed. Is that all this man could think about? Of course it was. Didn't she have firsthand experience on that score? Well, she wasn't going to sit around and listen to his vile innuendos.

"John," she said as she came to her feet. "I've a need to walk. Would you like to join me for a stroll? Down by the river perhaps?" She turned to the young boy at her side. "Pedro, get that pole we were working on the other

118

day. Maybe together we can catch tomorrow's supper."

John was beside her in seconds. Youngblood scowled as he watched Morgan take the man's offered arm. Pedro raced ahead with pole in hand and Rusty barking at his heels. His eyes never left the couple as they strolled toward the river. He listened until the sounds of her laughter were only an echo in his mind.

"That wasn't the most brilliant thing I've ever seen you do."

Youngblood shot Cindy a hard, evil look and almost growled, "I suppose you're going to tell me what you're talking about."

"If you want her, why are you pushing her into Marshall's arms?"

"Who the hell says I want her?"

"You do. Every time you look at her."

"You're crazy."

Cindy shrugged. "You're lucky to have me as a friend, Youngblood. Another woman might not take kindly to being invited to dinner and then being ignored because you're unable to take your eyes off the woman you profess to dislike."

"As a matter of fact, I do dislike her. She's everything I despise in a woman. She thinks she's superior. She's haughty. Looks down her nose upon us poor folks."

"Poor folks?" Cindy laughed. "Why, you old fraud. Is that what you told her? That you had no money?"

Youngblood shrugged and shot her a sheepish look. "I guess she might have gotten that impression."

"I wonder why?" Cindy mused. "Could it be you want her to love you for what you are, what she thinks you are, a poor rancher?"

"You're talking like a fool." Youngblood came to his feet. "You ready to go home?"

Cindy laughed. Youngblood was a stubborn one. But she'd bet her last dollar he'd found his match in the woman he professed to dislike. "Sure. You'll remember to tell Morgan I said good-bye, won't you?"

"What are we going to do? He won't even consider
selling out. Came near to throwing me off his land, just
because I brought the subject up." George Harrington
wiped his sweating forehead with a rag taken from his
back pocket and replaced his hat. "Jesus, I can't imagine
a more coldhearted bastard. Just looking in his eyes gives
me the goddamned shivers.

"He asked me about his fence. Wondered if I've seen
anybody hanging around. Seems he don't take kindly to
the notion that someone keeps cutting it." Harrington
shook his head as he continued. "Jesus, you should a'
seen his eyes. All you're doin' is makin' him mad. Mad
and suspicious."

"Don't worry, I've got everything under control,"
Marshall said with more confidence than he felt.

Harrington shot his partner a look of scorn. "Seems to
me I've heard that before."

"That was before the girl came." Marshall put his feet
up on his desk and leaned his chair back on two legs.

"What the hell has she got to do with it?"

"She's half owner, ain't she?"

"So?"

"So, the man she marries will share her property,
right?"

"You fixin' on marryin' the girl?"

"I figure I can swing it all right," he said, his chest
puffed up with confidence. Yesterday might not have
turned out exactly as he'd planned, what with Pedro
falling and cutting a gash in his knee that Morgan had to
see to; and then later she'd gotten that headache.
Marshall shrugged. After a few more visits he was sure to
soften her up to the point where he could get his kiss and
a lot more.

"Yeah, well, you'd better work fast. Talk has it
Youngblood's got his eye on the girl."

Marshall took his feet from the desk, knocking a pile of papers to the floor. The chair thumped forward. "I'll cut the bastard's balls off if he does as much as go near her."

Harrington laughed at the empty threat, knowing Marshall hadn't the guts to do anything of the kind. He was scared shitless of the man and they both knew it.

"She's a lady," Marshall continued almost to himself. "He ain't fit to wipe her boots."

"What about your brother?"

Marshall shot George Harrington a murderous glare. "How many times do I have to tell you to stop calling him that?"

Harrington grinned. "And how many times do I have to tell you that if you changed your attitude, we could have worked something out by now."

"My attitude! He's hated my guts since we were kids. Don't you think he'd grow a little suspicious if I started kissing up to him all of a sudden?"

Harrington sighed with disgust. He wasn't listening to another boring story of the sorrows Marshall suffered while growing up. He didn't give a shit if his mother loved the older brother more. He didn't believe it anyway. The thing to do was to get the man's mind off his childhood, or become stuck here for the rest of the afternoon while Marshall ranted on, with a half-insane gleam in his eyes. "I reckon. So let's have it. What are you planning?"

Marshall smiled. "Simple. I marry the lady and he meets with an unfortunate accident."

Harrington's eyes narrowed with disbelief. No doubt he'd have to do the job himself. He'd never met a man so damn scared of his own brother. "Why didn't you just take care of him when we found out about the copper? You would have inherited it all."

"Jesus, are you really that stupid? Do you imagine Popé would ignore the fact that someone murdered his son?" Marshall shook his head in disgust. "I don't care how peaceful the Hopis seem, Popé would never rest until he found out the truth." Marshall couldn't prevent the sudden shiver that ran up his spine. "If he ever got his hands on me . . ." He left the sentence unfinished, for both men knew well the cruel justice the Indian would impose. Hanging would seem a blessing in comparison.

"If the Hopis start something, the Shoshoneans and Paiutes might just join in. We don't need another uprising on our hands."

"So, what are you goin' to do?"

Marshall shrugged and allowed a small, sly grin. His voice lowered measurably. "How many ways are there for a man to die by accident, do you think?"

Harrington's eyes lit up with greed. This might just work. Marshall didn't have the balls to confront Youngblood, but to bushwack a man wouldn't take much guts. "And you'll inherit it all."

"Probably not." Marshall shrugged as if it were of little importance. "The Hopis will get their share if they're willing to take it. I doubt they'll bother, though, since it will mean leaving the reservation." Marshall breathed a long, supposedly weary sigh. "So that leaves me. His only living relative. Of course, I'll feel it my responsibility to step in and handle my dear late brother's estate." Marshall grinned. "After all, it's the only right thing to do."

"How rich is he?"

"Who knows." Marshall shrugged. "He lives like a pauper, but I know for a fact he got a million when he sold the mine in Eureka. No tellin' how much he made while he worked it." Marshall grimaced. "Stupid bastard could have made triple that if he'd worked the vein out himself."

Marshall shook his head. "None of that matters now. After we own the ranch, we'll be richer than either of us ever dreamed."

"Yeah, well, you'd better be quick about it before word gets out."

"It's not going to get out. The geologist has been paid

well for his services and is already back East. Only you and I know."

"Suppose he's wrong? Suppose—"

"He's not wrong, damnit! And even if he was, I think Youngblood's bank accounts would more than make up for any disappointment we might suffer."

Marshall leaned back in his chair again, his feet raised to his desk once more. Six hundred and forty ounces of silver per ton. A smattering of gold, just enough to make it interesting—he grinned at the thought—and copper. Mountains of the stuff. And all lying wasted on Youngblood's precious ranch.

Harrington's lawyers, with the geologist's report in hand—minus the exact location, of course—were already in discreet discussions with the Guggenheim family. Marshall knew to expect millions from the pending deal. All he had to do was get control of the land upon which the copper stood.

Soon, he promised himself. Soon he was going to have everything he'd ever wanted.

The house was dark, for the sun had yet to rise over the horizon, when Youngblood heard the scream. He nearly flew from his bed, stopping only to pull his trousers over his nakedness. He didn't even take time to secure them, but dashed out of his room into the hall. His heart was pounding with dread as he shook the last of his sleep away and watched with unbelieving eyes as a white blur with flying blond hair raced by him, muttering, "Kill it, kill it, kill it!"

An instant later the blur returned, holding a broom like a spear as it dashed by again, slowing only when it reached Morgan's bedroom door.

His heart had yet to cease its thundering as Youngblood closed the distance to her room. His eyes widened with shock as he watched Morgan scamper from one side to the other while swinging the broom in wild wide arks.

Suddenly, like a woman gone berserk, she threw the broom aside and attacked the bed, flinging quilt, bed sheets, pillows, and finally mattress to the floor. And when that seemed to bring about no satisfaction, she grabbed at the wooden bed frame, lifting it with the strength of two men clear off the floor, and succeeded in sending it crashing to the opposite end of the room.

"What the hell are you doing?"

Morgan glanced behind her at the sound of his voice. "What?"

"I said, what are you doing?"

"Don't just stand there. Help me!"

"Help you do what?"

"Get it out!"

Youngblood growled with annoyance. "Will you calm down and tell me what's happening here?"

"There's a lizard in here! I felt it crawl over me." She shivered uncontrollably as the grizzly memory returned.

"Don't kill it."

Morgan laughed a low mocking sound of ridicule as she picked up the broom. "Of course, why didn't I think of it. I'll invite it to supper."

"Morgan," he sighed, trying hard to overlook her sarcasm. "It eats bugs."

"I don't care if it eats mountain lions. I don't want it or anything crawling on me."

Youngblood smiled at her obvious disgust. "Put down the broom. I'll get it."

The feat was accomplished in record time. Youngblood held the tiny lizard cupped in his two hands. "You've scared him half to death."

"Only half? That's too bad."

Youngblood grinned as she struggled to move her bed back into place. "What's the matter now?"

"I can't—" She grunted as she tried to shove the suddenly immovable object back into place. "It won't move."

"You didn't seem to have a problem a minute ago."

Morgan sighed as she leaned against the bed post. "I guess I need something else to scare me before I can put it back."

Youngblood laughed. "Wait a minute. I'll be right back."

When he returned, Morgan was attempting to pull the mattress back on the bed. He moved the frame to its original place. They worked amicably together and moments later the room was in order, her bed remade.

"It looks comfortable."

"It is," she remarked with shaking fingers as she realized they were totally alone. Amazingly the noise hadn't awakened Martha or Pedro, both asleep in their rooms upstairs. She smoothed the satin spread into place.

Youngblood grinned at her nervousness. This was the first time in weeks they had been alone. The first time she had offered him more than icy contempt. He watched her a long moment, knowing he was the cause of her slight trembling. "When are you going to let me share it with you?"

"Never." Morgan's breath caught in her throat, but she answered him as calmly as if he had asked for the time of day. She wasn't going to let this beast get to her again. She'd suffered enough mental anguish at his hands. She didn't glance his way as she busily fluffed her pillows. "Now, if you don't mind," she said as her gaze moved toward the door, silently inviting him to leave.

"Not even a thanks for my trouble?"

"Thank you."

"Ever heard the expression 'Talk's cheap'?"

"Meaning, of course, you'd prefer something more substantial in the way of thanks?"

Youngblood grinned. "You're a smart lady."

Morgan laughed. "Smart enough to know there's nothing cheaper than your kisses, Youngblood. I take it a kiss was what you had in mind?"

"What do you mean my kisses are cheap?"

Morgan laughed again at his afronted look. "I mean, of

125

course, that they hold no value. I mean you give them away to anything wearing a skirt."

"You think so?"

"I know so."

"You wouldn't believe it if I told you that some women actually beg me to kiss them?"

"I wouldn't believe it if I saw it with my own eyes. There's little else you seem to think about. Why would you hesitate?"

Youngblood grinned. "I never said I hesitated. It's just that sometimes my mouth is busy elsewhere." His gaze came to rest on the soft outline of her breasts as he spoke. Morgan's chest heaved with agitation, thereby offering a more interesting sight as her breasts moved against the loose nightdress, for she had no doubt as to what he inferred.

Her voice was weak and ragged as she finally managed, "As I said, there's little else you think about."

"When I'm around you."

"When you're around any woman," she corrected.

"I swear I never think about it when I'm around Martha," he said, his straight, thin lips twisting into a grin.

"Bully for you. At least one woman is safe from your debauchery."

Youngblood laughed as he came around to her side of the bed and leaned against the post. "Suppose we strike a bargain?"

Morgan gave him a suspicious glance, her gaze moving hurriedly away from his opened trousers and the dark inviting shadow he didn't bother to hide. "I told you once before, you can't buy me out."

"I wasn't thinking of buying you out. There are other things we might bargain." He shrugged. "Unless you're afraid."

"Of you?" Morgan snorted, a most unladylike sound. "What kind of a bargain?"

"Correct me if I'm wrong, but you seem to be growing

126

particularly attached to this place."

Morgan nodded. "So?"

"So, you have three months before you're due to leave, right?"

"Three months and four days," she corrected.

Youngblood grinned. She was counting the days. Was it because of him? Did he bother her that much? Did she, too, lie awake every night, her body aching for his touch? "It's simple. If I persuade you to go to bed with me during that time, you give up your share of the ranch, and never return." Youngblood heard his heart pound with dread as the words came. Jesus, he was more desperate than he had thought. Whatever possessed him to offer her so outlandish a proposal? No doubt it would only strengthen her determination never to give in to his wants. For a moment Youngblood simply didn't care. Every day she was becoming more important in his life. No matter how he might rage, or deny the fact, he wanted her here. And the worst of it was he was beginning to believe he might want her here forever. The thought brought terror to his heart. He had to do something! Even if it meant chancing his ownership.

Morgan's eyes widened with astonishment. "You really are a cold-blooded, rutting pig." Her eyes narrowed with disgust. "One would have to search far to find greater conceit." She gave a flippant shrug. "Just for my own information, what would happen if I didn't give in to such romantic persuasion?"

"I'll deed my share over to you. And by the way, that was simply the offer, not the seduction."

"By seduction, I imagine you'll be making an effort to be nice for a change?"

Youngblood grinned.

"Watch out, Youngblood, you might be forced into behaving like something resembling a human being. You wouldn't want to do that."

"You think I'm not?"

"I think you have a way to go before laying claim to

that standing."

"What do you think of my offer?"

Morgan felt a moment's surprise to find she was mildly tempted. There was a glint in her eyes as she imagined the pleasure of living here without this rogue. Still, she'd never agree to such an outrageous plan. "I think you're out of your mind. I don't need this ranch."

"No," he agreed. "But you like it here enough, I think, to consider staying." *And make my life a living hell for as long as you stay out of my bed,* he finished in silence.

Morgan shrugged. In truth, she more than liked it here. She didn't miss the city, the parties, not even her friends. For some time now she'd been toying with the idea of, if not living here, at least coming often for long visits, if only she didn't have to contend with Youngblood. Idly she wondered how Bradley would take to the notion.

To her surprise, Morgan found herself silently considering his offer. If she agreed to his plan, he'd pull no stops in trying to bed her. Morgan couldn't deny her intrigue, for she couldn't imagine how he'd go about seeing his ends met. If she was smart, and she knew she was, in three months she could be the sole owner of this ranch. The question was, was she up to doing battle with this man? Did he want the sole ownership of this ranch enough to use trickery?

Morgan's eyes narrowed. "I don't trust you."

"I swear, you've got nothing to fear. You've got to come to me and willingly, or the deal's off."

"I'm afraid that to agree would only intensify your campaign to see me in your bed." Morgan shook her head, knowing she'd never be a party to his debauchery. "I'm afraid that won't do."

"If you ask me, I'd say you're afraid period."

Morgan would later realize it was the dare that did it. The moment she said the words, she knew she'd have many opportunities to regret her rash statement. But Morgan never was one to let a slight go by. Gritting her teeth in sneering anger, she extended her hand, and before she thought, the words came pouring out. "Say hello to the new owner of the Red Rock Ranch, Mr. Youngblood."

Youngblood grinned as he grasped her hand. "Confident, are we?"

Morgan snorted and shot him a superior glance. "Your offer only reaffirms my decision. I had no intentions of ever going to bed with you, no matter what arguments you might have come up with. Now I have something substantial to gain if I don't. I think you just lost yourself half of a good ranch."

"You think so?" he asked as he pulled her closer.

"No, I don't think so. I'm positive," she returned as she pulled her hand free.

"It wouldn't matter then if we sealed our bargain with a kiss?"

Morgan barely managed, "Good night, Mr. Youngblood," between gusts of hearty laughter.

Youngblood grinned as he left her room with a decided lightness in his heart, for this was the first time he had brought laughter, real laughter, to her lips. It might also be worth losing the ranch to hear her laugh again. Only Youngblood had no intentions of losing. He was going to win and listen to her laughter as she wrapped her legs around his hips.

Morgan swung her leg over the saddle and dismounted, thankful once again that she had listened to Jenny Holbrook's advice. Jenny, whose husband owned the Emporium, had suggested during one of Morgan's shopping excursions that unless Morgan was satisfied to use a buckboard or spring wagon as her only mode of transportation, she should consider the purchase of a split skirt.

Morgan could find no fault with the advice, for the slender, high-waisted skirts that were currently in fashion prohibited riding a horse astride. And unless she wanted to use her heavy, full-skirted riding habit, which would surely cause her to be unbearably uncomfortable in this heat, Morgan had to admit to the logic of the suggestion.

In fact, she had bought two complete outfits, each with matching vests, boots, hats, and leather gloves. Worn with a white long-sleeved blouse, the outfit made Morgan a feast for the eye. In truth, the outfit exposed no more flesh than one of her sedate dresses. Less, in fact, for she was covered from foot to throat. Still it provided many a man the pleasure of gazing upon slender hips and a rounded backside before the skirt split into wide demure legs. It had taken Morgan some time before she had grown accustomed to the costume, for the skirt came only to midcalf, but Morgan's boots fit almost to her knees and effectually covered the lower part of her leg.

Actually the outfit wasn't terribly unusual for the modern woman in this year of 1886. Morgan had seen more than one lady dressed so. Why then, she wondered, did she receive so many long appreciative looks when venturing into town? Actually "appreciative looks" was a charitable phrase. More often than not she was stared at and quite rudely. Morgan could attribute the men's gawking only to the shortage of women in these parts. No doubt she'd be stared at no matter what she wore.

Morgan laughed softly as Pedro fumbled with the reins as he tried to tie the horse to the hitching rail before the Emporium. "A slip knot, darling," Morgan said softly. "Or we'll be hours trying to free the reins."

Morgan untied the huge knot and patiently showed the boy how it was done. A moment later the two entered the store.

Morgan was disappointed. Jenny, in the last stages of her pregnancy, was feeling poorly today and Mr. Holbrook's check in the living quarters behind the store confirmed the fact that she was sleeping. Obviously the lunch and the afternoon they had planned to spend together were not to be. Morgan left Pedro to play with Jimmy Holbrook for a few moments as she walked toward the sheriff's office. If John wasn't busy, perhaps her trip to town wouldn't be wasted after all.

Morgan pushed open the door to Marshall's office and grinned. "I was hoping you'd be free for—" The words died in her throat as she noticed Youngblood, his back to her, staring out the window.

"For what?" he asked as he turned from the window, knowing full well she'd never tell him. He couldn't resist adding with a smirking grin, "Sex?"

Morgan lips thinned into a sneer. "You never fail to reaffirm my low opinion of you, Mr. Youngblood."

"What are you doing here?"

"I might ask you the same question, honey."

Morgan allowed the door to swing shut behind her and moved into the small office. Her eyes never left him as she leaned her hip on the corner of the desk. "But you wouldn't get the same answer, would you?" Morgan shot him a superior grin.

"Looking to Marshall for protection?"

"From you?" She laughed coolly. "Hardly."

"Maybe you're thinking about getting even."

"For what?" she asked, truly puzzled.

"I didn't come home last night."

"Didn't you? I never noticed."

Youngblood's dark eyes twinkled merrily. She couldn't lie worth a shit. She'd noticed all right. But what she couldn't know was that he'd spent the night cold and alone as he lay in wait for whoever it was that kept cutting his fences.

"Meaning, of course, you were with yet another of your women."

Youngblood only grinned, allowing her to believe his deliberate impression. What would she say if he told her he hadn't touched another woman in the three months since she'd been here? She wouldn't believe him, of course. He didn't believe it himself. All he knew was his pants were near to bursting every time he saw her, thought of her, and although he'd tried to get her out of his mind, tried in fact to bed others, he had finally come to realize no other would do. It was she alone he wanted, for only she could ease the torment.

Morgan breathed a long weary sigh. "One can't help but marvel at your unbelievable arrogance." She hoped her soft husky laughter gave credence to her words. "But the fact is, I'd have to care what you do in order to want to get even. And since I couldn't imagine anything less probable . . ." Morgan shrugged, leaving the sentence unfinished.

Youngblood didn't for a minute believe her show of unconcern. The woman had a long way to go before she perfected the art of lying. Still this wasn't the time to push her into telling the truth.

"Where's the sheriff?" she asked finally.

"Somebody at Daisy's decided he'd rather not pay his bill. Marshall went over to see if he could convince him otherwise."

"Why are you here?"

Youngblood shrugged. "Ranch business."

"Since I fully expect to be the sole owner in three months, would it be too much to ask you to tell me?"

Youngblood grinned at her haughty attitude. God, but he wanted to touch her, to kiss her. To kiss her until she forgot how to speak with that educated, well-bred, clipped Eastern accent and cried out low, aching, carnal words, begging for his touch. Youngblood forced the wild thoughts from his mind. In a minute she'd only have to lower her gaze to his crotch to gain proof of his thoughts. "Someone's cut our fence again. I wanted Marshall to know in case I have to . . ."

"What?"

"In case I have to take care of it."

"Do you mean to use violence?" she asked, clearly aghast at the idea.

"I mean to use any damn thing I have to, in order to

stop my cattle from dying."

"Why would someone want to kill the cattle?"

He shrugged.

"You know. I can see in your eyes that you do. Tell me."

"I've been getting offers to sell the ranch."

"You've refused them?"

He nodded.

"And then the cattle started to die?"

"And then the cattle started to get killed."

"It's very simple then," she remarked reasonably. "The one who offered is likely the one who's doing—"

"Which one?"

"What do you mean?"

"I mean I've had three offers. All from different people."

"Why?"

He shrugged.

"Why would three different people want the same ranch? Land is easily available out here, isn't it? Why do all of them want the Red Rock?"

"Beats me," he said while shaking his head.

Suddenly Morgan shifted. The movement brought Youngblood's gaze to her body. For the first time he noticed her attire. His eyes widened with shock. "What the hell are you doing wearing that?"

"What?" Morgan asked as she looked down her body.

"You lookin' to see every tongue in these parts scrape on the ground?"

Morgan raised one brow in a look of scorn. "You are being ridiculous."

"Am I?" he sneered, his gaze fastened to the sweet curve of her slim waist and the smooth line of a rounded hip. "Tell me no one even noticed you."

"What I'll tell you is to mind your own business. What I choose to wear is no concern of yours." Morgan heaved a great sigh of annoyance. How dare this man criticize her style of dress? He, of all people, who paraded around half naked! Lord, the man's gall was not to be believed! She shifted again, suddenly nervous under his unrelenting stare. The movement caused her vest to move farther apart.

"Jesus!" she heard him mutter in a voice that sounded almost strangled.

"What now?"

"Do you realize how your breasts press against your shirt when you breathe like that?"

"Mr. Youngblood!" she admonished, aghast that he would even mention such a thing.

"If I can see your nipples," he was almost shouting, "I'll bet half this town is panting after your ass. No doubt there's a line of horny bastards just waiting outside that door to get a free look at a woman's ti—"

"Don't say it! Don't you dare say another word!" Morgan was off the desk, her face beet red. She was jerking on her gloves. "I'm not staying here and listening to this gutter talk. I'll find the sheriff myself."

"Don't go to Daisy's." Youngblood cursed, knowing it was a mistake the moment the words left his mouth. "There are a lot of rough characters that hang out—"

"Anything is better than staying here with you."

Only it wasn't.

Morgan knew she'd made a mistake the moment she entered the saloon. Silently she brought all manner of curses upon the head of the man who had forced her into this. All right, perhaps he hadn't actually forced her. It was her own stubbornness that had done that. But he should have known the moment he'd said the words she would do exactly the opposite of his commands.

Now, as she stood in the center of the hazy, smoke-filled, whiskey-smelling room, she tried to ignore the hungry, speculating looks that were bestowed upon her by the leering clientele. Bravely she walked toward the bartender and cleared her throat. "Excuse me. Could you tell me where I might find the sheriff?"

The bartender nodded toward the stairs that led to the second floor.

Morgan looked up to see four doors, all closed. She wasn't about to go banging on any of them looking for the man. She bit her lip. "Could you tell the sheriff Miss Wainright is waiting outside?"

Mr. Small, the man who worked the day shift, nodded. "I expect he'll be down in a minute." There was no sense telling this lady what he was doing up there. If the sheriff took an occasional free toss in the afternoon, why should he care? The girls weren't doin' nothin' anyway. This was their time.

Morgan was moving toward the door when a heavy arm suddenly circled her shoulder and pulled her toward the chest of a tall man. "You don't have to run right off, do you, honey?"

Morgan shot the man a glaring look that probably would have freed her instantly. It would have, that is, if the man hadn't been eight drinks into an afternoon. "I'm afraid I must."

"Naw," he returned as he guided her away from the door. "We're a friendly sort. You ain't got nothin' to worry about. Why don't you join us for a drink."

"I'm sorry, I don't drink." He was almost dragging her now, obviously heading for the stairs. Morgan shot the bartender a pleading look, but the man only lowered his eyes, not at all sure what he should do. No decent woman had ever come in here before. Was her getup an act? Was it purposely done to excite the men? If so, she was doing a right smart job of it. He'd never seen the men so eager. Not even when one of the usually half-naked girls came down from upstairs to sit awhile.

"Not even a little one?" He grinned as he pinned her against the wall with his hips. His hand held her chin as he suddenly caught her mouth with his.

Morgan heard someone laugh. She swung her hand and contacted with his cheek, but she might have been

135

hitting a door for all the notice he gave her. His mouth moved to her neck. "Leave me alone!"

The man chuckled as he suddenly swung her over his shoulder and started up the stairs. Morgan screamed for help, but received only male laughter in answer to her plea.

"The lady doesn't want to go with you, Charlie."

Morgan didn't immediately recognize the voice, for it was tight and low with rage, but apparently the man did. He stopped and turned to face the man who had just entered the saloon. "She yours, Youngblood?"

"She ain't yours, Charlie. Put the lady down."

"If she's a lady, what's she doin' in here?"

"I'm not tellin' you again, put her down."

Beneath her belly, Morgan could feel the man's shoulder shrug and then a moment later she was suddenly dropped to the floor. She moaned as her head hit the first step. Her legs were shaking, but she came slowly to her feet.

Morgan's eyes widened at the sight before her. The two men stared at one another, their hands hovering over the guns in their belts. "Wait! Don't do it! He's drunk! He didn't know what he was doing."

It didn't take an instant for Morgan to realize that nothing she said would make any difference. All she could see was the hatred in those dark eyes. All she knew was that Youngblood might get shot. God, she couldn't let that happen! Without thinking, she stepped between the two men at the exact time both guns were drawn from their belts.

Only one shot was fired. Morgan screamed *"Noooo!"* at the sound and lunged at Youngblood. Youngblood cursed an ugly word but didn't dare pull the trigger for she stood directly in his line of fire. He felt the bullet hit his arm. The force knocked him back several steps. No doubt he would have fallen what with the extra weight of Morgan's lunge, but he slammed instead against the wall.

His ears were ringing, for the blow his head had taken

against the wall had not been minor. For the moment he felt no pain. He knew he'd been hit, but the only thing he seemed capable of really noticing was the delicious softness of this woman pressing against him as she sobbed into his neck. "Don't kill him. Don't kill him." And Youngblood realized, with no little astonishment, she was begging for his life.

"Jesus, Youngblood, I'm sorry," came the ragged sound of a man instantly sobered by the shock of what he'd done.

It was clear to Youngblood that Morgan was hysterical. She couldn't seem to let go of his neck. She pressed tighter against him. Youngblood groaned as his arm began to throb, only he couldn't honestly say if the sound was caused by pain or the pleasure of her closeness.

"Let me get you to Doc Franklin."

"Don't touch him!" Morgan lashed out, the loathing in her voice unmistakable. Her eyes dared him to disobey her command, and when the man lowered his now sheepish gaze to the floor, she continued, "I'll take him to the doctor."

Youngblood was sliding down the wall. It took all her strength to keep him up. How was she going to get him to the doctor? She couldn't let this monster touch him, and no one else seemed ready to help.

Suddenly Marshall was standing there, his eyes wide with incredulity. Morgan never noticed he was still adjusting his clothes. "What are you doing in here?"

"Sheriff, I want you to arrest this man." Morgan pointed to the man called Charlie as she turned her body so her back was pressed against Youngblood's chest.

Youngblood couldn't decide which side of her he most enjoyed.

Morgan sent Charlie a scathing look. "He tried to abduct me and when Mr. Youngblood interceded he was shot for his efforts."

"I was just havin' a little fun, Sheriff. I swear I didn't mean nothin' by it."

Marshall looked at Morgan, obviously waiting for her to relent. "Well? Are you going to do your job or not?"

In the meantime, Youngblood found he was more than enjoying this confrontation. In truth he was delighted. Not only was she leaning on him, in the hopes of keeping him from falling, but she was protecting him. The fool had even thrown herself between them to prevent him from being killed. At first he'd thought she was telling him not to shoot, but he had finally realized she was pleading for his life. He'd never have believed it if he hadn't seen it with his own eyes.

"He drew first," Charlie said in a sulky voice. "What else could I do?"

"Is that right?" Marshall asked Youngblood.

"He was touching her."

Marshall forgot there was a woman present and cursed. "Come on, Charlie, let's go."

"You and you—" Morgan pointed to two men, commandeering them from their tables, after the sheriff left with his prisoner. "Help me get him to the doctor."

Without a word, the men scrambled to their feet and did her bidding.

Morgan never left Youngblood's side. Under doctor's orders, she administered what was left of a half bottle of whiskey to the patient. Youngblood began to relax as the doctor went about his business. Morgan made herself busy, cleaning the wound and keeping a tight compress on the ugly gaping hole. Actually, for a woman who had never seen more blood than that caused by a splinter in her entire life, she was amazingly calm. But when the doctor had to dig into the bleeding wound with a pointed instrument in order to extract the bullet, Morgan turned white as a sheet and had to sit alongside him as he lay upon the table, lest she fall to the floor in a dead faint.

Youngblood almost broke her hand as he clung to her fingers, for the pain was excruciating. Beads of perspiration broke out over his face and body as he strained against the scream of anguish that tried to escape his throat.

Morgan spoke in low soothing tones, wiping at his face and chest with a cool wet cloth. She never remembered what she'd said, nor did the man who lay in agony hear her.

Sewing up the wound wasn't all that much better. Morgan felt dangerously close to disgracing herself. Bile rose to her throat as she watched the needle pass through his skin, the thread gathering the rough edges of torn flesh together.

After he was bandaged, Doc Franklin brought out a second bottle of whiskey. All he managed to say was "Here" when Morgan snatched it out of his hands. She took three huge swallows before she uttered a whispery "Thank you." She was gasping for air, clutching at her throat. Her lungs were on fire, her belly had probably melted, but amazingly her nerves came under some sort of control. Her hands hardly shook at all when she handed the bottle back to the doctor.

Both men looked at each other with some surprise and then grinned, for Morgan had never realized the bottle was obviously meant for the injured man.

Morgan never noticed their smiles. "Can he be moved?"

Doc Franklin nodded. "Let him rest a bit. I'll get Mackey at the livery to ride you back."

"That was a damn fool thing to do," Youngblood said the moment the door closed behind the doctor. "You could have been killed."

Morgan, who had felt nothing but tenderness for this man, suddenly shot him a scathing look. "And you couldn't? I told you to leave it be. The man was drunk."

"He had no call to touch you and I can take care of myself."

"You've certainly proven that," she remarked snidely.

"How could I prove anything with a hysterical woman in my arms?"

"Hysterical! When was I hysterical?"

"Who the hell was sobbing in my chest, 'Don't kill him, don't kill him'?"

"I never said any such thing. You were probably delirious with pain."

"I remember it quite clearly."

"Well, I was probably pleading for Charlie's life," she lied, quite badly. "The day I get hysterical because of you, sunflowers will grow on the moon."

"Yeah, right. And the next time I defend your honor, Thunder will have puppies." Thunder was his horse.

Morgan's lips thinned in anger. Why in the world had she been so worried? What did she care if Charlie put a bullet between his eyes? Actually that could only have made him more appealing. At least his mouth would be shut. The man was a brute, nothing but. He didn't deserve her consideration, never mind her concern. She hated him and would till her dying day.

Morgan spun away from the table and nearly wrenched the door from its hinges as she yanked it open. She shot him a look of pure venom, and just before she slammed the door, she drawled out the exact words she'd often heard the men at the ranch use: "Go piss up a rope."

Youngblood gazed up at the ceiling as a grin curved his lips. Despite the throbbing ache in his arm, a soft chuckle escaped his lips. His eyes twinkled merrily. And this from a woman who railed at him every time he used a nasty word? He laughed out loud. Damn, if she wasn't the most delicious woman he'd ever met. He couldn't wait to get home. With a few well-chosen grunts and groans, she'd be fussing over him, her angry words forgotten. She was going to nurse him back to health. And God, was he going to enjoy it.

Chapter Eight

The wagon rolled over a large rock and came down with a hard, bone-rattling thud. Youngblood hid his grin in the softness of her breast as he allowed another groan. "I know. I know. We'll be home soon," Morgan comforted as she held his head to her chest and smoothed shiny black hair away from his dark perspiring face.

From the back of the wagon, Morgan glanced up toward the man who slowly wound the heavy wagon over the rough countryside. "Can we go a little faster, Mr. Mackey?"

"No," Youngblood groaned, more than content for the moment to rest against her softness, knowing he wouldn't be granted this pleasure again for some time. "The bumps," he said, his voice slightly breathless. Although it was true that he suffered a measure of discomfort, the pain in no way necessitated his exaggerated portrayal, and if his voice was a bit unsteady, he could only hope she would attribute the sound to pain, rather than a most natural reaction to the present positioning of his head.

Youngblood shot her a pleading look. He almost grinned as her easily read expression showed her warring emotions. No lady would allow a man's face to be pressed to her breast and yet how could she deny him this small comfort when he suffered so? Youngblood forced aside

141

the urge to laugh and instead managed a look of helplessness.

"All right," Morgan relented. "Never mind, Mr. Mackey. Your present pace is fine."

"Is he going to be all right?" Pedro asked from his seat beside Mr. Mackey.

"The doctor said everything will be fine. Mr. Youngblood only needs to rest. He's weak. He's lost quite a bit of blood."

Youngblood grinned again. If she only knew how strong he felt, she'd be cursing him to hell. He wished they were alone, so he could show her the true extent of his strength.

Youngblood waited for the next bump before he grabbed at her inner thigh. Morgan stiffened and gasped even louder than when he had, uninvited, laid his head upon her breast. She covered his hand with her smaller one, her obvious intent being to move it away, when he muttered, "The pain," and then groaned again, only tightening his hold.

Morgan sighed, her features a study in pity at his obvious agony. "Shush," she whispered, and without thinking, kissed him at his temple, never realizing how the lingering of her lips belied the kiss as medicinal.

Youngblood almost turned his face up so his lips might meet hers, but wisely forced the instinctive response away. His fingers splayed and relaxed so that they posed no immediate threat. But every bump and rock of the buckboard tightened them again and somehow brought them closer to the juncture of her thighs.

Morgan was alarmed to say the very least. Her nipples grew hard and achy, longing for something she couldn't put a name to. Her body was stiff and trembling, her breathing erratic as every nerve and muscle concentrated on that portion of her anatomy he unconsciously clung to, as she awaited the next lunge of the wagon. To her shame, Morgan couldn't honestly swear if she prayed for another bump or not.

Prayers aside, it came.

Morgan never noticed the soft groan that came from her lips. Her hand moved again to his, her intent once more to remove his fingers so immodestly placed. But Youngblood groaned again, this time while rubbing his fingers against the juncture of her thighs and his face freely upon her breast. "I can't stand it."

Morgan felt her heart twist at his suffering and only held him tighter against her. Obviously he didn't realize what he was doing. She felt a wave of shame. Here she was worrying about the innocent placement of his hand while the poor man suffered in the throes of unbelievable pain. How could she be so self-centered?

Youngblood rubbed his face against her again and groaned, though not from pain—at least not from the kind of pain she supposed. Lord, this was heaven, or would have been if he could only manage to undo a few of those buttons. He could feel her nipples grow hard. He was dying to take one into his mouth. Even through the cover of her shirt, he knew he'd love it. But he'd have to wait for that. What he wanted couldn't be accomplished here and now. No, he needed the privacy of his room to carry this position to its rightful conclusion.

Youngblood felt not the least bit of guilt in this underhanded and yet advantageous manipulation of her concern. He wanted this woman, had wanted her since the first night they'd met, and reasoned that any means that could bring about her capitulation was justifiable. After all, she stood to gain as much pleasure as he from their eventual coupling. And that there would be a coupling, he had no doubt.

His bed had never seemed colder or emptier since she'd begun sleeping under his roof. His temper never so quick since she'd come to taunt his senses with a gentle sway of her skirt or the sweetest of smiles. He couldn't remember a time when a woman had so appealed. How often had he stood quietly by and watched her as she went about one chore or another? When had the beauty of a slender back

143

and trim waist come last to possess? How had he missed till now the fascination of form when an arm was raised to reach for something overhead?

Damn, but he'd tried to slack his passions on others. How many times had he visited Daisy's only to find himself incapable, even in a drunken haze, to take another? He didn't know why no other so tempted, but simply and finally faced the truth. There was no way to rid himself of this growing obsession but to have her and be done with it. To fight this need was a useless endeavor. This was the woman he wanted. What he had to do was make her want him equally.

The ride to the ranch was accomplished in two hours, but it seemed to Morgan to take forever. She was shaken and weak from the hours spent pressed so closely to Youngblood. She trembled at the mere thought of his touch. Of wanting him to touch her even more? Ridiculous. The man was ill, seriously ill, and her mental ramblings and secret thoughts were nothing less than disgraceful.

Thank God, he had given up her breast as a pillow and removed his ever-reaching fingers from her thigh the moment the wagon rolled beneath the sign that boasted the entrance to Red Rock Ranch. How could she have faced the men if they found her and Youngblood in so seemingly a compromising position? Morgan shivered at the very thought.

By the time the wagon rolled to a stop, Youngblood had released her completely. He was now lying on his side, his legs bent, hiding the state of his arousal. His head was resting on her knee.

Gently the men moved him to the house and placed him on his bed. Youngblood kept his eyes closed, feigning sleep. Someone covered him with a light coverlet. He heard footsteps recede.

No doubt he dozed, for the next thing he realized was someone pulling off his boots. Youngblood hid his grin in a sleepy groan. He could feel himself getting hard again.

144

She was taking off his clothes.

Strong arms gently raised him to a sitting position, his face was crushed against softness, only it wasn't the same softness he'd known these last two hours. Youngblood pulled himself back, blinking with surprise. "Where's Morgan?"

Martha grunted as she finally got his arms free of his vest. "She's making you some broth." Then pointing, she said, "Now your trousers."

"Leave them," he answered immediately and with no little alarm. "I'll get them off."

"Nonsense, you can't do it with one arm. The men are just outside, shall I send one in to help?"

Youngblood shook his head, the expression in his eyes bordering on terror as he pulled the covers nearly to his chin. Jesus, there was no telling what his men would think if they saw him hard and ready. "I'll take care of it."

Martha shrugged. "Have it your way." She was halfway to the door when she stopped and asked, "You want a cup of tea?"

"I want a shot of bourbon. Make it a double."

Martha nodded and left the room. In the kitchen she prepared his drink. "Lord, I've never seen a man so modest."

"Who?" Morgan asked, her mind still on the unusual arousal Youngblood's fumblings had brought to her body.

"Why Mr. Youngblood, of course."

Odd. Morgan certainly would never have associated modesty with that man. Not with the way he paraded half-naked around this place.

"He wouldn't let me take his trousers off. Wouldn't let me call one of his men either. Swore he could do it on his own." She shrugged. "Men don't usually make no mind to who takes their clothes off." Martha grinned wickedly. "As long as someone does."

"Martha!"

Martha laughed. "Speaking of taking off their clothes, Johnny asked me to marry him."

Morgan gasped her surprise. She'd known Martha enjoyed the company of the men, and although she'd seen her once or twice take an evening stroll, she hadn't imagined she was seriously interested in any one of them. Morgan studied her longtime companion and her eyes widened as realization set in. How had the woman changed so drastically in so short a time? She seemed somehow younger and more eager in spirit. Easier to laugh. Eyes twinkling, she held a certain contented beauty that had never before shown itself.

Martha was and always had been a handsome woman. Her features were good. Her skin unlined. Her eyes a soft, gentle brown. Even with the few strands of gray at her temples, she looked a good ten years younger than the forty Morgan knew her to be. She'd kept her figure, adding to it only a few pounds since Morgan was a young girl. And those pounds had landed in just the right places. "Do you love him?"

Martha grinned. She imagined she did. In any case she sure did love the way the man made her feel. God, but she'd never known pleasure like this existed outside of heaven. He was the best lover she'd ever had. Martha grinned, not that she'd had more than one and that one being her husband.

It was amazing how she had managed to live all those years back East in stiff formality. God, the joy she'd missed! She couldn't remember a time when she and Harry had made wild ecstatic love. It was always the same movements all done in silence. Always clothed and under the cover of darkness he'd come to her.

What would he think now if he saw her and Johnny naked and frolicking in the light of day? A small smile curved her lips. What would he think if he knew they loved everywhere, even outside, protected from inquiring eyes only by a small corpse of trees, or a large rock?

Martha almost laughed. Her friends wouldn't recognize this new Martha. Gone forever was the straitlaced puritan she'd once believed herself to be. And Martha couldn't be happier about the stuffy lady's demise.

"I guess I do, honey," Martha finally answered.

"Oh Martha, that's wonderful. When are you going to—"

"We haven't decided exactly when, but it will be soon. I promise you that." There was no way she was going to let a man like Johnny get away.

The soup was hot. Morgan fixed a tray including the drink Martha had poured.

"You'd best be bringing him in his food." Martha grinned, for she wasn't ignorant of the attraction between the two, although it usually showed itself in an argument. She shrugged. As long as the man was too ill to do anything about it, her Morgan would be safe. Her eyes twinkled with mischief. "Maybe you will have better luck than me."

Morgan's cheeks grew pink. "Mr. Youngblood can sleep in his clothes for all I care. If he's uncomfortable, I'll call one of the men to see to him."

Morgan found Youngblood wet with perspiration. He was just pulling the covers to his waist after the long struggle to push his trousers down his legs. He lay there gasping. Damn, but he was a lot weaker than he'd thought.

"Are you all right?" Her voice shook. The real question was, was she? For Morgan hadn't missed the fact that the man was naked beneath his coverings. She'd had the misfortune to open the door just as he was pulling the covers up, and hadn't even a moment to avert her eyes before realizing what she'd seen.

"I'm exhausted. I didn't know I was so weak."

"Why didn't you let your men do that?" Morgan nodded toward his pants lying crumpled at the bottom of the bed.

"Why didn't you offer?" Youngblood grinned. "I would have let you."

"Because I was in the kitchen. Because I'm not married." Her temper was instantly aroused that he had the audacity to ask her such a thing. "Because unmarried women never administer to men. Because judging from your usual dirty talk, you are apparently well enough to take care of yourself." She slammed the tray onto the bed, the force almost splashing the hot soup all over him.

Youngblood grabbed her wrist. "But I'm not." He shot her a look of contrition. "I'm sorry. I was only teasing."

Morgan studied his face for a long moment before she was satisfied he meant what he said. She nodded stiffly. "Can you feed yourself?"

"I think so."

Youngblood struggled to a sitting position. The problem was, the tray at his side held the sheet in place and when he moved, he almost exposed himself completely.

Morgan swallowed the groan that nearly escaped her lips and moved the tray to the bedside table, thereby allowing the sheet to be raised.

The room swam around his head. Youngblood supported himself on his good arm and grunted a curse. "Damn. I really am weak. Maybe I'd better get some sleep. I'll eat later."

Morgan retrieved two pillows from the closet and propped them behind him. "Lean back. I'll feed you."

Youngblood sighed as he swallowed a mouthful of chicken broth. "Did I tell you, till you came here, I'd never tasted food like this?"

Morgan smiled. "No, you didn't. I hope you mean that as a compliment."

Youngblood nodded. "I think I've gained about ten pounds."

"You must have needed them, because you look . . ." Their eyes met over the spoon that hovered near his mouth.

"What?" he asked softly, his voice low with yearning,

148

his eyes hungry despite his weakness. "Tell me how I look."

Morgan flushed. "Healthy," she said finally in a voice that sounded almost strangled, for both of them knew that wasn't what she was going to say. "You look healthy."

"I don't feel healthy. I feel like shit."

Morgan smiled, recovering quickly from her near blunder. Lord, whatever could she have been thinking to nearly blurt out how devastatingly attractive this man appeared to her? "Mr. Youngblood." Morgan shook her head as she reprimanded in her most prim and proper tone. "You really must do something about your tendency for vile language. I realize it is a habit used in particular in the company of men, but can't you control yourself when a lady is present?"

Youngblood grinned. And this from a woman who only a few hours ago told him to go piss up a rope? "I guess it's all right to say some things in the heat of anger, but not in idle conversation?"

"It's best, I think, not to say them at all."

If he'd had the strength, he would have grabbed her then. Never had she looked more kissable than when she was performing her lady act. Well, that wasn't entirely true. She sure looked delicious when she was cursing at him. At the moment, Youngblood couldn't rightly say which appealed more.

Youngblood was sadly mistaken if he thought Morgan would be the one to nurse him back to health. Mentally he had played out one scene after another of how she might comfort him. But over the next three days he hardly saw her at all. Mostly it was Martha who saw to his needs. And when she couldn't—for there were some things a man couldn't allow a woman to do, no matter how clinically she performed her duties—it was Johnny who helped.

Youngblood lay in his bed, bored. He'd slept more these last three days than when he was a baby. He had to get out of here. He couldn't stand this room another minute.

The house was quiet. He knew everyone was in bed, for although he'd been reading, he'd listened to the sounds as one by one they retired for the night.

Youngblood swung his legs to the floor. God, it felt good to sit in a normal position for a change. With his good arm he reached for the robe that was flung across the bottom of his bed. Gently he slipped his arm inside and brought it over his shoulders.

He stood and gritted his teeth as a wave of dizziness assaulted him, but a moment or so later he heaved a sigh of relief as it faded.

He stepped into the darkened kitchen lit only by the banked fires in the stove and the glowing embers in the fireplace. Twice he tried to pump himself a glass of water, but the stupid glass kept falling over and he couldn't hold it in his other hand. Youngblood cursed and gave up.

He walked to the table, pulled out a chair, and sat. In doing so, he banged his arm and uttered a round of painful curses.

"What are you doing up?" came the soft voice behind him.

"I couldn't stand lying there another minute," he answered, not daring to look at her. "Go to bed. I'll get myself back in a minute."

"And if you fall and rip open the stitches?"

"I won't."

Youngblood rubbed at his arm. His mood wasn't particulaly good, since not one of his plans had worked out the way he'd wanted and he'd been too goddamned weak to insist. On top of his frustrations, he'd banged his arm and it was aching like the devil.

He must have moved his shoulder, because she suddenly said, "You should have asked Martha for a back

150

rub. She would have gotten rid of that stiffness."

Youngblood turned to find her framed in the doorway. He couldn't breathe as a sudden thudding began in his gut and ran directly to his throat. His hand trembled as he ran his fingers through his hair. She was so beautiful, almost as if she were a vision shining out of the darkness. Her hair, blond and curling, lay over her shoulders and down her back. Her nightdress was hidden beneath her robe, but he could tell from the tiny glimpse at her bare ankles and wrists it was frilly and almost sheer. Their eyes met and held for a long moment. Neither said a word.

She, too, fought a long inner battle. She knew the moment she'd said the words it was a mistake. It was one thing for Martha to give back rubs, but the very thought of her fingers on his warm flesh was too much to contemplate. But contemplate it she did. She couldn't think of anything else. Her heart fluttered, her breathing grew harsh and ragged. Her fingers ached to feel the smoothness of his flesh beneath them.

She tried to turn away. She tried to retrace her steps back to her room, for she knew if she were to give in to this need, all would be lost. And yet even knowing what the final outcome would be, she knew she couldn't resist. Somehow she'd known the moment she'd left her bed. Finally she shrugged, the movement belying the need she'd come to know. "I'll do it."

Her fingers were cool against his skin. Gently they massaged the tight muscles of his neck and shoulders, grown stiff from lying in bed so long. Youngblood groaned at the pleasure and welcomed the tugging as her fingers slid his robe from his shoulders and arms. It fell to his waist, held there only by the robe's loosely tied belt. "My God, is there nothing you can't do?"

Morgan chuckled behind him. "Many things."

"I don't believe it. You cook like a master chef—"

"Hardly like a master chef, Youngblood," she interrupted. "You'd know the difference if you tasted

Mr. Henry's creations."

"Your father's cook?"

Morgan made a sound of agreement. "I like cooking, but it's simple fare I do best."

"Jefferies tells me you play the organ at the mission better than old man Peters and Peters doesn't like it a bit. Pedro says you hit almost everything you shoot. You ride as well as any man and give the best—" He groaned, growing weak or strong, he couldn't decide which, with the pleasure of her touch. "The best back rubs."

Morgan fought back the swelling hunger that filled her. He smelled so good. Her stomach tightened with the need to rest her face upon gleaming bronzed skin and luxuriate in the pleasure of both his touch and scent. She laughed, the sound ragged and soft as she leaned toward him and whispered near his ear, "Have you been checking up on me?"

Youngblood shook his head in denial. "People just seem to spout your qualities at every turn. I think you're becoming a legend in a land where legends are hard to come by."

"Good Lord, not that!" She laughed again, the sound this time almost a choke. Lord, what was she doing here in the dark of night alone with this man? Was she out of her mind? "Aren't legends supposed to be about people who are dead?"

"Not in this case. I couldn't imagine you more alive."

"Tell me your name." Her voice was a low sultry whisper. "Your Christian name."

Youngblood said nothing for a long moment. He'd heard the trembling in her voice, felt the shivering in her touch. His heart swelled with some unnamed joy that she should want to know him better. His body trembled as he reached behind him and grasped her hand. Slowly he brought it over his shoulder to his mouth. His lips lingered on the pulse at her wrist. "Joseph," he murmured against her sweetly scented flesh.

And when she seemed capable only of gasping at the

heated touch of his mouth, he murmured again, "Say it. Say my name."

Morgan didn't think to resist the slight tugging on her hand but moved to stand before him. Her heart thundered in her chest. Her breathing grew nearly nonexistent. With her free hand she pushed a lock of straight black hair from his forehead: "You should go to bed, Joseph. It's late and you've not yet recovered."

With a low groan Youngblood released her hand and suddenly buried his face in the softness of her belly.

Morgan gasped at the erotic contact, staggering as liquid heat rushed through her veins. From somewhere in the far recesses of her mind, she realized the danger. This shouldn't be happening. She shouldn't allow him to touch her like this, but she couldn't seem to find the strength to push him away. Indeed, it took every ounce of her strength not to hold him closer.

God, the agony of wanting! His arm circled her waist and brought her closer, so that she stood between his parted thighs.

"Morgan, Morgan, my God," he groaned as he twisted his face side to side. "I've never known what wanting was till I saw you," he murmured into her softness. "Touch me. Please touch me."

Morgan struggled to breathe. What kind of spell had this man woven? How had she become so weak and pliant under his touch? How did his softly spoken plea cause her knees to wobble even as he held her closer, more firmly against him?

Her fingertips tingled, for she had never wanted anything more than to do as he asked. She trembled with the need to feel his skin again, to hold him in her arms. To feel him hold her in return. Her breasts ached with the loss of his mouth, even now, days after he'd last touched her. She wanted him to kiss her there, to touch her until she knew nothing but the sweet heaven and blazing heat of his mouth.

Slowly she lowered to her knees. Facing him, she

watched the hunger flaming hot in his eyes as her hands reached timidly to his chest. The soft groan that spilled from his tight lips only spurred her on. She became more daring. His head fell back upon his neck as her inquiring fingers touched from shoulder to shoulder and then, eager for more, slid to his chest, to comb through the beckoning hair and at last his stomach. A low, hissing, indrawn breath stopped her exploration. Instantly she pulled her trembling finger away. "Did I hurt you?"

Youngblood's lips twitched into a tender smile. He could hardly breathe with the need for her to continue. Gently he took her hand and pressed it again to his stomach. "It hurts good." He gave a shuddering breath. "God, it hurts so good."

His fingers tilted her chin, bringing her mouth up to his. Slowly he brought their lips together. Gently he brushed his mouth against her. Again, again, again, until she murmured a small sound of pleasure. But it wasn't enough. He didn't want her acquiescence. He wanted her hungry and demanding. He wanted to feel her grow wild in his arms. He wanted the very depths of her soul, with nothing held back. He wanted it all.

With one hand he untied the belt to his robe and spread his legs as he gathered her closer. He was naked, never more vulnerable, never more in need, hard and aching as she lowered her hand.

Was there a pleasure greater than this? he wondered as her fingers moved down, down to thread into the rough hairs that nestled his sex. He was hard, almost bursting with need as her fingers bypassed his aching thickness and slid to the hard muscles of his thighs. Slowly, as if she'd done this a thousand times, her exploring fingers slid to his inner thighs and retraced their path.

Her shock at her daring wouldn't come till later. She felt no modesty, no shyness as she explored this man. Had she a moment to think she might have run for safety, but Youngblood hadn't allowed her the moment. She trembled as he teased her mouth to near insanity. Her

154

lips parted as she silently begged him to complete the kiss.

His hand threaded through golden curls, bringing her mouth closer. And she sighed when at last his tongue came to penetrate beyond parted lips and smooth teeth. Gone was the teasing sweetness of a tender kiss. They groaned in equal pleasure as their mouths opened and clung. He devoured her lips, drank of her mouth, ate as if his soul had been dying of hunger and perhaps it was, for he felt a newness, a swelling of spirit, for she was light, she was beauty, mystical and serene, she was an extension of his life. His tongue delved deep, hungry for every nuance of her taste and scent. He reveled in the wet, slippery heat. He couldn't get enough. Suddenly he knew he never would.

He cried out, the sound muffled against her mouth, as she touched him at last, and felt the last of his being, his very soul, lost in her.

His hand released the knot of her robe. Gentle fingers eased it from her shoulders. His mouth was instantly there, luxuriating in the exposed flesh, licking at her, kissing her creamy white softness, breathing her luscious scent.

Once his lips had discovered the sweetness of her neck and throat, she bent her head and moaned with the thrill of touching her mouth to his chest. Lower she moved, mindlessly hungry to taste what her fingers had known.

"No," he gasped as he tugged her mouth from him. Glassy-eyed she stared into the strange tightness of his face. His breathing was choppy, his skin flushed. "Later. Do that later," he soothed as his mouth took hers again in a kiss that united both body and souls.

Her gown was pulled over her head and flung aside. Again he joined his mouth to hers, desperate, aching, wild for more of her taste. His hand moved slowly from her shoulder to her chest. Down, inch by incredibly slow inch to the gentle sloping of a heavy breast. She was exquisite. Hot, silky, so deliciously sweet, he wished this

155

moment would never end.

He'd never felt stronger in his life. There was nothing he couldn't do, nothing! Youngblood brought her to her feet and nuzzled his face into the warmth of her belly. He couldn't believe this. Nothing he'd ever known was this good. Gently he pushed her back until she sat naked upon the table. The sight of her took his breath away.

A groan of hunger was torn from his throat. He leaned forward, unable to resist the temptation.

Morgan cried out as the searing heat of his mouth contacted with her moist flesh. She trembled and pressed her hands to his shoulders. "No!" She gasped as his tongue found her delicious entry and cried out in a soft whimper of embarrassment, "Please, don't."

Youngblood raised his head, realizing at last her stiffening, her frantic whispers. He rose to his feet and pressed her back upon the table. "Later," he promised, his smile so tender it squeezed at her heart. He moved the inches it took to bring him against her.

He kissed her again, leaning over her now, and Morgan moaned as the taste of her own body was brought to her mouth. Strangely enough it brought no disgust, but only intensified her need for more, for the taste mingled magically with his own.

Morgan closed her eyes and shivered with delight as his mouth, sizzling with heat, lowered to her breasts. He teased her nipples, rolling his tongue around the hard nubs. She whimpered, a soft aching sound, as he drew her deep into the flames. He sucked and bit at her as if her scent and taste were his only means of life. Suddenly he knew it to be true, for he'd never felt so alive.

His mouth moved lower to sample all he could. Her flat stomach, her waist and again to the juncture of her thighs. And at her murmured protest again to her mouth.

He entered her then, his muscles shaking with the need to absorb her softness, to savor the beauty. He felt the restriction. His eyes widened with amazement, but it was too late. He couldn't stop. Now now! Not when his

156

body was likely to die if it didn't drive deep into her.

Youngblood gave in to the need that had been building since the first moment they'd met. He drove hard into the softness of her, his mouth on hers absorbing the startled cry. Morgan gazed with something like shock at the man looming above her. "I'm sorry, honey. It won't hurt again."

In truth it had hardly hurt at all. Actually it was only a bit of discomfort, and when he kissed her again she forgot even that.

Youngblood remained very still as he waited for her body to accept his. His mouth wasn't still though; it moved voraciously over hers, ravenously absorbing her taste, while every nerve in his body trembled, screaming for him to continue. Still he held back, until he felt her softening. Until he felt her slight restless urgings for him to go on.

Godalmighty! She was so tight. He wondered if he'd survive such pleasure, such torment. His voice was low, ragged, gasping for breath as he murmured, "Put . . . put your legs around my hips."

Youngblood's eyes squeezed closed with the incredible pleasure of the moment. His skin was flushed and drawn tight over his features. His lips parted as he breathed a gasping ragged groan. He'd never known. Even with all his experience, he'd never imagined it could be this good. He started to move, forcing himself to think. *Think, man,* he silently swore. *Think about the ranch, think about the work that needs to be done tomorrow. Think or you'll never be able to . . .* "God," he choked. He couldn't. He couldn't. He'd have to wait for another time. It was already too late.

Morgan was dazed with feeling. Floating in an almost euphoric state. She never felt the hardness of the table on her back. All she knew was this man, the strength of him, the taste and smell of him. So much feeling. So much she hadn't known. He was moving inside her now. Thrusting hard and urgently against her body, bringing uncon-

157

scious moans with almost every movement. There was no pain at first, but she felt it now. And it was growing tighter with every thrust.

She felt a moment's panic. Was it too much? Would it be the end of her, if she allowed it to come? Her fingers tightened on his shoulders. She couldn't tell for a second if she was pulling him toward her or pushing him away. It didn't matter. She couldn't stop it. It was coming.

Her head twisted violently back and forth. She was gasping for her every breath, until even that was an impossibility, for her lungs didn't have the capacity to draw air. Something was grabbing at her insides, forcing them to grow tighter. Fiercely she strained against and then into the need, but it came nonetheless. Tighter, tighter, until with a moaning insane cry it shattered into ecstasy. His mouth was there, absorbing her cries, adding his own muffled sounds of fulfillment.

They breathed together, mouth to mouth as the aftershocks dwindled to soft, sweet, delicious pleasure, and their moans of delight softened to tired sighs, their bodies absorbing it all till the slow languid end.

Chapter Nine

"And just what is the meaning of this?"

Morgan snuggled closer to the delicious warmth at her side, burying her face in his muscled chest, cuddled still in his arms. Her eyes opened with sleepy happiness, a smile lingered still from the delight she'd suffered last night. They were in his room; Youngblood had brought her there only moments after their wild episode in the kitchen.

At the time, Morgan had thought herself so utterly devoid of strength she'd never be able to move again, but she had. Oh yes, she had. Morgan smiled with tender memory of how they had explored the wonders of each other almost till dawn.

Her slender form was hidden now from the door by his large body and the rumpled covers of his bed. Youngblood turned and came up on his elbow. He glared at the woman who stood in his doorway. "What do you want?"

Martha's gaze dropped to the garments held in her hands. Youngblood's gaze moved as she extended them forward. He cursed for neither he nor Morgan had remembered their clothes left in the kitchen. "Are you going to tell me why these things were in the kitchen?"

Youngblood sighed with disgust. He hadn't particularly wanted to hide the fact that Morgan was now his woman, but he hadn't wanted to broadcast the news either. Well, maybe he had, he reasoned. He wouldn't mind it if Marshall and any other man who had ideas about her knew what had happened between them. But for some reason he just didn't want Martha to know. Youngblood scowled. "It's none of your business."

"Isn't it?" Martha's mouth tightened. "You've taken advantage of my Morgan. What are you going to do about it?"

Morgan moaned, fully awake now, and tried to make herself as small as possible.

"Do about it? There's nothing much I can do. It's a little after the fact, wouldn't you say?"

"Not if your intentions are honorable."

"What the hell are you talking about?"

"Are you going to marry her?"

Youngblood laughed in ridicule. "Not likely."

Morgan groaned again as shame came to stain her cheeks. She didn't move a muscle. Her eyes were tightly shut, pretending sleep. Maybe if she pretended hard enough she could imagine herself somewhere else. Somewhere where Youngblood and Martha could never find her. Never in her life would she know a greater degree of mortification.

Martha made a sputtering sound as if she couldn't find the words.

Youngblood heaved a tired sigh. "Look, lady, we might as well get this straight right now. I ain't a man who can be forced to do anything. And I don't listen to women." His mouth twisted into a grimace, knowing Morgan was listening to every goddamned word. "Now get out."

"You're going to marry her."

Morgan gave the slightest moan. She couldn't bear it. She was getting up. She was getting out of here.

Youngblood felt her move and pressed his hand to her backside and held her in place. He raised his leg, so she couldn't be detected beside him.

"Well?" Martha said when he didn't respond.

"Well, what?"

160

"Are you going to marry her?"

"I don't think so."

"Oh you don't, do you? Well, we'll just see about that. I wonder what your men will think if I tell them you took advantage of her."

"What the hell are you talking about? She's a grown woman. I didn't force her into anything. She wanted it as much as I did."

Morgan groaned once more. She couldn't take another minute of this.

Martha shook her head at the unimportance of his declaration. "Johnny will believe me."

"Not after I talk to him."

"He'll believe his future wife, Mr. Youngblood. And after I'm through, so will everyone on this ranch." She shot him a knowing grin. "Do you think even one of these men will stay, knowing the disgrace you've brought upon my Morgan? Do you think you can run this place alone?"

Youngblood bit back a curse. He knew the honor expected among his men. They wouldn't for a minute put up with him messin' with a lady and not seein' right by her. Youngblood felt his anger rise to the boiling point. He didn't take to being blackmailed. "You ain't holding this over my head, lady. I don't need this ranch. I don't need any of this bullshit. And I especially don't need no woman. Nobody's ever going to tell me what I can and can't do."

He grabbed the covers, his obvious intent to get out of the bed. "Now get the hell out unless you want to see more than a lady should."

The door slammed shut.

Morgan lay there for a long moment wondering why Martha had done such a thing. Granted, it had probably come as a shock to find their clothes in the kitchen, but Morgan was after all of age 'and answerable only to herself. She was no longer a child and certainly didn't need Martha looking after her welfare.

Morgan had never known this degree of humiliation. It wasn't as if she wanted to marry Youngblood. Perish the thought. Why, the idea alone was enough to make her ill. She didn't even like the man! But to hear him refuse to marry her, even at Martha's insistence and then threats, was too much for her to handle.

He was pulling his pants up his legs when she came from the bed. The light coverlet was pulled around her shoulders as she walked toward the door.

"Where the hell do you think you're going?"

"To my room."

"Look, Morgan," he began, not really knowing what he was going to say. He hadn't meant half the things he'd said, except for the part about marrying her. And it didn't have anything to do with her personally. He didn't want to marry anybody.

"What?" she asked in a voice as dull and lifeless as a shriveled flower. Youngblood looked down at her. He'd never seen her so small, so delicate. Shoulders slumped, head bowed, she looked as if she were getting smaller before his eyes.

"I didn't mean . . ."

"Yes, you did." Her eyes lifted to his, huge and filled with . . . what? Pain? "You meant every word of it." She smiled softly. Don't worry. I don't renege. The ranch is yours."

"What?" he said as he dropped his boot and moved toward her. "Renege? Renege on what?"

"Our bargain." And at his baffled look, she smiled again. "Oh, don't tell me you've forgotten?" She laughed softly. "Of course you haven't. Good luck with the ranch, Youngblood," she said softly as she moved out the door.

Motionless, Youngblood stared dumbly at the closed door to his room. He stood there silently cursing as a strange tightness formed in his throat, for all he could think was last night she had called him Joseph.

*   *   *

Morgan forced a brightness to her smile as she bent low and spoke to Pedro. "You'll love it, I promise," she said as she waved the two tickets for the stagecoach before his eyes and tweaked his nose. She felt suddenly desperate to bring a smile to someone's face, for Martha and Johnny both looked as if they were about to attend a funeral. Morgan went on to tell about the train ride and the exciting city he was about to see for the first time in his life.

Her efforts proved fruitless. "But what about my horse? Who's going to feed him?"

"I'll get you another horse. There's a stable about three blocks from my house." Morgan felt as if her face were about to crack. She'd been smiling for days, trying to keep up her own spirits, terrified that if she allowed the smile to fade, she'd burst into tears and never stop.

What she couldn't understand was why she felt this state that bordered on panic. She had no reason to be upset. Why did she think she might? Why did she have this endless need to cry? She was going home. Wasn't that what she'd wanted from the first? Of course it was! She didn't feel a special tenderness for this dry, windy, barren land. She held no softness in her heart for the pretty house she was leaving behind. A house was a house and nothing more. Why, her father's mansion in New York was at least five times the size of the house she'd worked so hard to . . . Don't think about it. That was the key. Everything was going to be fine. Just fine. Just don't think.

"What's a block?"

Morgan smiled again, happy to have her mind taken from the terrifying direction her thoughts seemed to be wandering toward. "It's a measure of distance. It's not far. You'll see."

"I don't want a new horse. I want Bullet," he said while eyeing the horse already tied to the back of the buckboard.

Morgan graoned. She hated the name. Why couldn't he have called the animal Flower, or Honey, or

163

something? Why did he have to listen to Youngblood who, while examining the horse, remarked that the animal was sure to go as fast as a bullet. So the name. "All right, if you want Bullet, I'll have him brought to New York. Will that make you happy?"

"Why can't I ride him to New York?"

"Because it's too far. The train will take him."

"I didn't get to say good-bye to Mr. Youngblood."

"I know." Morgan's bright smile vanished at the mention of the man's name. He'd been gone almost a week. Left the very morning of his confrontation with Martha. No one knew where he went, or when he was coming back. And she most of all didn't care. "You can write him a letter."

They were outside the ticket office, waiting for the stagecoach. It would be there within minutes. And then the seemingly endless ride to Elko, where they could board the train. Their luggage was still on the back of the buckboard. Martha stood nearby, her eyes covered with a sheen of unshed tears. They'd never been apart. Morgan was the child she'd never had. How was she to bear letting her go?

She had cared for her from birth. And when her mother had died, it was Martha who soothed the young girl's tears. It was Martha whom Morgan had turned to when she needed solace. And Martha who had slowly become more than a companion, more than a friend.

"You're going to miss my wedding," Martha murmured, dangerously close to tears. Johnny dipped his head, finding no little interest in the tip of his high-heeled boot.

Morgan took the older woman in her arms. "Darling," she said, "I wish things were different, but you know it's best if I leave now, before it's too—"

"Late?" came the voice from behind and above her. "I'm afraid you didn't quite make it."

Morgan jumped at the sound of his voice. She hadn't heard his approach. She turned, her hand on her pounding heart. She had hoped to avoid a confrontation.

164

Actually she would have been relieved never to see this man's smirking face again. She snarled, "Is your horse Indian as well? I didn't hear it sneak up behind me."

Youngblood grinned at her fury. This was probably the way he liked her best. Well, he reconsidered, she wasn't half bad when she was all soft and warm and cuddling in his arms either. Youngblood almost laughed aloud at the understatement. His mind slid back to the moments when she was hot and straining against him, begging him to . . . Shit! Youngblood squirmed slightly in his saddle. He'd better get his mind off that right now.

Morgan glared at him. Her eyes spit blue fire. For some reason that she couldn't define, she felt more anger than the moment called for. She took a deep calming breath, swearing this beast would never see her lose control. "Good morning, Mr. Youngblood. Pedro was hoping to see you before we leave."

Youngblood's mouth tightened and his eyes narrowed as he studied her cool expression. How the hell did she do that, when only a second ago she looked ready to tear his heart out? "You goin' somewhere?"

Morgan smiled. "As a matter of fact, I am. Pedro and I are going home."

"Good. I'm headed in that direction myself. I'll go with you."

"By home, I meant New York."

"I don't think so."

"Don't you?"

"No, Miss Wainright. I think you're goin' to get on this horse and let me take you back to the ranch."

Morgan laughed. For just a second he thought she was going to explode. Youngblood almost grinned as he imagined the fight she'd give him. Suddenly he bit out a vicious curse as he watched her emotions close off, her expression suddenly shuttered.

"Really?" she said, more calmly than he could have imagined. Her tone marveled at and simultaneously ridiculed his audacity. "And why should I do that?"

Youngblood knew they could stand there and argue for

165

the next year and it would serve no purpose. "Johnny, take your lady and Pedro back to the ranch." He turned his head. "Seth, turn the wagon around. She's not going anywhere."

Morgan shot Pedro a stern look as he squealed his delight. This was too much. Who the hell did this man think he was? Morgan's hands positioned themselves on her hips. She faced him with murder flashing in her eyes. "Just a minute," she said softly. "Seth, I want you to take those bags off the back of that wagon, right now."

Seth shrugged and finally did as she said, not at all sure which one he was supposed to obey, while Johnny grinned, knowing without a doubt the outcome of this argument. His boss wasn't going to let her leave, no matter how she might rant and rave.

As it turned out, Morgan had no time to see the outcome of this standoff. She was suddenly caught up in his good arm and held alongside his dancing horse, her feet dangling in the air. "No sense listening to her, Seth. she's comin' with me. Now do as I said." The horse turned slightly. Youngblood grinned at an astonished Martha. "I expect we do things a bit different out here. But you will accept my apology, ma'am?"

Youngblood nodded his head and grinned at Martha's wide-eyed expression of amazement.

"We'll see you later. Morgan and I have to stop at the mission before we go home." And with those words he spun his horse around and was riding off.

"Good Lord, what was that all about?"

"I expect she'll be married by the time you see her again."

"Married! You mean—"

"I sure do, honey. I reckon Youngblood ain't takin' no for an answer."

Martha blinked and, to Johnny's delighted laughter, breathed a sigh, "Thank God."

*   *   *

The trouble was, Morgan couldn't find one thing to be delighted about. The man had kidnapped her and not one of those fools was doing a thing to help her. Youngblood had flung her upon her stomach and over his saddle as he made good his escape. The ground passed by at a frightening rate of speed. She was terrified and reached a desperate hand to the long silky mane, holding on to the moving horse as if it meant her life, which surely it did.

She was breathless with the force of the animal's pace. Every time the horse's hooves hit against the ground, she was bounced mercilessly upon his back, the air knocked from her lungs. Morgan finally managed the courage it took to release one hand from its deathlike hold and punched Youngblood's leg as hard as she could.

He slapped her backside in retaliation. "You monster!" Morgan screamed, outraged, and hit him again, this time swinging wildly up and behind her, contacting with his rib. She might have smiled in satisfaction at the sound of his grunt. She might have had she the time, but she most definitely did not, for Youngblood didn't hesitate to slap her bottom again.

"If you don't stop, you're going to fall off this horse."

Morgan had never resorted to violence in her life, but she was like a woman gone mad. No one hit her. No one! She turned her head and bit him just above his knee.

Youngblood pulled the horse to a stop. Her teeth were still firmly attached to his leg, her hold as far from comfortable as one could get. "Let go, Morgan," he warned softly. "I don't want to hit you."

"You don't want to hit me?" she asked in outrage, forgetting for the moment that in order to rail at him, she'd let go of his leg. "What did you think you were doing?"

"I was simply trying to calm you down."

"You maggoty piece of cow dung. I'm going to kill you. Nobody hits me."

"Is that right?" Youngblood had to bite back his laughter. "Well, you hit me first. You might think about

167

that the next time you're tempted to try it."

"You kidnapped me! For God's sake, what did you expect?"

"I expect you to act like a lady who's about to be married."

Her neck twisted. Morgan stared up at his seated form for a long moment. She was so shocked she couldn't seem to form a word. Finally she realized there were no words. There was nothing she could say. The man was obviously out of his mind.

With a grunt she was off the horse. A second later she was running. Of course it was impossible to get away. If Morgan had had her wits about her, she'd have known as much. A moment later she was tackled to the ground. Before she had a chance to realize her face was pressed into the brown sandy earth, he'd already spun her to her back and knocked the air from her lungs with the force of his weight.

"You little wildcat," he grunted as she raised her hands, nails extended like claws, ready to rip into the sides of his face. Instantly her arms were brought over her head and held in place.

"Stop it! You're going to hurt yourself."

"Maybe," she grunted, her teeth locked together as she bucked against his weight. "But a little pain won't matter much as long as I get to kill you."

Youngblood grinned down at her. "So you're going to kill me, are you? And just how do you figure you'll commit murder flat on your back?" He laughed at her helplessness. "Will you smother me with kisses? Kill me with lovin'?"

"You beast! Let me up," she hissed, almost insane with the need to do him bodily harm.

The close proximity of their bodies was having some startling effects on him. And the way her hips were thumping against his as she tried to throw him off wasn't helping matters any. "I'll let you up, if you promise to calm down. We've got some things to discuss."

168

"Really?" she gasped, trying to get enough air into her lungs, not an easy task since all of Youngblood's two hundred pounds were squashing the life out of her. "What kinds of things?"

Morgan groaned as the world swung dizzily around her, for he had suddenly jumped free, ever careful of a possible kick, and had yanked her into a standing position. He stood close by, but not close enough. She'd have to lunge at him if she had further intentions of violence. "About getting married this afternoon."

Morgan smoothed her horribly rumpled skirt. The blue traveling dress was covered with a fine layer of light brown dust. She smacked at it, concentrating solely on her task.

"Did you hear me?"

Morgan's head came up and she gave him a blank look. "Why? Were you talking to me?"

"Is there someone else standing here?"

Purposely Morgan looked around her. She shrugged her shoulder. "Not as far as I can tell." And she almost did a dance on the spot as she saw his scowl.

"Let's stop the games, shall we? We're getting married this afternoon."

"I thought you said to stop the games."

"I suppose that's your subtle way of saying no?"

Morgan shot him a mean grin. "My, my. You're not as stupid as you look, after all."

"But you must be." He shrugged. "Either that or hard of hearing. I didn't ask you, honey. I said we are getting married this afternoon."

"Drop dead, Youngblood. If you do me that tiny favor, I might consider it."

"Oh you'll consider it all right. You'll not only consider it, you'll do it."

"You're going to look mighty foolish when the priest asks 'Do you take this man' and I say no."

"And how do you think you'll look if you're having a baby with no husband?"

"Who says I'm having a baby?"

"Who says you're not?"

Morgan had thought of nearly nothing else this last week. She was almost thankful to be able to speak her fears aloud. "As a matter of fact, I don't know if I am or not. But you can relax, Youngblood, I pay my own way."

"Meaning?"

"Meaning, if I have a baby, I'll take care of it." Morgan didn't feel half as confident as she sounded. Modern though she might be, she knew well enough the standards of her time. She knew unmarried mothers were held in disgrace, shunned from society. Her friends would turn from her. Her father would die with the humiliation. But this monster didn't have to know that. She wasn't ever going to let this man have that kind of a hold over her. She'd gladly die before she allowed him that control.

"If you have a baby, it will be half mine."

"It will be all mine," she countered angrily, and took a threatening step toward him.

"It will be called a bastard."

"I'd kill anyone who dares," she snarled protectively.

"Children?" Youngblood taunted, his mouth curving into a sly grin. "Will you kill children, when they only repeat what their parents say?"

"I'll tell them the father died."

Youngblood laughed. "Since you wish me dead already, I imagine that won't be too great a chore." Suddenly his eyes narrowed dangerously, "But what happens when I come for visits?"

Morgan said nothing.

"I will want to see him, you know. I imagine I'll be coming quite often, as a matter of fact. Do you think your father and I will get along?"

Morgan only groaned. She couldn't imagine a less likely happening. And she'd be caught in the middle. She had to think! She had to get herself out of this mess.

"We're getting a bit ahead of ourselves here. There might be no child."

170

Youngblood nodded, his arms folded across his chest. "That's a possibility, of course."

"I'll let you know. I'll write."

Youngblood laughed, for the first time with real merriment. "Of course you'll let me know. But don't bother to write. You can simply tell me, since we'll be living in the same house."

"I don't think so."

"You don't?"

"No"—she glared at him—"I don't."

"Married couples usually live together, don't they?"

Oh God, he was back to that. "I thought we had that all settled."

"I reckon we don't."

"Youngblood," she said softly as if he couldn't be expected to truly understand, "There's no need for us to get married if there's no baby."

"I think there is."

"Do you?" she asked, eyes wide with ridicule. "Whatever for?"

"Because I've already wired your father, in your name, that the deed is done. And the possible reason for our haste."

"My God," Morgan moaned, and staggered back a step, turning a ghostly shade of white. "You didn't. Tell me you didn't!"

"All right."

"All right what?"

"I'll tell you I didn't, if it'll make any difference."

Her teeth gnashed together. She took a deep calming breath. "Did you or did you not telegraph my father?"

"I did."

Morgan moaned and buried her face in her hands. "He's going to be so upset. I'll have to wire him immediately. He's got to know the truth."

"I told him the truth."

And when she glared at him, he shrugged. "Well, almost. I made it sound as if you're already married,

171

instead of about to be."

Morgan began to pace. "I don't believe this. Why would you do something like that?"

Youngblood shrugged, barely able to hold back his grin. "I was just trying to do the honorable thing."

"Honorable!" Morgan snorted a sound that was somewhere between a growl and a laugh. "You wouldn't know honor from apple pie." She was pacing. Suddenly she came to an abrupt stop and gave him a long knowing look. "I'm beginning to understand. You want my money, right?" She laughed softly, never realizing the anger that was growing quickly out of control in the man she faced. "All right, what will it cost me? How much do you want?"

"Get on the horse," he said, at least she thought he did. She certainly hadn't said it, but his lips hadn't moved. Morgan's eyes widened at the sudden stillness of him. His eyes narrowed to mere black shining slits and his skin was growing a scary shade of red, beet red.

"I thought we were talking."

"We're finished. And if I ever again hear you mention money, I'll beat your ass black and blue."

"There's no need to threaten me, Joseph." She shrugged, a bit shamefaced. "My mistake, all right?"

"No, it's not all right," he said, but his tone softened measurably at the way she'd said his name. "Get on the horse."

"Are you taking me back to town?"

"I'm taking you to the mission."

"But why? I thought we had it settled. There's no need to get married if I'm not having a baby."

"Your father will expect to see a ring on your finger. He's coming."

"What?" she gasped, almost reeling with shock.

"That's right. He wired back. He's leaving immediately."

She began to pace again. "I'll explain everything when he gets here. He'll understand."

"Will he? After I tell him what you and I did?"

172

She came to a sudden stop. "I'll deny it."

"Martha will confirm it."

"You bastard."

"That's right. But nobody will ever have the chance to say that to my kid."

"What do you mean that's right? Are you a—"

"My mother and father never married. Is that what you want to know?"

"I won't do it!" She was sitting on his horse, her back against his chest. "Bring me back to town."

"You'll do it, all right. I figure the one person in this world you don't want to hurt, besides Martha, is your father."

"My father will understand." And when he didn't respond, she went on, "Word will get out. You'll be a laughingstock when I refuse to say the vows."

"We'll see."

"I won't say them. I swear it."

But she did.

Morgan listened to the familiar Latin prayers as the kindly priest bestowed God's blessing upon the happy couple, wondering for a minute who he was talking about. The priest finished and Youngblood's mouth pressed hard against hers. They were standing by the railing to the altar. Without thinking, she accepted Father Mendez's congratulations. She even smiled, but she never knew it, for her mind was in a daze, unable to fathom the reason behind what had happened, what she'd allowed to happen.

All right, so she had done a terrible thing. She'd had carnal knowledge of a man before marriage. It was a sin. She knew that. But she didn't have to marry him to make things right! All she had to do was go to confession.

So how come she was now Mrs. Joseph Youngblood? How had she allowed him to convince her this was the right thing to do?

Morgan could have faced her father. Even if she couldn't have lied her way out of this mess, he would have eventually forgiven her this one indiscretion.

Oh Lord, she silently lamented. She'd only made matters worse. So much worse.

It was all Youngblood's fault. Everything was his fault. He never should have gotten out of bed in the first place. If she hadn't heard him messing around in her kitchen, she'd never have gotten up. He shouldn't have touched her. He'd had no right. *So why didn't you stop him?*

Morgan ignored the question.

The man was so thick-headed. Once he got himself an idea, there was no way to talk him out of it. Lord, she felt sorry for the woman who got stuck with . . . God! What was she thinking? That woman was her!

No it wasn't! All right, she reasoned, as she tried to calmly catalog her thoughts. She'd married him, but only under duress. And if the marriage was never consummated, she'd be able to get an annulment. Morgan began to smile. For the first time in almost a week, she actually felt lighthearted. One idea stood out among all the rest. When her father came, she was going back to New York with him.

Chapter Ten

Morgan leaned back with a weary sigh against Youngblood's warm hard chest as Thunder meandered its way back to the ranch. She yawned.

"Are you tired?"

Morgan nodded. "I've been up since dawn. I didn't sleep well last night."

"Preparing for your trip to New York?"

She nodded. She was silent a long moment before she murmured, almost to herself, "If I'd have left yesterday—"

"It wouldn't have mattered," he interrupted. "I would have found you."

"The day before, then."

Youngblood sighed at her insistence. "Morgan, you might as well understand one thing. I wouldn't have hesitated to take you off the train, if you made it that far. And if I had to go to New York to find you, I would have done it."

"But why?" She glanced up at him, her eyes so big and round they threatened to swallow her face. "You don't even like me. Why was it so important that we marry?"

Youngblood shrugged, unable to tell her the reason behind his declaration, for he didn't know himself why this woman had to stay. Still she'd have an explanation. Youngblood said the only thing he could think of. "Once you shared my bed, you became my woman. And who said I don't like you?"

"Became your woman?" Morgan exclaimed, her blue eyes wide with fire, her lips tight with anger. "The idea is ridiculous. Where have you come from, the Stone Age? Good God, this is 1886! A woman has the right to choose her own mate. A man can't simply claim a woman as his own anymore."

Youngblood chuckled as he snuggled his nose in the warm curve of her neck. "Can't he? It feels like I already did."

Morgan denied the sudden lurching of her heart. "You might as well know this. When my father comes, I will be returning to New York with him."

"Will you?" he asked softly, while forcing aside the sudden anger her words brought to mind. Under the deception of guiding his horse, his hand brushed against the curve of her breast. He grinned at her sudden stiffening and listened to the harsh intake of her breath. "Will your father agree that marriage vows are to be taken lightly?"

"I didn't mean a word of it. I was forced into saying them and you know it."

"Did I hold a gun to your head?"

Morgan shot him a hate-filled glare.

Youngblood chuckled. "So why didn't you refuse to say them as you promised?"

Morgan groaned. "How should I know?" And at his low, sensual chuckle she continued, "I probably didn't want to embarrass you."

"You were very kind to worry about my feelings."

"Too bad I can't say the same about you."

"Can't you? Why do you think I don't care about your feelings?"

It was Morgan's turn to laugh. Her tone was filled with sarcasm when she remarked, "It came to me in a dream."

Youngblood grinned. "I suppose you know by now, dreams aren't always to be trusted."

So what was that supposed to mean? Was he telling her he cared for her? Nonsense. She knew the truth behind this hasty marriage. Martha had forced his hand. She'd insisted they marry or he'd suffer the loss of his men's respect and perhaps the loss of his ranch as well. Morgan knew he wouldn't chance that. So he had forced her into marriage simply to keep things running smoothly.

Youngblood had put aside his supposed accidental touching. His free hand roamed in earnest now over the flat smoothness of her stomach and ribs. "I'd appreciate it if you'd stop that," Morgan grunted as she squirmed uncomfortably before him.

"You don't like it?" he asked, a grin spreading across his mouth.

"As a matter of fact, I don't."

"Maybe I'm not doing it right."

"Youngblood . . ." she threatened.

"Is this better?" he asked as his fingers moved higher and cupped a heavy breast.

She refused to answer, but simply removed his hand.

"Oh, I know." His fingers moved back to her jacket and undid the buttons. A moment later her blouse was opened as well, but not without some struggling on Morgan's part.

"Will you stop that?"

"No. I want to touch you and I think you want me to. Don't you?"

"I most certainly do not!"

She was tearing at his hand now, but to no avail. It slipped easily inside her blouse beneath her lacy chemise and cupped the softness of her breast. Morgan bit back a moan as instant heat penetrated every fiber of her body. Gently he lifted the sweet mound free of material and leaned forward slightly so he might watch his thumb run back and forth over the rosy tip. "You have beautiful breasts, Morgan."

Morgan swallowed hard, desperate to fight the longing he so easily instilled. She tugged at his arm. Nothing happened. "I want you to stop this, Joseph. Stop it right now."

Youngblood almost moaned with delight. He'd never

get enough of her saying his name. He'd never before heard it said so softly, so tenderly. "Your whole body is beautiful. I love the way your waist curves, so tiny I can span it in my hands. And your hips, rounded and yet so slender and smooth. It's unusual, I think, to have breasts so large when the rest of you is so small."

"Will you please stop touching me?" she asked, her voice shaking with the need for him to go on. Her head fell back against his shoulder. She was gasping for every breath.

"I love to touch you. For months I lay awake at night imagining what it would be like to have you naked in my bed. Your skin is so soft. The night we spent together, when my hands moved over your body, I had to keep looking just to make sure it was really you I was touching."

Morgan moaned, a low aching sound as her mind drifted to the long sweet loving of that night. They couldn't seem to get enough of one another. He was so careful of her. At first refusing to love her again, afraid she'd be sore in the morning if he took her as often as he wanted. She had stumbled to his room on trembling legs, never thinking to part from him and return to her own room. He'd taken a cool wet cloth and cleaned her, and she had offered herself to his ministrations, without the slightest shred of modesty.

Youngblood had taken her in his arms and insisted they sleep, smiling at her disappointment, for his simple ministrations had enticed and inflamed her body until she ached for his touch again. He had promised more in the morning. But she had rubbed herself against him, unable to fathom the joy of this newly discovered sensation and had demanded more, until he was unable to refuse her silent plea. Morgan's face turned red at the thought of her daring, but not for long. His busy skillful fingers were fast making her lose her train of thought.

"Someone will see."

"No, they won't. We can see a rider miles away."

Youngblood let go of the reins. The horse would have

to find his own way back, or wander these plains for the time being. He needed to touch her. Needed it more than his very breath in order to live.

Youngblood slid his hand beneath her skirt and petticoat. Over her stocking and under her long-legged drawers, he followed the long curve of her thigh until his seeking fingers encountered the moist heat of her. His arm lifted her inches from the saddle so his fingers might penetrate the sweetness of her.

Morgan gasped as he entered her body, with first one, then two fingers. Again and again he moved, faster, faster, until she thought she might scream with the need for him to go on.

It happened so fast. One minute she had been pushing him away, cursing him for his daring, and then she was suddenly hungry for him to go on. Demanding that he finish what he had begun. Praying that he wouldn't leave her now.

She moaned, she gasped, she struggled to breathe. And then she cried out her relief. So fast. Oh God, she didn't want this to end so fast.

Morgan was gasping for breath, her body slumped against his. She didn't have the strength to think on his disgraceful action or her equally disgraceful responses.

"Sit sideways," he whispered near her ear.

"I can't move," she murmured, slumping weakly against him.

Youngblood chuckled as he helped her into the position he wanted, her one leg over the pommel, so that her thighs were parted slightly. He didn't remove his hand, but went on to touch her gently in the most sensitive of places.

"That was too fast, wasn't it?"

Morgan looked up to dark eyes alive with yearning and yet filled to overflowing with tenderness. Shyly she nodded her head.

"This will take a little longer."

Slowly he massaged the tiny nub to hardness. She squirmed slightly. "I don't like it when you touch

179

me there."

"Don't you?" he asked, a smile lingering at the corners of his mouth as he watched her brows lower in a slight frown. "Why?"

"I don't know. It doesn't feel very good."

"It will."

And it did. Good God, but Morgan couldn't imagine anything feeling better.

Morgan began to move ever so slightly. "Is it feeling better?" Youngblood asked.

"I don't know." She faced him, her eyes opened widely as she boldly allowed the intimate caress. Not even slightly amazed that they could talk so openly while he touched her in so private a place. She felt no modesty with this man. Her shyness was a thing of the past. "It's very sensitive."

"It would be better if my finger was my tongue."

Morgan made a tiny sound and squirmed again, unable to release the thought his words had brought to mind. Unable to decide if it was the idea of his mouth on her that made her feel so oddly shaken.

"Would you like me to do that? Do you want my mouth here?"

"You did that the other night. I didn't like it then."

"But you would now."

"I don't know." Her eyelids were beginning to grow heavy. She was having a hard time concentrating on what he was saying.

"Does it feel good now?"

Morgan moaned as she pressed her face into the warmth of his throat. "Yes. It feels good. It feels wonderful." She strained against his hand, tipping her hips up slightly. "But it's not enough. I feel like . . . I feel like I want more."

"It's supposed to feel like that. More will come, you'll see."

Morgan's hand raised to his chest. She opened two buttons and spread her fingers beneath the fabric. "Don't touch me, Morgan," he warned. "If you do, it

180

won't be enough. I'll need you to touch me in other places. I can do this only if you don't touch me."

Morgan looked into his face gone tight with need. He was breathing heavily, almost as heavily as she, but Morgan hardly noticed. All she knew was the sweetness that was flooding her body. Twisting at her insides, causing them to grow tight with some unnamed need.

Youngblood smiled as he felt the nub grow soft and then moments later hard again. She was nearing the end and she hadn't the least idea what it was all about.

"Joseph, please. I need . . ." Morgan never finished her plea, for the soft breathless sound of her voice and the sweet sound of his name was enough to bring his head forward. With a desperate groan of longing, his mouth captured hers and clung as if both their lives depended on this in order to exist. Feverishly he penetrated her parted lips with his tongue and moaned again as she mindlessly, instinctively sucked him further inside.

They were gasping for breath when he raised his head.

"I can't," she mouthed silently, her eyes filled with panic.

"Don't be afraid. Let it come," he soothed as he kissed her again. "You won't be sorry," he murmured into her opened mouth.

Tiny desperate broken sounds were escaping her throat. Her lips parted as she breathed short shallow gasps. Her tongue moistened suddenly parched lips. Her face grew flushed. She felt light-headed as blood raced from her head to the part he massaged. She throbbed there, grew more sensitive than ever, while her belly tightened, reaching for something, reaching, reaching until she closed her eyes, her body stiffened, and she cried out.

She was breathing as if she'd run miles. "Oh God," she choked as the first of many blinding waves of aching wonder throbbed through her. "Oh God," she cried again as another washed over her, tightening her body beyond belief, beyond bearing. Stealing her breath, her mind, her soul.

"Let it come," he coaxed, feeling her straining in his arms, enthralled at the exquisite pleasure of watching her. Her lips tightened into a grimace that bared her teeth, resembling pain and then delight and then, like magic, ecstasy.

Her head fell back, her body relaxed in his arms, her lips parted in a half smile, her eyes were closed as she relished with the softest of moans the last of the blissful sensation.

"Tonight, darlin'. Tonight, I'm going to do that with my mouth." He kissed her hungrily, savagely taking the last of her will into his mouth. "Do you want that?"

"Oh yes," she murmured, still caught in the afterglow of his magical fingers and the powerful persuasion of his mouth.

"I'm going to kiss you everywhere, everywhere," he murmured as he kissed her again.

Morgan shivered, her mind caught up in his promise. His threat? She pushed the thought aside. He wasn't threatening her with anything, was he? Morgan allowed herself to succumb to yet another of his hungry kisses, a kiss filled with promise, with yearning, with the tenderness of love. She had thought nothing could compare to the night they had spent together. Now she began to wonder, as her imagination took hold and raced on to when they would be alone in his room.

Hot and moist, his mouth ran a path from her lips to her exposed breast. He was teasing with teeth and tongue the pliant softness, and she cried out as he sucked the tip deep into the heat of his mouth. He released her moments later and smiled smugly. "That was to let you know that if you have any ideas about not sharing my bed, you're wasting your time. A hot little piece of a—" He caught himself, but not before Morgan realized what he'd been about to say. "You won't last long now that you know what's waiting down the hall from you."

Morgan stiffened. Her eyes widened with dread. If he'd splashed cold water over her, she couldn't have become more lucid any faster. He was proving his power over her and had done a masterful job of it. And she'd carry the shame of allowing it to her grave.

"You bastard!"

Youngblood chuckled, almost whispering a prayer of thanks at her scorn. She was dangerous, this one, more dangerous than he'd first realized. He hadn't imagined what it would do to him to take her to his bed. He'd only wanted her as a woman, the way he'd wanted a dozen others, but he'd gotten much more. Too much!

He didn't want this feeling of softness, of tenderness, to come upon him when his mind drifted toward her. He especially didn't want it when he held her in his arms. He wanted sex. Pure and simple. No emotion. No words of love attempting to tumble forth. He didn't love her. He never would. It was best they got that straight from the beginning.

He laughed as she straightened her clothes with quick, hard movements. "Should I have whispered sweet nothings, darlin'? Don't you like to hear the truth? You are a hot piece. I don't think I've ever had any hotter. A lot of women would be delighted to hear that."

"You can rot in hell, Youngblood. Hot or not, I'll never come to you."

Youngblood shrugged. "That's all right, darlin'. I ain't particular. I'll come to you."

Morgan thought about the gun she had been using for practice. Starting tonight and every night from now on she'd be sleeping with it tucked under her pillow. "I hope you try it. I swear to God," she said with vehemence, "I hope you do."

Youngblood ignored her threat and chuckled as he nuzzled his nose in her neck. "No matter how hot and sweaty you get, you always smell good."

The truth of it was she smelled better than just good. There was something about her scent, even when her perfumes faded away, that drew him like a bee to a flower. He couldn't seem to get enough of smelling her, touching her, watching her, whether her eyes were flashing as they were now in anger or glazed over with passion, she was a glorious sight. He wondered if he made love to her enough, would he finally tire of her body? Jesus, he hoped so.

Thunder brought them at last to the ranch. Morgan couldn't get there fast enough. Silently she urged him to hurry his pace. She wanted to be free of this man. She wanted his arms to come from around her. She wanted to breathe a deep breath that didn't hold his tantalizing scent.

Morgan's eyes widened with surprise as they finally passed under the triple R sign. The ranch was swarming with people! Who in the world were they? And what were they doing here? Vaguely she heard Youngblood's curse. There was a party going on. Why?

Morgan didn't have long to wait for the answers to her silent questions. The moment Thunder came to a stop, the young couple was bombarded by well-wishers. It looked as if the whole town had come to offer their congratulations. Morgan could have told them they were wasting their time. There was nothing to celebrate; this was but a sham of a marriage. But she never got the chance.

Almost immediately she was pulled from Youngblood's arms and swooped up into Johnny's embrace. He kissed her on the mouth and so did the rest of the men that worked their ranch.

Morgan's head didn't stop spinning until Youngblood came to rescue his bride. She leaned weakly against him, holding on to his waist while the men laughed at her rosy cheeks. Nearer the house some of the men from town were playing music. There were makeshift tables with white flowing cloths covered with food in the front yard.

Someone slapped a glass of whiskey in her hand and Morgan drank at it then choked as the burning liquid slid down her throat, but took yet another large sip, determined to join in the festivities, no matter the mockery.

A moment later Morgan excused herself. She was filthy, hot and sweaty and covered with dust. A half hour later she left her room in a high-waisted, black silk skirt and a lacy white blouse that was buttoned at her wrists and up to her throat. Her hair was piled neatly into a knot at the top of her head. Her face was scrubbed clean. Her eyes twinkled with determination. She was going to enjoy herself tonight. It was probably the last chance she'd have until she returned to New York.

The dancing came to a stop. The music fell off to odd pieces of sound. Morgan looked behind her, wondering why every eye in the crowd seemed to be looking her way. No one was there. Were they all looking at her? Why?

Suddenly Youngblood's hand reached out to take hers. "They were waiting for the bride. This is our dance."

Morgan blinked as she looked at her husband. Could this be the same man she had married? Was this sensitive, tender man the arrogant beast who had married her only to keep his ranch? Was this her husband smiling down at her as if he thought she was the only woman in the world? How had he become so artful at deceit? How did no one else see the mocking laughter behind the dark eyes? How did no one else know the sham of his celebration?

Youngblood had changed also. He was dressed entirely in black. Black pants and shirt, opened at his throat. Boots gleamed in the sunlight. He smelled clean and manly and wonderful. Morgan closed her eyes as he swirled her around in huge circles in the yard and wondered why he couldn't always treat her so.

"Smile, honey, people will think you're not happy."

"But I'm not happy, Youngblood." She smiled prettily. "I won't be happy till I see the last of you."

Youngblood grinned and leaned his head down as if to whisper something wonderful in her ear. "I take it you expect that to be soon."

"It can't be soon enough to suit me." She glared at him a long moment before she suddenly grinned, a wicked smile curving once sweet lips, while a light of retaliation danced in blue eyes. "This hot little piece has some traveling to do. I think I'll join my fiancé in Paris."

Morgan was thrilled to see Youngblood stiffen. He

looked as though he'd taken a blow. He was crushing her hand in his, his fingers biting into her waist.

"I wouldn't think about that too much. It might not be healthy."

"Are you threatening me?" she asked, while blinking in innocence.

"Not you, just any man who comes near you."

"Oh I see. You don't want me, but no one else is allowed to have me either."

"Who the hell said I don't want you?"

"Are you telling me you do?"

"Isn't that what you're mad at? Didn't I say you were the hottest piece I've ever had? Why wouldn't I want you?"

Morgan blinked her astonishment. Could it be this man cared for her, really cared? Could it be he just didn't know how, or couldn't say the right words? "What do you want, Joseph? Tell me."

"I want you."

"For how long?" Say it! Say it, she prayed. Tell me so I can believe there's a chance for a relationship.

Youngblood shrugged. "For as long as it takes."

Morgan blinked her confusion. "What takes?"

"To get you out of my system."

Morgan's knees wobbled with shock at his blunt words. She took a deep breath. A small, hard smile touched her lips; her eyes were as cold as ice. "At least the man is honest."

"Come on, Youngblood. You've got her for the rest of your life. Can't you give one of us poor fellas one dance?"

Morgan smiled at Doc Franklin, ignoring the man holding her. "Of course I'll give you a dance," she said merrily as she turned into his arms. She tried to smile, she truly did, but the words kept repeating themselves in her mind. 'For the rest of your life. For the rest of your life.' Morgan couldn't stop the shiver of horror. What a gruesome thought.

*   *   *

"Why did you marry him? You must have guessed how I felt. You never even gave me a chance. You never said anything . . ."

"John, please," Morgan returned, her hands twisting together as she faced the obviously distraught man.

"Do you love him?"

Morgan shrugged and murmured an out-and-out lie. "We get along."

"Is that a reason to marry? Because you get along?"

"John, I . . . I . . ." Morgan didn't know what to say or how to explain. How could she tell him why she'd married Youngblood when she didn't know why herself? Morgan groaned, knowing she'd curse her actions this afternoon for the rest of her life.

Suddenly a hard arm encircled her waist from behind and drew her back against an unyielding frame. Morgan sighed with defeat. She'd never be able to explain now, especially since Youngblood's handling of her implied an intimate loving relationship, a relationship that didn't exist.

"There's no need to be shy, honey. You might as well tell him you married me for the same reason anyone gets married." Youngblood's eyes turned hard and cold in a silent dare as they stared at the man opposite him. "You can see for yourself we're in love."

Morgan closed her eyes against the fury and pain of his lies. Why was he doing this? He held her as if she were a prize taken in battle. Why was it so important that he claim her as his own?

Morgan and Marshall had been standing just outside the barn, almost lost in the shadows of the dark night, when Youngblood had come upon them. It hadn't been an accidental meeting. Youngblood had watched them closely while they danced and then casually left the circle of light that lit the party. His mouth had grown grim at the thought of them alone in the dark. He had followed, with murder in his eyes.

"You dirty bastard. It's never enough, is it? You always have to take what belongs to me."

"Morgan never belonged to you. She was mine from the first."

"Is it true?" Marshall's lips curled with disgust. "Did you let him touch you?" he asked, his body stiff as he awaited her answer. And when she couldn't find the words to deny Youngblood's boast, Marshall laughed. "You have no call to worry. She let a half-breed touch her. That makes her less than nothing." He shot them a look of disgust. "I could kill you both."

The two men stared at one another for a long moment, Marshall's hand poised above his gun. Gently Youngblood moved Morgan to his side. "If you shoot me, you'll hang. I ain't wearin' a gun."

Marshall was quick to realize the truth of that statement. He wanted this man dead, but not at his expense. Patience, man, this isn't the time, he silently reasoned. His arm relaxed at his side at last, and Morgan allowed a long breath she hadn't until that moment realized she was holding as she watched him walk away. Seconds later, out of the darkness, came the sound of his horse pounding the earth as he raced back to town.

"He won't face me like a man. Never would. That makes him dangerous. I don't want you to leave the ranch alone for a while."

Morgan shook her head. "John wouldn't hurt me."

"You're wrong there, Mrs. Youngblood. He hates me enough to hurt you. I'd say we both have something to fear."

"Why? Why does he hate you?"

Youngblood shrugged. "He has this crazy notion that my mother loved me more than him."

Morgan's confusion was obvious. "What do you mean?"

"We're brothers, Morgan."

Her eyes widened with surprise. "But he's not Indian. How—"

"Our mother. We have the same mother, different fathers." Youngblood sighed as he watched her shake her head.

"Why didn't you tell me?"

He shrugged. "It's common knowledge around these parts."

"Tell me now."

Youngblood took her hand and began to walk. They were down by the river before she realized it, so engrossed was she with the story. "My mother was white. Her father owned this ranch. She met my father one day, not far from here, when she was out riding. She found him half dead. He'd been clawed by a mountain lion. He'd traveled a great distance and had lost a lot of blood.

"He was very young, as was she, but he was a Hopi Indian. Most of them live in northeastern Arizona. But not all. His family lives a few days' ride from here, in a pueblo; that's a village built on top of a mountain," he added for her information.

"Anyway, she met my father and despite her parents' objections nursed him back to health. She had to sneak out and bring him food and medicine. She ended up pregnant with me. They wanted her to give me up. She wouldn't hear of it. She probably went through some real rough times. By the time I was born, she had given her parents an ultimatum. If they allowed her to keep the baby, she'd never see my father again."

"Why didn't she just marry your father?"

Youngblood shook his head. "He was Hopi, a chief. He couldn't leave his people. If the council granted him permission to marry an outsider, she'd have to give up everything and live his way." He shrugged and said bitterly, "I guess it was too much to ask."

"Don't be so hard on her, Joseph. You said yourself she was young. Can't you imagine her fear of leaving everything she knew?"

He only shrugged for an answer. "Anyway a few years later she met Marshall's father. He was a prospector and not very particular that his woman had been touched by an Indian. He bought her a little spread, just south of town. They lived there for a while, before he got the itch to go looking for gold again. He never came back."

"So why does John hate you?"

Youngblood lifted his hands palm up and shrugged his shoulders. "Who knows? He's always wanted this place. Maybe that's it."

"What about the spread south of town?"

"Oh, he got that when my mother died. Never worked it much though. Finally lost the whole thing in a card game."

"Enough about Marshall." Youngblood grinned as he took her suddenly, unexpected, into his arms. "I want to talk about us."

"There is no us," she grunted as she broke free of his hold. "I'd never stay with a man who only wants to use me for a time."

Youngblood laughed as he followed her back to the party. His voice was low as he whispered teasingly near her ear, "Folks are bound to get suspicious if we don't look like a pair of lovebirds at least for today."

Morgan stopped in her tracks. She looked up into his smug expression and sighed with resignation as she took his arm. "Don't get any ideas. I'm only doing this so neither of us will be embarrassed."

Youngblood chuckled as he moved her into the circle of his arms. "Oh, I'd never do that. But I'd better kiss you. People will expect you to look properly kissed especially since we were gone so long."

Her arms held him away as he bent forward. "There's only just so much I'm willing to do to save face, and that's not one of them."

Youngblood laughed again and hugged her tighter to his side. Back at the party they danced, they smiled, they laughed with their friends. And there wasn't a one among the merrymakers who didn't notice the change in Youngblood. Already he'd lost that hardness that seemed a natural part of him. It seemed to folks that he treated his lady in an adoring fashion. Later they'd wonder if they'd ever seen a man so smitten.

Only Morgan knew the game they played.

Chapter Eleven

The last of the townsfolk had left hours ago. The house had quieted soon after. It was very late. Morgan lay awake, waiting for him to come to her, for him to insist on his husbandly rights. Her gun was within reach, as she had mentally promised herself. Her whole body was stiff as she imagined the moment of confrontation.

Would she go through with it? Did she have the nerve? Could she shoot her own husband? And if she did, how would she explain that she'd shot her husband because he had insisted on what were by law his rights?

Morgan sighed as she gazed up to the dark shadows on her ceiling. She tossed and turned, restlessly waiting, waiting while he played some terrible sort of game with her mind. When would he come? Why was he taking so long? When would it be finished between them? She couldn't wait much longer and survive this kind of tension. Morgan turned over again, her eyes straining through the dark to watch the door to her room. At any second she expected it to open. She fought off the need to sleep. She had to stay alert, or be caught off guard. Morgan shivered at the horror of being used to relieve Youngblood's lust, knowing that's all there was between them. Never, never would she succumb.

Morgan's next conscious thought was of the early morning sounds of the men outside.

She blinked in confusion as she glanced fearfully at the opposite side of the bed. Empty. She heaved a great sigh of relief. But her relief vanished as she began to wonder why he hadn't come to her. Why hadn't he insisted on his right to share her bed? What in the world was he doing?

He was lulling her into a false sense of security. That was it! He figured he'd get her to lower her defenses, perhaps to trust him—Morgan laughed at the absurdity of that idea—and then he'd take advantage of that weakness.

Morgan dressed quickly. Breakfast had yet to be started and she was late. She grinned as she patted a loose curling tendril into place. Well, he could plan to his heart's content. He wasn't going to ever penetrate the protective shield she'd place around her heart. She knew the beast for what he was. Hadn't he told her clear out he wanted her for his bed only until the day came when he tired of her? Good Lord, did he actually expect her to stay around and wait? Did he think her so weak in spirit? So manageable in mind? Of course he did.

Morgan grinned as she mentally prepared herself to do battle. Mr. Joseph Youngblood had a thing or two to learn about his new wife.

She wondered what new trick lay in store. Would he be his usual grumpy self this morning? Or would he try to confuse her with a suddenly even disposition? Morgan shook her head. Even if he knew how to sweet-talk her, which she doubted, she wouldn't believe his sudden attempt at civility.

Morgan opened her door as she silently mused, "Do your worst, Youngblood. I'm ready." Only she wasn't.

The hall, as always, was dark. Morgan took two steps toward the kitchen before she realized she was not alone. "You're late," came the low tender whisper against her neck as warm arms slid around her middle and pulled her to lean back against him. "I've been waiting for you."

"I overslept." Morgan tried to pull away, only to find his arms securely in place. Her body tensed, awaiting his

192

next step at seduction. Morgan felt almost disappointed when he did nothing more than hold her. She would have loved to have shown him how unsusceptible she was to his charms. His warm sigh against her neck breathed his content. Morgan only wished she could find the same emotion.

"Did you have trouble sleeping, honey?" His voice held an annoying touch of laughter, for Youngblood was not unaware of her longing to be free.

"Not at all. I slept very well, thank you." Morgan swore she preferred death to admitting the truth.

"But you waited long into the night for me, didn't you? Were you disappointed when I didn't come?"

"Hardly." Morgan managed to shoot him a somewhat hostile look of incredulity. Unhappily her show of defiance was lost in the darkness of the hall. "If you remember, we settled the question of our living conditions yesterday."

"Did we?" he crooned as he continued to caress her neck with tender, enticing kisses.

"Youngblood, let me go."

A soft chuckle tickled her neck and sent chills down her spine. "Honey, there's nothing wrong with a man holding his wife. Is there?"

Morgan tried to push aside his easily spoken endearment. She knew he used it unconsciously. She knew it meant nothing. And yet she couldn't stop the pleasure every time he chose to bestow a gentle phrase. "Probably not. Except we are hardly man and wife."

"You don't think so? Simply because I've yet to press my cause?"

"There's no sense in pretending. You want one thing, I want another."

"As two rational adults, we should be able to come to some kind of a compromise."

"I'm afraid that's impossible."

"Do you think so?" He seemed to think on it a moment and then continued, "All right, honey, no compromise.

193

But suppose I ask no more of you than an occasional hug and maybe a kiss? Would that be such a hardship?"

Morgan shrugged as she turned to face him. "Why would you ask only that? Do you think a hug and kiss will entice me into your bed?"

"Who said anything about enticing you into bed?" he asked, his teeth flashing with a grin. "If I'd wanted you in bed, I would have come to your room last night."

"I'm going back to New York when my father gets here."

Youngblood forced aside the unreasonable anger those few words instilled. Valiantly he fought against the need to crush her to him, to insist she stay. To demand she put aside her ridiculous intentions. No. If he wanted to coax this woman into his bed, it wouldn't be done with either threats or anger. Her capitulation would take a more subtle, sensuous effort on his part. "So? Does that mean you can't enjoy yourself in the meantime?"

Morgan's laughter was brittle and strained as she looked up at his dark handsome features. "Enjoy myself in your bed, you mean?"

"I don't mean anything of the kind. I simply meant for us to be friends."

"My friends and I only kiss or hug when we say hello or good-bye." Morgan lips twitched. She forced aside her grin as she teased, "Are you going somewhere?"

"As a matter of fact, I am. Kiss me good-bye," he said just before his lips absorbed the soft murmuring sound of her protest.

His mouth was tender and sweet as it held to hers. Morgan squeezed her hands between their bodies, her palms pressing against his shoulders, but the effort proved futile. It was like pushing against a boulder. Indeed, Youngblood's mouth only grew more demanding. Gently he rubbed his lips back and forth, waiting for her to relax and accept his kiss.

Morgan sighed, knowing her silent battle useless, for the feel of his mouth against her was heaven. She might

194

have sworn this would never happen again, but once it had, she only hungered for more.

She made a soft sound of denial when his tongue sought entrance, but the temptation was simply too great for her to resist. Her lips parted on a sigh, while Youngblood's hungry mouth eagerly sought out the warmth of her.

His body trembled with the need to rub his hips against hers, to drag her into his room, to tear away the clothes that prevented his hands from touching warm naked flesh.

He had to stop, or lose the last of his control.

"Unfair," Morgan moaned as she leaned weakly against him, her breath coming in short jerking gasps. "What kind of a kiss is that among friends?"

"A very thorough one, I think," he said, as breathless and shaken as the woman he held so close. He cuddled her softness within the circle of his arms, his mind leaping ahead to a time when she'd willingly offer what he was now forced to take. Youngblood wondered, with no little amazement, at the need he felt for this woman. When was the last time he'd so desperately wanted? When had a woman's kiss driven him beyond all rational thought? When had a body promised to ease all and no other could be substituted?

Morgan allowed herself the luxury of leaning against him. For just a moment more, she swore. Just long enough to regain her normal breathing. Just long enough to regain the strength in her shaking legs. She could hear his heart pounding beneath her ear and murmured almost drunkenly, "Where are you going?"

"I thought you might like to see my father's village."

"*I* might like!" Her head tipped up as she glared into his gently amused expression. "You mean you want me to go with you?"

Youngblood murmured a soft sound of agreement as he pulled her against him again and completely destroyed the neat knot she'd made in her hair as he buried his face

195

in the softly scented silkiness.

She was stiff again. "Then why the kiss good-bye?"

He chuckled. "I'm leaving, aren't I?"

"But you want me to go with you."

"You're right. That means you'll need a kiss good-bye as well."

Morgan tore herself from his embrace. Her first impulse was to rail at the man for forcing an unwanted kiss on her and then to sizzle his ears for the trickster he was. Suddenly she laughed at his sheepish expression. She'd never imagined to see that particular look on this man, and if it hadn't been getting later and later as they stood there, she might not have ever seen it. "Underhanded, sneaky, wretched creature," she murmured as she preceded him into the kitchen.

She was really late now. The sun was up, the men gathering impatiently in small groups outside.

"It looks like Martha overslept as well. You need some help?"

"You're not offering?" Her eyes widened with surprise as she taunted, "Not you? I thought you said this was woman's work," Morgan asked, as a sly smile played about her lips.

Youngblood slapped her bottom and grinned. "I think one should accept an offer of help with a bit less ridicule, lest that offer be rescinded." He was laughing as he pumped water into a huge coffeepot. "I figure we'll make good time if we leave within the hour. You're going to need some help feeding the men first."

Morgan grinned as she took a giant bowl from the shelf and began filling it with flour, eggs, and water.

The kitchen was filled with the warm scent of baking biscuits and frying bacon by the time the first man stumbled into the room. Youngblood and Morgan stood side by side as they both cooked up breakfast.

To their credit, or perhaps merely to guard against the sudden loss of teeth, not one man mentioned the fact that Youngblood had one of Morgan's ruffled aprons tucked into his belt as he deposited a huge skillet, filled with crisp bacon, upon the table.

"I imagine you think you've pulled off quite a coup."

"Me?" Youngblood asked, while shooting her an innocent glance from the saddle of his horse. He grinned at her stern expression. "What is it you think I've accomplished?"

"You know very well what. I wanted to take Pedro with us."

"Did I stop you?"

Morgan shot him a hard look. "No, you didn't, but neither did you take my side in the argument."

"What would Martha have thought if I insisted you take a chaperone on our honeymoon?"

"First of all, this is most definitely not our honeymoon. And I certainly do not need a chaperone. That's not why I wanted Pedro to come along. He would have enjoyed the trip and you know it."

Youngblood shrugged. "Probably. Shall we go back?" he asked as he brought Thunder to a stop. "If you really want him with you, I'm sure I can convince Martha."

Morgan eyed him suspiciously. "There's not a doubt in my mind that this is yet another of your wily tricks to get me into your bed."

"Tricks?" Youngblood found himself biting the inside of his lip in order not to smile.

"Since when have you been so easy to get along with?"

Youngblood laughed. "You are a suspicious one, aren't you?"

"Joseph, for three months you've treated me like I was poison. You can't blame me if I grow suspicious at the sudden change."

"I think there's less suspicion than fear. You're afraid to be alone with me."

"Afraid!" Morgan gave a wild, high-pitched laugh. She wasn't afraid. She was terrified. No matter how she constantly swore she'd never again give in to the need that constantly plagued, he only had to touch her to set her heart beating wildly out of control. How was she going to fight this need if she was alone with him? "Ridiculous!"

"Do you want to go back?" he asked.

Morgan knew he'd do as she wished. And that knowledge gave her the courage to discard her fears and go through with this trip. After all, they were only spending two days each way on the trail. Surely she could control her baser instincts for a grand total of four days. Morgan shook her head in answer to his question. "It's too late. Let's go."

They traveled some distance before she spoke again. "You don't speak like the rest of the men. Well, you do, but not all the time. What is that accent I sometimes detect?"

"Harvard." Youngblood grinned at her look of astonishment. "I thought I'd lost it all by now."

"You went to Harvard?"

He nodded.

"What did you study?"

"Law."

"Law? Are you a lawyer?"

Youngblood drawled in a lazy tone. "I reckon I could practice it some if I wanted."

Morgan's mouth hung open in surprise. Why in the world would an educated man choose to put aside that education and take on the running of a horse ranch instead?

Youngblood shot her a knowing grin. "If you don't shut your mouth, something's goin' to fly in it."

"Why?" she asked, her expression one of complete bafflement.

"Why don't I practice law?" He shrugged at her nod. "I like ranching."

"So why did you study it?"

"More than anything, my mother wanted her sons

198

educated. There was no money, but I made her a promise to do my best. After she died, I did some prospecting. Got myself a little stake and went East to school."

"A little! You must have had more than a little. Harvard isn't cheap."

"I did all right."

"You don't like to talk much about yourself, do you?"

He shrugged.

"I sometimes get the feeling the men around here are all hiding something."

"They're not," Youngblood said with a chuckle. "Although I'll bet they'd like you to think so. Makes them seem more mysterious, right? I reckon it's just the work we do. We're alone so much that it becomes a habit not to talk. You won't find a friendlier sort, though."

"Really?" she asked, her brows raised in disbelief. "I didn't notice anyone particularly friendly. Especially when I first arrived."

Youngblood grinned. "I suppose that was meant for me?" And at Morgan's if-the-shoe-fits look, he continued, "The men were probably afraid of you, you being so beautiful and all. Ain't that many women around these parts and beautiful ones are a mite hard to come by." His grin turned suddenly sly and teasing. "As for me, I could have been real friendly, only you didn't seem too happy about the idea."

"And I'm not happy about it now," she shot back, suddenly flustered. He thought she was beautiful. Morgan couldn't believe he'd said it so easily, as if discussing the weather or the time of day.

Youngblood was still laughing when, moments later, he brought his horse to a stop.

"Why are we stopping?"

"There's something behind that rock I want to show you," he said as he took his canteen and strapped it to his belt.

"Rock? You mean that mountain?"

"Aw honey, that ain't no mountain." He wanted to tell

her he'd take her farther west to the base of the Sierras someday. Then she'd know what real mountains looked like. But he knew she'd only remind him of her plans to leave. Ten minutes later they scaled the large rock. Morgan gasped her surprise as her eyes widened in astonishment.

"Valley of Fire," Youngblood announced as he pointed below to the huge flaming red rocks, some of which stood ten stories tall.

Morgan had never seen anything like it in her life. She'd never even imagined it. "It's beautiful," she whispered in awe, almost afraid to speak, for the silence of the desert had never been so thick, nor its view so majestic. The silent almost ethereal quality brought a soothing balm to her soul.

"I thought you'd like it. My great-great-grandpappy built his house with rocks brought from this valley."

Morgan breathed a long sigh of delight as her eyes took in the different shades of red. His arm came around her at her smile of delight and she looked up into dark, suddenly burning eyes. Morgan moved quickly away and nervously locked her lips. "Show me," she said. "I want to see more."

Together they skidded across the face of the rock and into the depth of the valley. From the floor Morgan could see hieroglyphic writings of some lost tribe embedded in rock high above them. "What does that say, I wonder?" she asked as her head tilted at such an extreme angle that her hat offered no protection from the sun.

"Most likely it's probably just pictures depicting a way of life. You want to climb up and see?"

Morgan returned his grin. "No, thank you."

"You want me to climb up and yell down what I read?"

Morgan laughed, a pure sweet sound that brought an instant ache to Youngblood's stomach. "I don't think so."

"Are you afraid I'll get hurt?"

"Not at all. I'm afraid you'll get killed."

"Aw honey, you worryin' about me?"

"Indeed." She smiled prettily as her eyes took on an impish light. "I might be lost for days if I had to find my way out of here alone."

Youngblood shot her a look of supposed disappointment. "Not exactly the answer I was looking for."

Morgan laughed again. She hadn't felt this good in months. From the beginning there had been this sexual tension, but she had grown angry at each and every confrontation. Why, she wondered, was she suddenly able to laugh? Morgan dismissed the thought as she climbed another rock and gasped at still more flaming color. "I can't believe this. I wonder why this part of the desert is red."

Youngblood, who had followed her up the rock, only shrugged, having no answer. He pointed below them. "There's a cave. Want to investigate?"

Morgan smiled for an answer as she led the way. Her hand held firmly in his, she half walked, half slid down the rock. Beneath them was a shallow, dried-up gully that gaped about six feet wide and ran three feet and better deep. Apparently it had once held water, for it snaked through an otherwise flat valley floor for some distance in a weaving pattern.

Youngblood jumped into the dry riverbed and warned, "Stay here until I call out. I want to make sure the cave is empty."

She nodded and obediently sat, her legs dangling over the sharp edge of rock. Morgan, so enthralled with her vivid surroundings, never noticed the gleam in his eyes. From the edge of her peripheral vision she saw him test the ease with which his gun slipped its leather holster, but took no real notice. Later she'd realize she should have suspected him up to no good, for she knew enough about his character to expect the worst. Because of her surroundings, Morgan wasn't as alert to him as she could have been.

Youngblood was determined to correct that oversight.

201

And maybe, if he was lucky, she might even reevaluate her feelings. After she got over her anger that is.

He was gone a long time. At first Morgan was too busy looking at the amazing colors and shapes of rocks to take much notice, but soon enough she began to realize she'd been alone for an unusual length of time. "Youngblood," she called out as a sudden burst of nerves rushed through her body. Where in God's name had he gone off to? The cave didn't look large enough to get lost in, but of course she couldn't tell for sure until she entered it. Had he fallen down? Was he hurt? A chill of fear slid over her and caused a shiver to race down her back.

Morgan jumped the few feet that separated her from the gully floor. Seconds later she was walking into the cave. "Youngblood!" she called out again, but she needn't have bothered, for the cave was so small and well lit due to its large entrance, she could see it was empty. About to turn and continue her search elsewhere, she noticed a shadow to her left.

Morgan followed the direction of her gaze and was surprised to find the shadow another opening, only this one was barely large enough for one person to squeeze through. She was in another cave, a small chamber of some sort off the main room. Here there were smooth slats of rock a foot off the floor that she imagined might have been used as beds, if this place had actually once had occupants. Along one wall was still another opening to another room.

Only this one was very dark. Morgan peered into the opening. She couldn't see a thing. "Youngblood," she called out fearfully, her heart thundering in her chest. Had he gone this far? Had he entered this darkness only to find a maze, and lose his way? Was it possible that there were many rooms like the two she'd already found? Another chill ran down her spine. If he was in there, would he ever find his way out? "Youngblood! Can you hear me?"

The moan came almost at her feet. Morgan gasped and

jumped back. "Joseph, is that you?"

He moaned again.

"Oh my God, are you hurt?" Morgan nearly flew into the room, heedless of the dark and the danger that might lay in wait. No sooner had she entered the room, than she tripped over his prone figure. Morgan, with a startled cry landed on her hands and knees. The problem was, her knees landed on him. One knee in a particularly vulnerable area.

The force of her fall brought Youngblood immediately alert and any grogginess from the falling rock that had struck his head was instantly forgotten. He couldn't think of anything but the burning pit of fire that had opened up in his loins. He rolled over in agony, clutching at his groin. Finding no relief, he rolled on his back again, his knees bent nearly to chin, his hand wedged somewhere in between.

"Jesus, God! What did you kick me for?" he asked between gasping, anguished breaths.

"I didn't kick you. I fell over you," she returned, somewhat stunned to find herself on the floor beside a writhing man so obviously in pain. "What were you doing on the floor?"

"Taking a nap," he snarled, still in the throes of unbearable agony. "What the hell do you think?"

Morgan continued to watch him squirm, knowing instinctively there was no comfort she could offer. Suddenly she realized or thought she realized, why she'd fallen over him. "You were waiting to scare me, weren't you?"

Youngblood took a deep breath, trying to will away the throbbing ache that refused to give up. He shot her his meanest look, the very one that had caused many a man to wonder if he'd live to see the sunset of that day. The threat had no effect on her, however, since the lighting, even from this angle, was barely enough to see him, never mind recognize his anger. And even had she recognized it, Morgan wasn't afraid of this man, no matter

203

his moods.

Morgan simply placed her hands on her hips and waited for her answer.

Obviously none too happy to admit to his folly, he finally grunted somewhat sulkily, "That was the idea at first. I was leaning back against that wall, waiting for you to come looking for me, when a rock fell and hit me on the head. It knocked me senseless."

"Good. God punished you for trying to scare me," she declared righteously.

"Your sympathy is greatly appreciated," he grated out between clenched teeth. "Did I deserve a knee in the groin as well? Jesus"—he flexed his legs gently—"I think you maimed me for life. I'll be lucky if I can—"

"Don't say it!" she snapped, coming to her knees and leaning threateningly over him.

"Say what?" Despite his pain, Youngblood grinned at the anxious expression in her eyes.

"Whatever it was you were going to say."

"Why?"

"Because knowing you, it's probably some vile curse and I've had more than enough of your dirty talk."

"Honey," he drawled softly, "I haven't talked dirty to you in weeks." Despite his pain, Youngblood chuckled wickedly. "Seems to me you might be needin' another dose."

"You rogue," Morgan managed in a voice suddenly tight. She was more than a little thankful that the shadows of the room hid cheeks that grew hot at the sensual sound of his voice.

Youngblood laughed as he allowed his legs to return to the floor. The pain was still there but bearable. "I'd be happy to give you another dose, if that's what you've a hankerin' for."

"Actually, Mr. Youngblood, I think I'll forgo the pleasure."

Youngblood watched her as a tender smile played upon his lips. If he weren't in such damn awful shape, he would have caught her to him and hugged her breathless. He moaned as his hand reached for his aching head. "All I was going to say was I'll be lucky if I can walk again."

Morgan eased back to sit on her feet. "That was not what you were going to say and you know it."

"It was. I swear it," but his grin belied what should have been solemn words.

Morgan moved so that she sat near his head. Carefully she raised his head to her lap. Gentle searching fingers found what was fast becoming a good-sized bump.

"Ow! That hurts!"

"You'll have to help me, Joseph. I can't get you out of here alone." She bent, and tenderly, without a thought, kissed his forehead.

Youngblood suddenly decided he wasn't all that uncomfortable after all. Even the sharp edge of a rock digging into his back suddenly mattered not in the least. "In a minute," he sighed, more than happy for the moment to accept her small ministrations.

"Come on," Morgan said as she came to her feet. "We'd better get outside. If a piece of this ceiling fell, there's no telling when another might come crashing down."

"Probably all right now," he grunted as he came to shaking legs. "A chunk was loose and I was fiddlin' with the damn thing when it came down on my head."

Morgan gave a low chuckle. It was beyond her imagination why a grown man would hide in a cave in the first place, never mind play with part of its ceiling.

"Don't laugh at me, honey. My head is killing me."

"Poor baby," she crooned, as she slid his arm over her shoulder. Morgan held on to his side and guided him from the dark room.

In the second chamber she had him sit on one of the slats of rock. "Are you dizzy?"

"A little."

"How little?" she asked with a definite edge to her voice.

"Don't worry. I'll give you directions back before I die."

"Youngblood, don't be a beast."

"It's just that I know how you worry over my welfare."

Morgan wasn't about to tell him she did indeed worry over his welfare. No doubt the man would use the information heartlessly. And she certainly wasn't going to add to the arsenal of weapons he already possessed. Still, she couldn't deny the terror that gripped her heart when she watched him try to come to his feet. There was no way he could scale those huge rocks. Not in his present condition. "We're staying here tonight," she said as she easily pushed him back to the rock bed. "I'll go get our things."

Youngblood shook his head and then moaned at the stupid action as a wave of dizziness almost dumped him on the floor. "It'll be cold. The desert is freezing at night. We won't be able to build a fire in here."

Morgan looked around. He was right. There were no openings in the roof, no windows. Nothing but the door that led to the outside room. She shrugged, knowing she had no real alternative. Youngblood couldn't possibly climb this rock, not in his present condition. "Stay here. I'll be right back."

Morgan took some time retrieving their things. First she had to unsaddle both animals, tie them as best she could to the weakest-looking cactus she'd ever seen, knowing they needed but one pull to set themselves free. She rubbed them down. Gave each a few mouthfuls of oats and water.

Saddlebags over her shoulders, both bedrolls and her canteen tied around her neck, two coats under her arms, she finally stumbled back into the cave, only to find Youngblood, soaked with sweat, leaning weakly against the wall, one step from the narrow opening. "What the hell took you so long?"

Morgan gave a grunt of annoyance as she threw the

206

articles to the floor. "Didn't I tell you to lie down?"

"Actually, no you didn't. What you said was, 'Stay here.'"

Morgan shot him a withering glance. "Now you'll have to change your clothes. You're soaked."

Youngblood slid down the wall to a sitting position. "Can't. Too weak," he mumbled as his head fell forward, his chin resting upon his chest. He couldn't stay awake.

Morgan hurried with her chore. She made up a bed of sorts with their two blankets, knowing she was about to spend the most uncomfortable night of her life, as she eyed the rock floor. She emptied the bags as she glanced toward the opening to the room. She'd have to hurry. Soon it would be dark, and without a fire she'd never even find this makeshift bed.

Morgan knelt at Youngblood's side. "Joseph, wake up. I can't do this by myself," she said as she unbuttoned his shirt and pulled it from his trousers. The shirt came off easy enough, but she had a time of it getting his arms into another. Then came the coat.

Morgan was sweating herself by the time she yanked off his boots and replaced his socks with a clean pair. "Stand up so I can get these pants off."

Youngblood managed to do her bidding, but not without some effort on Morgan's part. She was leaning against him to keep him in place as she fumbled first with his gun belt and then the buttons of his trousers. Finally she opened his pants and slid them down his legs. She bent to pull them free of his ankles when she came to a sudden stop. "Youngblood!" she gasped, "for god's sake!"

Youngblood chuckled. "Guess it works after all."

Morgan, with cheeks ablaze, glanced up into dark eyes that twinkled momentarily with amusement. She never noticed the cloud of pain as another wave of dizziness rocked him. "You fraud! Think you're very funny, don't you?" She shoved his clean trousers into his hands. "Finish it yourself."

Youngblood might have explained, but decided against it, for the moment. He was too tired and she'd never believe he had no control over the arousal her fumbling fingers had brought about. Even knowing that in his present weakened condition he couldn't do a damn thing about it, he'd been helpless as she rubbed against him.

"What are you doing?"

"I'm lying down," he said as he moved almost drunkenly toward the blanket, after dropping his pants at his feet. "What does it look like?"

Morgan might have laughed at the ridiculous sight of a man dressed in nothing more than socks and a coat. A coat which did nothing to disguise the fact that he wore not a stitch below his waist. She might have laughed if she hadn't felt terror as she watched him move. He was hurt. Seriously hurt, and all she could do was watch and pray he'd soon get better.

Suddenly her eyes rounded with horror as she realized what he was doing. Dumbly she watched him slide between the blankets. "Get dressed!" she said, the panic in her voice unmistakable.

"This is more comfortable."

Morgan muttered a most unladylike curse. "You are a beast! How am I supposed to sleep with you dressed like that?"

"Aw honey," he moaned as he clutched his head. "Don't yell at me. My head is killing me."

"Youngblood," she said more softly. "There's no fire. We have to sleep together. You must get dressed."

"Don't worry. I'm too sick to bother you."

"You didn't look very sick a few minutes ago."

Youngblood chuckled and then moaned as his laughter threatened an explosion inside his head. A moment later he was snoring.

Morgan watched him for a long time. Suddenly she realized the light was almost gone. Quickly she changed her shirt and slid into her sheepskin coat. It was dark by the time she moved carefully beneath the blanket.

208

Chapter Twelve

Four hundred miles west in Virginia City sat two men. It was dark. They sat quietly, straining hungrily for that all-important sound, hearing only the rapid beatings of their heart in the stillness of the small cramped cell. The almost suffocating heat coupled with nearly debilitating anxiety coated their bodies with sweat as they watched the seconds tick by into minutes and those minutes speed along with the agonizing hurry into hours. Hours that brought them ever closer to sunrise and the hangman's noose awaiting them.

It had to be tonight. Their brother had to make good on his promise. This was their last chance.

A guard, at least they supposed it was a guard, for the density of light forbade knowing for sure, walked on near silent feet. Eyes wide, they watched his shadowed form pass the door to their cell. Something small and metallic, from the sound of it, fell to the stone floor. Jake whispered a round of nervous curses, for the soft clink sounded as loud to his ears as a cannon blast. Instantly he was down on his knees, his fingers trembling as they hurried, brushing against uneven stone as they searched.

A thin stream of moonlight filtered through the high barred windows into the cell, its meagerness bringing no real help. Jake cursed as his fingers reached on, feeling for the one thing that could bring freedom. He found it! A wide slow smile showed missing and blackened teeth while the scar that ran from the corner of his eyes to his jaw deepened.

Slowly, carefully, silently, he inserted the key into the lock. The well-oiled tumbler turned easily. Jake motioned for Mike to follow. The two men stood in the dark corridor. Without the aid of the moonlight, they might have stumbled along blindly in their desperate search for freedom, but in their case there was no need for light. Each man had endlessly counted the steps. Twenty-three to the right stood a door. Beyond that another corridor. Fifteen more and the last obstacle to their freedom.

They might have been barefooted, for not a sound was heard above the choppy snores and sleepy grunts of those who slept beyond the barred doors.

Jake removed the gun from his belt. He'd had the Colt 44 almost a month. It had been smuggled in to him inside one of those blankets the charitable ladies from the town occasionally brought to the prison. Jake grinned. The guards never checked those blankets. Somehow, he didn't know how, the basket meant for him had reached the right cell.

The guard never knew what hit him. The moment he moved out of the tiny area of light, a soft grunt escaped his lips as the steel of the gun barrel came crashing down to contact with the back of his skull.

Careful of any excess noise, Mike caught the man before his unconscious body hit the floor. Gently he lowered him, but not before Jake made a quick search.

The keys! The goddamned keys! Where were they?

Jake spent a silent near hysterical moment as he continued his search. He couldn't believe it. To have come this far, only to be stopped midway because he couldn't find the keys! Sonofabitch! What was he going to do?

More clearly than ever Jake imagined the rope tightening around his neck. In frustration he slammed his hand against the metal door. It took a moment before he realized it had moved. Christ! The door was open! Jake almost sagged with the wave of relief that assailed him, but he pushed the emotion aside. It was too soon. He wasn't out yet. He and his brother had yet another checkpoint to master. One more door.

Again they moved, hugging the wall as they closed the distance between them and freedom. A guard sat at his desk in a soft pool of light. A glass kerosene lamp hung overhead suspended from the wall by a nail, giving off more than enough light for the guard to read his penny novel.

The keys were sitting in plain sight this time. Thrown carelessly upon the desk, waiting, just waiting for him.

Silently the two moved up behind the guard. It was over in seconds. Jake hadn't meant to kill the man. It was just that he was so anxious to reach the door. He'd hit him a bit too hard.

Jake shrugged, feeling not a twinge of conscience at the unnecessary death. In truth he had no qualms about killing anyone. Especially the law.

Outside!

Jesus, what a relief to breathe the smell of clean air. He hadn't realized how fetid the stench was inside until he took his first lungful of cold desert air. Silently he swore his days of incarceration were at an end. They'd never get him again. He'd die before they took him back.

Carefully his eyes searched out the dark yard. Two guards stood off to one side smoking a cigarette. Four more at their individual posts, one at each corner, atop the wide wall. The light was faint at best. He couldn't see more than vague outlines. Still he knew they were there.

Bent over, almost hugging the ground, the brothers ran from the darkly shadowed building straight to the center of one wall between two guard posts. A stone wall eight feet high and two feet wide was easily mounted. First Jake was boosted up. He lay along the top ledge. The five rows of barbed wire were barely noticed, even as they cut into his back and chest. He reached for his brother's

211

extended hand, pulling him up beside him.

A second later they rolled off the top and jumped to freedom.

Ten yards from the wall stood a small copse of trees. Beyond the trees sat a man upon a horse. In his hands were the reins of two more horses. "What the hell took you so long?" Larry, the last brother, inquired. "I've been waiting for hours."

"Let's ride," Jake said, ignoring the question. He was free! Jesus, he'd waited months for this night. Exhilaration filled every fiber of his body. He wanted to laugh with the sheer joy of being free at last, but he didn't. He remembered instead the treatment he'd received while inside. There was no room for laughter amid the hate.

His mouth turned grim. He was going to get the bastard who had put him there. An evil smile touched his lips as he imagined the pain the man would suffer. He would find him, of that he hadn't a doubt. But not tonight. No, not tonight. Tonight they would ride. Ride until their horses couldn't go a step farther. He wondered if he'd ever feel he was far enough away.

Morgan came slowly awake. Her hips and shoulder ached something awful, but at least she was warm. During the freezing night she'd had cause to wonder if she'd live to see this morning. God, she couldn't remember when she'd known such cold.

In her sleep she had turned to Youngblood, unconsciously seeking his warmth. Now she was loath to leave the comfort of his arms. Silently she reasoned that it couldn't hurt to remain there for just a few minutes. She snuggled closer, her head pillowed on his arm, her nose against his warm chest.

Apparently, sometime during the night he had awakened, for his coat was rolled into a ball, used as a pillow, while his shirt lay open. His arm was thrown over her waist, holding her close to his otherwise naked body.

212

Surprisingly Morgan felt none of the alarm this comforting closeness should have caused. Even realizing his nakedness brought no qualm to her sleepy mind. In truth she allowed herself a stolen moment of pleasure, snuggled securely in his arms.

She pressed her face closer, breathing in the warm, musky, male scent of his skin, and sighed her pleasure. His arm tightened, bringing her closer against him, when she unthinkingly kissed the flesh that lay so temptingly close to her mouth.

Morgan glanced up and realized he was still asleep. Daringly she kissed him again, this time her lips and tongue lingering with enjoyment.

He shifted closer. She kissed him again.

Youngblood moaned.

Morgan jerked to awareness at the sound. Lord! What did she think she was doing? She moved hastily from his side and leaned up on her elbow. The sudden movement brought Youngblood's eyes open. "Are you in pain?" she asked, referring to the sound he'd just made.

He only closed his eyes and groaned again.

"Is there something I can do?"

A smile touched the corners of his mouth. "You can keep on with what you were doing. You were about to make it all better."

"You wretch," she said as soft color tinted her cheeks, her eyes tender, her lips smiling. She should have known he was awake. When was she going to learn not to trust this wily Indian? Morgan sat up and rubbed her hip. It was killing her. She'd known the night would bring no comfort, but till she'd actually lain down, she hadn't imagined how hard a rock floor could be. She only prayed she wouldn't have to sample it again. "Are you feeling better this morning?" she asked hopefully.

"Fine."

"No more dizziness?"

"If I don't move my head."

"And when you do?"

213

"Just a little."

"Well, a little is too much." Morgan's sigh was heavy with disappointment. "We'll have to stay here another night."

"Not likely," Youngblood grunted as he came up to his elbow. "I'm not spending a whole day cooped up in here. This place is like a goddamned tomb." He groaned as he came into a shaky sitting position. And at her worried look, he said, "It'll pass."

"No doubt, as will you, if you don't lie still," Morgan said as she pushed him to lie back again.

"Morgan, honey, I'm not stayin' here. It's too cold."

"You can't climb the rocks."

"I want some food. I want coffee, damn it!" He was as close to whining as Morgan could imagine. A smile touched her lips and lit up her blue eyes with delight, for this was the first time Youngblood had allowed her to see a side of him that was as far from his strong manly image as one could get. "How do you suppose we'll get it without a fire?"

"We can move to the outer room. I'll build a fire there, while you rest."

The man was a good deal weaker than he'd admit. Morgan wrapped the top blanket securely around him when it became apparent he hadn't even the strength to pull on his trousers. She had cause to wonder at her easily spoken comment when she finally managed to get him to his feet, for his weight nearly buckled her knees.

Morgan gasped as she was shoved back against the wall. Lord, how was she to manage this chore? The man didn't have the strength of a kitten, and despite his trim form, he weighed a ton. If she had any sense, she would have insisted he stay put.

His hands groped blindly as he strove for balance, brushing, she assumed by accident, over her breasts. Morgan never saw the wicked gleam of laughter in his eyes for he closed them the moment her head snapped up. Then he covered his actions with a deliberate groan, pretending even greater dizziness and pain than he actually endured.

Youngblood denied any guilt that might have come to another, that he should so callously take advantage. She was his wife, damn it! No matter her wishes to the contrary, the fact remained. And even if he didn't have his usual strength, he'd have to be dead before he was weak enough to resist the allure of her lush curves pressed enticingly against him.

It wasn't without some effort, for the walls swam around him with every movement, but Youngblood managed to hold on to her, while Morgan grabbed at the walls for support and inched her way at last to the outer room of the cave. They were both exhausted and gasping for breath as she allowed him to slide into a sitting position, and she breathed a sigh of relief as he leaned his head back against the wall.

Her legs trembled from exertion. "I never realized you were so heavy."

"Or you so strong," he mumbled thickly just before he drifted off to sleep.

It was evening. Morgan sat before a small but hot fire of fragrant sagebrush, a fire that provided them with all the heat they might need against the chill of the desert night. She was sipping at the last of her coffee, her gaze beyond the fire, her thoughts on the man who sat to her right.

Youngblood sighed as he finished the last of his bacon and beans. He put his empty plate near the fire.

"Are you feeling better?"

Youngblood nodded; having slept most of the day, he could honestly say the dizziness had finally gone. "Fine. We can leave in the morning." After a few minutes of silence he added, "You take well to this hard life."

Morgan shot him a look of annoyance. "Is that astonishment I hear in your voice?"

"Well, you can't blame me for being a bit surprised. You didn't complain once all day."

"Complain about what?"

Youngblood shrugged. "Your trip to feed and water the horses, preparing our food, gathering enough sagebrush to cushion our beds, starting a fire." He shrugged again. "Everything."

"That wouldn't have done much good, would it? Someone had to do it."

"I know, but considering where you came from . . ."

"Are you about to insult me again?" she interrupted.

Youngblood smiled. "Actually, I think I was complimenting you."

"Thank you." She shot him a suspicious look. "I think.

"Why do you hate people from the city? Or is it ladies from New York City you hate?"

"I don't hate them."

"Oh really? I wonder why I got the impression you did."

"I'm sure I couldn't say."

"You didn't like me when I first got here, did you."

"It had nothing to do with you. I didn't like you *before* you came here."

Morgan smiled, her eyes widening with surprise. "Why?"

"I thought you'd be a typically spoiled, rich young lady. Someone who wouldn't dirty her hands with honest work. No doubt ready to look down her nose upon us peasants and eager to order everyone to do her bidding."

"I am rich," she returned honestly. "And I hadn't worked a day in my life till I came here. Why doesn't that bother you anymore?"

"I reckon being rich isn't the worst thing in the world."

"And spoiled?"

"You're getting better."

"Thanks," she said dryly. "It couldn't be, of course, that you easily recognize my faults because yours are much the same."

"Certainly not," he remarked with some vehemence, but his dark eyes twinkled as he glanced her way.

"I didn't think so," she agreed. "No doubt that swagger you have and the orders you bark out are merely figments of my imagination."

"Do I swagger?" Youngblood grinned.

"Like a man who owns the world."

"Well, I do own my small part of it."

"And as far as being stubborn, thick-headed, and—"

Youngblood was laughing. He reached his arm around her and pulled her against him until she was suddenly sprawled over his lap. "Aw honey, I wasn't that bad."

Morgan shot him a nasty look. "Actually, you were far worse."

"Why did you stay then?"

"Because you told me I should leave."

"Stubborn," Youngblood nodded as if she'd just confirmed his suspicions.

"Pig-headed," she returned.

Youngblood grinned. "Determined."

"That's not an insult."

"No, but a determined brat is."

Morgan giggled and leaned comfortably into him. "Mean-tempered, grouchy, arrogant . . ."

"Beautiful."

Her lips parted, but the words wouldn't come. He'd suddenly changed the game and Morgan marveled at how easily this new tension between them had come about.

"Nothing else to say?" she asked tenderly.

"Are you fishing for compliments?" she asked as she strove to keep the moment light. Morgan was all too aware of the comfort she felt in his arms and she wasn't sure she liked it one bit.

"Are you nervous?"

"Of course not," she returned quickly, but she was. Morgan knew he was naked beneath the blanket that was thrown carelessly over his lap. He'd slept most of the day. Time and again she'd found herself covering him, since he constantly threw his covers off in sleep. Her mouth grew dry and a tightening formed in the pit of her belly as she remembered the long brown muscular length of him.

"Do you like it when I hold you?"

"It's all right." She shrugged.

"You don't mind, then?" he asked as his hand caught a length of her hair and pulled the sweetly scented mass of curls toward his mouth. His mind returned to a time when it had flowed so beautifully over his stomach. Idly he wondered how much longer he'd have to wait to feel it again.

"I guess not."

"Are you afraid of me?"

Morgan shot him a look of utter disbelief. "Hardly."

"Then why are you so stiff?"

"Because we both know you shouldn't be holding me like this."

"I thought we agreed it was all right for us to hug and kiss."

Morgan shrugged, saying nothing.

"I won't demand my husbandly rights if that's what you're afraid of."

"I told you I wasn't afraid," she returned quickly and not without some annoyance. "Why?"

Youngblood grinned. "Why won't I demand my rights?" he asked, and then smiled at her nod. "Because I think it's time my wife came to me."

Morgan stiffened even further, clearly aghast. Suddenly her eyes widened with amused incredulity, while a smile touched her lips. "You mean you want me to . . ."

There was a long moment of silence before Youngblood laughed. "Can't you say it?"

"Of course I can say it," she said softly. "You want me to seduce you."

"Not at all, although I wouldn't fight you should you set your mind to it. I want you to make love to me. There's a great difference."

"And unless I do, nothing will happen between us?"

she asked, never realizing the odd mixture of amazement, hope, and dread in her whisper.

"And unless you do, nothing will happen between us."

Morgan couldn't honestly say if the idea made her happy or sad. She should feel a measure of relief, shouldn't she? So why then did she feel anything but? She forced a cocky grin. "Take my advice and don't count on it."

"Why?"

"I wouldn't want you to suffer undue disappointment."

"Meaning you're not about to make love to me?"

She laughed with all confidence. "Sometimes you show remarkable insight."

"Then it wouldn't matter all that much if I kissed you and touched you."

"You shouldn't. It will serve no purpose."

"Aw, honey, be fair. I ain't askin' much, am I?"

Morgan sighed, having no argument to offer. The man certainly had rights. He was her husband, after all. And he wasn't asking all that much. What harm could there be to allow him this request?

"Suppose I'm not having a baby. What are we going to do?"

"What do you want to do?"

Morgan shrugged. "Go back East, I guess." Morgan appeared to have forgotten her plan to return to New York with her father and Youngblood wasn't about to remind her. But she hadn't forgotten. Idly she wondered if her plans were at all possible. Would her father accept the situation? Would he allow her to return to his house? She knew he'd be less than pleased with this whole affair, but would he be angry enough to not forgive her this?

"You miss living there?"

"Not at all. Actually, I love it here."

"So why wouldn't you stay, no matter what happens?"

"Joseph, we couldn't live together. Not if we were divorced. And where else could I go but back East?"

"And you're planning on dissolving the marriage if there's no child?"

"Of course. It's the reason we married, isn't it?"

Youngblood didn't answer her question. He didn't know the reason why they married. All he knew was he wasn't about to let this woman go. "Morgan. I think I should tell you something before you make any specific plans."

"What?"

"There isn't going to be a divorce."

"Meaning?"

"Meaning, you're my wife. Things aren't going to change."

"I didn't want to marry you in the first place," she stated firmly as she pulled out of his arms. "You can't keep me a prisoner here."

"But you did marry me."

"And if there's no baby?"

"There'll be a baby eventually."

Morgan came to her feet and walked to the edge of the cave. She looked out upon the black night and waited for the anger to come. Oddly enough it did not. Certainly she should feel something, shouldn't she? Annoyance perhaps at his unwavering insistence, his arrogance, his daring to dictate her life? She wanted to leave here, didn't she? She didn't want to stay as his wife. Lord, most of the time she could hardly stand the man. So why was it she felt this confusion? Why wasn't she furious? Why did she feel so thoroughly dissatisfied? What exactly was it she wanted?

Morgan glanced behind her to find Youngblood had dozed off to sleep again. He wore only his shirt. The blanket came to his hip, while one long brown leg was left uncovered. Morgan's gaze moved over his form. God, he was something to look at. It had been impossible to keep her eyes off him as he slept today. His body was beautiful. Hard, strong, perfectly shaped, deliciously unyielding against her own. She gave a weary sigh as she realized the direction her thoughts had taken. She hoped he was better in the morning. She didn't want to stay here any longer. And most of all, she didn't want to think.

Morgan cleaned up the remains of supper and added to the fire before she settled herself upon her mat. It wasn't as hard as last night, what with the sagebrush gathered and crushed beneath the blanket. Still it had a way to go before it could be considered comfortable. It was warm by the fire. She rolled up her coat and used it as a pillow. Morgan thought she'd lay awake for hours worrying over his last words, but to her surprise, she drifted almost immediately off to sleep.

She didn't consciously feel him slide into her bedroll, but her body turned to welcome his warmth. Morgan snuggled herself against him and sighed with contentment as his arms came around her.

Youngblood watched his stubborn young wife in the light of the fire and wondered what it was about her that so intrigued. She was a beauty, yes. But there were other women equally beautiful and not nearly as stubborn. Why then was it he wanted her and only her? Was it because she refused him? Was his intent merely to conquer? Youngblood shook his head. No. She had come to him once. That night in the kitchen and then afterward in his room, she'd been eager to learn all. He'd come to know her body that night, better perhaps than she did herself. And still he'd wanted her. He didn't know how, but he knew there'd never be a time when he wouldn't.

Youngblood cuddled her closer and sighed with delight at the ecstasy of her along the length of his body. Whether she liked it or not, she belonged to him. She wasn't going anywhere, not as long as he lived.

She was dreaming that dream again. She'd been haunted by its sensuality almost every night since she'd first discovered the delicious pleasures shared between men and women. Morgan groaned. She didn't want to suffer this again. The dreams always left her so empty, so hungry. She didn't want to feel the aching dissatisfaction

221

that always came upon awakening.

Morgan tipped her face up as he teased her lips with a gentle brushing of his mouth. Warm lips moved down her throat to intensify the heat that was growing to life in her belly. She arched her back ever so slightly, aching for this sweetest of tortures, no matter the disappointment she'd be sure to know, and then sighed with delight as his mouth took the tip of her breast deep into its flaming heat.

Morgan sighed with sadness as his mouth left her breast. She'd awaken now. And as always, she'd suffer the ache her dream left behind. But no, not this time. The dream was going on. Morgan groaned with satisfaction as the damp heat moved to her other breast. "More," she murmured, still more asleep than awake. "I want more."

"Do you, honey?" came a deep voice close to her lips and then he was kissing her, deeply, desperately, hungrily, as if he'd never get enough of the taste of her. "I'll give you more tonight, if you want."

"Joseph," she murmured as his lips left her mouth and returned to her breasts. "What are you doing?"

"I'm waking you up, sweetheart. It's time for us to be going." Youngblood was greatly tempted to stay put for yet another day, but knew the impossibility of the notion. The idea, although appealing, wasn't feasible. Breakfast would see the last of their supplies.

Morgan gave a dreamy smile. "Is this the way you usually wake someone up?"

Youngblood's mouth released her breast and he grinned down at her. She wasn't trying to cover herself. Her arms were around his neck, her hips pressed tightly against his. "The only people I wake up are my men and I think they'd shoot me if I tried this."

Morgan giggled at the thought. "Either that or give you some peculiar looks."

"No," he said as he dipped his head for a final delicious tasting. "Now that I think of it, they definitely would

222

shoot me."

He kissed her again.

Her head was spinning when he finally slid his lips across her cheek, his tongue finding great delight in the shape of her ear. "They don't know what they're missing," she murmured softly.

"And they're never going to find out."

He kissed her again.

"Coffee's ready, honey. We'd better get dressed. We have a long ride ahead of us."

Morgan sighed her obvious disappointment as he left her. The sigh, however, became a strangled gasp as Youngblood came to his feet and loomed over her. He yawned and stretched without the slightest thought to his nakedness, nor the fully aroused state of his body.

"Joseph! For God's sake!"

"What?" he asked, glancing down at her reddening cheeks.

"Do you have to walk around like that?" she asked, trying valiantly to ignore his nakedness.

"There's no one here to see."

"I can see."

"You're my wife," he said with a shrug that clearly discounted any complaints she might have made. "You'll have to start getting used to seeing me like this." Youngblood felt a slight shiver as her gaze was helplessly drawn to his body. He watched it move over the length of him, her admiration obvious. Jesus, if she kept looking at him like that, they might not leave here for a week, food or no.

"I can't imagine ever getting used to it."

"Don't worry honey. I'm sure after forty or fifty years, you won't give it a thought."

"It just might take me that long," she grunted as she turned away and adjusted her clothes.

Youngblood felt his heart leap with gladness. She wasn't arguing with him. She wasn't threatening to leave. She hadn't made one comment disputing what he'd just

223

said. She seemed to accept it. He couldn't be more amazed or pleased, but judging from the way she'd welcomed his kisses, he wouldn't have long to wait on that score.

The river was wide, the water wild and muddy as it tore everything from soil to small trees and even an occasional rock from its sharp banks into its path as it raced along the desert floor.

"There must have been a storm in the mountains. This gully is usually dry," Youngblood said as his gaze slid over the turbulent waters.

"Gully? You mean this isn't a river?"

Youngblood smiled. "It'll probably be dry tomorrow. The trouble is, we can't wait. We can last a day without food, but the horses need their feed. We'll have to cross it."

His gaze moved to the water again. "It's not deep. Don't be afraid." He was wrong. It was very deep, for the force of water had ripped away the bottom of the gully until it was at least three feet deeper than usual.

"I'm not afraid," she returned with a trusting smile. "You want me to hold your reins?"

She shook her head in the negative.

"Maybe you should sit with me till we cross."

Morgan smiled at his concern. "I'll be fine."

Youngblood nodded, his lips tight with worry. "Just go slow and stay at my side."

Morgan returned his nod, her eyes bright with excitement as she urged her horse into the churning waters. A moment later the horse was swimming, the water coming clear to her saddle. Morgan laughed, but the laughter was from nerves, the sound disguising well her fear. The trouble was, Youngblood didn't recognize what he heard over the rush of water. He looked at her smiling face, a face that hid well her anxiety and frowned.

One moment she was at his side, the next her horse was

pulling ahead. Youngblood cursed as he tried to reach out and take her reins, but she moved again, just out of his grasp. She was having a terrible time controlling the animal, but her expression gave not a flicker of her distress. She smiled brightly at Youngblood's scowl.

They were halfway across when a huge, sharp rock slammed into the side of her horse, cutting deep into both the animal and her leg. Morgan never felt the pain, so startled was she as the animal lurched beneath her. She yanked at the reins, trying desperately to bring the panicked horse under control, but the horse screamed its fury and panicked further. Wildly it lunged ahead, trying to free itself from the torment. Morgan held on for dear life. Even when he went under, his leg crumbling from the agony that filled his side, she couldn't seem to let go.

In an instant she slid beneath the rumbling churning water and disappeared from view.

His first instinct was to jump in after her, but despite his near panic state, Youngblood knew enough to remain on his horse. It might mean both their lives. He had to keep his wits about him. Without his horse, he'd never be able to win a battle against raging water like this. *Find her!* his mind screamed as panic threatened to close over him. *Find her! Find her!*

He saw her booted foot come to the surface and immediately disappear into the muddy thick water. Jesus, she was going to die! She was going to die if he didn't get her out!

He guided Thunder further down the gully, praying with every step that she wasn't somewhere beneath the water, already dead, trampled by his own horse.

Amazingly a cloud of silver and gold suddenly brushed against his leg. In an instant his hand had reached for the filmy stuff, never realizing, at first that it was her hair. His look was pure amazement as her head cleared the bubbling, rolling surface.

His arm reached down then, circling like a band of steel

beneath her breasts, lifting her to lean against his horse as he made for shore. He was off his horse in a flash, crushing her limp form against his.

He heard her moan and was filled with a relief that held no bounds. He felt tears sting his eyes, just before a righteous rage filled his being. How could she have done this? How could she have so casually endangered her life? Never mind the horse. Didn't she care what happened to her? Didn't she know he wouldn't have been able to stand the pain if she had died?

"Damn you!" He shook her hard, her head snapping weakly back and forth. "Damn you," he almost bellowed into her dazed face. "Why didn't you listen? Why do you always fight me?" He shoved her hard. Her legs, unable to support her weight, crumbled beneath her. She hit the ground.

Morgan came slowly to her senses and then groaned as the nausea hit. A second later the dirty water that had been helplessly drawn in as she instinctively screamed out for help came bubbling up into her throat. She was doubled over, her stomach emptying itself of the dreadful water. She shivered at the ghastly taste, the harsh wracking heaves hurting almost as much as Youngblood's apparent unconcern.

A horrible crushing weight settled itself somewhere in the region of her chest, but Morgan's pride wouldn't allow herself to give in to its breathless promise. The beast would never know his careless disregard bothered her in the least. She had almost died. She'd been flipped about beneath the water's surface as if she weighed no more than a feather, turning somersaults until she grew unsure which direction was up and which down. And what did he do? He turned his back on her suffering. Morgan's smile was bittersweet. He had saved her, yes, but it was obvious her life meant no more to him than one of his horses. She sighed as she pushed aside the hurt that knowledge brought about. After all, it wasn't his fault. One couldn't force another to care. Still, he could have pretended some compassion, especially since they'd shared such tender moments only this morning.

Morgan came unassisted to her feet, the pain in her chest so great she never felt the agony in her leg. She wiped her mouth on the edge of her shirt and tucked it neatly into her waistband. It took a moment, but she finally forced herself to ignore the trembling in her arms and legs. With her fingers she combed through her hair and squeezed out the excess water. A moment later it was pulled from her face as she plaited it into one thick braid that hung to her waist.

She wouldn't think of her beautiful horse, or she'd surely cry. Then Youngblood, of course, would assume she cried for herself. Despite his beliefs, she'd suffer the ravages of hell before she'd allow herself that weakness. Her hat was gone, her coat, her bedroll, all her supplies plus a change of clothes. Morgan knew the desert sun would soon find her dry, but clean? She wondered when she'd again be allowed that luxury.

Youngblood stood still, his back to her, his heart twisting with pain, especially at the sound of her gut-wrenching heaves. But he wouldn't go to her. No! She had to be made to understand that he was her husband and as such he expected to be obeyed. Her foolishness had nearly cost her her life. Damn her! He felt the panic rise again. What would he have done if he hadn't found her? Or worse yet, if he had found her dead?

He shivered with horror. The subject didn't bear thinking on. It wasn't as if he loved her or anything. He didn't, of course. It was anger he felt, nothing more. Anger and concern, but no more than he'd feel for any human being. There was a principle involved here. In times such as these she should have simply obeyed his orders. He swore in the future she would.

Youngblood turned to face her at last. She looked so small, so utterly forlorn. Shorter wisps of blond hair hung loose and clung wetly to her face. Beneath the layer of mud, her skin was terribly pale and she trembled so badly he wondered if she'd be able to stand up much longer. Youngblood felt a sharp pang in his chest and almost reached out for her then, but pulled himself back as he remembered the deliberate act that had nearly cost her her life. She had thought it a lark. He could tell by the glow in her eyes. So she had deliberately disobeyed his orders. Yes, he knew her appearance to be deceptive. She was a strong woman, strong and more willful than he would have liked. Her white shirt was streaked brown to a shade that almost matched her split skirt and vest. Her creamy skin was hidden beneath mud and her hair was dulled with none of its usual golden-silver glow. And yet she'd never looked more beautiful.

Youngblood forced aside the tenderness that assailed. His lips tightened as he allowed the rage, almost thankful that it should come upon him now. "Because of your foolishness, your horse is dead. You'll have to walk the rest of the way," he said roughly, seemingly without care as he turned and mounted his horse and began to trot away. He couldn't trust himself to look at her for another minute, lest he take her in his arms and babble like a child the terror he'd known.

Morgan, in a state of shock at her near miss with death, merely nodded, her gaze held to the ground, refusing to witness his gloating at her misfortune. Her back stiffened with pride. She'd walk, all right. She'd walk all the way to Russia if she had to and never ask him for a thing along the way.

Morgan snickered evilly. Amazing, wasn't it? When he was injured, she hadn't hesitated about seeing to his care. Now that misfortune had fallen upon her, he turned his back and rode away, never bothering to ask how she fared. Morgan bit back the tears of self-pity that threatened and raised her chin a notch. What difference did it make? She didn't need his concern. She'd lived twenty-four years without it. She could live another twenty-four . . . forty-eight, for that matter, before she'd turn to him for comfort. In truth his treatment mattered not in the least.

Chapter Thirteen

It was hot. Morgan knew it was hot. Hot enough to have dried her clothes within minutes. Odd then that she should be shivering with cold. Vaguely she wondered why that should be.

She'd been walking perhaps ten minutes. Youngblood kept his horse at an incredibly slow pace, never more than twenty-five feet or so ahead and yet he might have been miles in distance, for Morgan knew she had no chance to keep up. Every step she took became a study in concentration, the effort so great she beagn to hope he'd simply forget her existence and leave her behind. She didn't want to face his scowls, for whatever the reason this time. She merely wanted to sit down and rest in peace. A low giggle bubbled up from her throat at the oddly appropriate phrasing.

She glanced again at his straight back. Ramrod straight, she knew, from anger. Indeed he had been angry; it would be closer to the truth to say he'd been enraged. What she didn't know was why. Could it be he was upset because she hadn't died when her horse went under? If so, why had he gone to the trouble of searching her out? Why had he crushed her to him in a hold that bespoke his desperation? Desperation, even her dazed mind had no trouble understanding, only to turn his back on her?

She trudged along, her every thought and effort on taking the next step. Her leg was badly bruised. She'd suffered numerous bruises and scrapes over nearly the entire length of her body, but her leg felt on fire.

She stumbled and found herself suddenly on her hands and knees, staring for a second with incomprehension at the desert floor. For just a moment she played with the thought to remain where she was forever. She needed to rest. Her whole body was trembling and this time it wasn't due to the shock of falling into those deadly waters, but weakness. Lord, she'd never known such absolute and utter weakness.

But Youngblood would never know. She'd gladly die before she let that happen. He hadn't once glanced behind him since he'd callously left her to follow. Morgan hadn't a doubt in her mind that he cared not at all for her welfare.

She took a deep breath and tried to get up, but the pain in her leg suddenly caused her to gasp. Something was wrong. Why should her leg hurt so terribly? Her blue gaze moved to the aching appendage. Morgan heard the low sound of surprise only to realize it was herself as she nearly swooned at the startling knowledge that her skirt leg was covered with blood. Blood that had dried and had now turned a brownish red as it coated her leg and puddled in her boot.

Her first instinct had been to call out for help, but she remembered in time his careless treatment since he'd dragged her from the water and knew the uselessness of that notion. She bit back the words while tears of self-pity and exhaustion stung her eyes. Her hands shook as she raised the leg of her split skirt. A buzzing sounded in her ears and the desert landscape seemed to swim at a crazy angle before her eyes.

Forcing her hands to move, she found the injury high on her thigh. There was a deep gash, perhaps four inches wide. She dared not investigate further, knowing she hadn't the stomach to know just how deep. It was enough to realize she was bleeding still and badly. Morgan had attributed her uncharacteristic weakness to the shock of being swept under water. Now she realized the reason she felt so particularly light-headed. She shivered just imagining the amount of blood she'd already lost.

Her hands were shaking, but between chattering teeth and trembling fingers, she managed to tear off a good-sized length of cloth at the hem of her drawers. Gently she wrapped the none too clean bandage around her thigh and smiled, albeit sickly, but smiled nonetheless when she realized her efforts had done much toward stanching the pumping flow.

Youngblood headed toward the buttes and the golden, flat-topped mesa beyond. Although he refused to look back, he watched Morgan's hobbling strides from his peripheral vision as he guided his horse in a wide zigzagging path. He slowed his horse again. She was falling farther behind, her movements growing more uncoordinated, almost drunken as she struggled to keep up.

Damn her stubbornness!

Why hadn't she simply apologized? Why hadn't she shown a moment's regret over her foolish actions? Had he seen a flicker of remorse, he'd never have felt this unreasonable rage. But no, not her. She'd never show by word or deed that she was sorry for what she'd done.

"God," he groaned softly as the near catastrophe played again in his mind's eye. Didn't she realize how close she'd come to dying? Didn't she know that he had been out of his mind with fear for her? Couldn't she imagine his pain if he'd found her too late?

Youngblood sighed in defeat as he brought his horse to a stop. At that moment he couldn't think which of them was more the fool. Granted she'd been walking only fifteen minutes or so, but it might as well have been years for the guilt that assailed. "Damn," he grunted as he turned his horse around.

Morgan was coming to her feet when she realized Youngblood had turned back and was now riding toward her. No doubt his mission was to further berate her for yet another unknown infraction. Well, he could rant and rave, scream if that was his want, to his heart's desire. She wouldn't listen to a word the beast had to say. She tried to control the need to limp. Silently she prayed Youngblood wouldn't notice.

He didn't.

All he noticed, in fact, was the blood-soaked leg of her split skirt. His eyes widened with the shock of it, his mind unable to fathom why she should bleed. Had she been bleeding when he'd taken her from the water? No, he silently swore. Surely he would have noticed. *Would you have?* came a distant voice from the far recesses of his mind. *She was soaked, covered with mud. Would you have noticed merely a slightly darker discoloration?*

He was off the horse and standing at her side in seconds. "What happened?"

Morgan saw the direction of his gaze. She shrugged as if the matter was of little importance. "The rock that hit my horse must have cut me as well. I didn't notice it at the time. I imagine I was too upset."

Had she thought on it, Morgan couldn't have said anything that might have cut deeper into his soul than her all so simple explanation. Youngblood closed his eyes and hissed an indrawn breath between clenched teeth against the pain. He'd never known such utter wretchedness. For a moment he was tempted to throw himself at her feet and beg her forgiveness. There'd never be a time when he'd know so great a measure of guilt. He'd accused her falsely. He hadn't asked, but had simply assumed she played a dangerous game and nearly lost it with her life.

Morgan looked at him blankly, as if they were strangers. As if they hadn't shared a night of intimacy that had bound them together forever. As if he didn't love her with all his being. Youngblood almost smiled at his thoughts. There was no point in denying it. He understood at last his obsession, his need to keep her here, to marry her despite her objections. He loved this woman beyond all reason, beyond all thought. He'd been a fool not to have realized his feelings sooner.

"Damn it, Morgan!" he took a step closer. "Why didn't you tell me?"

"I've only just realized it myself."

"And how long would you have gone on without saying something?"

Her blue eyes rose to his. They were hard and cold, without a flicker of the tenderness they'd known only this morning. "For as long as it took to get to your father's village."

Youngblood's lips tightened. He rubbed a hand over his face and muttered, "Damn, but you're a stubborn woman."

"And you, Mr. Youngblood, are an insensitive beast," she instantly returned, just before her eyes rolled upward and her body suddenly crumbled to the ground.

Youngblood's eyes widened in astonishment. For just an instant he couldn't imagine what was happening. Why should she be falling? Somehow he managed to pull himself from his stupefaction in time to save her from yet another injury, for her head would have surely hit hard against the rocky desert floor.

On his knees, her small form heavy against him, Youngblood was nearly overcome with a debilitating sense of terror. She had fainted! Without the slightest warning, she had collapsed. He trembled as he settled her more comfortably in his arms. Why hadn't she told him she was injured? Why had she needlessly put herself through this? God, she'd lost so much blood. Why? To prove a point? To show him she could take whatever punishment he imagined her due? Jesus, had he ever known a woman with more pride?

Youngblood's lips tightened with the horror of what he'd done. He might try to shift the blame, but he knew the truth of the matter. She hadn't told him because he hadn't given her a chance. She hadn't told him because he'd turned his back on her. What did he expect? God, what had he done?

With a helpless groan that bespoke his remorse, Youngblood buried his face in her neck. "Morgan honey," he said softly, his heart breaking at the sight of her skin, almost gray beneath the streaks of mud. "Wake up, darling. Tell me you'll be all right," he pleaded as he slowly lifted the blood-stiffened material of her skirt. Youngblood muttered a curse upon spying the dirty bandage she had used. He left her for a quick trip to his saddlebags. Within minutes he'd cleaned and rewrapped her wound. Finished, he came to his feet, never releasing her from his arms. A moment later he mounted his horse.

Morgan moaned with the pain as her eyelids fluttered open. "I'm cold," she managed, her teeth chattering uncontrollably. "I don't think I should be cold in this heat." She looked up at Youngblood's fierce expression, an expression aimed at himself, and quickly turned away.

Youngblood saw the brief look of dread in her eyes before she turned away. He felt her stiffen and crushed her tighter to his chest. "Don't be angry with me. You're right, I am a beast. I'm a monster to have done this to you."

Morgan blinked her surprise. She'd never expected this man to speak humbling words. She'd never expected to see that gentle look in his eyes. With no little amazement, Morgan found herself defending the very man she had cursed only moments before. "You didn't do it. It was a rock."

Youngblood shot her a disparaging grin as he reached behind him and untied his bedroll. A moment later his blanket was tucked around her. "Was it the rock that forced you to walk? To lose so much blood?"

Morgan might have gone on to further defend him, to point out that even she had no knowledge of her injury, but the effort was too great. She muttered an unintelligible sound and snuggled her face into the warmth of his throat. Almost instantly she slept.

Morgan continued to sleep throughout the remainder of the ride. Her eyes fluttered only slightly as she felt the horse come to a stop and heard Youngblood converse with another in a foreign tongue. A moment later he was walking. Cuddled close to his chest, held securely in his arms, she again drifted off to sleep.

Morgan never saw the fertile fields that surrounded the forbidden cliffs. She wouldn't know for many days that he carried her up the steep narrow path cut into the side of the mesa. She was more deeply asleep by the time he reached the honeycomb of stone houses that made up his father's pueblo, atop the mesa some five hundred feet above the desert floor.

Popé's dwelling, according to custom, belonged to his wife and was crowded with children, Youngblood's half brothers and sisters. They had little enough space as it was. Youngblood had long ago decided he wouldn't force his presence upon them as well. With Mara's permission, he built a small room attached to his stepmother's house to accommodate his visits. It was to Mara's house he now headed.

A crowd immediately gathered as Youngblood entered the village plaza. The amazement on their handsome faces was obvious, for it wasn't an everyday occurrence that one should suddenly appear carrying an unconscious woman in his arms, and yet polite to a fault, not one among them thought to question him.

Youngblood did not hesitate as he walked through the villagers, but moved on even as he offered many words of greetings to his longtime friends.

At last he reached Mara's home. As in most pueblos, but not all, these homes boasted no windows or doors. The entrance to each house was through a small opening in the roof. Carefully he lowered himself and Morgan into the opening and down the wooden ladder to the dark cool interior.

Mara was there to greet him, of course; his father was more than likely tending the fields or in the kiva, an underground room where the men went to pray. She was round with child again and, upon spying the woman in Youngblood's arms, quickly shooed the children outside to play.

Morgan awoke from a deep sleep to find Youngblood leaning over her, pulling at her boots. "What are you doing?" Her gaze moved around the tiny dark room, taking in the soft mat of furs beneath her. "Where are we?"

"We're at my stepmother's home. And I'm trying to make you more comfortable. Can you sit up?"

Morgan nodded, but soon discovered she hadn't the strength for even that small effort. Vaguely she wondered how she'd grown so terribly weak. "I can't," she whispered as she slumped back to the softness of the furs.

Youngblood smiled as he sat upon his bed. "Be still, honey. I'll see to it."

Morgan was sleeping again by the time he unbuttoned her shirt and slid her leather vest, mud-streaked shirt, and chemise from her. She never awakened when Mara brought in an earthen bowl filled with warm water and Youngblood began to cleanse her of the muddy remnants of her nearly disastrous fall. During the rest of the day and evening, she awakened occasionally. Once she was made to swallow, with some insistence, a vile-tasting brew, again a few drops of warm broth, and then twice more some water.

It was late at night when she awoke again. She was lying on her side, the furs beneath her soft and comfortable. Youngblood's warm body curved against her back and legs, his arm draped over her, his hand cupping her breast in sleep.

Most of her weakness had disappeared. Morgan imagined that emotional shock and fear had debilitated her as much as a loss of blood, for now, safely resting at Youngblood's side, she felt immeasurably stronger. Slowly she came to a sitting position. It was only then, when the cool night air hit her body, that she realized she was naked.

She jumped slightly at the sound of Youngblood's voice. "What are you doing?"

Quickly she grabbed at the furs and held them to her breast. "I didn't know you were awake."

Youngblood came up to lean on his elbow. "Where do you think you're going?"

"I need to . . . I need to use the outhouse," she whispered sickly, her face flaming at the sensitive subject.

"There's a pot in the corner," he returned in an odd tone. The flash of a white smile in the dimness confirmed her suspicions of laughter. "You want help?"

"No!" she answered instantly and with no little vehemence. "I want you to leave."

"Leave?" he asked, clearly astonished at her appeal. "Why?"

"Because I can't do what I have to do, if you're here."

"Honey, you want me to leave this nice warm bed and go outside, just because you have to take a piss?"

"Oh God," Morgan groaned, mortified at his crass language. "Must you talk like that?"

"Sorry," Youngblood muttered as he threw aside the covers and came to his feet. He stood before her, unconscious of his nakedness as he slid his legs into his trousers. "I hope you know this is ridiculous."

She didn't answer. There was simply no way she could make light of such a personal, private necessity.

"You'll have to get used to it sooner or later. I'm not leaving our bed every night for the next forty years."

Again she offered no response.

Youngblood sighed as he lifted her, cover and all, from the bed and strode to the corner of the room. "Now don't fight me, honey," he said as he felt her stiffen in his arms.

"You're not strong enough to be on your own." He lowered her to her feet and held her against him until he was sure she was able to manage the feat on her own. He touched her cheek with a gentle stroke of his fingertips. "Hold on to the wall if you feel sick and call me when you're finished."

Morgan nodded and then sighed with relief as he turned and walked away.

Morgan awakened at the end of the next day as he raised the furs and exposed her injured leg. Youngblood smiled as he leaned over her. "It looks good. No sign of festering. I've been keeping a poultice on it. You'll probably be able to get up in a day or so."

"Where are we?"

"Don't you remember? I told you we're at Mara's house. She's my father's wife."

"Don't your father and Mara live together?"

"Of course," he answered, slightly puzzled at the question. "Why?"

"Why do you call it her house and not your father's?"

"The Hopi women own the houses and have complete control over everything that goes on in them."

Morgan's eyes widened with astonishment. She hadn't imagined anything so obviously female-favored. "Pretty smart of them, don't you think?"

He shrugged, while allowing her a wicked grin. "I don't know. I suppose that would depend on what they had on their minds to do."

"You can get that grin off your face. I can well imagine what you have in mind."

Youngblood laughed as he gently washed her injury and the surrounding area. "It's not so rosy a picture. They might own it, but they have to do all the work. The men are treated like royalty."

"Not unlike most families, I expect. At least these women get to own their own homes."

238

"And the crops. The men work the fields, but the seeds and harvest belong to their wives."

Morgan smiled, her eyes widening with interest. "I'm beginning to believe I could take to this sort of thing."

Youngblood chuckled. "I thought you might."

"Tell me more."

"Well," he shrugged. "The men do all the hunting and farming. Also, they're the only ones allowed to handle the looms."

"You mean they do the weaving?"

Youngblood nodded. The women make the clothes, but most of them are made from deerskin. The men make the more colorful things like blankets and ceremonial sashes and kilts."

"That's fascinating."

"Is it?" He shrugged again. "I can see how it might be, if you're not used to it."

"How come the women get off so easy? All they have to do is cook and sew."

"They don't get off easy. It's their job to clean, make the pottery and baskets, and grind the corn into meal. Besides cooking and cleaning, and caring for the children, that's a pretty full day."

"I guess so," she said, sounding unconvinced.

Youngblood laughed as he leaned down and gave her a quick kiss. "Maybe we should stay on here. You seem to like the idea better than I would have thought. I could get used to being waited on hand and foot."

"Would you like that?" she asked seriously. "Staying here, I mean?"

His eyes grew distant as his mind returned to the ranch. "No. I love the Mustangs too much to leave. There's nothing"—his eyes twinkled with sudden humor—"well, almost nothing to compare to the thrill of riding them until they're broken in to a saddle. I'll always feel a bond to these people, but I much prefer the ranch."

Mara, a dark, handsome woman somewhere in her mid-thirties with long flowing black hair, came in bearing a large bowl filled with water. The two women smiled at one another as Mara left the water beside the bed, said a word or two to Youngblood, and moved gracefully out of the room.

Morgan eyed the bowl with some suspicion. "What is that for?"

Youngblood grinned. "I thought you'd be more comfortable with a bath."

"I'm comfortable enough, thank you."

"Are you going to be good and allow me to give you a bath?"

She shook her head. "No, I'm not."

Youngblood sighed. "I didn't think you'd cooperate. It will make you feel better, you know."

"I feel fine."

"Morgan," he said, his voice deepening with authority.

"I can do it myself."

"You can't. You're not strong enough."

"I am."

"You're not."

"Then I'll wait until I am."

"Come on, honey. Mara went to the trouble of warming this water. She'll be insulted if it's not used."

"You use it then."

Youngblood grinned at her sulky expression. For a second he imagined he knew exactly how their children would look. "I bathed while you slept."

Morgan shook her head again. "It's not a good idea."

"I'll be done in a minute," Youngblood said, ignoring her reluctance. "Roll over."

Morgan gave a long weary sigh as she finally gave in to his demand. "Be quick about it."

Youngblood chuckled at her gruff order. He washed the entire length of her body in slow swirling strokes. Morgan couldn't help the soft moan of pleasure that escaped her lips.

"Didn't I tell you it would feel good?"

"Shut up," she murmured, her face pressed into the soft fur bedding.

Morgan couldn't help grinning at Youngblood's laughter. "Now all I need is a way to massage your nasty disposition."

"My disposition is just fine, thank you."

Youngblood chuckled, his mouth close to her ear as he whispered. "I could make it better." And when Morgan didn't respond he went on, "Do you want to know how?"

Still she said nothing, which only caused Youngblood to laugh again.

With soapy hands he began to massage the stiffness from her shoulders and back. Moving down, his hands did the same to waist, buttocks, and legs. It felt wonderful. Morgan couldn't imagine anything more wonderful. She almost sighed her disappointment when he dried her and rolled her suddenly on her back.

Instantly she grabbed at the furs and covered herself.

"Now for the interesting part." He grinned wickedly.

Morgan giggled, her eyes bright with amusement as she clutched the furs to her. "You are a beast. Here I was all relaxed and comfortable. You completey destroyed the mood."

"Ahhh, but there's another mood I'm trying to create."

"Really?" She laughed as a tug of war over the covers began. "What kind of mood?"

"I want to see your eyes grow heavy, your lips parted and wet, like when I kiss you, your skin flushed, burning hot to the touch."

"That sounds like someone ill with fever."

"Does it?" Youngblood grinned. "Now that I think of it, you're right. It is something like a fever."

"Well, having a fever doesn't sound the least bit appealing to me."

"It could be."

"I doubt it." Morgan couldn't keep the grin from her lips.

241

"I could show you," Youngblood returned, suddenly all boyish charm.

Morgan felt her heart lurch and a pulse ticked in her throat as their eyes locked in a sizzling look. "You're very dangerous, Mr. Youngblood. Do you realize that?" she asked, her voice whispery soft.

"If you were well, I might be tempted to show you just how dangerous," he countered softly. "Let go of the covers."

Morgan did as she was told. He soaped her face and neck, rinsed the suds, and dried her skin before lowering the cloth to her shoulders and arms.

"Don't close your eyes," he breathed, his voice low and gravelly as he pulled the protective covering away. "Watch me."

Morgan swallowed, her eyes wide as she lay exposed to him.

"Do you know how beautiful you are?" he murmured, never knowing he'd spoken. He began to wash her then, but soon the soapy cloth was discarded and his hands continued on with the delicious chore. Again and again warm brown fingers moved over ivory skin until his dark eyes dilated and his breathing grew harsh and labored.

Morgan's body came alive under his ardent ministrations. She shuddered and gasped as he took her breasts and massaged them with soap. The tips formed hard nubs in his palms. She almost cried out her disappointment as he slid his hands lower to her midriff and waist. Gently he smoothed the already smooth skin of her belly and hips.

Heat. Blazing heat seeped into her veins, almost melting her from the inside out as his fingers moved to the juncture of her thighs. Her legs parted as she mindlessly urged further investigation. Her hands tightened into balls as she clutched at the fur bedding. Her eyes closed. She hadn't the strength to keep them open as her head moved restlessly back and forth. Her hips raised slightly from the furs as she strove for more of this torture.

He was nearly gasping for breath, the skin drawn tightly over his features, as he suddenly and quickly rinsed her free of soap and dried her skin.

With a groan Youngblood turned suddenly away. His back to her, he sat with his elbows resting on his knees, his head hanging low. The sound of his gasping breath filled the tiny room. It took some time, but he finally managed to bring his emotions under control. "That wasn't the smartest thing I've ever done."

Morgan reached a weak, shaking hand for the covers and pulled them back into place. Her whole body felt on fire, trembling with need. She, too, gasped for her next breath and tried to force the pounding of her heart under some control.

A moment later a smile curved her lips at his obvious suffering. "You have only yourself to blame."

Youngblood shot her a weak grin, his dark eyes alive with fire. "Actually it's you I blame. Were you another, I wouldn't be suffering this degree of pain."

"Unfair, Joseph. You insisted."

Youngblood groaned as he turned on the bed and faced her. He lowered his head, his lips inches from hers when he asked, "Do you know what it does to me to hear you say my name?"

"No. What?" she asked as he moved closer, her eyes bright with pleasure at his obvious struggle to regain control. She felt all powerful at the knowledge that this strong man had so little strength against her.

"Maybe I'd better not tell you," he reasoned. "You have enough weapons against me."

"Maybe you'd better not kiss me then. I might inadvertently say your name." She blinked, trying to look her most innocent and succeeding only in looking more sultry. "And then where would we be?"

His eyes narrowed with supposed menace. "I can see I've already said too much."

Morgan laughed at his ferocious look.

He growled and kissed her then, lightly, quickly. A

moment later he was standing beside her. "Go to sleep now. Tomorrow you can go outside for a bit."

"Aren't you coming to bed?"

"In a minute. I want to talk to my father for a while." He looked down at her, his eyes narrowing as he watched her struggle to keep the smile from her lips. "If I were you, I would get rid of that cocky look. It's bound to get you in trouble."

Morgan shrugged. "What have I got to be afraid of? I have you to protect me."

"It's me you're supposed to fear."

Morgan's grin only broadened and Youngblood was helpless but to join her in laughter.

"Joseph, these people are beautiful! No wonder you're so . . ."

"What?" He grinned as her words came to a sudden end. His eyes widened at her obvious embarrassment and watched in fascination as she grew a lovely shade of pink. "What am I?" he prompted.

"If you must know, you're an arrogant beast," she snapped, her eyes flashing her annoyance at the knowing look he was giving her.

"That wasn't what you were going to say."

"Actually, it was." She blinked in supposed innocence and smiled primly.

Youngblood chuckled as he pulled her into the circle of his arms, breathed deeply of her sweet clean scent, and hugged her before the gentle smiles of half the village.

Morgan's eyes widened as she moved about the plaza. All the houses bordered on the smoothed area. The village was enormous, taking up the entire surface of the mesa. The people were friendly. Although Morgan couldn't understand their tongue, they seemed not to hesitate to offer her greetings. Youngblood interpreted the words when necessary. Usually a smile was enough to ensure her welcome among them.

Some of the women cooked on their roofs, a slab of smooth stone over their small hot fires serving as a stove. Quick agile fingers formed piki, a paper-thin bread made from corn to be dipped into stews of deer and squash.

Others were busy crafting pottery, while still more wove baskets of many sizes and shapes.

Morgan, her eyes wide with amazement, took in the entire lively scene. "Is there a reason why all the women I see with child have their hair down, while the others are braided?"

"Very good." He looked down at her, his smile of amazement slowly being replaced with the tenderest of expressions. "A woman with child keeps all forms of knots from her hair and clothes. A knot might tie up the child during birth."

Morgan nodded as if this was the most normal of attitudes.

"You nod as if you believe it."

"No, but I can see how they might."

Youngblood's expression grew gentle as he pushed a loose curl behind her ear. His heart ached with the need to hold this gentle woman, to kiss her until he knew nothing but the sweet oblivion of her mouth. Instead he took her hand and said, "I want to show you how the men use the looms."

"Come over here, honey. I want to cuddle against you." It had been close to two weeks since their arrival and Morgan had almost completely recovered from her injury. Except for the fact that she tired easily, she was her usual self.

Morgan, her back to him, moved an inch closer.

"Is that the best you can do?" he asked, the laughter clear in his voice.

"Why are we sharing the same bed?" she whispered softly, not wanting those in the next room to overhear.

"Because we're married, of course."

245

"I thought we agreed that nothing would happen between us," she said, her mind going back again to that morning and the passion they had shared. Passion that had left her shaken and almost begging for more.

"We agreed nothing would happen that you didn't want," he corrected gently. "As I remember it, I'm permitted hugs and even an occasional kiss."

"Is that what you call it? An occasional kiss? Every time we awaken, it's getting . . ."

"Better?" he offered, and she could hear from the sound of his voice he was barely controlling his laughter.

Morgan sighed. She wasn't about to say better, although she couldn't deny the truth of his way of thinking. She'd almost said harder—harder to stop herself from begging him to go on. But she knew the comment would have given him yet another reason to tease. The truth of it was that it was growing increasingly harder to leave his arms. They hadn't made love since that one night at the ranch, but they were coming closer to it every morning. Especially since they slept naked and so close a flea couldn't find space between them.

"I think it's better if we don't sleep so close."

"Do you?" he asked as he moved the distance needed to bring their bodies together. "Why?" he whispered. His breath, warm and clean, sent chills down her back as it struck her neck.

"Because I don't want to make love."

"Are you sure?" he asked as his fingers moved familiarly over her breasts, bringing the tips instantly to hard nubs.

"Yes, I'm sure," she returned as she removed his hand and placed it on her waist. Oh Lord! How much longer was she going to be able to resist this man? How had she managed so far when he teased and taunted her to near madness every morning? More than half asleep, she would feel his hands moving over her. Soon his lips would follow the path already explored until she'd turn into his arms and sleepily sigh her delight. Only then, when she pressed against him, unable to get enough of the feel of him, would he kiss her. A quick, hard, hungry, almost devouring kiss, just before he would bound from the bed, laughing at some unspoken joy, leaving her trembling, aching with need.

Morgan felt his body hair scratch against her back and legs. Without thinking, she wiggled closer, unconsciously delighting in the differences between their bodies. Where had her chemise gone? she wondered. Youngblood claimed not to have seen it since he'd taken it off while she was ill. She didn't believe him, of course. He'd probably destroyed it, just so she'd have nothing to wear at night. Why, if she wore Indian garb during the day, wasn't there something to wear to bed?

She had tried at first to sleep in the pretty doeskin dress Mara had given her, but Youngblood quickly showed her the folly of her intentions. Without a word and despite her obvious reluctance, he had twice pulled the garment over her head and thrown it across the room. She hadn't bothered to try again. Idly she wondered if the whole Hopi nation slept naked.

"Why don't you want to make love, honey?"

"Joseph . . ." Morgan felt herself stiffen. It was hard enough to fight against this need, but when he was gentle like this, when his hand moved slowly in teasing strokes over her waist and hip, she wondered if it was possible to keep her resolve. "We've been through this before. I won't be a portal for a man's lust until he gets me out of his system. I'd never allow myself to be used like that."

Youngblood chuckled. "Suppose it doesn't happen?"

"What doesn't happen?"

"Suppose I can never get you out of my system? What then?"

Morgan shrugged. "Then you'll have to suffer through it, I imagine."

"Suppose I told you that I loved you." He pulled her tighter against him, his words as warm and silky as his breath as it brushed her neck. "What would you say?"

Morgan's heart began to race. She could hardly

breathe. Did he mean it? Was he playing yet another game? Could she trust him to speak the truth? Her voice trembled as she forced herself to remain in place. She'd be lost if she turned in to his warmth. "I'd say you were trying to get what you want and using any means at your disposal."

"You wouldn't believe me?"

"I'm afraid not."

"And of course, you could never love me."

"I'd be a fool to allow that, don't you think?"

"No, I don't. As a matter of fact, I think you already do. You're just afraid to admit it."

Morgan turned to face him at that remark. Rising up, leaning on her elbow, she glared through the darkness. "That's ridiculous."

"No it's not." Youngblood grinned confidently as he lay beside her and stretched. "You're stubborn, but not stupid. You know a good thing when you've got it."

The gall of the man! "Oh really? I suppose you're telling me that you're the good thing?"

"I am."

Lord! She couldn't imagine anyone with half this man's conceit. "First of all, Mr. Youngblood, you're as far from good as one could possibly get."

Youngblood chuckled. "Which only makes me more appealing, I think."

"I think you're an obnoxiously conceited boor."

"I think you love me."

"I don't. I'm smarter than that."

"But love isn't ruled by intelligence."

"Or lust."

"But lust can play an important role."

"The truth is, lust plays no role at all. It doesn't enter into my situation."

"You mean you're content with our morning romps? You don't want more?"

"You're right on one count, I don't want more."

"Why is it I don't believe you?"

248

"I'm afraid I couldn't say."

"I could."

"No doubt. You'll forgive me if I have better things to do than listen." She was about to lie down, but his next words brought her immediately up to her elbow again.

"I have to tear myself out of your arms and you know it."

"You do not!" She hotly denied the undeniable.

Losing patience, Youngblood muttered, "Right, it must be someone else whose been humpin' against my—"

Morgan gasped. "You beast! Can we never have one conversation without a disgusting display of your foul mouth?"

"Deny it then." He came up on his elbow and leaned toward her. Almost nose to nose, they scowled at one another. "Tell me I'm not driving you crazy every morning. Tell me you don't want me to touch you. Tell me you hate my kisses, and you're a goddamned liar.

"And for your information, this is not a conversation. This is a fight. I trust you know the difference.

"I hate you!"

"Yeah, well, that's tough, because I love you and I don't give a shit if you believe it or not." With that astounding bit of news, Youngblood turned on his side, his back to her, and promptly went to sleep.

Morgan was in shock. She lay down on her back and stared with wide-eyed amazement at the ceiling. What kind of man was this? How could he suddenly declare his feelings with no more emotion than if he were discussing the weather? No, that wasn't true. He'd displayed emotion, all right. He'd been furious. She almost laughed at the absurdity of it all. Whoever heard of someone telling another of their love with angry scowls? Where was the romance? Where were the tender words? The moonlight? The magic? Morgan sighed. Would she ever learn the workings of this man's mind?

Chapter Fourteen

Morgan awoke to the soft muffled sounds of giggling children in the next room. A quick glance to her right confirmed her suspicions. Youngblood had left their bed, probably at the first sign of light. Morgan couldn't deny the crushing disappointment that filled her being. Was he still angry? Is that why he'd gone before she'd awakened? Morgan might profess her dislike of their morning lusty rituals, but after finding herself alone only this once, she knew she missed the closeness she was becoming accustomed to.

Another giggle came from close by. Morgan turned toward the sound, her eyes widening with pleasure as Youngblood's half sister Ninna, an adorable chubby two-year-old with black eyes and hair and an angelic grin, greeted her.

The child reached a tentative finger toward Morgan's golden hair spread out upon the bed. It was obvious she was curious. No doubt she'd never seen hair that color before.

Gently Morgan patted the bed of furs and the child climbed up beside her. Smiling, Morgan sat up and returned the compliment by sliding her fingers through the child's silky hair. "Pretty," she said.

"Pretty," the little girl returned.

It wasn't often that Morgan got a chance to visit alone

with the members of this family, for Youngblood was almost always at her side. Gently she offered a long lock of her hair for the little girl's inspection and smiled again as a chubby hand touched the golden tresses.

"I see you're getting acquainted with my sister."

At the sound of his voice, Morgan looked up to find Youngblood leaning against the doorway.

"She's beautiful, Joseph."

"She seems to find your hair interesting." He came into the room and sat beside her, gathering the child into his lap. "Can't say I blame her myself," he drawled, reverting again to his lazy, sexy, Western twang. "I know how I felt the first time I saw you." Youngblood spoke, his attitude one of nonchalance, while the direction of his gaze remained on his sister as he smoothed her hair beneath the headband she wore.

"How did you feel?"

Youngblood's gaze met hers over the child's head. His dark eyes grew darker still at the memory of their meeting. "Terrified."

Morgan hadn't expected that. Her eyes widened. "Of me?" She laughed softly. "Surely not."

"Oh, but I was," he countered easily. To her amazement Morgan realized once he'd decided to allow her insight to the workings of his mind, he had relaxed all barriers. His mouth curved into a grin. "I knew the moment I saw you my life would never be the same again."

"Were you right?"

Youngblood shot her a cocky grin. "I usually am."

Morgan's eyes narrowed with warning as she returned, her voice dripping sarcasm, "That kind of attitude will surely ensnare many a lady's heart."

"I care little of many ladies or their hearts. I've already ensnared the one I want."

Morgan swallowed against the lump in her throat. She had no retort to his calmly spoken statement of fact. Her cheeks flushed as a multitude of emotions, confusion not the least withstanding, came to assault. Did he mean that his almost carelessly spoken words last night were the truth? Did he love her? Was it true she loved him in return?

She had lain awake for hours last night hotly denying his words. She hadn't known what to expect this morning. When she found herself alone, she'd imagined he was still annoyed. Morgan knew she could better handle his rages, for the tender warmth she now read in his dark eyes left her suddenly afraid.

"We'll leave you to get dressed," he said as he came to his feet. He tickled Ninna and flipped the now laughing child over his shoulder. "Are you hungry?"

Morgan nodded, suddenly shy at the warmth of emotion in his dark gaze. Her cheeks grew pink as he bestowed a gentle smile and left her to her privacy.

Morgan smiled, her heart filled with some unnamed joy as she eyed the short ornamental dress. She'd worn the Indian costume since the first day she'd left the bed, but in the weeks spent here, she had not yet grown accustomed to feeling so exposed. The dress was sleeveless and came only to midway between ankle and knee. The deerskin wrappings from feet to knee did little toward waylaying her feeling of nakedness. She needed underclothing. No matter how she might otherwise cover herself, she felt naked without it.

As she dresssed, her mind returned to the man who most always occupied her thoughts. Lord, but she was so confused. Every time she thought she was coming to know this complicated man, he changed like a chameleon before her eyes.

How many facets of his personality were there left to discover? Who, in fact, was Joseph Youngblood? Was he the angry savage of her first acquaintance, furious because an outsider had come to lay claim to the ranch he loved? Was he the arrogant taunting cowboy, who could so easily fill her with fury? Was he the heartless stranger who had carelessly discarded her after saving her from certain death? The teasing boy-man who had hid in a cave to scare her? Or was he more dangerous than all that had come before? Was he a would-be lover? The man who spoke easily of his feelings and now watched her with dark passionate eyes. Eyes ablaze with the sweet promise of the very paradise she had once sampled in his arms.

Morgan shook her head and sighed with defeat, finding no answers to the dozen or more questions that assailed. She ran her fingers through her hair and twisted the heavy golden mass into one thick braid, tying the end with a small piece of rawhide. She splashed water on her face and scrubbed her teeth with her finger and tooth powder taken from Youngblood's supplies. A moment later she joined the others in the main room.

A smile curved her lips as she watched the two boys tumble in rough play as they awaited their morning meal. The baby was chattering happily, perched upon her older sister's lap, while Youngblood sat in the far corner in quiet conversation with his father.

Mara was bent over a fire, her quick fingers preparing piki and deer meat for her family's morning meal. Apparently Morgan made a sound, for Mara suddenly lifted her eyes from her chore and gave a sharp exclamation. A moment later she spoke a word to her oldest daughter, who quickly resumed her mother's task, while the Indian woman came to Morgan's side.

The chiding words might have been no more than gibberish, but the meaning behind them was clear enough. With gentle but forceful words of reprimand, she worked Morgan's hair from its braid and with a wooden comb began to free it of any knots.

The meaning behind her action was clear. Morgan's eyes widened with shock as they met Youngblood's astonished gaze across the room. Mara continued to speak in her native tongue as she smoothed the long blond tresses into soft waves down Morgan's back. How? How could this woman know what Morgan had only begun to realize?

Morgan's cheeks darkened with embarrassment as Youngblood's gaze turned warm and then alive with excitement and what? Joy?

Silently Morgan thanked whoever was responsible for the presence of the others. At the very least it kept Youngblood seated. She wondered what her reaction would be if he'd come to her at that moment and shook her head, unwilling to imagine her reaction if he took her in his arms.

She was going to have his baby. It had been almost a month since she and Youngblood had shared that passionate night and she'd yet to come into her monthly time. For more than a week she'd refused to acknowledge the obvious sign, pretending the delay of her monthly flow was caused by travel, or perhaps the shock she'd suffered at her near brush with death. But in her heart she knew the truth of the matter. And now Youngblood knew as well.

"How do you feel?"

"Fine, thank you. I think I've completely recovered." She glanced at the rock trail cut into the side of the mesa they had just descended and gave a small shiver, for it was unbelievably narrow at some points. "But I don't know if I'll be able to climb back up, now that you've brought me down here."

Youngblood held her hand and grinned. "I'll carry you if you feel tired. But I'm not talking about your injury, honey. Are you upset because of the baby?"

Morgan shrugged. "I don't know. A little, I suppose." She hesitated a long moment before she went on, her eyes taking in the fields of corn and vegetables and the men bent over their tasks. "It certainly takes all options out of my hands. I'm not sure I like that."

"I'm afraid all options were taken from your hands the moment you left New York."

Morgan smiled at his dark hungry look. "You believe in fate then?"

Youngblood shrugged. "I only know I decided you were mine the moment I saw you."

"That's not true." She shook her head. "You couldn't wait to get me off the ranch and out of your life. If you felt anything at all, it was lust."

Youngblood laughed. "I won't deny it. I did lust after you. I didn't want to want you. I knew you'd change everything."

"How?"

"I was content with my life. I didn't want to marry."

"You certainly could have fooled me." Her brow lifted with disbelief, her eyes narrowed with remembered anger. "Who was it then that dragged me off to the mission?"

Youngblood laughed and then hugged her close to his side. "I mean at the beginning."

"What you mean is, not until Martha's threats."

Youngblood pulled her to stand before him. His gaze studied the almost dull expression in her eyes. "Is that what you think?"

Morgan shrugged and gave a slight shake of her head. "It doesn't matter."

"I'm afraid it does. You should know me well enough to realize no one can force me to do anything I don't want to do."

Morgan stared up at him, her brow creased with confusion. "What does that mean? I know she forced you to marry me. She threatened you. I was there."

His hands held her shoulders. "Morgan, listen to me. *No one,* with you being the possible exception, can force me to do anything."

"Really? Then why did you marry me?"

"I can't explain my reasons at the time, except to say when I saw you ready to leave I knew I couldn't let you go."

"And now?"

"Now I know why. I loved you, even if I didn't know it then."

"And you know it now," she said sadly.

"You're thinking I'm only saying this because of the baby."

"It doesn't matter. Can we talk about something else?"

Youngblood sighed, knowing she didn't believe him yet, but she would. "Tell me how you feel about the baby."

"I'm sure I'll be happy about it, once I get used to the idea."

Youngblood allowed her to escape his hold. As he walked at her side, measuring his steps to hers, his hand reached for hers. They walked in companionable silence for some time before he spoke again. "Are you afraid?"

"Of what?" she asked as she shot him a sidelong glance from beneath dark lashes.

God, she was so adorable it took every ounce of his restraint not to take her in his arms and crush her against him. "Of the pain."

She shrugged, saying nothing, but he could read the flicker of fear in her eyes as she allowed her thoughts to linger on the subject.

"There's no need." He meant to soothe. "Mara says, judging by the width of your hips, the birth will be easy enough."

Morgan came to a sudden stop, obviously stunned, her cheeks aflame. She shot him a hard angry look. Her lips barely moved. Her voice was tight with fury. "I'd take it as a personal favor if you wouldn't discuss the shape of my body with another woman."

Youngblood laughed as he again gathered her stiff form into his arms and lifted her high over his head. Her hands clung to his shoulders as he swung her in a circle. "I wasn't discussing your shape, honey. Mara mentioned it when she noticed I was worried."

Suddenly he stood very still, his eyes burning bright,

256

alive with a hunger that was never far from the surface. Her breasts were almost level with his mouth and Morgan watched with helpless growing fascination as he lowered her the inches needed to nuzzle his face in her tempting softness. Morgan never heard her soft moan of pleasure. She felt her body shiver with longing and then grow heavy with the desire he could so easily bring to life.

Slowly, almost regretfully, he began to slide her down the length of his body. Their breathing was erratic and labored by the time her mouth came even with his. Her feet dangled still above the ground, but Morgan never realized the fact, for her whole being concentrated on the solid heat of the man who held her against him.

She offered not a word of protest, but eagerly awaited the delight of feeling his lips upon hers again. Youngblood never thought to deny himself the sweet pleasure of her taste. His head moved forward just enough to allow his lips to capture the beckoning sweetness.

Gently he brushed his mouth back and forth across her lips, teasing her flesh with delectable, feathery strokes of his tongue until her eyes fluttered closed and she sighed her longing. The sigh came from parted lips and Youngblood took immediate advantage of their willingness. His tongue traced her mouth and slid just inside to tease the sensitive flesh and then move gently over small even teeth.

He felt her body yield against him as her arms came around his neck to hold his mouth closer. Groaning at her hungry response, he sucked at her lips, taking first the top and then the bottom between his teeth and rubbing his tongue over the captured flesh. Until at last with a low groan of yearning, their mouths opened wide, delighting in the taste and feel of each other.

His tongue delved deep into the sweet, dark warmth of her then and he groaned as she sucked him gently and then more hungrily, deep, deeper into ecstasy. His mind swam in a fog of wanting, of need, of a yearning so great as to tempt him to lower her now to the ground and take

257

what she so willingly offered. His arms trembled as he pressed her to his subtly moving hips. Her unbound breasts, separated from him only by the thin garment she wore, drove him mad as they seared his chest. He groaned with the pain of wanting to touch her, to weigh her softness in the palm of his hands, to tease the tips until they rose to hard aching buds. His hands cupped the lushness of her rounded backside. He kneaded the firm flesh, shivering with the need to slide his hands beneath her dress, knowing she wore nothing that would deter him from her warmth.

Youngblood realized, though not without some effort, that they stood out in the open. A harsh shuddering breath slipped from his lips as he took his mouth from hers. She'd been soft and yielding upon awakening every morning, but he'd refused to take her in that sleepy relaxed state. He wanted her to tell him with words or action of her longing, fully alert and responsible for her decision. Why did she have to do it now? Youngblood sighed a muffled curse while nuzzling his mouth into her hair and brought his hands to her back, while holding her still wrapped in the warmth of his arms.

"Were you?" she breathed on a trembling sigh once their lips parted. She never thought but to rest her head for a moment against his chest. And once she'd done that, her lips of their own accord and without any conscious thought began to sample the warmly erotic taste of his skin.

"What?" Youngblood asked, his unsteady voice husky and strained with the need to further this moment. The kiss combined with what her mouth was now doing to his chest caused him to lose track of their conversation.

"Afraid," she reminded him on a dreamy sigh.

"Did you think I'd already grown so comfortable with the idea of fatherhood that I wouldn't give it more than a passing thought?"

Morgan tipped her head back and looked up at this man who held her so gently in his arms. Her heart quickened at the heated look in his hungry eyes. "Have you given it some thought?"

Youngblood grinned as he looked down at her. "A bit," he said with a definite air of mystery as he forced back the words of adoration that threatened to burst forth. He'd already spoken of his love and she hadn't believed him. He wouldn't say more for the present, knowing time would eventually convince her of the truth.

"Just a bit?" she teased, her eyes wide with laughter, growing more confident by the minute that he had indeed thought of little else since realizing her condition. "Is that all?" Morgan giggled as she pulled free of his arms. "Have you suddenly reverted back to that handsome, brooding stranger I first came to know?"

Youngblood's dark eyes widened with pleasure. "Do you think I'm handsome?"

Morgan's saucy grin almost caused him to crush her in his arms again. "Ah," she said, "I see. In order to get an answer I must first fill your mind with words of praise." She laughed at his scowl. "What would you like to hear?"

"How about the truth?"

Morgan fought back her smile and shook her head, her expression almost sad. "Not an easy task, Mr. Youngblood, for there is much to your makeup besides your obvious good looks."

"So, you admit to my good looks then?"

"Oh indeed. You are most handsome." Morgan giggled, knowing she'd caught his full attention.

His eyes narrowed as he searched her amused expression. "Why do I feel as if there's a *but* somewhere left to be said?"

Morgan laughed and purposely, wickedly ignored his question. "Do you think we could ride for a while? It's been some time since I've sat upon a horse."

Youngblood sighed in defeat, knowing he'd get no more out of her as he allowed her to guide them toward the corral.

"Perhaps this wasn't such a good idea, after all," Morgan remarked as she measured the narrowness of her dress with widespread legs and realized mounting the horse would either split the fabric up the side, or push the entire skirt indecently high on her thighs. Neither option greatly appealed. Nor did the alarming and more dangerous fact that she would be expected to ride bareback. There were no saddles except for Youngblood's, and she didn't have the slightest idea how to remain upon a horse without the aid of stirrups. "I wouldn't want to overdo it."

Youngblood tightened the saddle under Thunder's belly. "Oh I don't think you should worry about that." He grinned, knowing her dilemma the moment she looked from her skirt to the horse and back to her skirt again. "I think we could both benefit greatly from the exercise." He sure as hell knew he'd benefit from just watching her. In truth, he couldn't imagine anything more beautiful than seeing her dress hiked almost to her hips, those long white legs straddling the horse, unless of course they were straddling him. His eyes darkened with undisguised hunger as his gaze traveled the length of her. "I know I would." He felt a definite thickness grow to life in his groin at his imaginings, and knowing she wore not a stitch beneath her dress only added to the constant ache.

"No doubt," Morgan remarked, a grin teasing her lips as she read correctly the way of his thoughts. She turned and began to walk toward the path that would bring her again to the top of the mesa. "But I'm afraid I won't be riding today. I'll see you when you get back."

Morgan gave a soft yelp of surprise to find herself suddenly in his arms, crushed against his chest as he walked back to his horse. Her eyes were wide. A smile played about her lips as she inquired, "Are you kidnapping me again?"

Youngblood grinned, marveling at how far they had come. "The idea doesn't seem to upset you this time."

Morgan shrugged. "One could say I'm growing used to

my husband's gentlemanly ways," she managed as he sat her atop his horse.

Her sarcasm wasn't lost on her husband. Youngblood grinned as he mounted behind her and pulled her close to his chest. "A wise decision, since you seem to have no other choice."

Morgan glanced up; the angry words at his cavalier attitude, ready to burst forth, were stilled at his taunting grin. She shook her head, giving him a secret smile, while deciding the wisest move on her part would be to ignore his high-handed manner. At least for the time being.

"Don't do that."

"What?" she asked, clearly puzzled.

"Don't smile like that. It gives me the shivers."

"Does it?" She laughed happily, unable to imagine anything that would instill fear in this man's heart. "I wonder why?"

"You look like you're planning some evil revenge."

Morgan played along with his teasing. "Not revenge. Justice perhaps?"

Youngblood groaned. "Have you no pity in your heart?"

Morgan chuckled. "Is the thought of justice so terrifying? Would you beg then for mercy?"

"Would you grant it?" His eyes were dark, the longing in their depths undeniable.

Morgan merely smiled for an answer, knowing their conversation had suddenly taken on a whole new meaning. She wasn't quite prepared to answer the unasked question.

"Joseph, I hate to ride like this," she remarked as the horse took a jarring step forward. "All it does is shake me to my bones."

"If you straddle the horse, you won't be bounced," he suggested, unable to disguise the leer in voice or eyes.

Morgan grinned at the wicked laughter in his eyes. "No doubt. But that would show an indecent amount of leg, don't you think?"

"I won't look," he said, trying to sound innocent. He failed miserably.

"I never imagined you would." She giggled at his sigh of obvious disappointment, for she wasn't about to expose herself, no matter how much he might have appreciated the view.

"All right," he said, conceding her this point. "I'll ride slowly. You won't be bounced." He gave a weary sigh. "I reckon I'm up to holding you in my arms."

Morgan shook her head, her eyes softly tender, and she sighed, knowing there was no use in fighting him. Once he set his mind to something, there was little she could do or say to convince him otherwise.

Morgan squinted against the glare of the sun, wishing for the relief her lost hat would have brought. A moment later, as if he'd read her thoughts, Youngblood's hat was placed upon her head. Morgan shot him an appreciative smile. "Now the sun will be bothering you."

"I'm part Indian, remember? I can handle it."

Morgan sighed and leaned comfortably into the circle of his arms. The heat was intense, almost stifling, but completely lacking in humidity. The beads of sweat that came to moisten her upper lip or ran down her sides dried almost as soon as they formed. Had she not taken notice, Morgan might have wondered how anything could live beneath the relentless rays of a sun so strong, but the obvious signs of life around her easily disputed the notion that the desert was merely a lifeless form of rocks and sand.

Morgan smiled as her gaze took in the beauty before her. Stark perhaps, but beauty of a majesty she could have only once imagined. Mountains, reddish brown in color, rose high above the earth in the far-off distance. Grass, wild flowers, cactus, and sweetly scented sagebrush dotted the desert floor. A jackrabbit scurried across their path. A lone eagle glided gracefully in a blue, cloudless sky.

"You do remember what happened the last time I held you like this?" Youngblood interrupted her silent admiration, his voice low and suggestive, near her ear.

Morgan knew well enough the workings of this man's mind. There was no need to look in his dark laughing eyes to realize the arousal that pressed into her hip. He had her exactly where he wanted her. But what he didn't know was that she was exactly where she wanted to be. All at once Morgan knew the folly of fighting against her predicament. She was married to this man and no amount of denying it would change that fact. She was having his baby. She wouldn't be returning to New York, now or ever. Why had it taken so long for her to come to this realization? Why had she fought it?

Because she wanted more than this. She wanted a man who loved her. Not someone who married her simply because he was forced into the act.

Granted, he'd told her he loved her. Rather he'd shouted he loved her, but Morgan had convinced herself that his words were untrue. She knew they had married only because of Martha's insistence, no matter his words to the contrary.

Still, she would have to be a fool to thwart the man's every advance. Wasn't she only adding to her own frustration? It wasn't wrong to indulge in the more pleasurable aspects of married life. Why should she deny herself any longer the delight of his touch? He cared for her. Maybe someday, she silently reasoned, he would come to love her.

Morgan didn't know what the future held in store. She only knew she wanted this man. Wanted him when he angered her. Wanted him when he made her laugh. Wanted him always to hold her as he did now. She'd be a fool to fight him any longer.

"If memory serves, you took advantage of me that day," she whispered in response, her eyes softening with the memory of that delicious encounter, her lips tempting inches from his.

"Would you like me to take advantage again?"

It took some effort on her part, but Morgan finally managed an astonished gasp. "Joseph! What a naughty thing to ask!" She schooled her features into a prim expression, her fingers playing with the fringe that ran the length of her dress, while Youngblood frowned with suspicion at the laughter he glimpsed in her glances. "Now," she continued in a most prudish fashion, "if I told you I would, I'd sound like a woman of no morals." A smile flickered at the corners of her mouth. "Then again, if I told you I wouldn't"—she hesitated—purposely dragging out the suspense, "you might not do it."

Morgan burst into laughter as Youngblood's eyes widened with shock. He growled, "Witch!" as he crushed her against him, his lips unerringly finding her mouth and holding it in a long sizzling kiss.

Morgan's arms came around his shoulders, her fingers brushing through his dark gleaming hair. "Am I terribly bold?" she asked as he released her mouth at last.

He was gasping for his every breath, his mind desperate to find a private place to take her. "Oh God . . ." His voice broke as he tried to speak. He cleared his throat and grated against the warm skin of her neck, "I hope so."

Morgan giggled as she cuddled against his chest. Her lips brushed whisper-soft kisses against his neck, her teeth grazed his collarbone, her tongue tasted with lusty enjoyment the flavor of his skin.

He was almost giddy with the knowledge that she wanted him to touch her. Dizzy with the feel of her eager mouth on him. There was nothing more on earth he could have asked for, except perhaps privacy. They were in flat Indian country. Anyone could see for miles from atop the mesa and there wasn't a damn rock of any size that could hide two lovers from even a casual glance.

Youngblood tipped his face up to the sky, calling on a power greater than his own to master this need. He gave a low, almost animalistic groan of pain. "Don't touch me," he gasped. "Jesus, I'm going to explode. I can't . . . I can't . . ." He never finished as her mouth moved against his jaw and his lips searched hungrily, helplessly, desperately for hers.

He sucked at her, starved almost to madness for her feel, her taste, her scent. The heat, the moisture, the texture and most of all the giving he found in her kiss took him to the edge of despair. He couldn't get enough and knew at that moment he never would.

"We've got to stop," he choked as he tore his mouth from hers and feasted on the delicate flesh of her neck as she leaned back against his arm.

"Do we?" she asked softly, am impish smile curving her lips and lighting her eyes. Her eyes flashed, her cheeks darkened at her daring when she whispered, "Why?"

Youngblood's lips grew thin, his jaw tightened against the pain of wanting her here and now. "Straddle this damn horse, Morgan. We're going to ride."

A cloud of dust and flying pebbles trailed behind the speeding animal as Youngblood urged Thunder to quicken his pace. He was heading toward the distant butte and he could only pray he'd get there in time.

He never had a chance.

Youngblood tried to ignore the creamy white thighs, naked from deerskin-covered knees and up, that rested so temptingly close to his own, but soon realized the futility of the effort. He hadn't known he was going to touch her, hadn't, in fact, realized he was touching her until he felt the softness of her flesh give beneath his fingers. He couldn't control his groan of pleasure.

Morgan jerked as his hand came to rest with bold possession upon her thigh. He pulled her back until her rounded backside was pressing against his arousal. The movement of the racing horse caused at least one particular part of their bodies to rub together with dizzying pleasure.

Morgan glanced behind her, only to find Youngblood's gaze trained over her head, his concentration on the buttes that lay in the distance. Did he feel it? Was he conscious of the fact that they were touching like this? Was his heart slamming into the wall of his chest, as was hers? Did he find it equally hard to breathe?

Morgan groaned as she felt his fingers move ever so slightly along the length of her thigh. She couldn't bear it. She wanted to feel him buried deep inside her. She'd wanted to touch him, to kiss him, to love him for weeks. She wouldn't allow even one more day to pass without knowing his touch again.

Youngblood instantly realized he had set himself upon an impossible task. Granted, he had done this once before and had suffered no staggering consequences. Yes, she had tantalized the senses. Yes, he had desired her, but not like this. Nothing had ever been like this. He had only begun to love her then and that emotion didn't compare to the need, the love he'd come to know since. And still, knowing the pain that would come to wrack his body, he was unable to resist her silent allure.

Morgan closed her eyes. Her body trembled in anticipation, for the pleasure was almost unbearable. Her head slumped forward as she watched his fingers inch closer to the juncture of her thighs. "Joseph, oh God," she murmured as her head fell back upon his chest. "Not your fingers this time. Please! I want you. I want to feel you!"

Youngblood thought he might die with the jolt of sensation that slammed into his groin. He was thick, throbbing, nearly bursting, straining with the effort it took to control his need. "I can't stop," he swore. "I have to touch you."

"Not your fingers," she moaned.

"Lean forward," he grated in a voice that sounded foreign to his own ears. "Just a little, honey," he instructed. Youngblood put to good use the space she created between them. In seconds his pants lay open, his

266

sex searching hungrily for its mate.

His arm came around her waist and lifted her from the saddle. His fingers moved briefly to the juncture of her thighs. He trembled at the heat and moisture found waiting there. Beyond the pounding of his heart he heard her soft gasp, felt her shiver and knew she was ready. Thank God! He couldn't wait a second longer. Without a moment's hesitation he brought her down upon him. The penetration was swift, hard, and blissfully total.

Despite his wordless cry of pleasure, Youngblood was conscious of her stiffening, of her sharp gasp of indrawn breath. He pulled his hat from her head and groaned into the soft cloud of her hair. "Did I hurt you, love?"

Sensation exploded. Lights flashed behind her closed eyes and she moaned yet another sound, this one guttural, as if suffering dreadful pain. Instantly he brought Thunder to a stop, lest his movements hurt her further. Jesus Christ! How could he have been so rough? Besieged with guilt, Youngblood attempted to lift her from him.

"No!" she choked as she tightened her legs upon the saddle, effectively preventing him from lifting her away. "Oh God, no," she gasped as her head fell weakly to his shoulder. She moaned as her lips sought out the warmth of his neck. "Don't put me from you, Joseph. Please. It feels so good."

Youngblood's mind swam in ecstasy as he realized she was nearly begging him to hold her, to make love with her. It was pleasure that had caused her to react, not pain. He relaxed his hold and growled a low hungry sound at the exquisite sensation of being deep within the softness of her body. She was so tight, so deliciously hot. It was better than anything he remembered. Better than anything he'd ever known.

Chapter Fifteen

Youngblood never knew how he'd managed the feat and remained upon his horse. His every thought was of the woman in his arms. He knew nothing but her scent, her taste, and the splendor of being deep inside her at last.

Their mouths clung together, imitating the movement of their bodies. Ecstasy! He never thought to wait until he found a more discreet moment to love her. He couldn't stop the passion that had already gone wildly out of control.

He felt her shudder against him, felt her body tighten unbearably around his, listened to her soft cry of pleasure and ground his hips forward for his final gasping release. His body stiffened, his teeth clenched together as if in pain, his eyes closed against the beauty of loving her.

Youngblood groaned, his face buried in the sweetness of her neck as the aftershocks of their wild lovemaking receded slowly into a mindless euphoria. "Oh God," he groaned, his breathing harsh and choppy. "I think I died." He nuzzled his face tighter against her, breathing deeply of her scent. "How did you do that?"

Morgan's laughter was closer to a breathless sigh as she leaned against him. "Did I do something?"

"I went wild, and you caused it." Youngblood shuddered as he remembered the frantic, mindless urgency he had just suffered.

"You deserved it, after all the teasing you've been

doing lately."

"When have I teased you?" His affronted tone might have worked had Morgan not known him well enough to recognize the laughter in his voice.

"What would you call the morning escapades these last weeks?"

Youngblood grinned. "I'd call them wonderful."

Morgan laughed and shot him what she imagined to be a stern look from the corner of her eye. "You wretch! You were making me crazy and you knew it. You did it on purpose."

"Did I?" he asked in supposed innocence, but one look at eyes that gleamed with wicked glee and she knew well enough the truth. "I only thought to awaken my wife in a proper husbandly fashion." Youngblood smiled, suddenly liking very much indeed the word *husband*. How was it he'd never before realized how wonderful it could sound? "I never for a moment thought it would make you crazy with wanting me," he lied unconscionably.

"Beast!" she returned, unable to hide her smile. "If you're going to make a habit of lying, you'd best do a proper job of it."

"Well, you'd better not show me how. You can't lie worth spit."

Morgan laughed. "You make that sound like a failing. Shall I take lessons from my . . . my husband?"

Youngblood noticed the slight stutter, but refrained from remarking on it. It was enough that she was thinking of him as her husband. If she stuttered a bit over the word, he couldn't find fault. She'd soon get used to it. "There'd be other lessons I'd be most willin' to teach you, ma'am," he murmured as he switched back to his cowboy jargon.

"Such as?" she asked, knowing exactly the direction of his thoughts from the sudden huskiness in his voice.

"I want to get you behind those rocks before I show you," he said as he urged Thunder again into a run.

Ten minutes later Youngblood pulled his horse to a stop, adjusted his clothes, and slid from the saddle. He helped her down and held her at his side as they left Thunder to graze on sparse short grass.

Youngblood moved to the scattered outcropping of tall rocks that stood in clusters before the mountainous butte. Hand in hand they walked over the rocky desert floor. The instant they were hidden from sight he swung her to his chest.

Morgan hit against him and laughed at the eagerness that shone boldly in dark eyes. There was obviously but one thing on this man's mind. A quick glance at her feet promised no real comfort, for the ground was littered with small sharp rocks. "We'll have to stand."

"I don't care," he returned. "I want to kiss you, really kiss you without the chance of someone watching."

"Who could be watching? There's no one out here."

There was no sense in telling her that anyone could see miles in any direction by simply looking down from the mesa. If she thought there was a chance someone had noticed what they had been about, she'd be mortified. "I know, just kiss me and stop stalling."

Morgan grinned as she inched closer to his hard form. Her arms slid slowly up his chest to his shoulders, her hands circling his neck. "Am I stalling?"

"You are."

"Strange, but I don't see you in any particular hurry."

"That's because I'm so good at lying, can't you tell?"

"I see," she remarked; her eyes matched his in laughter. "You are in a hurry then?"

Youngblood pulled her hips up and against his and moved suggestively against her. "What do you think?"

Morgan swallowed and found she had to clear her throat before she could go on. "Then why aren't you kissing me?"

Youngblood breathed a long weary sigh as he looked toward the heavens as if asking for help. "Do I have to tell you everything?"

"It appears you must."

"I want you to make the first move this time."

Morgan's eyes widened in surprise. She didn't know

what to think. This was the second time he'd remarked about her taking the initiative. She'd never heard of such a thing before meeting him. A lady did not kiss a man. A lady was kissed and submitted to her husband's kisses whenever he felt the need. Wasn't that the way of things? A frown marred her smooth brow as she realized the idea of taking the initiative was intriguing, to say the least. Slowly she came to realize she was partial to the idea. Very partial indeed. "Are you sure?"

"I'm sure," Youngblood grunted as she moved her shoulders just enough to allow her breasts to sway against him. Even through her dress the motion brought a groan from his throat.

She saw his eyes close with pleasure, and she grinned. "You are my husband, after all," she said with false submission. Her words grew whispery soft as she continued, "I imagine I've no alternative but to obey your commands."

"Oh God." He moaned his delight to find her lips brushing against his jaw.

"You'll tell me if I do anything wrong, won't you?"

"I'll tell you," he said, his voice low and tight with desperation.

"You're sure?" she whispered, her mouth less than an inch from his.

Youngblood was gasping for air. If she didn't kiss him, he was going to go out of his mind. He felt the feathery softness of her mouth brush over his and move away. "Damn you," he groaned as he tangled his hand in the lush softness of her hair. Holding the back of her head, he closed the distance between their lips himself. He couldn't stand another minute of her teasing. And the minute he was finished kissing her—say in, forty or fifty years—he was going to strangle her for the suffering she'd caused him.

"I wanted to go slow," he breathed on a gasping sigh into her neck the moment his mouth left hers. "I wanted to love you long and easy, but I've wanted you for so long, I can't." His breathing was coming in harsh jerking gasps. "Jesus, you're making me crazy."

"Later," Morgan said as she yanked at the hem of her dress until it reached her hips. "Love me slow later."

Youngblood couldn't help it. He had no control left. Not after the weeks he'd spent trying to seduce her into accepting him as her husband. Not after the mornings spent teasing each other to near madness. Now to find her willing in his arms, in fact more than willing, for she was as hungry for his touch as he was to touch her, was more than he could take. He had to have her and it had to be now.

His mouth slashed hungrily across her parted lips, his tongue delved deep into the silky, sweet warmth of her mouth. Youngblood shook with the urgency that filled his being. He was almost totally out of control by the time he felt her sucking gently at his tongue. He moved to lean her against the rock and lifted her legs to his waist. He didn't think much after that.

It was some time later before Youngblood got around to unsaddling Thunder. He cleared a small space free of rocks and spread his bedroll upon the mostly even ground. "Comfortable?" he asked as he gathered Morgan into his arms and pressed her head to his chest.

"I would be if I could wash up a bit," she returned. "You wouldn't be hiding a river or a lake on you anywhere, would you?" she asked with a wicked smile as her gaze quickly scanned his length.

"If I told you I was, would you search for it?" His eyes twinkled with amusement.

Morgan chuckled at the hopeful sound of his voice. "Wretch! Are you never satisfied?"

"With you so close?" he asked as if the idea were indeed impossible."

"Perhaps I'd better move away then."

"Don't," he said, the sound almost a plea. His arms tightened around her and held her fast. "I can bear it for now.

"There's water in my canteen, but I don't think we have a scrap of cloth to moisten between us."

272

Morgan hit his shoulder. "We would have, if you wore a shirt."

Youngblood laughed. "Use your own clothes."

Morgan looked down with pleasure at the prettily ornamented dress. "Doeskin? It's soft enough but I doubt it would absorb any water."

She shot him a glaring look. "I could have used my chemise or . . ." Morgan found no litle amazement in the fact that she could still blush, despite the intimacy shared this afternoon. "I could have used my unmentionables, if you hadn't hidden them."

Youngblood shook with laughter, knowing she couldn't bring herself to mention these unmentionables by name. "Me?" he finally managed. "Why do you think I have them?"

"Who else would take them? I haven't seen them since you brought me here."

"Are you accusing me of wearing lady's drawers?"

"Not exactly." She giggled at the picture his words brought to mind.

"What exactly?" His eyes were dark with supposed menace.

"Oh nothing," she said, unable to keep the smile from her lips.

He eyed her suspiciously and drawled out slowly. "You'd best not be thinkin' I get somethin' out o' playin' with them."

"The thought hadn't entered my mind," she professed with supposed amazement and then grinned. "Do you?"

"Only yours," he admitted, his mouth curving into a devastatingly wicked grin.

Morgan giggled. "You beast!" She came up to lean on her elbow and glared as best she could at his grinning, dark face. "I want them back."

"Why?"

"Why? What do you mean why? So I can wear them, of course."

"When?"

Morgan shot him a puzzled look and then suddenly

smiled as she realized his meaning. "I suppose you're worried I might take to wearing them at night."

"Ain't worried, honey. Was just thinkin' it sure would be a shame if they got ripped, is all. Them bein' so delicate and fancy with all that lace."

"Ripped?" Morgan laughed. "As in when you tear them off, you mean?"

Youngblood shot her a wicked look, never bothering to comment for they both knew how he expected her to sleep at night.

"All right. I'll only wear them during the day."

"Now I'm just a simple cowboy, honey. You wouldn't be tryin' to fool me, would you?"

She laughed softly. "Simple? You? I thought you were a wily Indian."

Youngblood grinned. "Only half." And then a moment later he asked, "Wily? Is that how you think of me?"

Morgan nodded her head. "A trickster."

"When have I ever tricked you?"

"I didn't want to make love and yet here I am."

"How did I trick you into it?"

Morgan shrugged and shook her head. Her voice echoed the confusion in her eyes. "I wish I knew."

He laughed again. "All right honey, you'll have them when we get back. Too bad though I kind a' like the idea of you wearing nothing under that dress."

"No doubt." She shot him an evil look that was immeasurably softened by the need to laugh.

"I like the idea of you wearin' nothin' at all even better."

Morgan watched him as he rolled from under her to a sitting position. His warm, dark gaze moved slowly over the length of her, from her deerskin-wrapped feet and legs to the very top of her shining hair. "Yes, I'm positive I'd like you wearin' nothin' at all."

Morgan's heart was suddenly pounding in her chest. Her tongue came to moisten her dry lips. Her cheeks flooded with color at her daring. "What are you going to do about it?"

Youngblood growled as he pulled her into his arms. "I wanted this time to be slow and easy, but I'll never make it if you look at me that way."

"What way?" she asked, her voice no more than a whisper as her gaze held to his.

"Like you want me to tear that dress off."

Morgan's lips curved into a soft smile. She shook her head and reached shaking fingers toward the hem of the garment. Slowly she began to draw it by mesmerizing inches up her legs. Had she been practiced in the art, her seductive disrobing couldn't have been more erotic. Youngblood barely breathed as the material slid up her legs and hips. He stared in fascination as the material moved over her silky skin, and he groaned a low guttural sound of pain as she flung the dress aside at last. "Shall I tell you what I do want?"

God! He wasn't going to live through this. For months he'd imagined her coming to him, her mouth soft, her eyes pleading, eager for his touch, and now that it was actually happening, he wondered if he would be able to stand the power of this moment. "Tell me," he choked, his heart pounding like a drum in his throat, nearly cutting off his breathing.

"Well, we could start with a kiss."

Youngblood jerked and breathed a shuddering sigh as her mouth came to press a fleeting kiss upon his.

"And then I could touch you," she said softly.

She smiled at the sharp intake of breath that hissed through his teeth and watched as his muscles contracted when her hands came to his chest and slid slowly over the wide expanse of shoulder and then down to his belly to hover at the opening of his pants.

Youngblood came to his knees. "Would you touch me everywhere?"

Morgan knelt before him. She appeared to be seriously thinking over his question while her blue gaze moved with great appreciation over his tempting form. She nodded. "Yes, I think that would be best. Would you like that?"

275

Youngblood could only choke out a ragged, "Oh God." His arms hung weakly at his side. He wanted to bring her closer, to feel her nakedness against his chest, to touch her, to love her, but couldn't garner the strength to put her hands from him.

Morgan rolled his still opened trousers down his thighs. With her eyes on his, her fingers boldly traced his sex, gaining courage as the low moan of dreadful pain was torn from his throat. She measured its length, its width, its firmness before moving to his hips and belly and back to his chest.

"I couldn't like anything more," Youngblood murmured, amazed that he'd found the strength to say his thoughts aloud.

"You understand I'm a novice at this kind of thing. You tell me if I do something you don't like."

Youngblood laughed, for there was nothing she could do to him he wouldn't love. "If you don't mind my saying it, you're very good. You learn fast."

"Do you think so?" She smiled and leaned forward so that her mouth could touch upon his shoulder and chest. Her tongue flicked out. She made a small sound of delight, while eagerly absorbing his taste. "I've got a marvelous teacher, you know."

"Do you think so?"

Morgan nodded. "I may not be much of a judge, considering the lack of experience, but I'd say he is the best."

Youngblood would never know how he managed to keep from crushing her against him. "Does that mean you like the things he does to you?" he asked as she leaned back and gave him a dreamy smile. He reached trembling fingers toward her waist-length hair. Gently he pulled it from behind her shoulders and draped it with great care over each sweet breast.

"Oh yes," she sighed, her back arching slightly, her body shuddering as the backs of his hands brushed over her flesh.

"What do you like most?"

"It's hard to say."

Youngblood glanced toward his obvious arousal and grinned. "And getting harder by the minute."

Morgan laughed as she followed the direction of his gaze. Her eyes were soft and shining as they returned to his. "You made me forget what I was going to say."

"You were about to tell me what you liked most," he said as his fingertips separated her hair so only the rosy tips of each breast shown through.

"Oh yes. It's har—" Morgan came to an abrupt stop and then began again. "It's difficult to pinpoint any one particular thing. But if I had to, I'd say it's his kisses. Yes." She nodded with confidence. "Definitely his kisses. He must have had years of practice. He's so very good at it."

"It's easy enough to appear practiced. The truth is when he's kissing you, he goes a little wild. You know sort of out of control."

"Oh I see. That must mean he likes it as well."

Youngblood's laugh was more a strangled groan. "You might be safe in believing that." From beneath the cover of her hair he lifted her breasts. He was weighing them in his palms as he rubbed the tips with his thumbs.

"Is it me, or does he simply enjoy kissing and any woman would do?" she asked. Her lips were parted. She was having some trouble with her breathing, and the more he touched her, the greater her effort to draw each breath.

"It's you. He hasn't kissed another woman since he met you."

Morgan shook her head, dislodging the hair he had so painstakingly placed upon her. "Not true. What about his women? What about Cindy?"

"He has no women. He lied about Cindy," he said as his head dipped forward.

"What about all those nights he didn't come home?"

Youngblood shook his head. "You. I only wanted you." His hands swept away her hair and his mouth took possession of her breast. He rolled his tongue over her

277

nipple and smiled at the soft, low moan that escaped her parted lips. Her head tipped back as she closed her eyes, relishing each luscious stroke of his tongue. "I let you think there were others, so you'd be jealous."

"That was mean of you." She nuzzled her face in his neck.

"I know. I couldn't help myself. I wanted you so badly."

"You could have had me a lot sooner if you'd changed your technique a bit."

Youngblood chuckled. "It took a while to figure that out."

Morgan pushed aside the thought that this was just another of his tricks. That he'd only treated her with kindness to get what he wanted. It didn't matter anymore. She wanted him just as much. "I'm glad you finally did," she breathed as he raised his head to gaze upon eyes warm and cloudy with wanting. Her lips were but a hairsbreadth from his, her voice low, husky with need, when she whispered, "Oh Joseph, I'm so very glad."

Youngblood's senses swam at the touch of her sweet mouth on his. His heart sang at the willingness he found in her arms. Rapture, bliss, ecstasy. Nothing came close to the wonder of having this woman press herself against him.

He realized then that no matter how many times he took her, it would never be enough. He knew at last that the ravages that had brought about untold pain and suffering since their first meeting were put to rest only in her wondrous kiss, in her sweet, sweet body. The joy he found in her was more than he could have hoped for, more than he could have imagined.

His tongue delved deep into the heavenly luxury of her mouth. God, he shuddered, hungrily absorbing the deliciousness of her taste. Would there ever be a time when he could take this woman without this trembling need? Could he one day sample a lazy, luxurious taste of her without being besieged with a sensation that threatened to shatter every ounce of restraint?

Youngblood's hands framed her face, holding it perfectly still as his mouth made wild love to hers. Gently at first, he sipped at her taste, but moments later only groaned as the need built almost instantly to raging insatiable passion.

"Slow," he breathed on a sigh as he tore his mouth from the enchantment found only in her. "Don't kiss me like that, or I'll never be able to do this."

Low, husky laughter bubbled from deep within her chest. "Kiss you?" she barely managed, knowing it was he who was doing the kissing. But any thoughts of blame drifted away like mist in sunshine when his lips and hands blazed a trail of ecstasy down the length of her trembling body.

Vaguely Morgan wondered why she had for so long fought the madness of this man's touch. Why had she refused them both the pleasure? His mouth at her breasts sucked the rosy tips deep into flaming heat. Morgan groaned as the suckling brought an ache to her belly. An ache for more, for everything he could give.

She arched her back and held his head closer as she breathed mindless, broken words of praise and pleasure. "Good! Oh God, that's so good."

Youngblood gasped as he pulled away, breaking her hold, not without some effort. It was imperative that he create some space between them. He needed a few minutes or this act would find its completion well before either had hoped.

Her eyes were glazed with passion as she stared up into his tight features. "What's the matter? Why did you stop?"

"Slow this time, remember?" he asked, his breathing ragged and strained, his voice husky as he forced a grin to a mouth tight with hunger.

"Joseph," she whispered as she reached for him. "Get back here," she demanded bossily.

Youngblood grinned. "Are you daring to tell me how to go about my business?"

"Not at all," she sighed as she moved the necessary inches it took to bring them together again. Youngblood growled at the contact, while Morgan's eyes lit with laughter. "I'm merely suggesting that while you're about your business, you might conduct that said business in as close a proximity as possible."

"Witch!" Youngblood grinned at her wicked teasing. "If you're so anxious to get on with this, perhaps you should do something about it." He rubbed his nose against hers and smiled. "If I remember correctly you were set on that course a few minutes back."

"Until a certain beast waylaid my thoughts," Morgan returned.

"Thoughts weren't all he laid," Youngblood countered with a smugness particular to the male species.

Morgan laughed. "Beast! I'm beginning to wonder if you can make it through one hour without bestowing upon this innocent maid your wicked thoughts."

Youngblood grinned as he gathered her close. He leaned back and pulled her to lie full length upon him. "Innocent, huh? There was a time when you might have convinced me, but not after that shameless display."

Morgan rested her weight on arms that crossed his chest and shrugged a shoulder. She didn't miss the light of interest that flared to life in his dark eyes at the movement. "Compared to you I'm as pure as snow."

"Meaning I'm what?"

"Well . . ." She grinned as a devilish glint entered her eyes. "Used up, might be a trifle strong."

"Only a trifle?" Youngblood laughed. "I would have thought experienced. I doubt you could say this was used up," he added as he guided her hand to his ever thickenig sex.

Morgan pulled her hand away. "You're impossible! Impossibly arrogant and . . ."

"And?" he asked, his eyes shining with delight as he waited for her to go on.

"And devastatingly attractive and handsome and oh-so-appealing."

Youngblood closed his eyes with pleasure. He hadn't realized till now how much he wanted to appeal to her. "Do you get hot all over when you look at me?" he asked, unable to keep the wicked gleam from his eyes. "Do you tingle all over? Do your nipples throb with the need for me to touch them with my mouth?"

Morgan shook her head with dismay and breathed a long weary sigh. "There's got to be a way to keep your mouth shut."

"I know of one."

"How?"

"You could kiss me."

She shook her head, her eyes growing smokey blue as her gaze lowered to his firm lips. "That wouldn't do at all," she murmured, her voice suddenly thick.

"Why?"

"Because when I kiss you, I most definitely don't want your mouth to be closed."

"God," he groaned as his arms nearly crushed her against him. "Kiss me, Morgan," Youngblood muttered in a voice gone tight with need.

Morgan did as he asked. Taking her cue from lessons learned, she teased his lips with light feathery touches, sliding her mouth back and forth. With little effort on her part, she felt his lips soften and move to accommodate the quick thrusts of her tongue.

Youngblood went wild. He'd never known a time when a woman had made her needs known. When she'd shown so obviously her hunger for him. He wanted to lie there to accept her sweet loving, but he couldn't keep his hands at his sides.

Tenderly brown fingers spread down the length of her, coming to rest at the juncture of her thighs. She kissed him wildly and moaned out her hunger as her body accepted the gentle touch of his fingers.

"I can't," she murmured roughly against his mouth. "Stop, I can't do what I want when you touch me like this."

"I have to touch you. I don't think I'll ever be able

to stop."

Morgan collapsed upon him with a moan as the gentle massage progressed. Her belly tightened with anticipation, her eyes closed against the magic.

Youngblood rolled her to her side and continued the sweet titillation. He listened as her breathing grew choppy and watched as passion-drugged eyes lifted to his in a helpless silent plea.

"Do you like that? Do you like what I do to you?"

A trembling sigh escaped her lips, but she couldn't find the strength to answer. Instead she only moaned again, her eyes fluttering shut.

Her body strained up toward his moving fingers. Her belly tightened further. Her face registered the ache that was growing by unbearable degrees into pain. "Joseph," she cried out as the waves of pleasure broke free at last. Again, again and again they came until she was mindless with the force of the surge.

She raised her arms, her intent to bring his mouth to hers, but found herself suddenly and dizzily swung up upon him. Her legs straddled his hips. He barely waited for her to steady herself before he joined their bodies in mindless ecstasy.

He heard her gasp as he lifted her to sit upon his erect throbbing sex. Her head tipped back, her eyes closed as if in the throes of agony.

His eyes widened with surprise and then narrowed as if in pain as he felt her instantly climax again. Her body shuddered, her muscles squeezed his inflamed sex, pulsating, drawing from him what he most wanted to give. He groaned as he closed his eyes against the helpless yearning that filled him, fighting against the need to join her in release. No. He wanted to prolong this pleasure. He needed to feel her soften and grow tight again. He needed to watch her response, to listen to her soft cries of pleasure.

He waited for the pulsating tightness that surrounded him to ease before he began to guide her into movements that allowed her full control.

His hands moved over her softness. From her waist, brown fingers moved over ivory skin, barely touching as they traced shoulders, chest, and arms. Centering his attention with her obvious approval, his fingers brushed back and forth over the tips of her breasts. He listened to her sharp intake of breath and groaned as she quickened her movement.

Her eyes closed. Her lips parted to accommodate her quickened breath. "God," she muttered as his one hand left her swaying breast to glide over a flat stomach, his thumb lingering inside the folds of her body where their flesh joined.

Out of her mind! He was driving her insane. Every time it was better than the last. The ache was growing into an agonizing pain. "Joseph, please," she begged breathlessly. "Help me. Oh God, help me," she pleaded as her body became slick with sweat and she strained harder, mindlessly trying to find the release her body craved.

Morgan felt the tension mount to insane proportions. "I can't . . . I can't bear it!" she cried as her head fell back, her hair brushing against his thighs.

Morgan shuddered as his continuously moving thumb brought on wave after wave of ecstatic sensation and then he joined her in her movements, straining up higher, higher, never satisfied but to drive deeper, deeper into heaven.

It was long breathless moments later before she could speak, and when she did, her voice was a weak almost drunken slur. "I'm bound to get sunburned in some very odd places if I stay in this position."

He sighed with pleasure at the soft kisses she was spreading over his chest. "No one will see it but me."

"I'm less worried about the look of it than I am the discomfort when I try to sit."

Youngblood breathed a heavy sigh. "God, I hate this. There's always a reason why I have to let you go. I'm beginning to wonder if I'll ever have you to myself for any appreciable length of time."

"Poor darling." Morgan laughed as she patted his shoulder.

Youngblood shot her a hard knowing look. "I might well be as satisfied if I climaxed four times to every one of yours."

Morgan gasped with shock. Her cheeks burned bright red. Her mouth thinned into a straight angry line. "For your information, it was three."

"It was four," he said confidently. "You forgot about my fingers—"

Morgan interrupted his calm calculations. "You know, you have all the sensibilities of one of those stupid animals you take such pride in."

Youngblood laughed and held her close as she tried to get up. "Don't go getting mad, honey. There ain't nuthin' for you to be ashamed of."

"Shut up!" she snapped as she continued her struggles to free herself, while her face turned redder than ever.

"I'm jealous, is all." Youngblood easily admitted. "You women have all the fun." He switched their positions by rolling her easily beneath him. His weight held her in place. "Don't you think I'd like to go four times in a row?"

Morgan squeezed her eyes shut. "I don't want to talk about it."

"Why?"

"*Why?* Because you're embarrassing me. Why do you think?"

Youngblood leaned on his elbows, his eyes warm as they studied her face. His finger grazed her cheek and outlined lips swollen from his kisses. "What I think is that you're adorable. But you have something to learn about husbands and wives." His head dipped forward and he licked at her softness. "There is nothing that can't be discussed. Nothing they can't do together if it brings both pleasure." He smiled as he watched her eyes and sighed with satisfaction when she seemed to accept his words. "And I also think I love you more than I ever imagined possible."

284

Youngblood smiled, knowing it would take a bit of time before she came to accept the truth of his feelings and more time still before she could answer in the same vein. Jesus, he'd made a mess of things. There was a time when she was ready to profess her love and he had ridiculed her for it. Since then he'd watched as she'd buried her feelings beneath a hundred of his nasty comments and a thousand angry looks. He had only himself to blame if she was afraid to admit the truth of it now.

"I don't mind getting burned," he said after a long moment of silence. Youngblood grinned as he watched her eyes widen with surprise when he moved his hips against hers.

A grin tugged at one corner of her mouth. "I thought you said you couldn't—"

"Go four times?" Youngblood grinned down at her amazed expression. "I guess I can. Only I wasn't talking about all within minutes of each other."

"Joseph!" she snapped, her hands coming to his shoulders as she tried to push him off. "Will you *stop* it?"

"No." His head dipped forward and his mouth nibbled at her lips. "I love watching you when it happens, knowing I'm the cause of your pleasure. I only wish I could join you every time."

Apparently he couldn't, but Morgan would first suffer the ravages of hell before she'd ask why.

He groaned as he slid his mouth over her pliant lips. "How many times do you think this time?"

"None. I'm exhausted," she said, unwillingly drawn into the conversation while avoiding the laughter in his eyes.

"Shall we try for five?"

Morgan chuckled, unable to resist the man when he decided to use his considerable charm against her. A softness invaded her eyes. "You really are a beast," she said, so gently it sounded like words of love to both their ears.

Chapter Sixteen

The Johnson brothers left the busy, rowdy, cattle town of Elko one week after their arrival. During their stay, they patronized the brothels and saloons exclusively, always careful to cause no trouble, lest the marshal or one of his deputies notice them among the hundred of cowhands that visited in their free time.

One important reason for moving on was the fact that their money had already begun to dwindle. It was time to replenish their meager store. Another reason, and perhaps the stronger of the two, was boredom. It was true that the whores in town, although mostly fat and ugly, were cheap enough and eager to accommodate. And after a man had spent months behind bars as Jake and Mike had, even a two-dollar whore had a certain appeal. But the fact of the matter was, these three men preferred women not quite so willing and a damn sight prettier.

Jake, Larry, and Mike traveled south. Their intent was to pay a visit upon a certain sheriff in Sweetwater, for they owed that fool for their months of confinement. It was in Sweetwater, while sleeping off a three-day drinking binge, that the sheriff had accidentally discovered their true identities. Unable to defend themselves, Jake and Mike had been carted off to the town's jail to await the arrival of the marshal and deputies from Virginia City. Larry had managed to escape the bungling efforts of the law as he had been occupied at the time and right nicely, to his way of thinking, by one of the town's whores. The whole fiasco might have made little impression on the men were it not for the fact that the sheriff took full credit as if he'd faced down a pack of wild dogs and brought them singlehandedly to justice.

Now, Jake and his brothers found no fault in being compared to a pack of dogs. Actually they, all three, took to the description well and weren't the least bit ashamed of the fact. What they didn't like was the sheriff's pompous attitude, and his declaration that outlaws had best learn by his quick judgment and keep out of Sweetwater.

Quick judgment, my ass. The sheriff had been over the saloon, pumping away in the room right next to Larry's, when one of the town's biddies, by relayed messages of course, interrupted his fun. She had insisted he come outside and do something about the two drunks whose feet blocked the sidewalk.

Ah yes, the brothers were eager to see just how brave the bastard was when the three of them stood, able to defend themselves, on his side of the bars.

On their way south, the brothers took no precautions to remain unnoticed. Indeed, they raised their usual havoc. They robbed. They plundered. Finally, traveling almost aimlessly, they found a small isolated spread. After murdering the owner and the one hired hand, it was there that they stayed for nearly another week. It took that long before the woman stopped fighting and lay docile with thighs spread beneath them. When she did, they grew bored again, slit her throat, and moved on. They felt no pangs of regret or guilt, for the Johnson brothers were without a shred of conscience. A woman was a convenience and no more, easily disposed of when no longer needed. A docile woman bored them as nothing else might.

* * *

Idyllic. There was no other word for the time they spent among his father's people. Morgan knew they'd be returning regularly, but she also knew they'd never know such a time again, a time of freedom, of laughter, of learning, of pleasure.

Granted she had none of the luxuries she had always associated with a honeymoon; she imagined this was her honeymoon. Their bed consisted of a mat of furs in a small underground room. There were no candle-lit dinners for two, no music, no expensive restaurants. Their privacy was at best limited and yet Morgan doubted she'd have enjoyed herself more at one of New York's finest hotels.

Dressed again in her split skirt and boots, and wearing Youngblood's hat to protect her face from the harsh rays of the sun, she waved a last good-bye to his family. A moment later she was following Youngblood as he descended the long, steep, narrow path along the edge of mesa that led to the desert floor.

Youngblood's father had given her a pony, but Morgan couldn't ride bareback. Youngblood had offered in a foolish moment of chivalry to switch horses for the trip back. Now he thought better of the notion.

Morgan shot Joseph a grin as she mounted Thunder, knowing by his expression he wasn't too terribly happy about the turn of events. Youngblood eyed the Indian pony with annoyance. "I would have preferred to ride my horse and have you sit before me."

Morgan's blue eyes twinkled with mirth as she forced her mouth into a severe line. Without a doubt she could see the appeal in his way of thinking, remembering clearly the last time she'd done so, but reasoned correctly, "I'm sure you want to make it home before winter sets in."

A grin tugged at his lips. "Meaning I'm apt to get a bit distracted with your luscious ass rubbing up against my—"

"Joseph!" she gasped, thankful that her cry had

288

stopped him in time, for her cheeks were already bright red. "I've asked you not to talk like that."

"Like what?" He grinned, his eyes rounding with feigned innocence. "What did I say?"

Morgan pretended great interest in the stirrups already holding her booted feet. She wouldn't look at him. "You don't expect me to repeat it, do you?"

Youngblood shrugged. "Only if you want me to know what you're talking about."

"A lady doesn't use those kinds of words and she most definitely doesn't need to hear them."

"A lady doesn't say 'go piss up a rope' either."

Morgan laughed with remembered surprise. Her cheeks darkened as she dared, "Well, you did give me cause."

"Oh, I see. It's all right for you, but not for me."

"I was very angry."

"I understand. As long as one is angry, it's permissible to use words like—"

"Joseph!"

Youngblood was laughing at her prim expression. "What a fraud you are, Morgan."

Morgan frowned. "That's a terrible thing to say. When have I given you cause to believe I'm not exactly what I appear to be?"

"When I have you naked and beneath me." His eyes glowed with remembered pleasure. "I can talk to you then as I please and you offer not a word of objection." He grinned. "Why, I wonder."

Morgan's cheeks were ablaze with color and her words were almost a mumble. "Perhaps I'm not paying all that much attention to what you're saying."

"Or perhaps you like it well enough, but feel some shyness in admitting it?"

They trotted the horses in a westerly direction away from the mesa. Morgan, having no intention of furthering this most embarrassing conversation, looked around her and smiled at the wild beauty of the desert.

The sky was gloriously blue. The sun shone a yellow circle of light behind them. The desert was just coming awake. Birds chirped chattily as they flitted from prickly pear cactus to mesquite, while lizards and an occasional jackrabbit dashed out of their path. "It's a beautiful day, don't you think? I like the mornings the best. It gets so uncomfortable later. Do you—"

Youngblood interrupted her babbling with the pressure of his mouth. He brought his horse alongside hers, circled her waist with his arm, and pulled her so she nearly left the saddle. Planting a loud, hard, smacking kiss on her lips, he declared, "I won't press you now, honey, but later you're going to admit you love it."

"That's not fair at all," she said, her voice taking on a soft pouting sound. "You can convince me to say anything when . . ."

"When what?" Youngblood grinned at her hesitation. It was obvious she hadn't thought before she spoke. "All I said was you're going to admit you love it. Did I say what position you'd be in at the time?"

"Mr. Youngblood, sir, you are a rogue. A beast," she teased, her eyes lowering as a smile played at her mouth. "But I can tell you what position I like most."

"Ah, maybe you'd better not."

"Really, why?" she asked, her blue eyes round with feigned innocence as she watched him squirm uncomfortably.

Youngblood heaved a long sigh. It hadn't been two hours since they'd left their bed and already he wanted her again. He'd never known a wanting like this before. There was a time when he'd believed having her in his bed would ease the torture she brought to both mind and body, but that was not the case at all. His need for her seemed only to increase at every taking. Slowly he'd come to realize that everything about her intrigued him. Her teasing words had him aching to bed her again. Her laughter was a balm to his soul, her kisses the sweetest of tortures. For a moment he was tempted to grab her from the horse and, despite any objections she might offer, hold her against him for the ride home, but he thought better of the notion. Later, he promised himself. Later they would enjoy each other under the stars, perhaps till dawn, for out here there was no one to hear her soft cries but him. "I'm not sure I can listen to this kind of talk and do nothing about it."

"I was only going to tell you I like—"

"Morgan," he growled a warning.

"—to sit upon my rocker at the close of a day and watch the sun set."

Youngblood laughed at her look of total innocence. "Shall I tell you what I like?" he countered.

"Oh dear, I'm afraid I've started something here," she almost moaned. But the look in her eyes and the tone of her voice were strangely lacking in disapproval. It was clear enough she was enjoying this teasing.

"I'd like much the same as you except instead of watching the sun, I'd like to watch you stand in front of me and take your clothes off."

"On my porch?" She blinked her surprise, and his dark eyes sent chills of excitement all the way to her toes.

"With the sun behind you."

Morgan shook aside the sudden need to do just that and to do it here and now. She found she had to force aside a definite longing in her voice. "Disgraceful. The men—"

"Wouldn't see a thing if they were gone for the day."

Morgan shook her head, knowing the impossibility of such a notion and said wistfully, "What about Martha and Pedro?"

Youngblood sighed. "I think I'll build us a little place, maybe at the foot of the mountains up on the north pastures, where we could go for a little privacy." He seemed to think about it for a moment and then smiled. "Yes, I think that's exactly what I'm going to do."

Morgan smiled. Her heart felt lighter than air. She'd never felt more beautiful than beneath his warm steady gaze. She knew he desired her. The hunger he felt was never far from the surface, but it wasn't hunger alone she read in the dark depths and that was what excited her most.

It was late by the time they crossed the now dry gully that had nearly taken her life and camped for the night. After a light supper of dried meat and piki bread, they sat before the fire and talked.

"I can't wait to get home," Morgan said as she rubbed the crumbs from her fingers on her split skirt. "I can't get used to living without a few of the necessities."

"Like what?"

"Like a napkin to clean my hands and enough water to bathe." Her eyes closed with the pleasure of the thought and she sighed, "I'm going to sit in the tub till I wrinkle. Do you realize I haven't bathed in weeks?"

Youngblood grinned as he gazed down at her. "Now that you mention it, I do detect a certain aromatic scent."

Morgan laughed at his teasing and came up on her knees. She pushed her very willing husband to his back and leaned over him. "Take the blame on your own shoulders, if that's the case. It's you who dragged me away from civilization."

"I'm not complaining. I happen to like the way you smell."

"I smell?"

Youngblood was laughing at her expression as he reversed their positions. "Yes, you smell, honey. Just like the rest of us earthlings. The only difference is you smell good."

Morgan reached up and touched Youngblood's face; her fingertips grazed his cheek and slid across the wonder of his lips. Lips that gave more pleasure than she'd ever believed it possible to know. "So do you," she said softly.

"What?" he asked, his voice measurably lower, his breathing growing steadily harsh and weak.

"Smell good. I love the way you smell."

"Do you?" he asked. "What else do you love?"

292

She hesitated and a mischievous gleam entered her eyes. "Apple pie, fried chicken, tiny babies, puppies . . ."

Youngblood shook her and growled, "About me. What else do you love about me?"

"Oh, you!" Morgan said with a bit too much surprise and then laughed at his fierce look. "Let's see. It can't be the way you order me about." She shook her head. "No, no, that's not it," she said, dismissing the idea. "Could it be your crankiness upon awakening, especially after you've spent the night deep in your cups?" She shook her head again. "I don't think that's it either." Morgan heaved a great sigh. "Let's see, there has to be something."

"You wretch!"

Morgan laughed. "No. It's definitely not the names you call me."

"When have I called you names?"

"Well, the first time—"

"Forget it," he interrupted, not at all happy at the turn of this conversation. "Think of something else."

He waited, silently if not patiently, for her to go on.

Morgan took in the almost hopeful expression in his eyes. Her voice and gaze grew suddenly soft. "I love the way you hold your sister. The way you smooth her hair. The way you laugh at her antics and play with her and cuddle her in your arms."

Youngblood's eyes widened. He hadn't imagined she'd watched him so closely.

"I love the way you care for your father's people. The smile that's never far from your lips when you see them, talk to them. I like the way you talk to the men who work for you. You're never above menial tasks. You work along with them. I like the way you treat Martha, as if she's a special lady. And your patience with Pedro, how you've included him, made him feel like he belongs." Morgan shot him a hopeful look. "Is that enough?"

"No," he said, the look in his eyes matching the tone of his voice in softness. "Go on."

"I like the way I feel when I'm with you?"

"How?"

"Like I'm safe." She shrugged. "You know, protected." She took a deep breath before she went on. "I like the way you kiss me."

"Do you?" And at her nod, he said, "But I kiss you many ways. Which one do you like best?"

"All of them. I like everything you do to me."

Youngblood's mouth lowered to hers. Her eyes closed in anticipation. She could feel his warm breath against her lips. Her heart fluttered.

"Sonofabitch!" he said, so low that Morgan thought for a second she must have imagined it. "Sit up real slow and nonchalant-like. Don't be afraid. I have to check out how many."

Youngblood rolled away from her, reached for his gun, and pulled it from the holster still tied to his thigh. "Hide this under your skirt," he said as he pressed the gun into her palm. His free hand already held his rifle as he faded silently into the darkness.

Morgan simply blinked, her look of surprise turning slowly into a frown. "How many what?" she murmured to no one.

The light of the campfire could be seen for miles. They were tired and lazy enough not to have stopped sooner to prepare their own camp. Too bad, Jake thought now, they shouldn't have killed the woman. They should have taken her with them. She could have made their camp right homey and then serviced them all after their bellies were full. Even if she had lain there like she was dead, it was better than nothing. He shrugged at the thought and promised himself the next woman they found would be put to better use.

It would have been better if they had a chance to come up on the campsite more quiet-like, maybe protected from sight by some trees or rocks. No tellin' who they were or what might be found around that circle of light. But whoever had stopped for the night had guarded against being surprised by purposely camping far from any cover.

Jake's eyes widened in disbelief as he moved his horse closer to the camp. The woman's hair shone gold and silver against the firelight. She twisted to her side at the sound of their approach and her coat fell open. Christ! How did such a little thing like that have such a pair of tits? Jake felt himself grow hard just at the sight of her. Jesus, but he ain't never had one that looked like this. He felt his mouth water and it weren't for a cup of that brewin' coffee.

What was she doing out here alone? A quick glance toward the two animals grazing nearby brought an answer to his silent question. She wasn't alone. So where was her man? Maybe he went off to take a piss, Jake reasoned.

Jake dismounted and walked toward Morgan, who had yet to realize what was going on. "Evenin', ma'am," he said as he lifted a hand to his hat. "You ain't out here all alone, are ya?"

Morgan felt a burst of terror send chills down her back. She was suddenly tongue-tied with fear. There was no mistaking the look in this man's eyes. And the two who came in with him were certainly no better.

Morgan fought against the shiver that threatened. Surely the man couldn't help it if he was ugly. Obviously he'd been on the trail for some time, for his hair hung limp and greasy to his shoulders. He was missing two front teeth, but that happened to many people and shouldn't have caused her to feel this degree of fear. It didn't. It wasn't even the scar that ran down the side of his face puckering the skin and distorting his mouth into a permanent one-sided grin. It was the look in his eyes that set her heart to hammering.

Morgan, stunned by the looks of the man, hadn't much noticed the other two who had come to join him, but

Youngblood had. He had circled the camp, making sure no others held back to surprise him later.

"Move back from them, Morgan," he said, his voice tight with anger that they, that any man, should dare to look at her with such blatant lust. He was standing suddenly directly behind her, his rifle aimed at the man standing in the middle. "Slide on off to the side, honey," he said, not trusting any of these three within miles of his wife.

Morgan scurried to her left and backed up until she stood almost even with her husband.

"There's three of us, mister," Jake said as he nodded toward his brothers. "You fixin' on killin' us all?"

"I'm fixin' on seein' you ride out of here. Now get." Youngblood motioned with his rifle.

"You ain't bein' neighborly, mister. People share their fires out here and that woman—"

"I don't share my women. Especially not my wife." His dark eyes bore into Jake's, sending chills down the man's spine. "If you want to stay alive, you'll forget about her."

Jake cursed. He should have taken it slower. He should have asked for food, and then when the man relaxed his guard, he could have killed him and taken the woman. "You ain't got no call to—"

"You got to the count of ten to mount and ride."

"And if we don't?"

Youngblood's lips curved into a sinister smile. "I figure I can take two of you right off." His dark glance encompassed all three men as he arrogantly promised, "And I'll finish the last one before he takes me out."

Jake's mouth split into an evil grin that sent chills down Morgan's back. She knew the men weren't going to back down. Someone was going to die here. She only prayed it wouldn't be Joseph.

Except maybe for pumping a woman, there weren't nothin' Jake liked better than a fight, especially one as unfair as this one promised to be. His hand slid down his hip and cupped the handle of his gun. An instant later he was rolling on the ground. Jake got off three shots before he heard Mike cry out. Sonofabitch! The woman had a gun too! And she was using it as if she were born with it in her hand. He rolled again, desperate to find cover where there was none, and fired another two shots before Larry gave a garbled bubbly groan.

Youngblood flung his body over hers, knocking her to the ground. All the while his gun continued to fire. It was over in seconds. One was dead, one injured, one pleading for his life. "Jesus, mister!" Jake screamed. "Stop shooting! I'll leave you and the missus alone. I ain't never meant no harm, anyways."

Youngblood wanted to kill him so badly his body shook with need. He stood, legs spread, over the sobbing quivering man and kicked his discarded gun aside. "Too bad you wasn't payin' attention a few minutes back. You got one dead friend. The other has a hole in his belly." His voice was low and as deadly as his aim had been. He didn't need to elaborate. There wasn't a doubt in anyone's mind what the future held in store for the injured man. He'd be better off with a bullet between his eyes, for he was as good as dead, only he had a powerful lot of suffering to do.

"They're my brothers," Jake whined in a voice that might have stirred pity in an ordinary man.

But Jake wasn't dealing with an ordinary man. Joseph Youngblood held dear the things that belonged to him, and his wife headed that list. "Tough shit," Youngblood grunted, feeling not a moment's remorse. Brothers or no, they would have killed him and brutally abused Morgan if given the chance.

"Lie facedown and spread your arms," Youngblood ordered. Within minutes Jake was tied, wrists behind his back, ankles together. It was only then that Youngblood turned to Morgan. But the sigh of relief he'd been about to breathe got stuck in his throat at the sight of her.

Morgan struggled to her feet, her legs barely able to

297

hold her weight, for her whole body trembled with the shock of being thrown to the ground. In an effort to protect her, Youngblood had inflicted his own damage. Her shoulder and arm felt numb from his abuse.

A large, wet, red stain was spreading slowly across her chest. Youngblood stood there unable to breathe, his heart pounding with terror. Before his eyes the stain grew while the whiteness of her skin took on a gray hue. His mind went numb. He couldn't think what to do. She'd been shot and she hadn't said a word.

Morgan's eyes followed the direction of Youngblood's gaze. Her fingers were suddenly too weak to hold the gun. It fell silently at her feet, forgotten amid the shocking knowledge. She'd been shot! She hadn't realized that fact at the time. It wasn't until the last shot had been fired that the jolt she'd taken just below her shoulder had grown numb. At the time she attributed the discomfort to Youngblood's rough tackle.

Morgan watched in some amazement as her blood seeped from the wound and soaked her shirt front. Odd that it didn't hurt more, she thought. She'd always imagined a bullet wound to cause excruciating pain.

Morgan's head came up at Youngblood's gasp. She tried to smile, to reassure him, to wipe away the terror that filled his eyes, but her lips simply wouldn't work. She looked down again, almost mesmerized by the stain, unable to pull her gaze away as she watched it continue to grow.

He was close. She could see the tips of his boots standing before her. His hands reached for her and still she couldn't summon any real alarm. It was as if another had been injured and she was merely a witness to it all.

"I've been shot, Joseph," she said unnecessarily.

"I know, honey," he said as he lifted her into his arms. "I don't want you to be afraid. Do you hear me?" he said as he laid her upon the blanket they had used earlier. "I'm going to take care of you."

She must have dozed, for he was suddenly kneeling

298

over her, covering her trembling form with a blanket and tearing a shirt to shreds. A moment later he pulled her into a sitting position and began to pull away her vest and shirt. "Turn away before I put a bullet between your eyes," Youngblood gritted out to the man tied at his right. Satisfied that his order was obeyed, he carefully slid her arms from the blouse.

Morgan made a moaning sound, deep in her throat. "It hurts when I move it."

"I know, honey, I know," Youngblood replied, his lips whitening at her obvious pain, his fingers trembling as he went about the job of locating the exact position of her wound. "But I have to clean it and bandage it. I'll be done in a minute. I promise."

Youngblood felt on the edge of hysteria as he strained to keep his voice low and soothing. He had to keep her calm, a herculean task considering he was as close to losing control as he'd ever been in his life.

With shaking fingers, Youngblood managed to free her of her shirt and vest. He sighed with overwhelming relief upon finding the bullet wound just below the shoulder. "Thank God," he murmured unknowingly.

"Is it bad?" she asked, her voice barely above a whisper, suddenly unable to look for herself.

"No," he said gently as he leaned over to examine her back. "The bullet went clean through. I just have to get this bleeding to stop."

"Suppose you can't?" she asked, knowing fear for the first time.

Youngblood leaned down so his eyes were even with hers. "Didn't I tell you I'd take care of you?"

Morgan nodded, her eyes huge, filled with trust.

"Why it ain't hardly more than a scratch," he drawled as he tried to smile. "I'll have you fixed up in no time." He was rolling the torn strips into thick pads. Gently he placed them over her wounds and wrapped them in place with more cloth.

"You wouldn't lie to me, would you, Joseph?"

"I wouldn't lie to you, honey," he soothed as he pulled one of his clean shirts over her bandaged chest and back. "I want you to rest now." His voice was calmer, his hands had lost much of their trembling. "I'm going to saddle Thunder and get you home directly."

"You always get what you want, don't you?" she said, trying to lighten the moment but finding it hard to keep her eyes open. Her trembling had stopped, leaving her exhausted.

"Do I?" he asked, a faint smile teasing his lips.

"I can't ride," she murmured. "Now I'll have to sit in front of you."

Youngblood chuckled as he smoothed her hair back from her face. "I promise I won't take advantage of you this time."

Morgan smiled at the tender look that filled his eyes. She sighed as she lay back already half-asleep and felt his warm lips against her cheek. "I love you, honey."

"I love you too, Joseph," she whispered, close enough to sleep that she never realized she'd uttered the words.

Chapter Seventeen

Jake closed his eyes and gave a silent groan as he listened to the shivery high-pitched cry. An instant later the three horses scattered. Oh Christ! No! He couldn't leave a man in the desert without a horse, without water. How did this bastard expect him to live if left like this?

Suddenly Jake imagined he knew the man's intent. Trembling with fear as he awaited the end, he cursed vilely, for there wasn't a damn thing he could do about it. Not even in prison had he felt this helpless.

He watched in breathless silence as Youngblood broke camp and closed his eyes with relief as he realized the man had completely forgotten his existence. He watched the half-breed lift the injured woman into his arms. A moment later he was on his horse. Soon the sounds of the horse's pounding hooves faded into the night, leaving the campsite silent but for Larry's heavy, labored breathing and Jake's low, steady stream of curses.

Mike was dead and Larry, from the sound of his breathing, was well on his way, while he was tied tighter than an old maid's ass. His arms strained against the ropes and he cursed again. He'd never get free. Not without some help.

Jake rolled to his back and groaned at the pain that shot up his arms. That sonofabitch was going to die for this. Somehow, someway, he'd get even. That half-breed should have known better than to mess with Jake Johnson. He was going to learn Jake always got even.

An evil grin split his already distorted mouth into a grotesque semblance of a smile as his mind raced on ahead. He'd find them. It didn't matter how long it took, he'd find them, and when he did he was going to kill them both. But first he was going to take the woman and use her till he was half dead from the pleasure. Jesus, he ain't never had a piece like that one. His mouth watered just thinking about how good it was going to be. A maniacal gleam of spiteful laughter lit up his eyes. Maybe he would make the man watch. That was always good for a laugh, especially if the woman fought him real hard and he had to get rough.

Jake glanced at his brother. Jesus! The hole in Larry's gut looked big enough to climb through. He had to get to him before it was too late. He rolled again, bringing his body within touching distance, but Larry was fading fast. Damn! He had to get help.

"Larry, wake up," he grunted, finding it no small feat to keep his face out of the dirt with his arms tied so tightly behind him. "Wake up! Can you hear me?"

Nothing.

Jake crawled on his belly and butted his brother's thigh with his head.

Larry groaned a low sound of pain.

"Wake up! You have to untie me!"

"Mmmmm."

"For Christ's sake, wake up! I can't stay like this all night."

"What?" came a low murmur.

"Untie me, damn it!" And when it seemed Larry was about to fall back to sleep again, Jake gave him another blow with his head. "Untie me!"

Jake was screaming his frustration in a string of vile curses as he tried to bring his brother around, but the words barely penetrated Larry's consciousness. He heard them yes, but from a distance. For a second he tried to fight his way back, but the struggle was too great, the distance too long, and the promise at the end only pain. He knew then that he was dying and yet he couldn't find it within himself to care.

Jake groaned with frustration. Even if he did get his brother to wake up, he doubted Larry had the strength to work the rope loose. A knife! He could do it himself if he had a knife.

Jake turned his back to his brother and twisted until his fingers found the knife Larry always kept hidden beneath his trouser leg. Sweat ran in rivulets down his face by the time he finally held the knife in his hands. He was gasping for breath, unable for a moment to begin the torturous movements it would take to free himself. He had to rest, but he dared not take the time. He was easy prey to anyone or anything passing by. He had to be able to protect himself. And in order to do that, he had to get free.

It was late into the night before Jake finally cut through the last of the rope. His arms were shaking, his wrists, fingers, and hands cut in a dozen places from maneuvering the knife. He quickly cut the bindings at his ankles and lay there for a long moment gasping for air, his body trembling with exhaustion from the effort it took. The sonofabitch was going to pay for this.

Jake might have sworn his vengeance, but in truth he was more upset that his plans for the woman and a meal had been thwarted than he was about his brothers' deaths. He wasn't happy to see them die, but neither did he feel any real grief for them. Actually, not one of the three brothers had the capability to care for another. So it couldn't be said that Jake acted out of character when he looked his brother over, gave a short snort of disgust, shrugged, and then left him to die in the desert alone.

It took Jake until well into the next day before he found his horse, thanks to that goddamned half-breed. His belly rumbled from lack of food. His throat was parched from thirst. His feet ached from the seemingly endless walking. He sighed as he mounted the horse and nearly emptied his canteen in one swallow. Someone was going to pay for this. Someone was going to pay real good.

Youngblood guided Thunder toward the ranch, holding Morgan in arms that strained in their effort to cushion her from the jarring movements of the horse. She moaned, deeply asleep and yet apparently suffering still from the pain. He'd ridden through the night, but the pace he'd set had been slow. They wouldn't reach home for at least another five hours.

Morgan gave another muffled cry and Youngblood's chest squeezed with sympathy. He had nothing with him to help relieve her discomfort and cursed his lack of proper preparation.

If only he'd thought beyond his immediate need to seduce his wife. He knew better than to travel alone in a country that was considered at the very best unfriendly, without some decent supplies. Good God, he couldn't believe he'd acted with such unbelievable arrogance! How had he dared to take it upon himself to chance a life so terribly precious? Why hadn't he brought one of the men along? Suppose it was he who had been injured or killed? How could Morgan have managed to get herself back alone? Where had his mind been? Jesus, if nothing else he should have packed a bottle of whiskey and a smattering of medical supplies.

Youngblood's muscles bulged as he held her limp weight high above the jarring of the saddle. His arms ached at the strain and finally arms, shoulders, and back grew numb. But no matter the pain and stiffness, he wouldn't give in to the need to rest. She couldn't be jarred. Bouncing upon the horse's back might cause further bleeding, and she'd lost enough blood.

Wrapped tightly against the chill of the night, Morgan had slipped in and out of a restless sleep, her head against Youngblood's broad chest. Now that the sun was beginning to warm the cool desert morning, Morgan instinctively snuggled into the heat, for the loss of blood had left her predictably weak and cold.

Something was bothering her; something more than the injury she'd taken to her shoulder. She'd awakened from time to time, unsure of the reason, knowing only a vague discomfort in her lower back. But the moment she awakened, it seemed to disappear and she almost instantly fell back to sleep again.

It was a little after dawn when the first real pain slammed into her midsection. Morgan gasped suddenly awake as a thick, heavy cramp tore at her stomach. Her eyes widened in confusion, for she couldn't understand why her belly should hurt so terribly when it was her shoulder that had been injured.

Youngblood heard her sharp intake of breath and felt her stiffen in his arms. "What is it?" he asked, his heart hammering with dread as he watched her lips tighten in pain. "Is it worse? Are you bleeding again?"

Joseph pulled Thunder to a stop and lowered the blanket, his eyes searching for any sign of fresh blood.

"No!" she gasped again, curling herself into a tight ball. "Here," she said, her hand moving beneath the blanket to her stomach. "It hurts here."

"Jesus," Youngblood groaned, his heart and mind filling with dread. She was curling tightly against the pain, her knees almost at her chest. He breathed a low horrified groan. The baby! She was losing the baby and he didn't have the slightest notion of what to do! His mind screamed in silent panic. How does one go about assisting a woman in this hour of need? Especially this woman!

He strained for calmness, forcing himself to think. Nothing could happen that fast, could it? Women suffered hour upon hour while birthing a child. No doubt the loss of one would take at least that long. Wouldn't it? Oh God, please! She wasn't going to do this to him here in the middle of nowhere, was she? God, there was no way he could help her. Nothing he could do. There were no clean shirts left and only a mouthful or so of water in the canteens. No! This couldn't happen now.

Joseph kicked his horse into a wild run. He had to get her back! Jesus God, he had to get her back!

Ten minutes later Youngblood realized the impossibility of the notion. No matter how he might hurry, it was already too late and the terrible jarring of the horse was simply adding to her agony.

"My back," she gasped as he pulled the horse to a stop. Still holding her, he dismounted and knelt at her side as he lowered her gently to rest upon the ground. "My back. It's killing me."

Youngblood had never felt so helpless in his entire life. This woman who meant more to him than the very air he breathed was in the midst of losing their child and he couldn't do a damn thing about it.

Weak from her loss of blood, fading in and out of sleep, Morgan never realized the reason she should be suffering this pain. "What's the matter with me?" Morgan groaned as another pain finally eased its wrenching agony. She collapsed weakly in his arms, gasping for her next breath.

"It's the baby, honey."

Morgan's eyes opened wide with fear as the truth dawned. "No!" Her eyes clung to his, silently pleading that he take back his words. But another pain came before she had a chance to speak her thoughts. Her eyes filled with tears as she realized the truth of it. "I don't want to lose this baby, Joseph," she said, her voice tight with anguish as she fought against the back-splitting cramp.

"I know, honey," he soothed as he held her upper body close to his chest and rubbed her back, praying this small effort would soothe her torment. He buried his face in her hair. "I'm sorry. I'm so sorry."

Now that she was on the verge of losing her child, Morgan realized nothing had ever been so important in her life. She wanted this baby. She needed it. It couldn't

306

be allowed to die.

"Help me, Joseph. Please don't let this happen," she begged, knowing he hadn't the power as she spoke the words.

Sweat beaded her forehead and upper lip as her uninjured arm reached for his shoulder. Her body shook as if palsied. So extreme was her shaking that Young-blood found himself hard put to merely hold her in place. Jesus! Oh sweet Jesus, what was the matter with her? What was happening? In a desperate hold, he pulled her tighter to his chest as if his strength alone could forestall this happening, all the while whispering disjointed soothing words that belied his terror.

She wasn't dying. No! He wasn't going to allow that. She had to live. She had to. Don't die, he silently implored. Please God, don't let her die.

Her mouth opened in a silent cry. With unbelievable strength her fingers dug deep into his back as her body stiffened and the last agonizing cramp threatened to split her back in two. She couldn't stop the overwhelming need to bear down. She was going to disgrace herself and she didn't care. She had to push. Her teeth gritted with the effort. She groaned and then pushed again. Suddenly a soft wet form was expelled from her body. She gave a low moan, her head fell back, and her eyes closed as she collapsed against him.

Tears streamed down her face to mingle with the sweat that already coated her skin. She trembled from the chill and wondered how she could be so cold and yet sweat. A dry, aching sob slipped from her lips. It was over so fast. One minute she was a woman expecting a child. The next, that child no longer existed. She hadn't imagined something so terrible could happen in just a few minutes. But it hadn't been minutes. She knew now that she had suffered throughout the night, only she had been so weakened from her injury, she hadn't realized at the time she was losing the baby.

Morgan turned and buried her face into the hard

307

warmth of his chest. It was so unfair. She was just becoming accustomed to the idea. She was only now beginning to enjoy the fact that she'd soon have a child. And now, now she had nothing.

Soft silent sobs shook her form as the enormity of the last few minutes hit her. She lay weak and trembling against him.

"Don't cry, sweetheart," Youngblood choked, his own tears making speech almost impossible. "There'll be other children. I promise, there'll be others."

But Morgan knew the truth of the matter and cried all the harder. He'd only married her because of the child. Now that the child no longer existed, there was no need for them to stay together. She knew he was just being kind. There would be no other children, at least not between them. She shook her head, and her voice was muffled as she spoke against his chest. "I don't think so."

Never realizing the direction her thoughts had taken, he hugged her closer. His face sought out the warmth of her neck as he whispered, "There will be. You'll see."

Morgan sighed, suddenly terribly weary. She bit her lip, too tired to argue as huge tears slid from glistening blue eyes. She wanted to tell him there was no need to pretend. She knew he felt bad, but the truth of the matter was they had only stayed together because of the child. Now that the child no longer existed, the reason for their marriage was gone as well. Morgan knew the sooner she came to accept that fact, the better off she'd be.

She was almost asleep when she heard him whisper, "After I make you comfortable, I'll take you home."

He lowered her flat upon the ground and proceeded to unwrap the blanket. Her split skirt was stained, but her drawers were soaked with blood. Youngblood fought back his gasp of shock. Was it normal to bleed so heavily? Would she be all right? His fingers shook as he pulled off his shirt and tore it in half. He rolled the material into a pad. After cleaning her as best he could, he discarded her drawers and gently pressed the pad between her legs. A

308

moment later he managed to get her into her skirt again. God, she was so weak she hadn't the strength to lift her hips for him. "Do you want some water?"

Morgan had never imagined a weakness so totally debilitating. She couldn't keep her eyes open. From somewhere in the back of her mind she knew she should feel some degree of embarrassment that Joseph should administer to her so personally, but she simply couldn't garner the strength. She never answered his softly spoken question, having forgotten it the moment he asked. She slid into a deep dreamless sleep.

Morgan was still sleeping when Youngblood pulled his horse to a stop some six hours later. It was dark. Light shone from the windows in cheerful welcome. He almost smiled at the sight of the large, homey structure. In his concern for his wife, he'd completely forgotten the beautiful house she'd created. A house that she alone had made into a home.

He dismounted, gathering Morgan close to his chest as he moved up the two steps to the porch. A shaft of light coming from the parlor window shone across Morgan's sleeping features. Youngblood stood still, gazing down at her for a long moment. God, he loved her so desperately. Why had it taken him so long to realize that fact? They'd had such a short time together. Nothing could happen, he silently swore. Now now. Not when he'd finally realized his need for her. Not after discovering what it was to truly love.

The door opened. Martha's full form moved out into the shadows. He saw her stiffen as he walked toward her. "Oh my God!" she said as her hand came to her breast as if to calm her heart. She slumped against the wall behind her, legs trembling, imagining her Morgan to be dead. "Is she . . . ?" Martha couldn't seem to get the rest of her sentence beyond stiff lips.

"She's hurt," Youngblood bit out, suddenly furious that she should dare imply more, "but she'll be all right." He moved past her through the hall, never stopping until he lowered Morgan to his bed. "Send one of the men into town for the doctor and then make her something. Some broth maybe. She hasn't eaten or drunk anything since last night."

"What the hell is the matter with her?" came a roar from the bedroom door.

Youngblood turned toward the sound of a strange male voice and spied an elderly gentleman coming to the foot of his bed. He'd been about to ask, "Who are you?" when it suddenly occurred to him that Morgan's father had arrived. Jesus, what a welcome!

He turned back to his wife and began to open the buttons of her shirt. "She has some gowns in the room down the hall. I'll need some towels and water as well. Let Martha know."

Despite his size, Andrew Wainright was gone and back before Youngblood slipped the blouse from Morgan's shoulders. He placed a silk nightdress on the bed, suddenly unsure of what to do next. What had his daughter gotten herself involved in? And why in hell had he sent her here in the first place? In order to avoid one situation, he'd foolishly sent her into another far more dangerous.

"Tell me," he insisted, obviously upset and feeling decidedly helpless and ill at ease as this strange man fawned over his only child.

Youngblood sighed. "She was shot. Three men came across our camp last night. There was some disagreement on who wanted her most."

Wainright turned pale at the thought and then a vivid red. His blue eyes shouted his fury as he whispered tightly, "Did they . . ."

"No they didn't. But she got shot during the discussion."

"Sonofabitch! Are you telling me she was standing there in the open? In the middle of a shoot-out?"

Youngblood said nothing.

Wainright could hardly speak so great was his fury.

310

"This doesn't say much for your ability to protect my daughter." Wainright nodded toward the makeshift bandage that covered Morgan's shoulder.

Youngblood grunted. He'd cursed his inability to protect her for the last twenty-four hours. He wasn't about to argue he could when obviously he hadn't. But he sure as hell wasn't about to listen to another throw accusations.

"She's going back to New York the minute she's able to travel."

Youngblood lifted his head, his black eyes glaring his resentment.

"Do you expect me to leave her here with a man who admits he can't protect her?"

Youngblood's fingers came to an abrupt stop in the midst of his task. He glanced up at his father-in-law. The man was livid with rage. A well-justified rage, as far as Youngblood was concerned. Still he wasn't about to take anybody's bullshit. "Morgan needs me right now, Mr. Wainright," he said coldly. With a nod toward the door which clearly bespoke his dismissal, he added, "We can always argue later."

Wainright cursed in frustration as he walked toward the door. "One more thing," Youngblood said, halting Wainright's steps. "You might as well understand this right now." His dark eyes narrowed and bore into his father-in-law's with fierce determination. "Morgan's my wife. There is no question about you taking her away. This is where I live and she'll be staying with me."

Youngblood held her close to his side during the long night. He couldn't sleep for fear of hurting her. Neither could he bring himself to leave her side. After he had washed and changed her, she had awakened long enough to take some beef broth and two glasses of water. No sooner had she swallowed the last sip than she'd fallen back asleep. The pattern was to continue for days.

Doc Franklin came at last and, much to Youngblood's relief, promised that sleep was what she needed most—and that all was well as long as a fever didn't appear. Even Martha had agreed with the doctor's opinion and still he had been unable to relax.

He watched her constantly, never leaving her side, sleeping only in short snatches and only in the chair at the side of the bed, lest he roll over and hurt her further.

"How long have I been sleeping?"

Youngblood heard the sound of her voice and came sharply awake. He reached again for her forehead as he had a thousand times during her illness and sighed with relief upon finding it cool and dry.

"How do you feel?"

"A little tired." She shrugged and then winced at the pain, having forgotten her injured shoulder. "A little sore."

Youngblood nodded. "You need to rest. Are you hungry?"

She shook her head. "Thirsty."

Youngblood sat on the bed and lifted her so she might drink from the glass he held.

"How long?"

"Three days."

"Three days? How could I have slept so long?"

"You lost a lot of blood," he said as he pressed her back to freshly fluffed pillows. He smoothed her hair away from her face. The doctor said you'll be just fine."

"Did he?" Morgan felt no little amazement at the tears that suddenly began to gather in her eyes. She brushed them away impatiently. Her hand fell to her side.

Youngblood picked it up and held it in his own. "You're tired, sweetheart. You'll feel better after you rest."

The sadness in Morgan's smile tore at Youngblood's heart. "You look terrible. You haven't slept, have you?"

He smiled at her concern. "I'll sleep. I wanted to make sure you were all right first."

"Well, I'm glad to see you're finally awake," came a deep booming voice from the doorway.

Morgan turned at the sound and smiled. "Father! How long have you been here?"

Andrew came to the bed and leaned down to kiss his daughter's cheek. "Long enough to wonder if I didn't make a mistake sending you here." He wiped at suddenly misty eyes and blew his nose loudly. "I've been thinking maybe you should come home when you're well again. Would you like that?"

Morgan felt Youngblood stiffen at her side. His hand was suddenly crushing hers. She turned to look at a face gone distant and cold. Morgan closed her eyes. She simply didn't have the strength for this right now. "We'll talk later, Father."

"Of course, of course," he said in his blustering way, already embarrassed at his show of emotion. "You go back to sleep. We can talk all you like tomorrow."

The door closed behind him. The sudden silence in the room was a palatable thing.

"Would you like that? Youngblood asked, his eyes remote and distant, his jaw and mouth harder than she'd ever seen them.

"Do you want me to stay?"

Youngblood shook his head. "No good, Morgan. You're going to have to say it," he remarked almost coldly.

"Say what?"

"That you love me and you want to stay."

Morgan would have gladly said just that, if it hadn't been for the fact that he didn't feel the same. Yes, he'd said he loved her, but Morgan hadn't believed those easily spoken words.

"Is that what you want?"

He shrugged. No matter how desperately he might want it, there was no way he was going to beg this woman to stay. "I've told you often enough how I feel."

"But that was before the baby died."

"And you think I only wanted you because of the baby?"

Morgan nodded, the look in her eyes bleak.

Youngblood sighed. "Morgan, I didn't know about the baby when we married. I'd only hoped."

"Why?"

"Because I wanted you. I only used the threat of a baby to convince you."

Morgan shook her head. "I don't know." Her eye caught his in accusation. "Martha insisted."

"I've told you before, no one can force me to do anything I don't want to do." And when she didn't answer, his lips tightened. He was growing obviously angry now. "Why did I tell you I loved you?" he almost shouted. "I didn't have to say it."

"I don't know," she said again, unable to believe his profession after all the weeks of believing he'd married her only because of Martha's threats.

"Because I do, damn it! Why can't you believe me?"

Tears of weakness and confusion slipped from her eyes. She didn't know what to believe anymore and right now she was too tired to bother.

Youngblood breathed a long sigh and rubbed his hand over his face. "I didn't mean to make you cry." He came to his feet and walked to the door. His hand was on the knob before he spoke again. "Look, I can't keep you a prisoner here. You'll have to make your own decision." He hesitated for a long moment, obviously waiting for her to say something. And when she didn't, he sighed again; this time his sorrow was mingled with anger. "I'll send Martha in with something for you to eat."

Chapter Eighteen

Youngblood's spurs jingled as he walked down the hall and outside into the dark night. "I don't mind telling you, you're far from what I would have chosen for her," came a voice from out of the thick shadows.

Youngblood cursed. He wasn't in his most civilized mood right now. He'd stepped outside feeling more than a little angry at Morgan's hesitation. He needed a few minutes to sort out his thoughts. What he didn't need was the confrontation that loomed ahead. Idly he leaned his hip against the porch railing and began to roll a cigarette. A moment later a match flared to life, illuminating a small corner of the porch. "I can imagine that much," he said in response as he exhaled a thin blue stream of smoke. "Don't exactly fit into your social circle, do I?"

Wainright's voice was a low purr of rage. "I wanted to kill you when I received that telegram."

Youngblood's eyes narrowed into dangerous slits, his body tensed, his mouth hardened as he waited for the man to make his move. The old bastard was just itching for a fight. Youngblood had never backed down from one in his life and he didn't feel particularly inclined to do so now. Actually he would have loved the chance to vent his frustration. Only the thought of physical combat with Morgan's father didn't sit at all well. He knew the man would come out the worse for it and Youngblood would spare Morgan that kind of hurt, if it was in his power to do so. He pushed his need to lash out aside and turned to face his father-in-law. "No doubt. Still, I'd hoped you could put aside your animosity, for Morgan's sake."

"Meaning she'd be upset if we came to blows?"

Moonlight glittered off Youngblood's wolfish grin. "I take it you'd find some pleasure in that?"

"Goddamned right I would. I'd say you deserve at least that for ruining my daughter."

"And by ruining her I suppose you mean the baby?"

"I do."

Youngblood sighed and flicked his cigarette into the yard. He watched as two chickens came to inspect the glowing tip. "We were married before either of us knew about the child."

"But—"

"I know," he interrupted with a wave of his hand. "The telegram said she was already expecting. I did that on purpose, so she wouldn't fight me."

"You sent it?"

Youngblood nodded. "In her name."

"To coerce her?"

He nodded again.

"You know, of course, that makes the marriage a bit less than legal. I could have it annulled since she was forced into it."

Youngblood shrugged. "She willingly said the words." He shot his father-in-law a hard look. "Lest you harbor a thought or two to the opposite, let me make myself clear. The marriage is legal. Morgan has lived with me as my wife."

Wainright was silent for a long time before he said, "I don't like you much."

Youngblood shrugged, knowing there was little he could do about that glaringly apparent fact. "I think all that matters is that Morgan does."

"Does she? Enough to stay here and slave for you?"

Andrew allowed a low, insinuating laugh. "I doubt she'll be so willing once the novelty wears off. Morgan has never been denied anything. She's come to appreciate life's luxuries."

"Such as servants?"

"Yes, damn it, such as servants and gaslights and shopping sprees and telephones and friends. In other words, Youngblood, money! How long do you think she'll be happy living like this?"

"I don't know," he said, his voice dangerously low. "Why don't you tell me?"

Wainright cursed, ignoring his son-in-law's gibe, and asked, "Would you mind telling me your financial status?"

"Actually I do mind. I mind very much, in fact." Youngblood leaned more heavily against the railing, his arms folded across his chest, his stance one of pure arrogance. "But seein' as you're Morgan's father, I reckon I could tell you. I'm worth two million, give or take a few hundred thousand."

Wainright leaped to his feet. "Damn it, man! This is not a time for flippant remarks. I have every right to make sure my daughter will be taken care of." And at Youngblood's grin, he cursed and stormed into the house. "I can see I'm wasting my time."

There was no love lost between the two most important men in Morgan's life. For almost a week they circled around each other like combatants, each waiting for the other to let down his guard before the final attack. Andrew Wainright was obviously furious that Morgan had married without his permission and married well beneath herself at that. Worse yet, she had done so because she'd been with child. He'd never known such impotent rage as when he'd received that telegraph. His first thought had been to kill the man who'd dared to force himself on his lovely, innocent daughter.

317

When she'd been brought back to the ranch, unconscious and seriously injured, it had taken some effort to restrain himself as he'd watched the brute bending over her, taking her clothes off as if that were an everyday occurrence.

Andrew might have put his dislike for the man aside and made the best of what he considered a bad situation, had it not been for the haunted look in his daughter's eyes. As a father, it was beyond his power to sit idly by and watch her suffer. That the bastard had hurt her and hurt her deeply was obvious. That she loved him was also obvious. What Wainright couldn't understand was why Youngblood didn't return the emotion.

And it was for certain he did not, for no sooner had Morgan been able to leave her bed, than Youngblood left the ranch. He'd been gone almost a week, without saying a word to his wife. No one in love acted like that.

Morgan drifted through each day as if in a trance. She couldn't seem to shake herself out of an almost debilitating state of melancholia. She smiled only when nagged into it by her father and Martha, but those smiles were wane and lackluster, an obvious effort. She sat for hours staring at the walls in Youngblood's bedroom, a bedroom they were to have shared. Only he was gone.

She felt on the very edge of despair. His disappearance was ample proof of his feelings. He might have professed to love her, but she knew the words now for the lie they were. The worst of it was she didn't care. She only wanted him back. How much longer would she have to wait before he returned?

Almost always on the verge of tears, she moved listlessly from the bedroom to the porch and back again. She slept most of every day away as if finding sleep the only escape from her pain. And yet if asked, Morgan couldn't have truthfully said why she suffered. She might have supposed it was due to the loss of the child, but in truth she rarely thought of the babe.

Youngblood's words echoed endlessly in her mind, bringing no end to her torment. Why had he said them?

Why did he insist he loved her, only to leave when she needed him most?

Morgan sat in the rocking chair, moving back and forth, and sighed as her gaze took in the workings of the ranch. A dozen or so of the hands were crowded around one of the corrals, watching another as he tried to break a wild stallion. Separated by only a few feet from the barn stood a shack where the equipment for the farm was made, everything from knives to hinges and horseshoes. Right now puffs of smoke drifted from its huge chimney as Seth's hammer echoed upon an anvil.

She loved it here and should have felt content, but she did not. There was an emptiness inside her, an emptiness that had nothing to do with her recent loss.

Morgan closed her eyes and leaned her head back against her rocker. Her expression was almost heart-breakingly sad.

Andrew Wainright ground his teeth together with the effort it took to force back the anger he felt toward his son-in-law. Judging by Morgan's forced smile, she suffered enough. She didn't need to hear his low opinion of the man's obvious lack of concern.

"How are you today, Morgan?" Andrew asked as he came to join her on the porch.

"Much better, Father. Thank you," she replied, forcing a cheeriness she was far from feeling.

"Have you given any further thought to my suggestion?"

Morgan gave her father an imploring look. She felt so torn. She didn't know what to do. Finally she spoke, her voice low as she fought back this continuous urge to cry. "Father, how can I leave? I'm his wife. Isn't it a wife's duty to stay with her husband?"

"Duty be damned," Andrew muttered in disgust.

Morgan shook her head. "Father, you don't mean that."

Andrew sighed and pushed his fingers through his dark gray hair. "All right. Perhaps I don't mean it. But there are two sides to every coin, Morgan. If we're talking duty here, what about his duty to his wife? Where the hell has he been this past week? You've been terribly ill. Are these the qualities you want in a husband?"

"He thinks I don't want to stay."

"So he thought to convince you by leaving you when you needed him most?"

Morgan shot her father a soft smile. He'd never understand a man like Joseph. Idly she wondered if she understood him herself.

Wainright sighed and again ran his fingers through his hair. "Morgan, don't make excuses for the man." He shook his head, already sorry he'd spoken so harshly as pain flooded her eyes. He gentled his voice considerably. "Listen to me. I have to go back, but I can't leave you here alone. Lord, what kind of a father would that make me? If he feels anything for you, he'll come after you. If he's the kind of man you seem to think he is, the kind you deserve, he'll do at least that much."

"And if he doesn't come?"

"Then you'll know for sure, won't you?"

"I don't know . . ."

Wainright gave a silent curse. He'd never seen his daughter so unsure of herself. Damn the man for doing this to her. She was almost totally without spirit. He tried a new tactic, praying his words would be the catalyst Morgan needed. "Morgan, isn't he cocky enough? Will it not only add to the man's arrogance to find you docilely awaiting his return?"

Wainright almost laughed aloud as he saw the fire enter his daughter's eyes again. God, but she was a beauty and so much like her mother his heart ached. Her shoulders straightened from their slumped, despondent position, while her lips tightened with determination. It was a long time in coming, but when it did, Morgan could barely control the rage that suffused her body. "When are you planning for us to leave?"

Andrew smiled at his daughter. "The moment you're ready."

"Then I'd best get at my packing," she said as she came

320

to her feet and kissed her father's cheek.

Morgan felt better than she had in weeks. No longer did she pine for the man who had insisted on becoming part of her life, only to come and go as he pleased. It was over. Finished. Even if he came for her, she wouldn't have him again. She'd never felt so confident, so sure of herself. Perhaps she wasn't deliriously happy, perhaps she'd never be, but she knew now that in time she'd find a degree of happiness that would satisfy her.

Morgan gave a quick glance over the room she'd used since returning to the ranch. She wouldn't allow a moment's yearning to thwart her new resolve. Her gaze skimmed over the bed. She denied the sudden twist in her chest. The bed held no real meaning for her. It was simply that, a bed. Except for one night, she'd never shared it with him and never would again.

Her bags were nearly packed. She checked the room for anything that might have been left behind. Morgan pulled a pair of lacy drawers from the dresser and frowned, wondering how they had gotten there. No matter that she slept here every night, all of her clothes had been kept in her room. Finally she shrugged. Martha must have placed them in there by mistake.

Morgan almost groaned as she opened his closet. His scent permeated the air in this room, but was the strongest here. Her fingers shook as they brushed past his neatly hung shirts and trousers, looking for anything that belonged to her.

On the shelf above stood a package wrapped in tissue paper. Morgan's brow creased. She couldn't remember putting anything here. Perhaps Martha had left it.

Morgan took the package down. Her knees wobbled as she unwrapped it and a soft sound of longing came from her lips.

He loved her! Of that she had no doubt. Damn the man and his stubbornness! Why hadn't he stayed? Why hadn't he insisted she believe him? Why hadn't he shown her this?

Morgan felt a lone tear escape suddenly misty eyes. Determinedly she brushed it aside and rewrapped her old bedraggled and thoroughly outrageous hat. A moment later it was once again on his shelf.

Yes, he loved her, she mused, for there was no other explanation for keeping it, lovingly wrapped and secreted away. But if the man thought she was going to allow this kind of mistreatment, he could think again. Her father was right. Joseph never should have left, no matter his damaged pride. His place was at her side. Now he was going to come for her. And for the first time, Morgan had every confidence he would.

Early the next morning the heavy wagon pulled to a stop just outside of the stage office. Again Seth had driven them to town and again Pedro, dressed once more in his Sunday finery, had followed on his horse.

The bags were unloaded from the buckboard and placed upon the wooden sidewalk just to the right of the office door.

While Wainright entered the small office to buy their tickets, Morgan glanced around the town's main street and its slowly moving traffic. Her eyes skimmed the wooden buildings, the uneven sidewalks, and hitching posts that lined both sides of town. She thought of the friends she'd found there and made a mental note to say good-bye to Jenny at the Emporium. Idly she wondered when she'd return. Odd how she'd come to love it here. A terrifying thought squeezed her chest. Suppose he didn't come? Suppose she never saw this place again?

Determinedly she shook her head. No. He'd come. She knew it as surely as she knew her name. And when he did . . .

Morgan's breath caught in her throat as she spied the man leaning lazily against the wall of a building. It was him! He'd come for her and far sooner than she'd expected.

Their eyes caught and held for a long moment before Morgan finally uttered a low curse and walked determinedly toward him. Her hands were on her hips, her feet widespread as she tipped her head up and glared her anger. "Well?" she asked as she faced him, her fury only just barely under control. "Are you going to stop me or not?"

Youngblood looked down at his wife and almost grinned, thinking her a particularly delicious bundle of fury. His hat was pulled low over his eyes and a cigarette hung from his lips. His arms were folded across his chest. His expression was lazy, ridiculously male, and all too confident. "Seems to me you're wastin' a powerful lot a' time packin'. When you suppose you're gonna realize you ain't goin' nowhere?"

"I imagine that means you're here to try and stop me?"

"You imagined right, honey. Only I ain't gonna just try. I am stopping you."

"And it took you till now to decide you want me to stay?"

"I always wanted you to stay. From the very first." Youngblood shrugged and shifted his hip as he rested his weight on one leg.

"And I was supposed to know that? I was supposed to trust you to return from God knows where?"

"I wasn't far away. I figured I'd give you time to visit with your father. When he left, I'd have come back."

"Afraid of a man twice your age, Joseph?" she goaded.

"Morgan, honey, the man was itchin' to get his sights on me. He's your father. I wouldn't want to see us come to blows. It was better with me gone."

"It wasn't better! How could it be better when I didn't know where you were? When you didn't think to even leave a note?"

"Did you miss me?" he asked, his eyes glowing with pleasure while an arrogant grin touched his lips.

Morgan couldn't imagine a man more wonderful to look at. Her heart skittered and then thumped wildly in

323

her chest, her breath catching at the dark hungry look he gave her through slitted eyes. She forced aside the things he did to her with just a simple look and gave a ridiculing laugh. "Miss you? Not likely."

"You shouldn't lie, honey. You ain't got the knack."

"And you shouldn't try to make believe you're an ignorant cowboy."

Youngblood grinned. "Is that what I'm doin'?"

Her eyes hardened with righteous anger. "You think that sexy cowboy jargon will do the trick, don't you? Well, I'm afraid you've gone too far this time. I'm leaving."

"Why?"

"Because a man doesn't leave his wife without a word only to come home a week later as if nothing happened."

Youngblood's heart thrilled at how easily she spoke of herself as his wife. He almost laughed aloud as he realized Morgan considered the ranch home. A moment later he flicked his cigarette away. "Are you punishing me then?"

"Do you think I'm going to make it easy for you?" she taunted.

"Honey, nothing's been easy since I first set eyes on you. You ready to go?"

For just an instant her mouth hung open as if in shock. He was ignoring her threat to leave in his usual arrogant fashion. She felt her anger suddenly fizzle away. Morgan's laughter was low and silky. She shook her head slowly. "Oh, you are a beast. Suppose I was gone before you came back?"

"Not much chance of that. I was watching the ranch the whole time."

"Suppose you missed me?"

He gave a casual shrug as if the idea didn't bear merit. "I would have stopped the stage."

"And kidnapped me again?"

Youngblood said nothing. His smile and the hunger that showed clearly in his eyes were all the answer she needed.

"Lord, that would have caused a ruckus."

"Probably." He nodded in agreement and then looked toward Thunder tied to the hitching post. "Get on the horse."

Morgan shot him a look of annoyance. "Seems to me you're getting awfully lazy. You want me to kidnap myself?"

Youngblood laughed, his arms aching to pull her against him, but he wasn't all that sure what might happen if he touched her right now. For himself he didn't care much, but he didn't want to embarrass her. "I think you'd be right smart to listen to me. If I have to do it myself, there's no tellin' what might happen."

"What could happen?" Morgan's eyes widened at the all too obvious sexual threat in his words. "We're in the middle of town."

Youngblood nodded slowly, a sly almost wicked smile curving his lips. "That's just what I was thinkin'. I wouldn't want to embarrass you."

Morgan licked her lips, her heart thundering in her chest. She should have known from the beginning. It was a useless effort to fight him. She wanted to stay. Wanted that easily as much as he. "I have to say good-bye to my father."

Youngblood nodded as he leaned back against the post again. "I'll wait." For as long as it takes, he silently added, watching the gentle sway of her skirts as she walked back up the street.

The wagon was pulling away, loaded again with her bags, a smiling Seth at the reins while a jubilant Pedro raced on ahead as Morgan hugged her father.

"I hope you know what you're doing," came the muffled sound of his voice against her bonnet. His thick arms held her in a bear hug.

"I know, Father. Joseph isn't the easiest man, but he's the one I love." Morgan grinned. Amazing. It was so easy to tell him the truth of it and yet she couldn't seem to speak the words aloud to her own husband. "In many

325

ways he's a lot like you." She hugged him again as the stage rolled to a stop. "Someday you'll get to know each other and you'll see for yourself."

Wainright grunted a sound that neither confirmed nor denied her prediction.

"I won't worry," he said, ignoring the misting in his eyes. "If you need me . . ."

"I'll come," Morgan finished for him and then smiled.

The stage took off in a cloud of choking dust. Morgan stood for a long moment and watched until the stage was no more than a dot on the horizon.

She moved into the arms that suddenly circled her waist and leaned her back comfortably against the hard frame, loving the feel of him against her. His words were soft and filled with a promise to last a lifetime as he bent and whispered near her ear. "You ready to go home, honey?"

Morgan smiled up into his dark eyes. "I'm ready."

Morgan sat sideways before him, her back supported by his arms as she leaned into his chest. They were traveling back toward the ranch when Morgan suddenly remarked, "You might as well know, I'm not going to forgive you anytime soon."

"For what?"

"For leaving like you did."

"What would you have had me do, Morgan? Should I have stayed and fought it out with a man twice my age? A man who was determined to see me suffer for ruining his daughter?"

Morgan shot him an impish grin. "Is that what you did?"

Youngblood nodded his head, a wicked gleam in his eyes. "And enjoyed every minute of it."

"Is that why you stopped me from leaving? To continue on with my downfall?"

Youngblood frowned. He wasn't sure she was going to be pleased, but he figured he'd best clear up any misconception on her part. "It's probably long past time, but I figure there's something you ought to know. You're my wife. You're always going to be my wife. I'm sorry if that don't much appeal to you, but that's the way things are."

"And there's no use in my fighting it?"

"No use at all."

"Then why did you tell me I'll have to make my own decision? You said you couldn't keep me a prisoner."

"Because I needed to hear you say you wanted to stay."

"I still haven't said it."

"Yes you have."

Morgan glanced his way. Her frown told clearly she couldn't remember when.

"You said it when you waved good-bye to your father," he said, so softly her heart twisted in her chest.

Morgan smiled, her eyes softening with emotion. "I love you, Joseph."

His arms tightened at her waist as he pulled her closer. "I know. I waited a long time for you to finally figure that out." Then he asked, grinning, "When can we make love again?"

"I'm not wild about your arrogance." She stiffened slightly and glared at him. "What do you mean, you know?"

Youngblood laughed. "You're not the kind of lady that goes to bed with a man unless you love him."

"I didn't love you that first time."

"Yes you did. You just didn't know it."

"Lord," she sighed as she shook her head in exasperation. "It's astonishing how a normal-size hat can fit a head so big."

Youngblood chuckled as he nuzzled his face into the warmth of her neck. "You were crazy about my body, is that it?"

Morgan decided it was safer to ignore that particular question, especially since it was uncomfortably close to the truth. But she might not have bothered, for the blush

327

that slowly stole up her cheeks answered him well enough. Youngblood burst out laughing and squeezed her tighter still. "I love you. It doesn't bother me none that you want my body. When did Doc Franklin say we can make love again?"

Morgan's cheeks grew to flaming red, remembering all too clearly the doctor's clinical advice. "He said he wouldn't advise us to try for another baby for a few months."

Youngblood gave a long whistle between his teeth and shook his head. "A few months? That ain't goin' to be the easiest thing I've ever done."

"What's that look in your eye mean?"

Youngblood grinned. "I was just thinkin' there are ways and then there are ways."

Morgan's cheeks stayed apple red for the entire trip home as he gave a detailed explanation.

Youngblood opened his eyes and groaned with delight at the warm softness of her body curved into his. It was very early. The sun hadn't yet broken over the horizon. The house was quiet. The only sound was Morgan's gentle breathing and the racing of his heart as he forced away the remnants of yet another erotic dream. Jesus, how much longer was he to wait?

Four more weeks. How was he to bear it?

Unable to deny himself, he suffered untold agony sleeping with her while not being able to do more than touch her. Youngblood grinned as he nuzzled his face into the warmth of her neck. There was a time when he would have done much for just this pleasure, the freedom to touch her as he might. But touching her wasn't enough. It had never been enough. He needed to love her as a man loves his wife. In every way possible. And he didn't think he could wait much longer.

His hand slid beneath the silk of her gown, over the smooth length of thigh and hip to dip into a tiny waist and at last to cup a soft, warm breast. He sighed with pleasure

328

as its weight filled his palm.

More than half asleep, Morgan squirmed her backside closer to his heat and sleepily sighed her delight.

The movement did little toward relieving Youngblood's need. In truth, the sweet softness of her against his arousal brought him all that much closer to losing control. He couldn't think but to have more. No matter their efforts, pleasurable though they may be, to ease the agony of this enforced waiting, nothing could take the place of loving her as she was meant to be loved.

She stirred and murmured a soft sound as he rolled the tip of her breast into a tight nub of desire. "Joseph," she moaned, but it wasn't until his hand slid from its prize, down over her belly to cup her gently, that she turned toward him. Her arm flung over his waist, her leg slipped between his, her face buried itself in his chest. "You feel so good."

Youngblood's chuckle was low and silky, filled with growing hunger. Her gown was slipped over her head and his hands returned to the pleasure, the sweet agonizing pleasure of her body. "Not as good as you."

He pulled her hard against him, pressing every inch along his length. His eyes closed with the perfection of her. Nothing was this good. Nothing was ever this good. His mouth lowered to hers and a whisper of a sigh came from his throat as he felt her warm lips part beneath the pressure.

Ravenous, starved for her loving, he kissed her until she was breathless and dizzy. He'd never get enough. He loved her taste, the texture of her mouth, the flavor of her skin. The way she sighed when he touched her and whimpered her joy when in the throes of ecstasy.

Morgan, her eyes still closed, smiled. "I love the way you do that."

"What?"

"Wake me up."

"Do you?" he asked as he brushed a heavy curl behind her ear. Unable to fight the temptation, his mouth replaced the wonder of his hands. "Should I do this every morning then?"

"Oh yes," she gasped as his mouth slid from her ear to her neck, along the sweetness of her shoulder, and down the delicious curve of womanly breast, taking her soft flesh into its blazing heat.

She rolled to her back as he came up on one elbow. "Do you think it's too soon? Do you think we can . . . oh Joseph! I don't think you should be doing that."

"Why?" came his muffled response as hands, lips, tongue, and teeth chartered a wondrous course down the length of her.

"Because I like it too much."

Youngblood laughed, a low, thrilling, erotic sound. "Do you? Then I think I should do it all the more."

"But what about . . . ? We were supposed to wait."

"We'll take it very slow and very easy. If you're uncomfortable, I'll stop." He groaned as his mouth ran a line of exquisite biting kisses inside her thigh. His voice was thick with need and a pulse throbbed in his throat, causing his breath to grow stilted and choppy. "Jesus, I don't know how, but I'll stop."

A low groan of longing escaped her lips. Her hips rose invitingly, her body stretching, opening eagerly to the glory in his gaze, to the wonder of his mouth, hungry for the temptation that was him. She almost cried out her pleasure as he put aside at last the agonizing teasing and gave in to her silent, desperate urgings. A low tormented moan was muffled against moist warm flesh as he drank greedily from her his life's breath.

Morgan shivered at the delicious contact. Her legs and arms tremored as he sought to absorb her very essence into the depth of his own being. "God," he murmured against her heat. "So good, so damn good."

Her heart pounded wildly as she strove toward the pleasure she knew to await her. She moved frantically beneath him. Begging with low aching wordless sounds, with gasps and groans for more, more, till she knew nothing but the pleasure/pain of this exquisite wanting.

Her belly tightened, hard, aching, desperate for the

ecstasy promised in this coming release. Her fingers curled, as hungry to touch as she was to be touched. They pressed, hard with desperation, deep into the flesh of muscular shoulders, moving in furious strokes over all she could reach, until they buried themselves in his hair, bringing him closer to her need.

"God, oh God," she moaned, knowing it was coming at last, eager for the moment. She stiffened, her fingers clawed, her legs trembled as she lost the last of her reason. "Yes. Yes. Oh God, yes" she cried against her fist as she felt the first shattering wave of throbbing ecstasy assail. Aching pleasure, deep, deep, it wracked her body from the inside out.

Youngblood absorbed the tremors against his mouth, sighing his delight, knowing he could bring this woman to such a state of total abandonment. He eased his body up the length of her. Her eyes were dazed, lost as she was in the throes of a rapture that went on and on. She never felt him ease himself deep into her slippery warmth. Easy, easy, he silently warned as he forced his mind to think of anything, anything that would soothe the aching need, lest he take her with a strength that would rock his very soul.

Propped on his arms, he leaned back and watched for any sign of discomfort in her eyes. "All right?" he whispered in a breathless gasp.

"Mmmm," she murmured, her eyes half closed in delight. "Better than all right. Delicious, luscious . . . oh Joseph," she cried as he moved to fill her to overflowing.

"I'm not hurting you?" he choked as he strained for a temperance he wasn't sure he could find, while his body clamored to take her with a viciousness that matched this unbearable need.

His fingers intertwined with hers as he held their hands out from their sides. Gently, with a tenderness he'd never before shown, he began to move. His eyes squeezed shut at the agony of muscles contracting around him in aftershocks. His dark eyes took in the loveliness of swollen lips, of creamy flushed skin, of riotous curls framing her face, the dampness and scent of sexual sweat, and her eyes as they began to grow cloudy again as her body succumbed to overwhelming need.

"Yes, it hurts," she said between weak, gasping breaths. Her blue eyes closed yet again as her body found delirium. "It hurts so good."

"Look at us," he said, the pulse in his throat almost cutting off his ability to talk. "Watch where we're joined. Watch, Morgan," he said as he leaned away from her.

"Beautiful," she said. "Oh God, Joseph, you're so beautiful."

He lost the last of his control then. He couldn't hold back. It had been too long. His need was too great. All he could do was pray it wasn't too much as he rushed into blind, mindless euphoria.

Endless moments later, Morgan sighed as he rolled them both over so she lay upon his relaxed body. "I think we should always wait two months between each time. That was the best yet."

Youngblood groaned. "You're hoping to be a young widow, I take it?"

Morgan laughed as her hand patted his cheek. "Poor baby. Was it so hard on you?"

"You felt for yourself how hard it was," he said, the corner of his mouth twitching with a grin.

"Beast!" she said, unable to control the laughter that spilled out. And then, spying his look of utter satisfaction, she asked, "Think you're pretty good, eh?"

"With all due modesty, madam, I was magnificent."

Morgan chuckled. "Modesty, eh? Well, I think . . ." Purposely she let the sentence hang.

With a growl, Youngblood reversed their positions. He glared down at her. "And you dare call me a *beast?*"

The sound of her laughter was muffled against his chest. "But darling, you are a beast," she said, trying desperately to control her need to laugh. "How can I deny it? A lusty, wild, dark, hungry beast. A lady doesn't stand a chance against you."

His dark eyes teased. "It might be in your best interest to soothe such a beast."

"Haven't I tried?" She grinned as she pushed him to his back and straddled his thighs.

"Not so that I've noticed."

"Well then, perhaps I should try harder."

"Mmmmm, that sounds interesting," he said as his hands began a slow path from her knees to her hips. "Have you a plan in mind?"

"That's the problem. I haven't a clue as to what to do."

"I could tell you how to win out against the beast, no matter his strength," he offered as his hands continued up her body to weigh and cup her breasts.

"Could you?" she asked, forcing aside the trembling that was beginning again. "I'd be ever so grateful. She smiled wickedly. "What should I do first?"

"You could call me darling again. This time without laughing."

Morgan leaned down, her breasts flattened against his chest; her hair tumbled in wild disarray around their faces. "Like this? 'Darling.'"

"Better," he said, "but you'll have to work on it a bit."

"Really? How long do you think before I'll get it just right?"

"Fifty years should do it."

"Oh." She smiled. "I see. You will tell me when it's right, won't you?"

"I will," he said, trying to hide the grin that insisted on curling his lips. "But that's not the whole of it. It'll take more than a word, no matter how softly spoken, to soothe this wild beast."

"Tell me, then, what should I do?"

"Make love to me, Morgan. Take all I have. Give to me all that you are."

"I'm not so practiced, Joseph," she said, her eyes soft, filled with love. "Suppose memory should fail?"

"I'll be here to remind you."

Chapter Nineteen

Morgan laughed as Rusty chased a chicken clear across the yard, stopping only when the bird managed to squeeze through the small hole in the bottom of the wire fence, turn, and squawk her outrage. "See what you've done?" She admonished gently as she glared down at the dog. "She probably won't lay for a week because of you," Morgan said, and then ordered, "Stop that barking!"

"Pedro," she called as she tossed handfuls of corn over the small enclosed yard, "come take your dog away from here."

Within minutes Pedro was there pulling a ready-to-play Rusty from the fence. "Why don't you get your pole and go down to the river? I'll join you as soon as I'm finished here," she said as she heaved a huge bucket of water over the fence and poured it as gently as possible into the long shallow trough. Instantly, amid fluttering wings and sharp squawkings that admonished her lateness with this particular chore, two dozen chickens came forth to drink their fill.

"And be careful," she called as the boy, already with pole in hand, eagerly obeyed her suggestion.

Fifteen minutes later, Morgan pushed aside the thick branch and smiled as Pedro sat along the banks of the river talking to his dog. Morgan made herself comfortable at his side and remarked, "I'll have to take you into town

334

soon. It's almost time for school to start."

"Aw, do I have to?" His expression was one of pure disgust.

"Yes, you have to," she answered in a no-nonsense tone.

"But—"

"Every boy your age should go to school. Don't you want to be able to read?"

"I don't like to read."

"But there might come a day when you'd like it." Morgan sighed at his continued disgruntled look. "Besides, everyone needs to know their numbers. How will you know if someone is cheating you if you can't count?"

"I can count."

"Yes, but do you know how much change you're supposed to get if you buy something that costs ten cents and you give the storekeeper a dollar?"

"Mr. Holbrook knows."

Morgan sighed. There was no sense arguing with a child's logic. "Pedro, you'll be going to school when the summer is over," she said with finality.

"But I like helping out around here. If I have to go to school every day, I might forget how to ride. Johnny is teaching me how to rope."

"You can continue to learn on Saturdays, after your chores are finished." Morgan grinned at his obvious lack of excitement about the work that would await him. "And you won't forget how to ride. You'll be riding Bullet to school every day."

He gave a long unhappy sigh.

"It won't be so bad, I promise. You'll meet the boys who live around here. Before long you'll have lots of friends."

"Does Jimmy go?"

Morgan nodded, knowing he referred to Jenny Holbrook's boy. "He's been going for two years. You'll have to study hard to catch up."

"He ain't so smart. I won't have to study that hard"

Morgan grinned. There was nothing like a little competition. Soon Pedro would be riding the hour it took to get to town every morning with hardly a word of complaint.

"You have a bite on your line," she said as she watched the end of the pole snap sharply.

"I know," he said, coming to his feet.

"It's a big one. You want some help?"

"I can do it," he said, his tone telling her clearly he wanted none of the pampering she was apt to bestow.

"Pedro, be careful," she said as he discarded the pole. His hand wrapped around the line, he walked into the water.

"Don't worry," he said just before his foot slipped on an unseen rock. Suddenly his arms were waving in the air as he sought his balance. To no avail. A moment later he plopped into the water.

Morgan was running without thought into the cold water. A moment later she, too, found the slippery rock and, after several stunned moments, began to laugh as the water covered her from the neck down.

"Must be a whale," came a deep voice filled with humor from the shore.

Morgan shot Youngblood a grin as she came to her feet. "Only a baby." God, he was beautiful. He stood leaning against a tree, his slim hips hugged in tight pants, his shirt opened a few buttons too many, exposing a tanned chest. Morgan felt herself tingle at the warm look he bestowed upon her.

Youngblood nodded as he watched his wife help Pedro from the water. Her clothes were plastered to her body. His eyes glowed with pleasure at the sight of her. "Seems even a baby whale possesses powerful strength."

"I imagine it does," Morgan agreed with a smile. "But it was a slippery rock that caused the dunking."

Youngblood laughed as he hauled in the small fish still attached to the line. "You sure?" he asked as he eyed the squirming fish. "Seems to me this little fella' is mighty strong."

Morgan was wringing out her skirt. "Thought you were working."

"I was. I heard Rusty barking and wondered what he was doing down here."

"You were working around here?" she asked, her eyes clearly puzzled, as she wondered what he could be about.

Youngblood nodded. "Why don't you go up to the house and change? Meet me back here. I want to show you something."

Morgan nodded and hurried back to the ranch. The water had been icy cold, and even with the sun's harsh heat, she was chilled to the bone.

Thirty minutes later Morgan parted the branches that lent a bit of shade to the river's edge. Youngblood was sitting on a small flat rock, watching the river. He didn't hear her approach.

She was standing almost directly behind him when his voice came suddenly, surprising to her ears. "I wouldn't. You can't sneak up on me." As he spoke, he turned and grabbed her around her knees, knocking her off balance and into his lap. Morgan was laughing, her shout of surprise smothered by his warm mouth.

"How did you know I was going to scare you?" she said, her voice holding a slightly dreamy quality, after a kiss that investigated quite thoroughly the heat of her mouth.

"You were too quiet." He grinned down at her.

Morgan shot him a confused look. "How can a person be too quiet?"

Youngblood ignored her question. "What were you planning?"

"I was planning to grab you and kiss you."

Youngblood chuckled as he nuzzled his face in her neck. "It seems our thoughts often run along the same lines."

"What do you want to show me?"

337

Youngblood grunted, not at all happy to see this moment pass so innocently. "Now that I have you in my arms, I can think of a hundred things I'd like to show you." His grin turned terribly wicked. "All of them involving the closest of contact and considerable fewer clothes."

Morgan laughed. "Here?"

Youngblood sighed and then nodded. "We'd better not. There's no telling who might stumble across us. I wouldn't want to embarrass you."

"That's the first I've heard of it."

Youngblood chuckled.

"The truth of the matter is, you love nothing more than embarrassing me."

"That's because you look so pretty with red cheeks." He came to his feet, helping her to stand. "Let's go."

"Where? Where are we going?"

"You'll see," he said as he took her hand and began to walk through the trees that lined the river. About a quarter of a mile upriver, they came to a small clearing. In the center stood a small wooden cabin. Its construction was almost finished.

"This is lovely," Morgan said as she took in the house that was perhaps twice as large as the original Red Rock had been. She shot Youngblood a puzzled look. "Are you building it?"

Youngblood shrugged. "I thought Johnny and Martha might like it for a wedding present."

"Joseph!" Morgan's eyes widened with surprise as she suddenly flung herself into his arms. "It's wonderful. They'll love it."

"Would you like to furnish it? I thought I wouldn't surprise them with it till it was all done."

"My God," she gasped. "This is so generous of you." She shot him a long searching look. "Can we afford it?"

Youngblood shrugged. "It didn't cost much. A few of the men in town owed me some favors."

Morgan laughed, unable to contain her excitement.

"This is wonderful. Martha will love it. I don't think she's ever had her own place."

Her eyes were wide with delighted laughter. "I can't wait for her to see it."

"After the wedding," Youngblood insisted. "You can keep a secret, can't you?"

Morgan shot him a look that clearly bespoke her disgust at his question. "All right," he chuckled. "I see you can."

"Is it finished inside?" she asked as she nearly ran up the steps of the wide porch. "Oh Joseph, it's beautiful." She danced a merry step as her gaze took in the stone fireplace that took up almost one whole wall. "I can't wait for her to see this."

Youngblood's arms came around her from the back and pulled her to lean against his chest. "Do you think they'd mind if we christened it for them?"

"It's a bit warm for a fire, wouldn't you say?"

"Not for the particular fire I have in mind," he grated, his voice heavy with meaning.

Morgan chuckled softly as she turned to look up at her husband's tender smile. "I'd feel terrible if we burned the house down."

"Imagine that much heat, do you?" he asked as he gave her a lazy, sexy look that set Morgan's heart to racing.

"Things often get a bit wild," she reminded.

Youngblood grinned. "I think I can keep the fire contained well enough."

"Are you sure?" she asked as she pulled his shirt from his trousers and began to open the last of his shirt buttons. "I wouldn't want to cause any damage."

"The only damage you could cause would be if you said no."

Morgan smiled as she nuzzled the tempting exposed flesh with her mouth. "There are no beds."

"We use a bed every night. We could stand or use the floor this time." And after a long pause, a pause where

339

she was sliding her hands down his chest and belly to boldly cup his sex, he almost choked, "Would you mind?"

"Mind what?" she asked, her voice a low ragged whisper as her mouth slid up his neck to nibble at his jaw and then finally to cover his lips with a kiss that threatened to incinerate him.

"I'm going."

"Morgan," he sighed as he secured his gun belt to his thigh. "It's dangerous work gathering a herd of mustangs."

"How dangerous can it be? Pedro's going. He's gone with you more than once. I'll stay at camp and watch over him, while I help out with the cooking."

"You've been ill and have barely recovered. I don't want to see anything happen."

"Nothing's going to happen."

"It's uncomfortable. I'd feel much better knowing you were back here waiting for me."

"And I'd feel much better knowing I could see you more often than once a month."

"It won't take that long. I'm never gone for more than two weeks When I get back, we'll celebrate. Maybe I'll take you to San Francisco for a week. Would you like that?"

"No, I wouldn't. When we get back, Martha will be getting married. She's put it off long enough."

"Morgan, don't force me to order you to stay."

"Joseph, don't force me to follow you."

"Jesus! You're enough to drive a man crazy." Joseph felt a chill shudder through his body at the thought of her alone in the wild country following him. And this woman was just stubborn enough, just fool enough, to do it. "You of all people should know it's dangerous country out there."

"I know and I'm going." She gave him a long

determined look and then, in a last-ditch effort, flashed what she hoped was her most sensuous smile. "Besides, think of the nights. You won't have to sleep alone if I'm there."

Youngblood gave a frustrated curse, knowing he didn't stand a chance in hell against her allure. "Wonderful," he remarked grumpily. "Except for one thing. There'll be no privacy. I'm sure my men would appreciate the show." He sighed, knowing she'd made her point. It was better to have her at his side, even if nothing could come of it, than to leave her behind, aching daily for the sight of her. "Well, if you're going, you'd better get your ass out of that bed. We're leaving in exactly ten minutes."

Morgan grinned as she watched him storm out of the room.

"I don't care what you say. This is the only way."

"You're out of your mind. You've seen the way he looks at her. Jesus Christ! Youngblood will go crazy."

Marshall grinned at his partner. "I expect he will. Actually, I'm counting on him not keeping his head. He'll follow our tracks. And we'll be waiting."

"You gonna bushwhack him after all?" Harrington asked. His amazement couldn't have been greater. "What about Popé? I thought you didn't want—"

"I don't see where we have a choice," Marshall interrupted. "He won't even talk about selling." He shrugged. "We'll take care of the Indians, if it comes to that."

"And the woman? What are you gonna do with her?"

Marshall's lips tightened with rage as he remembered how he had been taken for a fool. He'd thought she was a lady. He'd been so gentle with her, treated her as if she were special, when all the time she'd been sleeping with that half-breed. Marshall could well imagine the laugh they must have had at his expense. He forced a nonchalant shrug. "That's up to Morgan. If she cooperates, she'll be fine. She'll have to marry me, of course." Marshall contemplated the idea of Morgan as his wife and the hundred ways he could make her suffer. "There's no other way I can get my hands on that property."

"And if she won't?"

Marshall grinned, and an evil, vengeful light entered his eyes. He almost hoped she'd put up a fight. He wanted to see her suffer for how she'd led him on. He wanted that almost more than he wanted the land in question. "Then I'll be the only living heir."

"A very rich heir."

Marshall laughed as he put his feet up on his desk. "Very rich," he agreed.

Morgan tucked a lock of golden hair behind her ear and blew a puff of breath at the curls that stuck to her damp forehead. Her back ached from bending over a fire most of the day. Her hands were raw from washing dishes in pots in ice-cold water and the harshest of soaps and yet she'd never been happier.

A horse rode into camp and came to a sudden stop behind her. Morgan never glanced up from the huge bowl as she mixed its contents. "Is this the same city woman I found crying over a broken nail?" he asked as he brushed flour from her nose and cheek, while pushing the same heavy lock of hair behind her ear.

Morgan smiled as she put down the bowl and turned fully into the loving arms of her husband. "It's growing more obvious daily that there is very little of the city woman left. And it wasn't a broken nail. I hit my thumb with a hammer trying to repair that stupid chicken coop and you know it."

"You should have asked for my help," he said as his lips sampled the delicious skin beneath her ear, his voice low and tender as he remembered how hard she'd tried not to cry.

"Would you have helped me?" she asked softly.

"I would have done anything for you," he answered honestly.

"But not without a certain amount of grumbling."

"Probably," he answered honestly, and then kissed her hard and quick on the mouth. "What's for supper?"

Morgan shot him a saucy look. "Turkey with stuffing. Cranberry sauce. Buttered potatoes. Apple pie and ice cream."

Youngblood groaned at her teasing. "Biscuits, beans, and beef. I don't know why I ask."

Morgan laughed. "Go wash up. It will be ready soon."

While he cleaned up, Youngblood watched her as she moved around the camp. He figured bringing her along was just about the most brilliant thing he'd ever done. It might not have been his original intent, but he sure was glad he'd given in to her pleading. Well, maybe *pleading* wasn't exactly the right word. She'd given him a definite ultimatum. Either take her or she'd come on her own. The idea that he held so little control over his wife didn't sit at all well and yet he'd never been happier that she'd gotten her way.

She never complained about the rough living conditions. It didn't seem to bother her that she had to cook over an open fire, or sleep under the stars. A smile was never far from her lips and the men nearly fell over themselves to be in her company. He couldn't remember when he'd last looked forward to returning to camp. Life was so damn good, it almost scared him.

The next day, after the midday meal, Morgan watched as the horses were herded into the huge temporary corral fashioned of barbed wire and a few necessary posts. From the looks of the fire and the hot, red irons, it was almost time to start the branding. The best of the lot were chosen and seperated from the herd. All were to be marked with the Triple R brand, but these few stallions and mares were to be kept for the ranch. The rest of the herd, along with those already waiting at the ranch, would be sent to the stockyards in Elko and then shipped to various parts of the country by rail.

"Doesn't it hurt?" Morgan asked, feeling particularly squeamish at the cries of the helplessly bound animals. The hot iron was applied again and again to perhaps a hundred horses and she almost gagged at the stench of burnt horse hide permeating the air.

"A little," Youngblood answered.

"Why is it necessary to brand them? You're selling most of them."

"They're branded so people will know which of them belong to me." His eyes sparkled with enjoyment as he teased, "Kinda like the way I branded you. Now everybody knows where you belong."

"Too bad you don't go where you belong," she returned after a long, hot glare.

She was about to stomp off when his arms closed around her and held her to him. Youngblood chuckled at her anger. "I'm already where I belong. With you," he said easily as he pressed her back tighter against his chest.

She stood stiffly against him. It took no mastermind to know he'd annoyed her. His voice lowered and he leaned down to whisper near her ear. "In Elko they'll be put into holding pens with horses from a dozen different ranches. There's no other way to tell them apart." And without the slightest hesitation, he continued in one breath, "I love you and if you're branded, then so am I."

Morgan turned to give him a final stern look and then grinned at his tender smile. "Obnoxious beast."

It was late. The campfire was banked and would give off a measure of needed heat throughout the cool night. Morgan sat on a blanket next to her husband, while Pedro had fallen asleep at the blanket's edge. Rusty, his head upon Pedro's stomach, snuggled close to his master and sighed a whispery dog sound. Morgan smiled as she smoothed a heavy black lock of hair from Pedro's forehead and watched as it insisted on falling back into place. There was nothing she could do without pomade and a comb, both of which Pedro had professed to have conveniently forgotten. His face was dirty. His clothes were ready to throw away, but he'd never looked more adorable to her. "He's enjoying himself. I've never seen a boy so happy not to have to brush his hair or bathe."

Morgan received an incredulous look at that last remark. "You haven't seen many boys then."

Morgan laughed. "You're right about that." She watched him for a few more minutes before she spoke. "He's beautiful."

Youngblood nodded as he whittled at a piece of wood. "It won't be long before he'll have to beat the girls away with a stick."

Morgan laughed softly, the sound carrying sweetly over the camp. "I'll have to bring him to town next week. It's almost time for school to start."

Youngblood chuckled. He turned around, his back to the fire as he leaned on his elbow facing her. "He's going to love that."

"I know, we've had a discussion about it. But he'll soon realize I was right."

"Much like the rest of us poor simple males, he hasn't a chance against you."

Morgan laughed at his knowing grin. "He wants very much to be grown up. He's obviously picked you as an example. I've seen him trying to imitate your swagger and the way you sit your horse."

"I don't swagger." Youngblood shot her a dangerously sexy grin.

Morgan smiled. "Your walk then. Let's hope that's the only thing he copies."

"Meaning?"

"Meaning I'd have to wash out his mouth if I heard him repeat some of the things you say."

"That sounds vaguely familiar."

"I take it your mother did as much?"

Youngblood shrugged. "Didn't work."

"Obviously."

"Boys are gonna talk like boys. No amount of soap is gonna stop it."

"You're probable right. Only I'd better not hear it."

Youngblood watched her for a long moment. His dark eyes softened with longing. He couldn't wait to see her round with his child. To listen to the rules she set down for their children. He'd never wanted anything so badly than to hold their baby and to listen as she made sounds like a mother.

Knowing thoughts like these were bound to cause him a measure of pain, Youngblood rolled suddenly to his feet. Knowing it impossible, he nevertheless tried to shake himself free of a longing that would know no end as long as he lived, for no matter his efforts, it only took a softly spoken word, a gentle smile, or the sight of her to bring it back full force. "We'd better get him into his bedroll. It's getting chilly."

Shortly after they bedded Pedro down for the night, Youngblood and Morgan lay comfortable in their own blankets. "After Martha and Johnny get married, I think we'll take a trip to Virginia City. It would be a lot easier on us if we didn't have to travel so far," Youngblood sighed as he held his wife close to his side and gazed up at a velvet and diamond sky. "We can go to San Francisco next year. In the meantime, Virginia City has nearly everything you'd want to see. Theatres, restaurants, and hotel suites. I figure we can stay for a week or more. Would you like that?"

Morgan's head was cushioned on his shoulder, her leg thrown comfortably over his, her hand upon his flat stomach as she imagined the two of them alone in a luxury hotel.

"Is there anything you want to buy?"

Morgan laughed and tipped her head so that she was looking up at him. "You're asking a lady if she wants to

346

buy something? I want to buy everything, of course."

"Like what?"

"Like hats and shoes and gloves and dresses and—"

"I'm sorry I asked," he groaned.

"—pretty nightgowns and perfume and ribbons—"

"What kind?"

"What kind of what?"

"Nightgowns."

Morgan chuckled, a low sultry sound and then laughed at his instant reaction to the sound as his hand reached under their shared blanket for her breast. She shooed his hand away and remarked, "I hadn't planned on any particular kind. Maybe you'd like to suggest something."

"My suggestion is: It would be a waste of good money."

"Why?"

"You won't be wearing them long enough to warrant the expense."

"Does that mean you'll be taking them off?"

Youngblood chuckled, a low, wicked sound. "What do you think?"

"I think that's too bad. I was just imagining romantic evenings with the two of us having dinner sent to our rooms. Maybe eating by candlelight, while dressed, shall we say, as comfortably as possible?"

Youngblood's voice was obviously choked as his imagination ran riot. "And you'd be wearing one of those see-through things?"

"Actually I wasn't planning on see-through." Morgan allowed a moment's hesitation before continuing and then grinned at his obvious and oh-so-wicked thoughts. "But the idea is deserving of some merit."

Youngblood had to clear his throat twice before he finally managed, "Now that I think about it, I imagine you in something maybe black and cut low enough so that your ti—"

"Joseph!"

"—your breasts are almost showing," he corrected

347

without missing a beat, "well worth the money spent. I think I'll buy you a dozen."

"Darling, the trip to Virginia City will be expensive enough. I'll take care of—"

"I said I'll buy them," he interrupted, knowing she imagined him unable to afford such luxuries. It was time, way past time if the truth be known, that his wife knew of his financial status. "Do you have any idea what I'm worth?"

Morgan stiffened. She knew the subject of money, especially her money, annoyed him. She knew too that he didn't have much, for he never spent a dollar that wasn't ranch-related. "What difference does it make? I don't need the gowns. I don't care if you're not rich. If I wanted to marry money, I would have—"

"But you did."

"Did what?"

"Marry money."

Morgan caught herself before she laughed, but her voice was strained with the effort of keeping it even when she spoke. "Joseph, it doesn't matter. Really it doesn't. I love you, not your pocketbook."

"I've got something close to two million in the bank."

Morgan laughed now at the ridiculous statement. "Two?" She teased. "Not one million, but two? I had no idea a horse ranch could be so lucrative."

Youngblood sighed. "I got it by working and then selling my silver mine," he returned simply. His voice was obviously more annoyed as he went on, "What the hell is it with your family? I told your father and he got so angry I thought he was going to take a punch at me, and you," he accused, "you laugh."

"You didn't! Oh Lord, tell me you didn't?" She breathed a long weary sigh at his continued silence. "No wonder he was furious. Don't you want him to like you?"

"Why is it the Wainright's believe only they can have money?"

Morgan shook her head. "I've never said—"

"No, but you don't believe me when I tell you I do."

Morgan's eyes widened with shock. She came up and leaned upon her elbow as she watched his expression. "Oh my God! You're serious!"

"Why is it so unbelievable?"

"*Unbelievable?* That's putting it mildly, don't you think? Why were you living in what could only be called a hovel when I came here?"

"Because I only used the house to sleep in. I didn't need fancy."

"Fancy? You call it fancy to merely keep the rain off your head?" She was growing angry now, suddenly feeling very much the fool. "You let me spend hundreds of dollars to fix it up, all the while goading me with sly innuendos and nasty remarks about money and never once told me you could have done it with what you probably have in petty cash?"

He reached to pull her down beside him again, but she shoved his hands away. Her eyes glittered with anger as she glared at him. "Beast! Rogue! Impostor! Tightwad! You made me believe you were poor and all the while you were as rich as, no, richer than me. I want to know why."

Youngblood shrugged. "I don't take much to braggin'," he said in his lazy cowboy drawl.

"Bragging? You call it bragging to live in a decent house? To eat off dishes rather than out of a pot? Don't give me that."

"All right, so maybe I gave you the impression I didn't have much. I didn't do it on purpose."

"The hell you didn't!"

She was in a fine fit now. Youngblood cursed. He never should have told her. Better yet, he should have told her from the first. He couldn't figure out why he had waited so long.

"You looked your nose down on me and my money. You made me feel like I had the plague just because I could make my life comfortable and you're going to tell

349

me why."

"Am I?" he asked, his expression growing annoyed at her demand.

"Don't give me that superior male attitude, Youngblood. You're going to tell me. I have every right to know."

"I didn't want you here, damn it! And when you insisted on stayin' and spending all that money, I just . . ." He shrugged, unable to finish.

"You were scared," she said triumphantly.

Youngblood laughed in ridicule as he looked down his nose at her. "Scared? Of a little thing like you?"

"Scared I was making that shack into a home. Scared you might like it too much. Scared you might want it too much, want me too much."

"Jesus!" he said, ready to dispute her words, when it suddenly hit him. She was right. He'd been afraid of her and what she could do to him from the first. He breathed a long sigh as he ran his hand over his face. "You're right. I didn't tell you because I was afraid you'd stay. I didn't want a city woman, any woman in my life. I knew if you stayed, things would never be the same; I'd never be the same.

"I taunted you about spending money in the hopes that you'd leave and then later when I realized that stubborn streak you have, and realized too how much I wanted you, I taunted you in the hopes you'd stay." He shrugged again. "After a while it didn't seem to matter."

Morgan sighed as she lay down again. She wasn't touching him now. She, too, watched the velvety sky as she spoke. "You're a hard man to love, Joseph."

"But worth any effort?" he asked hopefully.

Morgan's laughter was low and silky. "I'm going to get even, you know."

She didn't elaborate, having no notion how she might back up her words.

Youngblood rolled to his side, his expression tender as he watched her profile. "You've no need to make me suffer further."

She merely glanced his way and then turned back to watch the sky, obviously waiting for him to go on.

"I didn't understand it for a long time. I only knew everything about you drove me crazy. I couldn't watch you laugh without imagining the sound coming soft with pleasure from beneath me in my bed. I couldn't watch you eat without wondering how your lips would feel moving under mine. I couldn't watch you walk without thinking of your legs and how they'd wrap deliciously around my hips. I couldn't enter the house without breathing your scent. I almost went crazy wanting to taste you."

"God!" she muttered breathlessly. Her eyes were wide with amazement as she turned to face him. "Do you always think along those lines?"

"Only about you. I love you, Morgan."

Morgan laughed softly. "Even though your suffering was brought on by your own evil thoughts, I'll be magnanimous and forgive you this time. And just to show you how forgiving I really am, I'll let you buy me everything I want."

Youngblood laughed as his arms reached for her again. He buried his lips in her hair as he pulled her tight against his body and vowed, "You little witch. I almost want to thank you for deciding to spend my money. How did you do that?"

Her only answer was to snuggle her face into his chest and laugh again.

Chapter Twenty

Youngblood slid his arm around her waist and pulled her close to his side. "Would you like to go for a ride after supper?"

Morgan grinned as she looked up into his hopeful expression. Knowing full well, just by his look, his intent. "Now why do you suppose a man who spends the greater part of every day in a saddle would want to go for a ride when there's no need?"

"Oh, there's a need all right." His eyes glittered with promise as his arms tightened fractionally.

Morgan laughed. "We are talking about riding, aren't we?"

"Of course," he returned with a miserable attempt at innocence. "What else could we be talking about?"

"I'm not sure, exactly. But I am sure what your men will think if they see us riding out after dark."

"They'll think I'm damn lucky, that's for sure."

Morgan laughed at his lecherous grin. "Feeling a little feisty, are we?"

Youngblood threw his head back and laughed at her choice words. "You too?"

Morgan had a time of hiding her grin. She shook her head at his teasing. "If you can think of a good reason, I imagine we can go."

"I have the best reason in the world. I want to make

love to you."

Morgan laughed and slapped his shoulder. "I meant a reason to tell your men why we'll be gone."

"Honey, they don't need an explanation. They know well enough the happenings between a man and his woman."

Morgan groaned. "You're hopeless."

"Mmmm," he murmured as he nibbled on her neck. "Hopelessly in love."

"We'll be back at the ranch tomorrow night."

"I know, but I can't wait that long."

Morgan sighed as she leaned into his strength. "I could ride up the stream a ways. If I took a towel and a bar of soap, they'd think I was going for a bath."

"And I could come along to watch over you. After all, there's some mighty treacherous parts to the stream."

Morgan giggled. "The only treacherous parts are where you'll be."

"I surely am lookin' forward to another taste of your apple pie, ma'am."

"Why thank you, Henry." Morgan smiled as the man emptied the pot of the last of the chili.

"Not that this food hasn't been mighty good. Matter a' fact, I don't recall ever eatin' so fine while on the trail."

Morgan smiled.

"You tellin' me my cookin' stinks, is that it?" Seth asked.

Henry grinned as he turned to the rotund man and wiped his plate clean with a biscuit. "Now Seth, far as I can recall, I ain't never said no such thing."

Morgan was suddenly swept away. "What are you doing?" she asked, flabbergasted by Youngblood's sudden presence and none too gentle movement.

"I'm getting you out of here. The boys are fixin' to have a little fun."

"What kind of fun?"

"Honey, they ain't been doin' nothing but workin' for more than a week. I imagine they're ready for a little ruckus."

"What?"

"A fight. They need to get rid of some of that energy they've been a storin' up."

Morgan was placed upon his horse by the time Henry threw the first punch. "Joseph! Stop them. Someone could get hurt."

"Yeah, and it ain't goin' to be me."

Youngblood turned the horse away from camp. "They'll be finished in a minute or so."

"Are you telling me this always happens?"

Youngblood nodded. "If they're out here long enough."

"And you never do anything to stop it?"

"Course not. What could I do?"

"You could order them to stop."

"Honey, they ain't doin' nothin' that'll hurt anyone. 'Cept for maybe a black eye or a missin' tooth. They're just havin' a little fun."

"Amazing." She shot an astonished look over her shoulder. "And men think that's fun?"

"Some men."

"Meaning you don't?"

"Oh, I've been known to hold my own, now and again."

"But not tonight."

"You got that right."

"I wouldn't want to keep you from enjoying yourself."

"You won't," he said silkily, his voice and manner pure male confidence.

Morgan chuckled, a low, soft sound. "You really are such a beast. Why is it I can never get the last word?"

"'Cause somewhere along the way we usually end up kissin'. After that, neither of us has much time for words."

"Is that what you intend to do now?"

354

"In a minute."

"But first?" she prompted.

"First I want to get you where the boys can't see or hear."

"We didn't need my plan and the towels after all."

"That was mighty nice of the boys, wasn't it?"

Morgan laughed. "Do me a favor and don't thank them, or they'll know for sure what we've been up to."

Youngblood laughed. "I wouldn't think of it."

Tonight they'd be sleeping in their own beds. Morgan couldn't wait to see the ranch again. She wasn't sorry that she'd insisted she come along, but she did so long for a bath, clean clothes, and a soft feather mattress beneath her.

Youngblood and the men had gone off this morning after spotting the stallion, the leader of the herd he'd captured. He had tried for days to corner the animal but his wily instincts had kept him safe from human hands so far.

Morgan and Seth broke camp as they waited for the men to return and begin the long journey that would bring them and the horses back to the ranch. She was tying Pedro's bedroll behind his saddle when Rusty began to bark. A moment later he was racing after some animal. From the corner of her eye, Morgan watched Pedro take off after him. "Don't go far," she called out a warning.

She smiled as she heard the already distant response to her call and continued on with her chores.

The wagon of supplies was packed and ready to leave by the time Morgan realized Pedro had not returned. Her brow creased with alarm. He'd been gone far too long. With a word to Seth, she set out to find him.

Morgan had been walking close to fifteen minutes before she realized she should have taken her horse. She called out for perhaps the hundredth time and still received no answer. Where in the world had that boy taken himself off to? Morgan silently promised herself she'd look for only a few more minutes and then she was returning to camp. She'd cover a lot more ground if she had her horse. Hopefully the men had returned to camp and they could search as well. With their help she had no doubt they'd find Pedro directly.

She was just about to turn back when she found his hat. A great shiver of apprehension spread throughout her body as she spied the mountain stream. It was deep and fast-flowing. And Pedro's discarded hat was far too close to its edge for her liking.

Panic filled her as her gaze darted to the stream. Terrified of what she might find, she nevertheless explored what she could. But for his hat, there was no sign of him. Morgan's heart thundered in her chest as she called out his name. She ran like a woman possessed up the banks of the stream and then back down. She couldn't find him. "Pedro!" she called again and again, her throat tight with unshed tears.

Finally realizing the futility of continuing this search alone, she turned toward the camp. If she hurried, if she ran, she could make it back in a matter of minutes. If the men hadn't already returned, she'd fire the signal that would alert them to trouble.

Morgan stumbled over the uneven ground. She fell to her knees and groaned at the horror her eyes took in. Rusty's dead body was lying barely covered by low weeds. If she hadn't fallen, she'd never have seen it. Her heart raced in dread.

She was up and running in a flash, not daring to further investigate the area. She couldn't face seeing Pedro in much the same condition. Again she fell to her knees as her booted feet tripped over sharp rocks. She neither heard the low aching sobs that slipped from her throat, nor realized the tears that were streaming down her cheeks, but wiped them away with an unthinking motion, with hands that were scraped raw and dirty from her fall. The result was to smear her sweating, dusty face with traces of blood.

She was nearly flying, her feet hardly touching the ground as she leaped over large rocks in her race back to camp. She was passing an outgrowth of shrubs when she fell again. A low unladylike curse of frustration barely slipped passed her lips, for this fall had knocked the breath out of her.

A moment later she realized she was not alone. A pair of boots stood directly before her. "Thank God," she almost moaned as she looked up. Her eyes widened with surprise to find John Marshall standing there. A puzzled crease marred her smooth brow, for she couldn't for a minute imagine what the sheriff was doing this far out of town. Was there trouble? Had something happened at the ranch?

Marshall squatted down on his haunches as he noticed her face. "Are you all right? Have you been injured?"

"No. I'm all right," Morgan said as he helped her to her feet. "What are you doing out here? The ranch . . ."

"Everything's fine. Nothing's happened at the ranch."

"I'm trying to find Pedro. You haven't seen—"

Marshall grinned. "As a matter of fact I have."

Morgan almost swooned with relief. She leaned against Marshall as relief caused her knees to grow incredibly week, while fresh tears gathered. "Oh, thank God. I was so scared. Is he back at camp?" she asked as she allowed the man to support her for a moment.

"No, he's up there." Marshall nodded, indicating the mountain that loomed above them.

"And he's all right?" she asked hopefully.

"He's fine."

Morgan realized her position and pulled away from Marshall's embrace, her cheeks coloring with embarrassment. "Then why didn't he answer me?" she asked, feeling the first sensations of a more ominous fear.

"Because I told him not to."

"John!" she exclaimed, her annoyance very much in

357

evidence. "Were you playing some sort of game? If so, I think you were being very cruel. You can't imagine how worried I was."

"No game, Morgan," he said, his voice taking on a hardness she'd never heard but for the confrontation he'd had with Youngblood on her wedding night. "The time for games is over."

"What do you mean?"

"I mean I've come to take what belongs to me."

Morgan took a step back, her annoyance gone, her fear returning full force at the look in his eyes. "What belongs to you, John?"

"The ranch for one."

"And?"

"And you."

Morgan closed her eyes for just a moment and took a deep breath, trying to calm the panic that suddenly suffused her body. "John, I don't belong to you. I belong to Joseph. He is my husband."

"He tricked you into sharing his bed. You don't have to protect him any longer." Marshall tried to reach for her again, but Morgan moved quickly from his arms.

"No! You're mistaken. He did not trick me. He loves me as I do him."

Marshall laughed. "Darling, you don't have to go on like this. I know you couldn't love one of his kind."

"What do you mean? Why couldn't I love him?"

"Because you're a lady and he's nothing but a half-breed savage. God, I couldn't imagine a more unlikely pair."

"You're wrong, John." Morgan shook her head and spoke very gently. "I might have thought that very same thing when I first met him, but I do love him. I love him very much."

Marshall's eyes darkened with anger. His smile sent chills down her back. "Do you?" He laughed at some private joke. "Then you're nothing but a whore. Fool that I was, I believed you to be different." He didn't give

358

her a chance to escape him this time, as his hands reached and held to her arms. A second later she was slammed against his body and held there, no matter her struggles. "If you fight me, you'll only get hurt."

"What . . . what are you going to do?" Morgan cursed the fear she heard in her quivering voice. It gave him even more of an advantage to know how much he terrified her.

Marshall laughed. "Do? Why, what I should have done years ago, of course. I'm going to kill that sneakin' sonofabitch, and then I'm going to have you and the ranch."

"John, listen to me," she said, but by the maniacal gleam in his eyes she knew any argument she might give to be useless. The man couldn't hear anything above his own insane hatred. Still she had to try. "John! Joseph won't calmly sit by and allow this. He'll come after you." She tried to pull away, but she might as well have saved her energies. His arms held her like steel manacles, impossible to break. "He'll kill anyone who touches me. I don't want to see the two of you—"

"Very touching," Marshall said as he began to drag her up the slope of mountainside. "But if you're worrying about me, don't bother. You can save your sympathies for my brother."

She was trembling now. Trembling so badly, in fact, that John almost had to carry her, for her legs were suddenly incapable of holding her weight.

"John," she said again as he crushed her against him. She was fighting for breath, fighting against the blackness that threatened. She had to talk to him, she had to try to convince him that this was madness. "What will you gain? You want the ranch. Do you think Joseph will give it over, once he knows what you've done?"

Marshall's laughter was low and evil. She shuddered as she felt his breath against her ear, while icy chills of terror raced down her spine at the sound. "I'm counting on his coming after you. I only hope I won't have to wait too long."

"He's not alone," she said, holding at bay the impulse to scream at him. "He won't come alone."

"Yes he will," Marshall returned unreasonably. "Once he finds Pedro's body, he'll come on looking for you. To turn back for help would show him less of a man. He won't do that."

"Pedro's *body?*" Morgan gasped as she flung herself out of his arms. She groaned as she hit the ground and then struggled to her knees. "My God! You said he was all right!"

Marshall was laughing now, the sound more terrifying than any she'd heard in her life. He is. I haven't done anything to him. Not yet."

"John, please," she said as he took her into his arms again. "Please," don't hurt him. I'll do anything, *anything* you say. I'll go away with you. I'll—"

"Your pleas for his life are very touching, but far too late. It's not only you I want. I want the ranch."

"Why? My God, why? You can have almost any piece of land you want. Why the Red Rock?"

"Because of the copper!" he blurted out in disgust. For a second he looked as if he was sorry he'd said so much, but then suddenly shrugged, knowing his slip wasn't important. It didn't matter anymore what she knew. She wasn't going to live long enough to tell anyone.

So that was it. All these months she'd wondered why there should be three offers for a piece of land no different than a thousand others. But it was different. The Red Rock held copper. No doubt in great quantities if she read the greed in his eyes correctly. Morgan took a deep calming breath, determined to bring some sense into a situation gone mad. "I'll talk to Joseph. John, I swear I'll convince him to give you the ranch. Just let Pedro and me go."

Marshall thought that was particularly funny. Actually nothing had ever seemed quite so funny before. He laughed until tears glistened in his eyes. "You'll convince him," he laughed again, and continued laughing until he had to stop and hold his hand to his side. "God, that's good. That's really good."

"I will!" she insisted. "He'd do it for me." Idly she wondered if that was entirely true. It didn't matter. What mattered was that John had to believe she could do it.

"Sure he would." Marshall couldn't seem to get control of himself. "You don't know him as well as you imagine, if you think he'd give up his ranch for a woman."

"John, please. At least let me try."

Marshall chuckled. "Oh yes, I can see you working your wiles on my brother. And he'd just turn the whole thing over to me because you batted those pretty eyes of yours."

"What have you got to lose, John? What could it hurt? It could save you a lot of trouble."

"No trouble, sweetheart," he said as he pulled her tighter against him and continued again his trek toward where George held Pedro. "First we're going to take care of the boy. We'll leave him where Youngblood can't help but find him, and then when the bastard comes after you, we'll take care of him as well."

We?" she gasped breathlessly as she was dragged over rough uneven ground. "Is there someone else with you?"

"You'll see. We're almost there."

They were beyond an outcropping of rocks now. The ground was smoother, more even. They faced a small copse of heavy-limbed trees and thicker underbrush that dotted the mountainside. A moment later they moved into the twilight of heavy shade.

At its center Pedro sat bound hand and foot, a dirty rag tied around his mouth. His eyes were wide and obviously terrified. He made as if to come to her but the movement would have been impossible considering the ropes around his ankles. Therefore, the kick George Harrington delivered to the boy's chest was entirely uncalled for, and Morgan had nothing to lose by letting him know.

"Tell him to stay in place then," Harrington sneered as he watched Morgan run to the boy's side. On her knees she instantly removed the rag from his mouth. "Did he hurt you badly?" she asked, touching his chest.

Pedro shook his head as tears came to glisten huge brown eyes. He hadn't cried, not once since they first grabbed him, but now that she was fussing over him, all he wanted to do was bawl like a baby. Valiantly Pedro kept his control. He had to show her he wasn't no baby. "Don't be afraid, honey. Joseph will find us. He'll take care of everything."

"She give you any trouble?" Harrington asked his partner.

Marshall shot him a look of incredulity. "And just how much trouble could a woman her size give?"

"I was talking about screaming," he said, his disgust showing clearly. "Did she—"

Marshall waved aside his inquiry. "No one knows I have her. Tie her up."

Morgan, in her concern for the boy, heard only this last remark. Her whole body tightened. She knew this was the last chance she'd have to escape. Once she was tied, she'd be as helpless as a child. It didn't bear thinking on what they'd do once they accomplished that much. "No!" she shouted as she came instantly to her feet. "No," she managed again as she began to run. "Help!" she screamed as an arm came around her waist and effortlessly lifted her from the ground. "Help!" she screamed again at the top of her lungs and then groaned an instant later as a fist came to smash against the side of her jaw.

Morgan didn't lose consciousness, but came dangerously close. She fought against the need to give in to the blessed ease of forgetful blackness. She couldn't allow it. There was no telling what might happen if she wasn't able to fight these men. Still, for the moment, she was so dazed she could only watch as ropes were being tied around her arms and legs. Too late she tried to struggle. Even then her movements were slow, almost dreamlike, and although she strained against Harrington's strength, she might have been a child for all the good it did her.

But every last ounce of fogginess instantly disappeared when she watched the men take the ropes from Pedro. She knew what they were planning even if the boy didn't. They were going to pretend to let him go and then they were going to kill him.

"Noooo!" she screamed, but the sound was little more than a moan against the rag that was tied around her mouth. Her heart pounded so loud she could hardly hear and yet she heard enough to instill terror. Vigorously she shook her head and screamed again as Marshall told the boy, "Go find Youngblood. Make sure you bring him back here, alone."

Pedro nodded and on shaking legs began to run toward the camp. An instant later she watched his body pitch forward as a shot rang out. Morgan screamed until her throat was raw. Tears streamed down her face as John walked calmly to the body and began to drag it down the mountainside to a place where it could be easily found.

There'd be no problem following the trail he'd left. A child could follow one so obvious. What he hadn't counted on was that more than one could follow a trail.

Jake Johnson watched from behind a rock as Marshall gave the boy's body a final shove and smiled as it rolled to a stop where the tracks of a dozen horses showed the way out of the canyon. Jake couldn't believe his luck. He'd followed the sheriff from town, but he couldn't do much of anything while the other man remained close by. Jake wasn't a fool. He wasn't about to go up against two men by his lonesome.

He'd waited for a long time. Sleeping in the alleys in town, staying out of sight as much as possible. He couldn't do anything with the sheriff staying in town; he had to wait to get him alone. At last he had his chance.

The other one was around here somewhere, probably with the woman. Jake cursed. He hadn't been close enough when the stupid bastard had taken the woman. His mouth watered as he remembered how pretty she was. He could feel his belly tightening just knowin' he was gonna have her in a few minutes. But first he had to get rid of these two. It didn't make no sense causin' a ruckus by usin' his gun. His knife would do just fine. After all, he only wanted the sheriff dead. It didn't mattter none how he died.

Jake crept close enough to where there was no possible way he could miss. A second later his knife flashed through the air to sink deep into the sheriff's back. Jake grunted with satisfaction as Marshall gave a low startled groan. Instinctively his hand reached behind him as if to find the reason for the pain he suffered and then he fell to the ground in a low cloud of dust.

Jake snickered as he approached the body. A moment later he was emptying the dead man's pockets. With a sickening sound of suction he pulled the knife from the body and wiped the blood from the blade on the leg of his pants. He followed the deliberate path left by the dragged body, knowing he'd find the woman at the end of the trail. A moment later he stepped, with gun in hand, into the small grove of trees.

Jake laughed as Harrington's eyes almost bugged out of his head. It was clear he wasn't expected. "Who the hell—" were the last words Harrington ever spoke, for his sentence was immediately cut off as he raised his gun and two shots were exchanged.

Morgan groaned in fatalistic horror as Harrington slumped to the ground. There wasn't a doubt in her mind what would happen next. As she contemplated her terrifying fate, she watched as Harrington's clothes were quickly gone over. His watch and a few bills were slid into Jake's pockets before he stood and walked over to her.

"Fancy meetin' you here, lady," Jake guffawed as he

slapped his thigh, imagining his statement particularly witty. "As pretty as ever, ain't ya?"

He loomed over her and Morgan forced aside the shiver of revulsion as he displayed blackened and missing teeth in a grin that was evil incarnate. Morgan held her silence, not that she had much choice since the gag was still in place. Still, she didn't struggle or show a flicker of the disgust she felt. She wasn't sorry to see Harrington, her neighbor to the north and a man she knew only slightly, dead. He was, after all, the one who had killed Pedro. But to be faced with this man was almost more than she could bear. Thanks to him, her baby was dead. Her eyes hardened at the thought. If she got the chance, she was going to kill him. Nothing mattered but that this coward should die.

He'd take her first. Of that she had no doubt. If Joseph found her at all, he'd be hours too late. She almost shrugged. It didn't matter. At the moment, Morgan could hardly find it within herself to care. All she knew was that the man was going to get his just reward for the heartache he'd caused.

"I'd like nothin' better than to stay awhile, but the sounds of those guns . . ." He shrugged and gave her a look indicating the matter was out of his control. A moment later she was flung over his shoulder and he began the slow descent down the incline of the mountain to where he'd left his horse.

Chapter Twenty-One

Youngblood grinned. As planned, the stallion ran directly into the boxed canyon. He was as good as theirs. All that was needed now was patience and extreme gentleness. It wouldn't be easy. The horse would be wild with fear and his fear could cause much damage.

They were heading into the canyon, surrounded on three sides by tall, stark, rocky cliffs, when the sharp, distant crack of gunfire echoed over the valley. Instantly Youngblood reined his horse in as he listened, trying to distinguish the actual shots from the endless, distorting echoes that followed.

There was trouble. It wasn't the right signal, but there wasn't anyone else in these hills, with the exception of those back at camp. And Youngblood knew there'd be no reason to fire a gun unless there was a problem.

His chest twisted with foreboding as terror for his wife's safety knotted his stomach into burning pain. With a stream of vile curses he spun his horse around, completely forgetting the rogue stallion just waiting for the taking.

Without being told, his men followed suit, knowing, of course, something was amiss, but Youngblood gave no notice of the hoofbeats that pounded the earth directly behind him. Two more shots were fired, this time in quick succession.

Youngblood cursed and pressed his spurs into Thunder's heaving flanks. It mattered not at all that he raced at breakneck speed down the treacherous slope of mountain, and then over flatter, perhaps more dangerous ground that boasted sharp rocks and hidden holes. He never thought of the consequences should Thunder take a fall. His only thought was of Morgan and the possible happenings at camp.

Amid a cloud of choking dust he pulled his horse to a stop before an obviously agitated Seth. "Where is she?"

Seth nodded over his shoulder. "Went after the boy. Sounds like the shots are coming from up there." He pointed to the mountain whose base bordered one side of the camp. The problem was that echo created in this small valley made pinpointing an exact location impossible. Youngblood cursed again, knowing it might be hours before he'd find her. Jesus, he couldn't bear the thought. What was happening? Obviously someone was shooting. Was it at her? Had the man already killed her? *No!* his mind screamed denial. She was alive and he was going to find her. If it was the last thing he ever did, he'd find her, for his very life depended on it.

Thunder reared up on his hind legs at Youngblood's sharp slap of the reins. A moment later the horse spun about and kicked stinging sand as he charged out of camp. A quarter of a mile around the base of the mountain he spotted Pedro's still form.

Youngblood moaned a low sound of anguish. His world was ending. If someone had killed a boy, surely they'd have no qualms about doing as much to Morgan. A wild mingling of unconscious curses and prayers fell from his lips as he jumped from the still-moving horse. He could hardly breathe. He certainly couldn't think, for panic filled him to the very core of his being. He took great gulps of air, trying to ward off the worst of his terror.

His dark eyes quickly scanned the area, desperate to find a sign of her and yet thankful beyond belief that her body was nowhere in sight. She was alive. He had to believe she was alive or go mad with crushing despair.

On his knees beside the child, Youngblood breathed a sigh of relief upon hearing the low moan. "Pedro," he whispered as he saw the boy's eyelids flicker. He wasn't dead. Dear God, please, don't let him die! Gently he rolled the boy to his back. Blood and dirt streaked one whole side of his face. The sight of it caused viciously muttered curses from the men who stood around the boy. Youngblood shivered at the sight, but upon further investigation found the wound in his hair. Apparently the blood had run forward when the boy fell. A long strip of hair and scalp was missing just above his ear. Already the injury was crusting over with blood.

"Dead?" one of the men ventured to ask.

"No." Youngblood couldn't hold back his sigh of relief. "But he's been hurt bad. Johnny, see to the wound and take him back to the ranch. Be careful with him."

Youngblood was already on his horse before he finished the last of his order. He was stopped from whipping his horse into a run with a loud "Wait!" Henry was pointing up the mountain. "Up there. It leads up there."

He turned in his saddle and noticed for the first time, thanks to Henry's pointed arm, the trail of a dragged body. The same trail showed footprints, not completely covered by the body. One set was small enough to be Morgan's.

It was obvious there had been a struggle. The smaller prints were dragged up the slope.

Youngblood gave a round of disgusted curses that he could have, in his panic, so easily missed such obvious markings. He had to get control of himself. He'd be absolutely useless if he couldn't rid himself of this need to give into hysterics.

He took several deep calming breaths before he realized that the horrible buzzing in his head was beginning to fade. Slowly, thankfully, a cold fury took the place of his fear. It enabled him to think. And his first thought was to find his wife. And when he did, he was going to kill the bastard that had dared to touch her. Whoever he was, the slime was going to beg for death by the time Youngblood was through with him.

He was off the saddle, moving carefully up the steep slope of mountainside. Youngblood used every bit of knowledge he'd ever gained from his father as he followed the trail. When all signs of a dragged body disappeared, he watched for turned-over rocks. Pieces of shrub torn from the rocky earth. Broken twigs, anything that could show him the way.

Youngblood's gasp was close to silent as he came across Marshall's body. A dark puddle of blood stained the center of his back. Youngblood hadn't the time to investigate further. So Marshall had been involved. What had happened? Had Morgan shot him in an attempt to free herself?

Youngblood shook his head. He doubted Morgan had it in her to kill. Still, one never knew what one might do, if faced with the fear she must have known.

He continued on, bent into a crouch position, moving slowly up the narrow path, ever alert for a trap, conscious of every twig that broke beneath a boot, of each harshly gasped breath and low murmured curse of the men who followed.

Gun in hand, he entered at last the small hollow, screened by heavily limbed pines. An instant later he muttered a stream of curses. The signs were clear. She had been here. Now all that remained was Harrington's lifeless body and ropes that had obviously been cut from someone.

She had been here. He could see the shape of her small boots in the soft earth. There had been yet another struggle. Had Morgan somehow gotten free? Had she killed Harrington as well as Marshall?

Youngblood called out and received nothing but silence for his efforts.

Youngblood's sharp eye found the spot where she had

been held. There was a slight imprint of her body there. But no footprints leading away. Someone had taken her. Jesus Christ! He'd wasted a good five minutes looking and she'd been gone all the time.

Youngblood moved ten feet beyond the hollow to the ridge and scanned the flat plain below. He could see for miles in all directions, except for directly behind the mountain, where they had camped. A tiny spot of dust could be seen upon the horizon. Someone was riding and hard.

She wasn't dead. She was on that horse. She had to be. Anything else was unthinkable.

He fell twice as he came down the mountain, so great was his speed. He never noticed the gash that laid open his cheek, nor the cuts and scrapes to his hands and knees. He was on Thunder riding in the direction of the small puff of dust before his men were halfway down the mountain.

Morgan held back the groan of pain as the saddle dug deep into her belly. The ground moved by at a harrowing pace as she curved her body around the horse, praying the terrible bouncing she was taking wouldn't knock her off. She'd die for sure if she fell now. And she couldn't allow that. Not now. Not when she had to kill this beast.

Morgan was amazed at how calm she felt. She knew the moment he had a chance, he'd abuse her terribly. She simply didn't care. It wasn't important that this man's dirty hands would touch her. That his body would violate her own. It was only important that she somehow find the opportunity to rid the world of this piece of filth.

Morgan grunted a low sound as the man pulled the horse to a stop. The animal danced for a moment, its sides heaving with the strain of its run. A trickle of fear slid down her spine at the soft evil laughter that floated above her.

"Looks like nobody saw us leave." He slowed his horse

down, thinking he had all the time in the world. No sense riding his horse into the ground. Nobody would find him now.

Jake couldn't have felt better. He had got the bastard that had put him behind bars. It hadn't taken near as long as he imagined it might. All he'd had to do was hang around town for a bit. It hadn't taken a week before the sheriff had ridden out. And he had followed. Damn! Who would have thought it would be so easy?

Not only had he done what he'd set out to do—his hand cupped the woman's rounded backside in appreciation—but he'd gotten himself the best little piece of ass he'd seen in a long time. Now that he thought on it, he couldn't remember seein' better. Jake gave a black toothless smile of satisfaction. He'd keep this one. He wasn't going to have to go looking for pussy when the urge hit again. He kind a' liked the idea of snugglin' up with a warm body on a cold night. Especially a body as round and pretty as hers.

He was tempted to stop and have himself a little sample right now, but shook his head at the thought. She wasn't goin' nowhere. He could wait. He had to get farther away, just in case that half-breed husband of hers was somewhere around.

Jake suppressed a shiver as he remembered the look of death in the man's eyes. No. He didn't want to go up against one of his kind. He'd put a bullet to his own head before he'd let that one get ahold a' him. A bullet would be a blessin'.

Jake moved his horse toward the hills. There were caves up there and enough growth to hide a campfire. He could make a right cozy camp with this here woman. Jake's mouth watered as he imagined the two of them enjoyin' the long night.

Youngblood cursed as he spotted the trail. It led to the hills. *Jesus, please*, he silently implored as he urged

Thunder to hurry his pace. He had to find her and soon. Light was fast fading. Before long it would be too late.

Jake grinned as his horse slid down the slight incline and he noticed the cave. It was perfect. Protected by hills on all sides, no one could see or smell their campfire. Not unless they were a goddamned bird. He chuckled a mean sound. He could have his fun tonight without worryin' someone might come across them by accident.

Jake dismounted and looked around. Sure was a pretty place, he thought with satisfaction. It was all cozy-like with plenty of grass for his horse. The only problen was, no water. Least none he could see right off. Jake shrugged. He had a couple a' canteens. One was full. That would have to do for a spell.

He eyed the woman still lying over his saddle, imagining the sight of that ass without a stitch, and he felt his crotch start to grow into action. If he was careful-like, maybe it would do for a long spell.

There was no sense waiting till later. He could have his vittles after he had some fun. And if she was good, maybe he'd even give her a bit as well.

"Come on, girlie, seems like we're home," he said as he pulled her off the horse and dragged her away from the animal.

Morgan was dizzy from hanging upside down. The world spun by her eyes as she was flung from the horse to the ground. She hardly noticed the blow to her head, for an instant later Jake's heavy body came crashing down upon her. The air left her lungs and she almost blacked out, but valiantly fought against giving in to unconsciousness. She couldn't faint. She had to stay awake. There was always a chance if she she could keep her senses about her.

His hand was beneath the wide leg of her split skirt. He cursed as he realized what she was wearing. "Who the hell was fool enough to invent this kind a' contraption," he muttered as his hands moved to her waist, fumbling with the buttons of her skirt.

He pulled away the gag from her mouth, but Morgan hadn't time to inhale one breath before his mouth was there. Morgan gagged at the stench of decayed teeth and a mouth that hadn't seen cleansing in years. She fought against the urge to gag as he forced his tongue into her mouth. Her teeth bit down. Hard.

Morgan knew she'd suffer greatly for her actions, but she couldn't allow herself to think about that now. She simply couldn't allow any man to touch what wasn't his.

Jake screamed as excruciating pain filled his mouth, his head. He tried to pull back, but it was she who held him now.

Morgan's sharp teeth clamped tighter. If he was going to take her, and surely he would, she wasn't going to make it easy for him.

Jake tried again to pull back, but she held on and bit down harder. Desperate for relief, he grabbed at her jaw. The bitch was gonna cut his tongue in two.

Morgan ignored, as best she could, the metallic taste of his blood, the altogether rancid flavor of his mouth. She bit further into the slippery softness.

A moment later her teeth released its hold and she moaned as his fist slammed into her cheek. Free at last, he sat upon her stomach and hit her again and again while calling her every vile name he could think of.

Her blood mingled with his as her teeth cut into her lips and the blood from her nose began to run back into her throat. His fists didn't stop for a long time.

Growing tired, Jake rolled from her, his hand holding his mouth as blood continued to rush through his fingers.

From somewhere in the back of her dazed mind, Morgan realized she was still awake. She felt no little amazement that she could have suffered such a beating and yet remain alive, never mind conscious. Apparently he had not hit her as hard as he could have. Certainly not as hard as his first three or four punches. No doubt his own shock and pain had influenced his ability.

Morgan rolled to her side. She couldn't breathe what with the blood running down her throat. She watched through an eye on its way to swelling closed. He was kneeling near her feet, while blood ran from his mouth.

Jake shivered with horror as he gently ran a dirty finger over the damage. The cut went deep. He didn't want to think how deep. The bitch had nearly bitten the damn thing off. His mind went on to imagine what she might have done if he'd stuck his cock in there like he'd wanted to. Jesus, he shivered again. He didn't want to think about that.

Jake got to his feet, stumbled to his horse, and reached for the canteen of water. He washed his mouth out and then groaned out a curse at the soreness. He shot her a vicious, hate-filled glare. This one was going to suffer and he was going to take pleasure in her every scream.

He watched her for a long moment before he figured out what to do. A satanic look gleamed in his eyes, while a smile curved bloody lips. He knew just the thing. Not only wouldn't he have to worry about her next attack, he could enjoy what he wished for as long as he planned and she couldn't do a damn thing about it.

Jake suddenly realized he liked his women to fight him, but without his brothers to hold them down while he was at it, he could get hurt real bad. This one wouldn't hurt nobody again.

Jake moved past her, kicking her hard in the center of her back as he did. He heard her soft groan and grinned. It wasn't much, but it sure was a beginning. Damn, this was goin' to be fun.

Youngblood was almost out of his mind with fear. The horse had disappeared into the hills. A body could get lost in those damn hills for days before finding his way out. Jesus, how was he supposed to find her? It was getting

374

dark. Soon he wouldn't be able to see the trail. But he wouldn't stop. He'd search these hills for eternity if need be. He was going to find her.

Morgan must have dozed, for the next thing she knew she was trying to blink her eyes open. Only she couldn't quite manage the chore. Something was holding them closed, or nearly closed. She gave a long silent moan as she remembered.

Gently she moved her tongue over her teeth. There was a chip in one bottom tooth. It stung just a bit when she opened her mouth to breathe. Morgan almost laughed as she realized she could still distinguish that small discomfort from the pain that wracked her brain. Her lips were stiff, impossible to move without excruciating pain. She stopped trying.

Her nose was probably broken. All she knew was she couldn't breathe through it. Apparently her eyes were swollen shut. Lord, she was going to be a mess for weeks.

Morgan giggled at the thought. She had been kidnapped by a brutal madman and was very probably going to die, and here she was worrying about how bad she was going to look.

"You awake, are ya?" came a gloating voice from above her.

Morgan didn't need to see to know that the monster was still here. She could hear him walking around her. She could probably have smelled him, if her nose worked.

Above the pain in her head and face, Morgan noticed the shivering cold. Why should she feel such a chill? She tried to move her arms, to curve her body into itself, but nothing moved.

She tried to see what the problem was, but her eyes wouldn't open far enough to focus. Again she tried to pull her arms to her body. Odd that they felt tight, almost as if they were pulled away from her.

"No sense you tryin' to fight it. You ain't goin' to get free." Jake chuckled as he watched her naked body squirm as she tried to bring her arms and legs together.

"Noooo!" Morgan cried out as she realized at last her position. It wasn't so much the fact that she was naked and this man could see what he wished. It was being bound that left her so distraught. She had to get free. She couldn't be left like this if she was to take her revenge.

"If'n you yell, I'm goin' to gag you. You want that?"

Morgan moaned from the pain as she vigorously shook her head. She was going to throw up. She took long deep breaths as she fought against the nausea. He couldn't gag her. She'd die if he did, for she could only breathe through her mouth. "No," she said softly, her head pounding with a dull immobilizing pain. "I won't call out again. I promise." Morgan almost smiled. Perhaps she might have if her lips could have moved. He didn't need to have gone to the trouble of tying her. What with the pain in her head, she couldn't have moved if her life depended on it.

Jake laughed. "You promise, do ya?"

"I promise," she repeated.

"That's good," he said almost conversationally. "You're a real looker, you know that?" he asked. "At least you used to be." Jake seemed to find that last statement extremely funny. He laughed loud and long as he sat between her legs and allowed himself the luxury of looking over her naked body. He was drinking from a flask he'd once stolen off some drunk. "I wonder what you'll look like in a few days, or a week maybe."

"Are we going to be here that long?"

"I reckon it'll take that long before I have my fill of ya."

"And then?" God, it was torture to speak. She could hardly keep the cry of pain from bubbling out of her throat. She cared not at all that she lay naked and spread-eagled before this man's lecherous eyes. It didn't matter. Nothing mattered, but that she be allowed to sleep. She'd never wanted anything more, but she knew she'd delay the inevitable if she could keep him talking. And with God's help, if she delayed long enough, help

376

would arrive.

"And after?" she asked. "After the week? Where are we going?"

"Why?" he asked, his voice heavy with suspicion.

Morgan groaned as she tried to keep her thoughts from flying away. She had to keep him talking. "A lady likes to know these things, is all," she said, trying desperately to keep from crying as pain sliced into her face with every movement of her lips.

"You figure on stayin' with me? Is that it?"

"I thought you wanted me."

"I know what I said! What the fuck did you bite me for?"

Morgan tried to shrug a shoulder. An impossible task since her arms felt almost pulled from their sockets.

Jake eyed her warily, wonderin' if he understood her correctly. Did she want to be with him? Was that it? He could feel his pants growin' even tighter with the thought. Jesus, he ain't never had a woman come to him, especially not one who looked like this one. Even the whores, who he had to pay anyways, so they didn't really count, were as ugly as sin. Jake gave a small shrug that she couldn't see. "Maybe I got a little rough."

Despite the pain, Morgan fought back the nearly hysterical laugh that threatened at the ludicrous statement. She was beaten to a pulp. She couldn't open her eyes wide enough to see. No doubt she had a concussion, if the dizziness and nausea she suffered meant anything, and he wondered if *maybe* he got a little rough?

"It doesn't matter. You can untie me now."

Jake chuckled. "Can I? And if'n I do, you goin' to stay?"

"I have no clothes, no food, no horse. Where would I go?"

Jake grunted. She was right about that. Only he didn't trust her. Not yet. "Maybe in the morning," he said as he released his sex from his pants. "But first I'm goin' to

377

have myself a bit a' fun."

Sweat ran down Youngblood's face. His every breath was labored as he forced his eyes to watch the trail. The light was almost gone. In minutes it would be too late. He couldn't follow it in the dark. All he could do was go on, hoping by some miracle he'd come across a camp.

Thunder mounted a hill and Youngblood felt a wave of relief mingle with a fury the likes of which he'd never known. He stopped at the crest for a long moment, knowing he couldn't allow his men to come this far. There was every chance the bastard would be on his horse and lost in these hills the moment he heard Thunder coming down the slope. He wasn't going to get away. Not this time.

Youngblood made a motion with his arms, indicating he'd found her and telling his men to circle the area to his left and right.

Slowly he dismounted his horse and began the long walk down to where Morgan lay. He didn't make a sound, at least not that any normal man could hear.

Jake was coming to his knees, his sex hard and throbbing as he leaned over the woman, when he felt the hard nose of a gun dig deep into his back.

"Easy," Youngblood said as Jake instinctively reached for his gun. "You ain't goin' to be needin' that."

With his free hand Youngblood eased the gun from the man's holster. A second later he tucked it into his belt. "Now stand up real slow." He was going to kill this man, but he wouldn't chance Morgan's safety while doing it. He could have killed him a dozen times as he moved down the hill, but the man was too close. He didn't dare fire.

Morgan heard the voice, but wondered if it was simply her imagination. Had Joseph truly come? Was she safe from this beast? God, she wanted to see so badly, but no amount of effort would open her eyes.

Youngblood gave a horrifying bloodcurdling cry as he

378

saw for the first time the damage this monster had done to his wife. Jake felt a chill ripple up his spine, knowing he was going to die. Funny thing was, he'd always thought he'd be more afraid at the end.

Youngblood felt no remorse, except perhaps for the fact that he had given in to Morgan's insisting and taken her with him. Jake had gotten off easy. Had he his senses about him, the man would have suffered long and hard.

It was days before the full story was known. According to Doc Franklin, Morgan had suffered a concussion and Youngblood had to hold back asking the hundred questions he was anxious to pose.

A week passed while Youngblood saw to the care of his wife. Early one morning, he entered the bedroom balancing a tray. He grinned when he saw her awake.

"That smells good."

"It is good. You're not the only one around here that can cook."

Morgan smiled and then breathed a sigh of relief to find the stiffness completely gone. She ran her tongue over her lips in anticipation of breakfast.

Youngblood shook his head. "The swelling's down." Actually, other than the slight trace of discoloration around her right eye, she looked wonderful.

"I know. I think I'll get up today. One whole week of lying in this bed is about all I can take. How's Pedro?"

Youngblood grinned. "He's harder to hold than a wild stallion. Martha and I are getting sick of his nagging to get up." He eyed her cautiously. "Are you sure you're ready to get out of bed."

"Joseph," she said, frowning at his concern, "nothing happened but that my face took a beating. I'm fine."

Youngblood looked down at his wife and silently cursed the fact that twice he had not protected her. If he had killed Jake Johnson at their first encounter, this never would have happened.

"After you eat, do you want me to comb your hair?"

Morgan shot him a look of annoyance. She didn't like the fact that he insisted on treating her as an invalid. Nor did she much appreciate the guilt that never left his eyes. "What I want is for you to act like my husband, not a nurse," she said as she bit down on a crunchy piece of bread. "Doc Franklin told you I was all right. I've told you the same. Why don't you believe it?"

"You don't know what your face looked like."

Morgan chuckled. "Yes I do. Martha brought me a mirror."

Youngblood bit his lip, his eyes downcast.

"Will you stop acting like that?"

"Like what?"

"Like you're guilty. Lord, one would think you were responsible."

"I was responsible, damn it! Don't you understand? I should have been there. It's my job to protect you. Christ! I can just hear your father ranting about how I'm taking care of his daughter."

"Rubbish. You killed the man responsible. What did the marshal say?" she asked, changing the subject.

Marshal Post had been summoned from Virginia City to oversee the legalities of the situation, since the town no longer had a sheriff. Only Morgan and Youngblood knew of his brother's involvement in the matter.

"He said he would have done the same."

Morgan's face broke into a beautiful I-told-you-so smile.

Youngblood grinned at her superior look. "Think you're real smart, don't ya?"

"Smart enough." A small frown crossed her brow. "Have you given any thought to the copper?"

"Yup."

"What are you going to do about it?"

"Nothing. I don't want this place overrun with prospectors."

Morgan nodded her agreement. "You didn't make this

380

coffee, did you?" she asked as she took another sip.

Youngblood laughed. "What makes you think so?"

"I can drink it."

"Meaning you can't when I make it?"

"Meaning there are many things you can do, Mr. Youngblood, but making coffee is not one of them."

Youngblood chuckled as he walked to their bedroom door. A moment later came the sound of the lock falling into place. "You interested in telling me exactly what you think I'm good at?" he said as he swaggered back to the bed.

Morgan grinned. "Well, for one thing, your riding is outstanding."

"Is it?" he asked as he sat on the bed. "What else?"

"I've never seen anyone better at roping horses."

"Have you seen many men rope horses?"

"No."

"Then that doesn't count," he said silkily. "What else?"

Morgan shrugged as a tiny smile touched the corners of her mouth. "Well, you can aggravate me faster than anyone I know."

Youngblood chuckled as he removed his shirt. "Come on, honey."

"Is there something in particular you want to hear?" she asked with supposed innocence.

Youngblood nodded as he began to lift her nightdress over her head. "I want to hear everything you think I'm good at."

"Well, you're very good at undressing ladies, aren't you?"

"One lady," he reminded as he pushed off his boots. His eyes were warm with appreciation as they watched the movement of her breasts as she breathed. His voice was lower now, filled with aching need. "What else?"

"Your kiss," she said, her voice growing slightly breathless.

"What about it?"

"You do that very well."

"How many men have you kissed to know I'm good at it?"

Morgan raised her fingers as if to count off. "Well, there was Bradley, of course. And then—"

Youngblood shook his head. "Never mind," he almost growled. "I don't want to know."

"Besides kissing, do I do anything else you like?"

"Oh, many things." Morgan sighed, her eyes closing with pleasure as he leaned forward and brushed his lips against her shoulder and neck.

"Will you tell me?"

"I have an idea, Joseph," she said as if the thought had just occurred to her. "Why don't we make love. If you refresh my memory, I can be more explicit."

Youngblood laughed as he gathered her close. "I don't know why I didn't think of that."

Epilogue

Morgan stepped out of her old room to find her husband lurking in the hall. "Is she ready?"

Morgan laughed at his worried expression as she dusted a piece of lint from his dark shoulder. "You weren't this nervous when we got married. What's gotten into you?"

"I've never been a best man before. Jesus! Where did I put the ring?" he said as he wildly attacked his pockets.

"I put it in your coat." She patted his chest, indicating his inside pocket. "Will you calm down?"

"Do you know how many people are out there?"

"Yes, I do. Martha and I made out the guest list, remember?"

"When the hell is she going to be ready?"

"She's ready now. Go inside, Joseph, and tell Mrs. Schmitt she can begin to sing. We'll be out directly."

Youngblood turned and walked down the long hall. He came to a sudden stop. His brow creased with a puzzled look when he turned again. "Doc Franklin's been giving me some real hard looks. Do you know what the hell is the matter with him?"

Morgan smiled and gave a slight shrug of one shoulder. "Pay him no mind. He's probably a bit upset because he wanted us to wait."

Her hand was on the knob as she prepared to tell

Martha everything was ready.

"What does that mean?" he asked, obviously confused.

"It means I wasn't supposed to get pregnant for another few weeks."

"Oh," he said as he nodded and continued on down the hall. For a second he appeared as if to stagger. His eyes held a wide range of emotion. Confusion and then shock. An instant later they gleamed with joy and then amusement. He grinned at her wicked expression. A long moment of silence followed while his gaze held hers and told of the endless depth of his love. Joy rippled thoughout his entire being. He had to force himself from touching her, lest the wedding be put off an hour or so. His voice was low, sexy, causing chills to spread down her spine, as he finally said, "You know, of course, I'm going to get you for that."

Morgan chuckled a wickedly delicious sound. "Darling, I'm afraid you already have."